Kurakex wo_____
bridge. *Were* _____
fight, and no doubt quickly. _____
picture the human commander as coward___
headed, rather. The human would *make* him catch
him. *Well*, he told himself, *I too am stubborn. And I
will have him alive.*

The warbeams beat relentlessly, multicolored
luminescence playing over the *Makor's* shield in
irregular waves. A salvo of torpedos struck, and the
outer shield layer collapsed.

The ship spoke. "Admiral, the Garthid commander
is trying to communicate with you."

Ferringum didn't hesitate. "Reject him."

They were the only words spoken. Kelmer
watched the battlecomp display Shield strength,
shield generator status, overall power status—all
were slipping. A fourth beam found the *Makor*, and
a fifth. The shield's mid-layer, the outermost now,
fluoresced more strongly, the waves quickening. It
pulsed once, twice, flared blindingly, then collapsed,
leaving only the inner. The afterimage on Kelmer's
retina slowly faded.

All but two of the Garthid beams cut off, but
generator status had dropped into the red zone. The
weakening inner layer replayed the event sequence
of the mid-layer. When it collapsed, it was not
cataclysmic, but power status fluctuated up and
down. Aft, hull metal boiled.

It would, Kelmer thought, be getting hot in the
engine room.

BAEN BOOKS BY JOHN DALMAS

The Regiment
The White Regiment
The Regiment's War
The Three-Cornered War

The Lion of Farside
The Bavarian Gate

The Lizard War

THE THREE-CORNERED WAR

JOHN DALMAS

BAEN

THE THREE-CORNERED WAR

This is a work of fiction. All the characters and events portrayed in this book are fictional, and any resemblance to real people or incidents is purely coincidental.

Copyright © 1999 by John Dalmas

All rights reserved, including the right to reproduce this book or portions thereof in any form.

A Baen Books Original

Baen Publishing Enterprises
P.O. Box 1403
Riverdale, NY 10471

ISBN: 0-671-57783-2

Cover art by David Mattingly

First printing, January 1999

Distributed by Simon & Schuster
1230 Avenue of the Americas
New York, NY 10020

Printed in the United States of America

DEDICATION

To Gail, Judy, Jack, Jill, Ian,
Ryan, and Kristen

with love

Acknowledgments

Thanks are especially due to MARY JANE ENG, JIM GLASS, and JIM BURK, for critiques of an early draft. And to the Spokane WORD WEAVERS for critiques of several chapters.

To CHRIS O'HARRA, the honcho of Auntie's Bookstore, for her great and constant encouragement of Spokane area writers.

And to ROBERTA RICE and her jolly crew at Dragon Tales, for their long and firm support of science fiction authors at conventions throughout the inland Northwest.

Foreword

Twenty-one thousand years before this story, eight large shiploads of refugees fled a vast war of destruction, an Armageddon in a distant part of the spiral arm.

They were wise enough to realize that being human, they carried with them the seeds of future discords and war. And in an effort to avoid those wars becoming megawars, they developed *The Sacrament*. This was a powerful system of pain-drug-hypnosis conditioning for all the refugees, and for all their descendants forever. It was designed to prevent scientific curiosity and investigation. They also stripped their ships' computers of scientific and technological information that might lead to development of megawar weaponry.

For several years the refugees traveled in hyperspace, emerging from time to time to explore some promising planetary system for a habitable world. Eventually they settled on one they named Iryala.

Over the following millennia, the Iryalans colonized other planets in their sector of the arm, always taking with them the Sacrament and its technicians. Their worlds and progeny remained under the dominion of Iryala, which retained to itself the exclusive manufacture of spacecraft, space drives, and space weaponry.

Despite new worlds, new conditions, new colonies, the Sacrament resulted in a technologically and mentally stagnant culture which increasingly stressed the concept of Standardness. And a shallow view of both past and future, without a great deal more curiosity about history than about the principles of how the universe works.

Each confederated world had its own ingrown interests and focuses, and they were too farflung to be closely ruled. What held them together was the Sacrament, and their dependence on Iryala for technology. Many of the colony worlds never achieved a central planetary authority, but developed autonomous states separated by rivalries and grudges.

The Confederation of Human Worlds, in its various historical formats, had never experienced space warfare. In fact, with one exception, all its wars had been surface wars between states that shared a common world. And in the more distant past, revolts against Iryalan authority.

It hadn't even made a show of force in space for over seven hundred years. Its naval equipment was of inherited designs, modified long millennia earlier to serve police functions rather than fight wars.

During the exodus, long forgotten now, two large groups of refugees had been purged for refusing the Sacrament. They'd been put down on two planets so difficult, survival seemed questionable and civilization impossible. As the Confederation expanded, those two forgotten worlds had been rediscovered. For a long time their primitive peoples were treated as anomalies, and not quite human. One of those planets was Tyss, also known as "Oven." Tyss was so poor that for millennia its only export was superb mercenary regiments, hired by states on worlds without a central planetary government, to help fight their many small wars.

The T'swa—the people of Tyss—had evolved a culture that eventually caught the interest of a small group of Iryalan aristocrats. Now the T'swa had a new export: ideas.

And those aristocrats formed the opening wedge in the stagnated culture of the Sacrament. The Confederation began a planned and gradual change, heretical and covert.

Meanwhile the ancient Home Sector had been terribly ravaged by the interstellar war the refugees had fled. Some planets had been literally destroyed, physically disrupted. Others were rendered uninhabitable for most lifeforms. On still others, the environment was sufficiently degraded that the demoralized humans who survived the war did not survive its aftermath.

Only three worlds retained human populations, and technology had died on them all. Eventually one of them, Varatos, reevolved science, redeveloped space flight, and discovered and subjugated the other two. On eight others, the ecology had adjusted sufficiently to be habitable again, and the Vartosi colonized them. The result was an interstellar imperium calling itself the Karghanik Empire.

Exploration had found no further habitable planets in their sector. Their religion accounted for this peculiarity as the will of God—the same God they believed forbade birth control.

Eventually, the worlds of the Empire grew seriously overpopulated. Finally one of its planets, Klestron, sent an expedition years beyond known space. There it encountered and skirmished with the alien Garthids. Later the expedition discovered and took possession of a very minor "trade world" on the periphery of the Confederation. Within months, however, they were driven from it.

But the expedition had broken the ignorance of both human sectors by whetting the appetite of the Empire, while pressing the Confederation to accelerate change.

And disturbing Garthid isolation.

Prologue

More than two hundred parsecs from Iryala, two figures stood on a high balcony of the Garthid imperial palace. Over the previous eighteen millennia, it had been built, damaged by internecine wars, rebuilt and expanded. All without basic change. It was far more than the imperial residence. It housed and officed the central executive function overseeing a loose khanate of fifty-three inhabited worlds. There was no compelling need for its centralization on a single site. Garthid electronics and cybernetics were highly advanced. But the palace suited the Garthid psyche.

The seven-sided wall enclosing it was more than six miles around, and tall beyond need, yet the structures it enclosed rose high above it, an intricately interconnecting complex of buildings, courtyards, jumbled roofs and high-vaulting towers, often irregularly stacked. There were arching walkways, some open, some enclosed. Turrets, landing platforms for floaters and shuttles, and innumerable and often unlikely balconies, large and small, partly in lieu of adequate windows. The architecture was more intricate and extreme than any Gothic cathedral, and far less orderly. Yet somehow stark, brooding, powerful. Nowhere was there a glint of silver, gleamstone, gilt, or even copper. The structures were black—hardsteel and poured blackstone—nonreflective as a military gunbarrel. The tall narrow windows were deep-set, of dark-tinted glass.

It was considered the most beautiful architecture in the Garthid Khanate.

The country surrounding it was a broad, tree-spotted grassland, broken by swales, shrubby knolls, and forested flood plains. Tradition called it the home of the species— a sort of racial shrine. Its local climate and ecology were as little changed over the millennia as Garthid science could keep them. The Garthids, even those whose families had dwelt for millennia on other worlds, felt a powerful, a *compelling* attachment to it. Garthid racial memory insisted that the species had evolved on that plain, lived and scavenged there. There or in a region and climate much like it. A savage Eden where predators large and predators fleet had struck down or pulled down hoofed prey. Often to be harassed and driven from their kill by robber scavengers, among which the foremost were the pack-roving protogarthids, and later the early Garthids themselves, tough, aggressive, relentless. Intelligent.

Now, after some two million years, the species looked not so different from its ancestors. Their crania were notably larger, their heavy fighting teeth a little smaller, their scaly skin less tough. But except for their crania, they were remarkably like their forebears—obligatory carnivores with powerful jaws and teeth. Their frames were still powerful, though their muscles seldom so sinewy and tough.

Two figures stood by the railing. The giant was the Surrogate of God, the smaller his chief counselor. The Surrogate was of the guardian gender, of course, seven feet tall and 440 pounds. His pantaloons were a sort of exaggerated plus fours, as wide as a Varangian's, their vividly colorful pattern at odds with the black motif of the city's architecture. His only other garb was a sort of vest, resembling a *kabe-shima*, its enormous padded shoulders ending in upcurved black horns. His counselor, a foot and a half shorter and only 40 percent of the

Surrogate's mass, wore nothing below his plain blue-green vest. He was of the healer gender, and had risen through the bureaucracy.

The evening was a pleasant 125 degrees Fahrenheit. Their balcony, a thousand feet above the pavement, overlooked the traditional landscape, its genetically restored herds of prey vaguely visible in the dusk. To the west, a molten smear showed where the sun had set. To the east, stars already gleamed. It was on these the two Garthids gazed.

"The aliens may not have arrived with bad intentions," the Surrogate said. "But suppose for a moment they did."

His counselor answered diffidently. "It is possible of course, Your Potency. But the reports suggest they arrived innocently, lashed out in fear, then fled. I doubt we shall see them again."

The Surrogate's parietal hood flared slightly, its fringe of vestigial "horns" rigid. "There are passing encounters," he said. "Mere armed incidents. But there are also wars. The difference is vast. We must be prepared, which includes being informed."

The chief counselor recalled a proverb: *He who snoops the canebrake may rouse the dragon.* But he'd said enough.

The Surrogate continued: "We must develop a sentry system which can monitor a zone at least a parsec across. No such thing has ever been attempted, but I am assured it is technically and economically possible. I may also decide to scout the intruder's extrapolated course, and perhaps discover its system of origin or destination. Our success in that depends on their having followed a constant course over a very long distance. And we will begin preparation for possible hostilities. To start with, this will consist of preparing an infrastructure for a full war effort, in case one is needed. Meanwhile the expansion of existing forces can be moderate."

The two old friends continued to gaze starward. Finally

the chief counselor spoke again: "We have not fought another species than ourselves since we destroyed the Chil-ness-pakth, in the time of the Ninth Khroknash, more than eighteen thousand years ago."

The Surrogate nodded. "In the pride of our youth. But perhaps it is time."

"I will pray on it."

The Surrogate grunted. "I have prayed. And it seems to me God had a hand in this. The probability that an intruder would emerge twice within reaction range of a patrol ship is extremely small." Laying a hand on the counselor's shoulder, he added: "We shall see. If God wills peace, we shall have peace. I do not intend to force war on anyone needlessly."

Part One
THE GATHERING
FORCES

Chapter 1
Return From War

The White Regiment arrived on Splenn with less than half its virgin strength. Arrived by ship. There Colonel Artus Romlar exercised his influence with the Confederation Ministry, and had his three civilians forwarded to Iryala in a ministry courier. The regiment itself gated to Iryala by teleport, arriving in a security area of the Landfall Military Reservation. The troopers were quartered there overnight, and the next day given a reception by the Office of Special Projects. The king himself attended, and a crew from Iryala Video broadcast the welcoming ceremony.

Interesting, Romlar thought. Apparently the government wanted to add to the regiment's reputation.

The next day the troopers were given new paycards that accessed the credits they'd accrued. Then they dispersed for a dek,[1] to vacation, and visit their families. It was their first leave on their home world in more than four years.

Colonel Romlar, however, began three days of debriefing by an officer from the Office of Special Projects. He'd

---

[1] A dek is a tenth of a year, and in the Confederation calendar occupies a role equivalent to a month. For ordinary affairs, its length varies from world to world. The Standard dek, like the Standard year and day, is that of Iryala.

11

expected the OSP debrief. What surprised him was having an audience, all of them obviously members of the Movement. The general from the Ministry of Armed Forces asked about the training Romlar had given to Smoleni rangers on Maragor. Apparently the army planned to overhaul its own training.

On the fourth morning, Romlar was picked up by limousine, for a trip to "the residence of Lord Kristal." He was delivered, however, to a high-rise government office building on the extensive royal estate. Lotta Alsnor met him at the broad steps, and they faced off, holding hands between them, looking at each other. He grinned. "How come I have such a pretty girl?"

Her laugh was light. "Bullshit, Artus," she said. "I'm a plain and scrawny little minx. Wiry anyway. I prefer it that way. It holds down the distraction." She grinned. "But say it again; I like it." She squeezed his fingers. "I suppose you're wondering why you were brought here. And what I'm doing here."

"It crossed my mind."

"Let's go see Emry, and we'll uncross it."

She led him into a large reception area where security personnel were conspicuous. The couple was not stopped; apparently Lotta was known to them. A wide main corridor took them to a glass-domed rotunda, some eighty yards across and fifty high. There, small groups of trees were surrounded by lawns, fountains, shrubs, and bright, many-colored flowerbeds. There was a fragrance of blossoms. Birds darted, twittered, sang. Apparently, Artus thought, tailored repellent fields kept them inside.

Lotta grinned at him. "Nice, eh?"

"My driver said he was taking me to Kristal's residence."

It was an inside joke, she explained. The building officed OSP headquarters and labs. As His Majesty's Governor of Special Projects, and a widower, Kristal lived there in a penthouse apartment.

So the OSP rates a governor now, Romlar thought. *It's risen on either the importance scale or the PR scale. Or both.*

They rode a lift tube to the top floor, where Lotta led him to a large reception room with offices on two sides. Its windows extended from floor to ceiling.

The receptionist looked up smiling. "His lordship is expecting you," she said. "Just a moment." She spoke quietly into a commset, then motioned toward a door. "Go right in."

The old man was on his feet to greet them. Taking one of Romlar's thick hard hands in both of his thin ones, he shook it. "Artus, it's good to have you back. It's spring where you've come from, right?"

"Going on summer."

"Well. And here you find summer half used up." His deep bright eyes examined Romlar's. "I have a new assignment for you. A new and *different* assignment, to start after you've had your leave. A short leave, I'm afraid, a few days."

He paused. "I take it your regiment came home in good mental and spiritual condition?"

"Most of them better than I did."

Kristal nodded as if he knew what Romlar alluded to. "The regiment will not be contracted out again," he said. "The Confederation has its own need for it. An imperial invasion armada is on its way, little more than two years distant. You'll help develop strategies and tactics to counter the invasion. Which will mean turning over regimental command to someone else—whomever you consider best suited."

Romlar wasn't smiling now, but his face was relaxed, his answer casual. "Coyn Carrmak," he said. "He's my best officer, the best leader, and the smartest man in the regiment. And the men know how good he is. Beyond that, he's also the luckiest person I've ever seen." He glanced at Lotta. "With the exception of your brother.

Jerym's come through more than anyone else in the outfit, unscratched."

He turned back to Kristal. "I'm not surprised. What specifically do you have in mind for it?"

"More training. Partly in techniques and tactics no one's invented yet. That's where you come in. Are you willing?"

Romlar grinned. "I'm your man. It sounds interesting."

"Good. To start with, you'll work right here. Your office will be two floors down."

Romlar put a hand on Lotta's arm. "Does Lotta have a role in this?"

Kristal laughed. "She'll take you to lunch and answer your questions. Meanwhile, I have a great deal to do here." His gesture took in not only his desk and monitor, but the whole building. "We'll talk again, very soon."

Lotta took Romlar to the second floor, to a dining room whose transparent inner walls bordered the Rotunda. There they took a table near a cluster of flowering fern trees, their fronds soft green through the glass. A waiter brought menus, took their drink orders and left.

"An impressive place," Romlar said. "What hat do you wear here?"

"I'm Emry's principal psychic resource, and the head of his Remote Spying Section."

"How about getting married then? Take an apartment and be together for a change."

"I'm afraid I can't take an apartment with you."

His eyebrows raised. "Why not?"

She laughed. "Because Emry's assigned me a guest house on the hill. As free from psychic disturbance as you can get, this near the capital. I'm one of a kind, he tells me. To be more exact, he said: 'Lotta, you're like Artus. You're one of a kind.' " Her smile softened. "There's lots of room, if you'd like to share it with me. Our schedules won't always match, but we'll be together a lot more than once every few years."

Romlar chuckled. "I love you, Lotta. Very much. I suppose I've mentioned that before."

"I seem to recall something like that. In the dim past." She grinned. "Would you like to see the house first? Before you commit yourself to anything as drastic as marriage?"

He laughed aloud, then leaned across the table and they kissed.

Chapter 2
Wedding

Artus Romlar's twelve-day leave was busy. Lord Kristal had had six days in mind for him, but he'd gotten an extension in honor of his forthcoming marriage. He spent a day in Landfall with Lotta, shopping for civilian clothes, then six days with his parents.

Having their son at home had been a strange experience for them. As a boy, he'd been considered marginally retarded. Big, fat, and dumb, his schoolmates had put it. But seldom to his face, because violent could easily have been added. Not that he'd been truculent. Actually he'd been self-effacing, tried to go unnoticed. But when he was angered, his big fists flew. It was that which, soon after his seventeenth birthday, had taken him from public school to reformatory.

Now he stood in their living room, bigger than ever but hardbodied. And even to them, charismatic! At age twenty-six, he was by far the Confederation's most famous military figure in centuries. Not in the army, but commanding the 1st Special Projects Regiment, the glamorous White T'swa. Still a teenager, he'd led the defense of Terfreya. Then the regiment's survivors had dropped out of sight for a few years, completing their training on other worlds.

Seeing him again, his mother was almost unable to

16

speak. Her love for him, her only child, had been blunted only occasionally by his troubles at school. Despite her usual meekness, she'd defended him as best she could, even against a father who had problems of his own. A worrier who sometimes attacked his son with abusive mouth, and less often with his hands, a troubled man who'd tried but too often failed. Whose saving grace was appreciation of his wife's goodness, an awareness that kept him from abusing her physically, and for the most part verbally.

Now Artus's calm, self-assured presence awed them. Years earlier they'd seen action videos of the guerrilla war he'd led on Terfreya. Now news television was showing cubeage of the defense of Smolen, in the forests of distant Maragor. They'd viewed a column of crude sleighs, loaded with munitions and supplies. The gaunt horses pulling them were coated with rime from their own breath. They'd watched other people's sons die in battle. Watched their own son, a large and imposing total stranger, leading a file of deadly White T'swa on skis.

To those who'd known him only as a kid, it was unreal. And more unreal to have him there live, a smiling man who seemed even larger than he was. At the terminal, he'd hugged first his mother, then his father. The hug had startled Darlek Romlar, and triggered guilt. There were no cameras standing by—only his parents had known he was coming—and Artus wore casual civilian clothes. To better ensure privacy, he'd arrived on a routine government courier flight.

He'd had few friends in school, but on the second day he'd visited two of them, and two of his old teachers who had treated him with sensitivity. The visits blew his privacy, of course, and that evening he was respectfully contacted by local television, which was, of course, government controlled. He put them off, scheduling them for his last day there. On the third day he'd taken his parents for a two-day trip to Cobalt Lake, and the Great Cascade of the Alvslekk. There they'd seen the sights from a horse-drawn carriage, and eaten in fine restaurants. His mother adored him, while silently worrying about the cost. His father began to feel more comfortable with him.

Lotta had stayed at Landfall. The Iryalan culture did not require that fiancés and fiancées be approved by, or even meet their prospective in-laws. And on the job there was always more needing her personal attention than she had time for.

They were married the day after Artus returned. On Iryala, weddings were personal and intimate. Thus the reception was small but elegant; Lord Kristal had paid for it. The regiment was widely scattered on leave, and few even knew of it. A dozen attended. Colonel Voker had flown in from the Blue Forest Military Reservation, along with his T'swa counterpart, Dak-So. The T'swa colonel was larger than Artus, his scarred black face set off strikingly by his white dress scarf.

Sir Varlik Lormagen was also there, with his wife and their son Kusu. Kusu was OSP's Director of Research and Development, while Varlik had been the original "White T'swi." He'd served as correspondent with the T'swa Red Scorpion Regiment, in the Technite War on Kettle, more than thirty years earlier. The concept of T'swa-trained Iryalan regiments had originated with him.

After the reception, the newlyweds left on the traditional "love trip," five days on the coast, alone at a guest cottage on Lormagen beach property.

That evening, after a swim in a backwater pool, they sat on a split-log bench beneath a darkening sky, holding hands, and watching the surf crash on massive basalt. The first stars were appearing in the east. Artus chuckled.

"A beautiful day," he said, and grinned down at the woman beside him. "Who'd have imagined? It's quite a world, at least for its luckiest man."

"Artus," she answered, "luck is made, more often than not. Remind me to give you my advanced lecture on 'the parts of man.'"

"Parts of man?" he said. "If you'll give me a lecture, I'll give you a demonstration."

She jabbed him with an elbow. "That's not one of the parts I referred to." She got to her feet, then sat astride his lap, leaning against him, her face close to his. "Although if you're up to it again . . ." she purred.

Chapter 3
Briefing

In his office in the OSP Building, Kusu Lormagen touched the switch on his desk communicator. "What is it, Lira?"

"Colonel Romlar is here for his briefing, sir."

"Good. Send him in." As the Director of Research and Development got to his feet, the door opened and Artus entered. Kusu gestured at a chair.

Artus took it. "So," he said. "Here I am, ready to be informed."

"I don't know how much you already know."

"Assume zero. You won't be far off."

"Right. Lotta told me she was in two-way communication with you psychically, while you were still on Maragor, and let you know then about the invasion Armada. How much did she tell you?"

Artus frowned. He'd been in a weird state at the time. Had confused the Armada with a war fleet of twenty millennia earlier, that he'd revisited in nightmares. "I know it exists," he said. "That it left their central system two or three years ago. And that it's bigger and better equipped than anything we'll have to meet it with."

Kusu nodded. "We've made major progress in matching its equipment, but they'll arrive with close to twice as many warships of every class. I'll give you a chart comparing forces; you can familiarize yourself with it after you leave." He got up and walked to his beverage machine. "Joma?" he asked. "Or thocal?"

"Joma."

Kusu drew two cups and set one of them in front of Artus. Sitting down himself, he sipped reflectively and began his lecture. "I suppose you know how we've learned what we know."

"From Lotta. And her staff."

"Right. They get it through a covert, long-distance mind meld, the sort of thing she did as your intelligence specialist on Terfreya. Some T'swa have been able to do it for a long time. For generations, some of our Ostrak masters have been able to meld too, but only with people they knew, and mostly face to face. Lotta bridged the gap. She may be as good at it as any T'swi. And she's testing other Ostrak operators for the potential, and having them trained.

"The tricky part of remote spying is the initial connection. She learned how to find, and meld with, a person she simply knows *about*. That was the critical step. From them she learns about others with the sort of knowledge she wants to tap, and melds with them. A chain of connections, so to speak. So far as we know, none of the imperials has any notion they've been visited. Except maybe their central artificial intelligence; she tried snooping it." He grinned. "It spit her out. That's how she put it.

"The first person she trained was her own old mentor, Wellem Bosler. Now Wellem does the training for her, at the Lake Loreen Institute. And she runs the shop here—assigns, coordinates, and oversees projects. And generally handles the most important contacts herself, though she's gradually farming those out too."

He took another swallow of joma. "Interestingly though, some of the most critical information we've gotten came through standard intelligence procedures. When the Klestroni occupied Lonyer City, they wanted to learn what they could about the Confederation. And you know what a backwater world Terfreya is. Anyway the Klestroni rounded up a number of people there—bureaucrats, technicians, teachers—and took them out to their flagship. Kept them separate from each other and interrogated them, to learn what they could. They worked on them for all the weeks they were there, then released them on the surface before leaving."

"Just a minute," Romlar said. "I'm not clear on the connection between the Klestroni and the Empire."

"Klestron is simply one planet in the Empire. They're all sultanates—semiautonomous theocracies. With major overpopulation problems. The Klestroni were looking for a world to colonize and milk. After you guys ran them home, the Empire put together an armada to come back and do the job right."

Kusu paused till he remembered what he'd been saying. "At any rate, the Klestroni returned their prisoners to Terfreya. Their rules of warfare don't allow holding civilian prisoners after hostilities are broken off. Which was fortunate for us as well as the prisoners, because Lotta had Ostrak operators sent there, who questioned them at length in an Ostrak revery. Debriefed them, so to speak, of the questions the Klestroni had asked. The Klestroni were particularly interested in our fleet, including some kind of protective shield they assumed we had—something that protects ships from warbeams and torpedoes.

"The apparency was, they had shields while we definitely didn't. So ship armor was one of the first things Lotta snooped. It turned out not to be armor in the usual sense of the word. The imperials call it 'force shields' in their language."

Artus interrupted. "She's learned their language?"

"Not really. She reads flows of mental concepts and images. But to some degree they're tied up with language, which imprints on her language center as a kind of side effect."

Blessed 'Tunis, Artus thought, *I knew she was a genius, but . . .* She'd never talked shop with him, and he'd never asked. She dealt with shop ten to sixteen hours a day. And that, it seemed to him, was enough.

"Anyway," Kusu continued, "my group worked on developing shield generators, starting with the information she gave us. But even before we could make them, we knew our older warships couldn't accommodate them. We knew that well before the Klestroni got back home. So most of our fleet is new.

"The most remarkable thing Lotta did was provide us with technical information on the imperial fleet. *She had to fish it from people's minds while they thought about it or used it.* She had to find out who to hang around, psychically that is, and where and when. It's still beyond me how she managed to do it all, and to integrate what she learned into something that made sense. She had no engineering background at all! Zero! Nothing! Not even drafting. Her patience and persistence astounds me." He fixed Artus with his eyes. "When the history of all this is written, I have no doubt your wife will be ranked among the most remarkable human beings our species ever produced."

Artus stared at him, mind-boggled.

"Our older ships fell into two categories: the frigates and the rest of them. The frigates are inadequate in various respects, but we may find limited roles for them. The rest are being used as training ships. We're phasing them out as we commission new ships, and cannibalizing them for useful parts."

The two men sipped joma, then Kusu continued. The Imperial Armada, he said, was organized into three war fleets and a huge fleet of transports and supply ships. Each warfleet had its own flagship, each with its own supercomputer. The Confederation had nothing to match those computers, and no prospect at all of building any.

"Our one technical advantage," he said, "is the teleport.

The recent ones are far more accurate than the model you had on Terfreya. And apparently the Empire doesn't know such things are possible. They redeveloped science and technology a few thousand years ago, then at some point lost their science again almost as completely as we lost ours. We're not sure why; they don't seem to have had anything like the Sacrament. Anyway they've used the same old technology over and over for a long time, without much change. Lotta suspects their supercomputer had something to do with it. It seems to do their technical thinking for them, but apparently doesn't do basic research.

"At any rate, we can now make teleport jumps to targets in space almost as accurately as to surface targets, even without the gravitational interface effect."

He sensed blankness behind Artus's eyes. "Don't worry about how," he said. "We can go into that some other time, if you want. The important thing is, we can do it. What we're working on now is scale: how to build a functioning gate large enough to transit warships. There are some real problems. We keep hoping we'll find a way around the topological enigma, too, but so far we haven't a clue to work on."

Topological enigma? Artus had no idea what Kusu was talking about. Before he could ask, Kusu took a video cube from a drawer and handed it to him.

"I want you to familiarize yourself with this. It's from talks I've given to the War Ministry. It'll give you the basics of how fleets function in space. We're not trying to make you an expert in space warfare, but there are things you need to know. Read them today, then sleep on them. We'll talk again tomorrow."

Chapter 4
Elements of Space War

Artus put the cube in his reader, read the abstract and summary, then skimmed through the complete text, slowing here and there. To him it seemed hopeless.

On an impulse he phoned Lotta. Mostly she worked at home, but calls went through her administrative assistant in the OSP Building. Before Lotta entered a trance, she activated a signal light. It wasn't on, so the assistant put him through.

"Sweetheart," Artus said when she answered, "I've got Kusu's cube on spaceflight and space weaponry. I'd like to bring it home and work on it. I'll keep out of your way. . . . Right now. Will that be a problem? . . .

"Thanks. I'll want to have it on audio, too, if that's all right. . . . Okay. Be there soon."

It was most of a mile from the OSP building to the small house on the ridgecrest. Much of it was uphill, and wanting to get in decent shape again, Artus speed-marched it, jogging all but the steeper stretches. Being in less than peak condition, he arrived winded and sweaty, his legs tired.

He'd thought Lotta might shut herself into her office suite: two insulated north-end rooms with an insulglass roof. Instead she met him at the door.

"Hi," he said. "I'll stay out of your way."

"I'll listen with you," she answered. "I've never heard one of Kusu's War Ministry lectures."

"Maybe I should shower first," Artus said. "I might not smell too good."

"You're all right. Shower later."

He dried the sweat from his face with a hand towel, and put the cube in one of the living room players. Lotta poured cool fruit drinks, a taste they'd both developed on Tyss. Then they settled onto recliners facing the wall screen, and he started the reader. After a brief introduction by Kusu, the screen split. The right side would show visual aids as appropriate. The text appeared on the left, synchronized with Kusu's clear baritone:

WAR AND WEAPONRY IN SPACE

Let me begin with two caveats: You are not going to understand this. Even the math provides only limited understanding. What you can do is become thoroughly familiar with it—get used to it—and that's good enough. For those of you trained in space flight, much of it is already familiar.

My language here will be slippery, imprecise, and roundabout. The only language really suited to the discussion of N-spaces, and the physics of faster-than-light travel, is an esoteric mathematics we have only recently reacquired. Since none of you know that particular calculus, I'll use the language of metaphor, which serves well enough for our purposes.

Keep in mind that we've been doing these things for thousands of years, using technology inherited from before the Sacrament. What's changed is that we now know how it works, which allows us to explore problems, and create solutions and new applications.

Some Key Things to Know About Space Travel

Strictly speaking, in most space travel, we do not travel in space-time as we know it. Instead we make use of "parallel" space-times, using hyperdrive for hyperspace, and warpdrive for warpspace.

Think of the various space-times as N-dimensional grids, with lines that are simultaneously explicit—both distinct and ordered—yet effectively contiguous, their separation infinitely small. N can be any one of a not yet fully explored and defined set of integers.

With existing technology, or even theoretical technology, only three sets of dimensions can be entered and traversed. They are termed "warpspace," with 10 dimensions, "hyperspace," with 16 dimensions, and our familiar, 4-dimensional "F-space." Warpspace and hyperspace are sometimes collectively referred to as "strange spaces." Only warpdrive and hyperdrive are practical for traversing interstellar distances.[1] Everything else is too slow. The equation which permits travel through 16-dimensional hyperspace allows extreme but not infinite "speeds." It also allows the hyperspace ship to track its own progress through F-space, and allows it to emerge into F-space at approximately the coordinates chosen.[2]

The high hyperspace "velocity" cap permits travel through considerable reaches of our spiral arm in reasonably short periods of time—weeks or years. Furthermore, mass does not increase with either "velocity" or "acceleration," because strictly speaking, in hyperspace (and in warpspace as well) there is no velocity or acceleration. Although changes in location take place over time, in hyper- and warpspace those changes are infinitely small. That is, virtually zero. Only when translated into F-space are they finite.

---

[1] The space technology left us by the ancients grew out of theoretical research on how the universe functions. At an intermediate stage in that research, a concept of interstellar travel developed, based on the notion that 4-dimensional space could be "warped." It was therefore termed "warpdrive." Though the concept would prove unproductive, the term became popularized in fiction.

Later, totally unrelated research led to the concept of 10-dimensional space as a means of bypassing the light-speed limit on travel in 4-dimensional space. The popular term "warpdrive," and by extension "warpspace," were quickly but inappropriately applied to it. The original concept of "warpdrive" does not at all fit the actual "warpdrive," which does not "warp" familiar 4-dimensional space.

[2] Theoretically the coordinate match is precise. However, for reasons not understood, the actual match is approximate, and the error unpredictable in both magnitude and direction.

Artus's lips had tightened. He wanted to be anywhere but where he was, doing anything but this. He flicked a glance at Lotta. She was looking intently at him, and his eyes flicked back to the screen. Meanwhile Kusu's voice had not stopped.

> I've been speaking metaphorically. Now I need to switch metaphors on you. If some parts of this discussion seem inconsistent with others, it is the fault of metaphor as explanation. As far as we know, reality is consistent, and so is its mathematics.
>
> Warpdrive requires far more time to transfer a mass a given F-space distance than hyperdrive does. Thus, loosely speaking, we can say that warpdrive is much "slower." In fact, the far greater "speed" of hyperdrive makes it the only really practical means for travel between widely separated systems.
>
> On the other hand, the distortions caused in warp-space by the proximity of stellar masses are far far less than the analogous distortions in hyperspace. By contrast, for a ship in hyperdrive to "emerge" into F-space deep within the gravity well of a star system, would be violently fatal to ship and crew. Thus warpdrive remains very important to insystem transportation.
>
> Hyperdrive and warpdrive do not generate matter, and hyperspace and warpspace do not contain matter. When they "contain" a ship, the ship is an "island" of F-space, so to speak, an island encapsulated by warp- or hyperspace but not part of them.
>
> Furthermore, the properties of hyperspace permit emergence into F-space from any hyperspace "velocity" *without generating F-space momentum*. Thus a ship newly emerged from hyperspace is always motionless in F-space. It is "parked," so to speak.
>
> Emergence from warpspace is less simple. Warp-speed must be cut effectively to zero before emerging. Otherwise momentum is instantaneously generated in F-space, proportional to the "warpspeed," with resultant inertial stresses on the spacecraft, and on any organisms in it.[1] To emerge from warpspace at only one mile per second would convert personnel

---

[1] There is, of course, neither actual speed nor actual momentum in warpspace or in hyperspace. However, in both there is what can be called "virtual speed" and "virtual momentum."

to mush. However, within warpspace, "speed" can safely be "slowed" from maximum to zero in picoseconds, an interval undetectable to human senses but nicely manageable by a navcomp. The ship can then be translated safely into F-space.

Reaction drives analogous to those used in fireworks could be built for use in F-space, but would serve no practical function. . . .

Then why ramble on about it? Romlar thought resentfully. He shifted in his seat, and did not look at Lotta. He also cut the audio and speeded the march of the text up the screen, skipping as he read.

Gravdrive is the usual means of maneuvering near planets and landing on them. And it permits hovering in relativistic motionlessness. . . .

Emergence from hyperspace into warpspace, or vice versa, is not possible. One must emerge into F-space as an intermediate step. . . .

Being relativistically immobile while flying encapsulated within strange space, a ship can carry out extreme maneuvers without inertial effects. As an experience, flying in strange space is much like sitting in an unmoving virtual reality game, pretending to fly. . . .

I will now shift gears and seemingly contradict some of what I've already said. . . .

Seemingly contradict . . . Artus swore inwardly. This was, he told himself, the most exasperating thing he'd ever read.

Hyperspace and warpspace differ importantly in almost every respect. But in a sense, neither strange space exists in "nature"—except as a potential. From the viewpoint of F-space, *they exist only in the fields generated by a hyperdrive or warpdrive.* They are artifacts! However, a hyperspace *potential* and a warpspace *potential* do exist in F-space. It is these which permit the generation of those foreign spaces.

Communication is a problem for hyperspace ships. Messages analogous to radio messages can be generated, and for example pass through the hyperspace potential from one hyperspace ship to another, with the transmission interval a complex function of their relative hyperspace potentiality coordinates, practical only when ships are traveling together on nearby parallel courses. . . .

"Artus," Lotta said, "kill it for a moment." As his Ostrak operator, she knew her husband's personality profile, and his history as a person and a student. His military studies had been under T'swa instructors—practical, hands-on studies with intuition emphasized and nurtured. And he'd been brilliant, both analytically and intuitively.

Earlier however, as a pupil in school, he'd been submarginal. Fortunately the problem hadn't been genetic, and his blockages against learning from books had been greatly reduced by Ostrak processing. But he'd had no successful experience in abstract studies. His successes had been in learning "how to do," and when.

"You told me you'd read it at your office," Lotta said. "How did you go about it?"

Shrugging he frowned, and described what he'd done—read the abstract and summary, but mostly skimmed the rest. "I wasn't getting it anyway," he added.

She nodded. "You had steam coming out your ears here. You need involvement while you learn." She cocked an eyebrow at him. "Why did you want to work on this at home?"

He stroked his chin thoughtfully. "I guess— No guess about it. I hoped you'd offer to help. I know you've got more than enough to do, but I hoped—I *knew* you'd listen with me, and make some suggestions."

She nodded curtly. "My suggestion right now is that we read, or skim, the rest of it, then eat lunch. After lunch I'll make further suggestions."

Again they sat back, and he continued the program.

Mainly About War in Hyperdrive

Two ships can actually encounter, detect, and even attack one another while in their separate hyperspaces—in a sense their own separate universes. Because hyperspace *potential* permeates all of F-space.

And hyperdrive can be thought of as propagating a moving hyperspace cell through that potentiality.

Conversely, to a ship in hyperspace or warpspace, F-space is only a potentiality, and objects in F-space have "degrees" of potentiality, depending on their mass. Mass and proximity are the basis for ships in hyperspace or warpspace detecting objects in F-space.[1]

If they are "near enough" to one another in the hyperspace potentiality, one ship can detect another through the hyperspace potential, "locate" and lock onto it, and destroy it with a torpedo. This is possible because a torpedo is an unmanned hyperspace craft which, instructed by its onboard navcomp, generates its own hyperspace cell, with its own "vectors."

Basics of Defense

A ship in strange space can generate a shield, reconfiguring its strange space to accommodate the shield. However, in any space, interactions between the drive, the shield, and the shield generator result in stresses on the drive and the shield generator. . . . Ships in hyperspace very rarely encounter blips of another ship, even in "heavy traffic" zones. . . .

In hyperspace, a ship fearing a torpedo attack can instantly cut field generation and emerge in F-space. . . . With existing instrumentation, a ship in hyperspace cannot, without emerging, detect something as small as a ship in either warpspace or F-space. . . .

It is futile to fire torpedoes into F-space at a computed emergence coordinate. All strange-space astrogational computations are approximate, and the errors, though expressed in nano- or picodegrees, increase proportional to target distance. Thus, at the distances involved, torpedoes emerging into F-space are virtually certain to miss their targets. . . .

Artus paused the program and looked at his wife. "Sweetheart," he said, "I can see how important this is to people commanding warships, and the subject *is* interesting, but why does Kusu want me to know it?"

---

[1] Actually it is not mass itself that is sensed by instruments in hyperspace, but mass-induced distortions in the hyperspace *potential*, which is distinct from hyperspace. Hyperspace itself is not coupled with either electromagnetism or gravity.

"You'll have to ask him. But I suspect it's a matter of knowing the larger field within which you'll be acting. That's my guess. Speed the scrolling, and slow it if something catches your attention. Maybe that will help."

Nodding, he followed her suggestion.

> . . . In warpspace, a ship's instruments can provide details permitting an image to be digitally synthesized and identified by a battlecomp. This is not true in hyperspace, where only a blip is discerned, along with its mass and location. . . .
>
> When a ship emerges into F-space, it produces an emergence wave in the hyperspace potential. This wave arrives at a system's planets and defense installations essentially instantaneously, warning them that something has arrived, approximately where, and with about what mass. . . .

Warbeams

> Beam guns have major advantages over torpedoes: First, a warbeam is effectively continuous while being fired. Secondly, a warbeam can be destroyed only by destroying the gun. Thirdly, except on scouts and other small craft, shield generators can produce topologically complex shields that permit ships to fire warbeams without "dropping" their shields.
>
> Beam guns also have major limitations. The greatest is, *they function only in F-space.* Beams do not propagate through the hyperspace or warpspace potentialities. . . . To fire beams is a major drain on a ship's power. . . .
>
> Shield protection is weakened if at some point a multi-layered shield is sequentially deactivated to fire torpedoes. . . . When an opponent's shield and shield generator are stressed by beam attack, a torpedo may more readily break them. . . .
>
> With existing technology, to escape from F-space into a strange space requires deactivating the shield generators, then allowing the shield to decay. Thus, once a ship engages in a beam fight, it is unlikely to have an opportunity to escape, except by running away in gravdrive, which of course is slow.

Torpedoes

> Torpedoes are armed with a disrupter charge,[1] and have greater destructive power than warbeams. Invariably, a torpedo's navcomp will be locked on a target before or quickly after launch. . . .

When Lotta saw the sentence on disrupters, she shifted her gaze to Artus. His aura had shrunken and turned cloudy. *That again,* she thought. Back when she'd been his Ostrak operator and he was still the fat dumb kid, she'd known he had some extreme incident sitting in his deep history, lives and lives ago. An incident too powerful to get at and defuse. Later she'd gotten a sense of it, and later still, parts of the picture. But not the key. Without it, his reaction to Kusu's lecture would have been much milder.

She returned her attention to the screen. Material about torpedoes was scrolling. Mostly it seemed fairly straightforward.

> Ships of about 7 to 12 kilotons can generate two-layered shields, and ships heavier than about 12 kilotons three or more layers, sufficiently separated so that hits on the outer leave the inner intact.
>
> Launching torpedoes from a shielded ship requires generating torpedo ports, which weaken the shield layers. Usually, torpedo ports are generated through one layer at a time to reduce the risk. This greatly slows a torpedo's launch speed, at the same time warning the intended target. . . .

The last page flicked from the screen, replaced by an image of Kusu's face saying: "End of program. Thank you for your attention." Artus's finger shut the reader off. He looked better than he had a few minutes earlier, but Lotta wondered what his dreams would be like when next he slept.

"Did it go better this time than before?" she asked.

---

[1] A disrupter charge is a small and very primitive analog of the planet killer of the ancients, which caused the long-term collapse of civilization in the Home Sector.

"Better?" He shook his head more in thought than denial. "I feel as if I know more. Because I've gone through it twice, I suppose."

Lotta got from her chair. "Go take that shower. I'll dish up some of the sea salad Arlana mixed this morning, and toast some bread."

When they'd finished their lunch, Artus started back to his office, and Lotta placed a call. "Kusu," she said, "what kind of response have you gotten on your space war lecture?"

His eyebrows raised. "Variable. At least when I've given it live."

"Elaborate."

He knew at once she'd watched it with Artus, and had found it lacking. "Some of them liked it. Others had trouble with it; too strange, I suppose. Maybe too much all at once? They tended to doze, or seemed—impatient. Maybe irritated. Did Artus have any trouble?"

"Yes he did. You have a particular kind of mind, and you've worked with the problems. The operative term being 'worked with.' In your lecture you've presented a whole stew pot of significances—and no doingness. It goes with the subject, I suppose. What's needed now is a program in which you stop after every major point or set of points, and ask questions. 'What if' questions. 'So what' questions. *Engage* them. *Involve* them. Call Artus in tomorrow and practice on him. Maybe have him diagram things. It'll do you both good. Then assign one of your people to do it with others."

Her face and voice were firm, definite. *I screwed it up,* Kusu told himself. "Will do," he said. "And thanks."

"You're welcome," she replied, and T'swa fashion cut the connection without another word, as if he was no longer there. For a moment Kusu looked ruefully at the blank screen. He was supposed to be the remarkable, the *powerful* mind in the OSP, and with regard to science, he was. But for breadth and depth of understanding . . .

He remembered her from one early summer day in his youth, on an institute staff picnic at Lake Loreen. He'd been the young hotshot reopening the long suppressed field of physics research, and Lotta had been a bright, carrot-topped little child in a crisp yellow dress. The only child there, flitting sure and unselfconscious among the adults. The other children—she was one of the youngest—had gone home for the solstice holidays. He hadn't known her name, but she'd caught his attention as some kind of unclassifiable but very special phenomenon.

If they pulled the fat from the fire, in this time of extraordinary danger, it would be she to whom the greatest credit belonged. He had no doubt at all of that.

He grunted, chuckled. She'd taken time from her own intensely full schedule to review and critique his work, had found it lacking, and given him his orders. *I'd better,* he told himself, *get busy on them.*

Chapter 5
Kurakex

Glaring, the killer lizard straddled her prey, while her young bit and worried the dead ungulate with their small jaws. About seventy feet away stood three bipeds, holding spears. Over thousands of generations, the lizards had evolved an awareness that bipeds stabbed at the eyes, and that their resonating hoots brought others. When enough gathered, they attacked.

Briefly she took her attention from them, and sank triangular serrated teeth into a haunch. Her powerful neck jerked viciously, then she tossed her head and swallowed before returning her gaze to the bipeds.

The Garthids watched patiently. Others of their pack would arrive soon; there'd already been an ululating answer from the edge of hearing. Peripherally one of them saw a movement, and murmured. The others turned their heads slightly. "Shafa," one guessed aloud, for the biped loping toward them was alone. As the newcomer neared, the hunters could see a sinew tied loosely around the thick neck, bones and feathers strung on it. A flute would hang between the shoulder blades. A shafa.

The newcomer slowed to a walk. The lizard watched, then returned her attention to the carcass. The shafa approached her without even displaying his parietal hood. After speaking quietly, he crouched by the kill, lowered his jaws and set heavy fangs, then tore a mouthful from a shoulder. Briefly he chewed, then swallowed. The young complained at the intrusion but did not stop their feeding. When the shafa had taken several bites, he stood, murmured again, and left.

Their voices guttural, the other Garthids spoke respectfully to him as he passed. He gestured a salute, and a moment later broke into his tireless lope.

They did not resent the performance. Shafan were shafan. They lived and traveled alone, attacking neither beasts nor other Garthids. Rather, they healed. They even healed animals. Now and then one stopped with a resting Garthid pack, and spent an hour or several. Fed with them. Healed wounds, infections, broken limbs. Chanted a tale or two, then left. It brought luck to have one stop.

In the packs, only an occasional offspring showed the gifts. Invariably these left as preadolescents, to learn from some older shafa.

The ululations of other pack members were much nearer now—two trios from different directions. The three gripped their spears in anticipation. They were hungry, and hoped the lizard would leave without a fight, as usual. When they didn't, Garthids sometimes died.

The lizard watched the Garthid reinforcements approach, and with a clawed forefoot slapped her young from their feeding. Her legs were longer than they looked, and she straightened them, raising her swag belly a yard above the ground. Expanding her frill, she opened her gape at the gathering thieves. Then, hissing like a steam vent, she backed away, dangerous head swinging from side to side, her young dodging nimbly underfoot. Finally she turned and left resentfully at a swinging trot, her young scurrying beside her.

❖   ❖   ❖

Approximately an imperial year after the Karghanik Armada left the Varatos System, it "entered" Garthid space. But only figuratively. It traveled in hyperspace, the only feasible means of crossing such distances. Its admiral had no intention at all of emerging into that sector of four-dimensional F-space—Familiar space—where a Garthid patrol might be encountered.

The Karghanik Empire knew next to nothing about the Garthids. Didn't even have a name for them. They called them simply the "aliens"—and wanted no trouble with a species whose military capacities were unknown. They knew, of course, that their Klestronu cousins had violated alien space and fired on alien patrol ships. And they assumed the aliens would remember.

They were correct. What they did not imagine was the vast sentry system the aliens had recently emplaced in the hyperspace potential of their sector.

Admiral Kurakex sekTofarko stood stoney-faced and rigid while the Surrogate gave him more instructions than any commander would ever want. Why should he be burdened with such constraints? The aliens had entered Garthid space. That in itself was an affront, and reeked of ill intent. And had fired on a patrol ship—first!—demonstrating ill intent without any conceivable doubt. Then they'd fled, displaying their cowardly, devious, cunning nature. Devious, cunning, dangerous.

Only to emerge again near the far edge of the Khanate. And who knew how many places in between, undetected? Any fool could see they were carrying on a reconnaissance, and the only possible reason was war! Raiding. Maybe conquest.

Yet here was the Surrogate warning him to avoid war unless the intruders displayed ill intentions. That question had already been answered, and war it would be! He'd have to be very careful, of course, cover his nape at all times, say the politically correct things . . .

That was the hard part—saying the politically correct things.

The Surrogate paused, his eyes drilling deeply. "Do you have any questions?"

"No, Your Potency."

The words were sour in Kurakex's mouth. Both were of the guardian gender, the admiral as large as the Surrogate, and perhaps stronger. Younger by more than a decade—still in his prime. It seemed to him he could take the old ruler, throw him, roll him in the dirt, kill him if it came to it. But politically it would be disastrous, for himself and his clan.

"Good," said the Surrogate. His gaze was intense. "I know you well, Admiral." Again he paused, then his heavy features relaxed a bit, though the red-brown, slit-irised eyes remained hard. "I am aware that my admonitions seem onerous to you, that you would prefer to simply attack in force. But we do not know what sort of beings you will find out there." The Surrogate gestured skyward. "Or in what strength, or how great their empire." He paused, and when he continued, the words were like slow drumbeats, measured and powerful. "*We must not make war needlessly. Unjustly. Recklessly.* Do you understand? But if we must make war, it is vital that we prevail."

His jaws, during his student days, had been famed for their strength. He clamped them now like a killer lizard's, their heavy muscles bulging from jawline to the crest of his skull. Finally he continued: "My instructions to you have been recorded in the central computer. Even now they are being distributed planetwide. Empirewide with the daily pods." He paused again, for emphasis. "So there will be no misunderstanding. When you return, I would much prefer to reward you than execute you."

"Yes, Your Potency!" The threat, and the hard-bodied imperial guards nearby, made Kurakex overheat. None were friends of Clan Tofarko. He had to fight the panting reflex.

"Good." The Surrogate's demeanor turned casual, despite what he'd just said. "I would send someone with a reputation for moderation, but if there is fighting, we must win decisively. And you are my best commander." Again he paused, his eyes half hooded now. "My misgivings are serious. Therefore I am sending someone with you, to help you maintain perspective. Someone who carries my full authority."

Kurakex felt his chest tighten. What could this mean?

"Esteemed Valvoxa will accompany you as your spiritual overseer and my personal representative. When he speaks, he will speak for me. And more importantly he will speak for *God!* Remember that well, Lord Kurakex! He will attend you at his personal will. You will keep nothing from him. He will have free access to all meetings, orders, records and instructions. You will yield to him in all matters except military strategy and tactics."

The Surrogate's rough lip callosities pressed briefly, meaningfully together. "And be sure that no harm comes to him. His life is your life. Understood?"

Kurakex's gut burned like coals. "Understood, Your Potency!"

"There must be no war unless the intruders are set on it. But if Esteemed Valvoxa agrees that war is necessary—*if he agrees!*—then you must move promptly. Send couriers back, crush whatever force confronts you, and from there, follow your own judgment."

At that, Kurakex had tingled from foreplate to heels. It took strong will to prevent his hood from flaring. There could be no doubt that war was necessary; anything less was wishful thinking. "Yes, Your Potency!"

"Good. You are dismissed."

Kurakex gave the deep bow of submission, holding for a moment at the bottom, exposed, should the Surrogate choose to strike. Then he straightened, turned, and left the Supreme Presence, already examining ways he could deal with the imposition of a shafa on his bridge.

Watching him leave, the Surrogate damned the clan politics that had forced Kurakex sekTofarko on him. Well. It was in the hands of God now. And God's servant Valvoxa.

Chapter 6
Confidences Shared Before a Journey

Somewhat more than a year earlier, and a very great distance from the Garthid homeworld, Shuuf'r Thaak, two humans sat in an arbor. In a palace garden, on a world called Varatos. Neither of them knew the Surrogate of God existed, barely knew the Garthids existed. One of the two was the Emperor Kalif of the Karghanik Empire, Chodrisei "Coso" Biilathkamoro. The other was his deputy, the exarch and Kalif-to-be, Jilsomo Savbatso.

The Kalif would leave the planet before lunch. Most of the things he would take with him had already been sent up to the flagship.

It was a lovely sunny morning, and from time to time the two prelates sipped iced tea. When the Kalif had said he wanted to speak privately with him, Jilsomo had supposed he had last minute observations and suggestions to communicate. So far, however, he'd seemed preoccupied, saying nothing beyond comments on the weather and garden.

For just a moment his obsidian eyes touched those of his deputy, then shifted elsewhere again. "What do you think of the language and literacy training the invasion troops have been given?" he asked.

The question surprised the deputy. The Kalif knew well what he thought of it. "I like it," Jilsomo said. "I like it very much. I intend to expand it, as feasible, to peasants outside the military."

By and large, army command had thought it a waste of time—time that might better have been spent in additional military training. Many from the Great Families considered it subversive, a continuation of reform.

After a moment the Kalif spoke again. "There is something I've kept from you, about the invasion expedition. It is not what it seems."

Not what it seems? Jilsomo's eyebrows rose. *What else could it be, that vast armada of warships and transports waiting some 60,000 miles out?*

"Since the coup attempt," the Kalif went on, "I've looked differently at war. Consider the destruction we suffered here, then imagine it extended over a planet." He shook his head. "I intend there be no conquest. No destruction, no killing."

Jilsomo had always felt uncomfortable about invading the Confederation, but wasn't it preemptive? There was, after all, the prospect of the Confederation invading the Empire, a prospect the Kalif himself had emphasized. Had made it seem quite real. The Klestroni, in their arguably illegal military exploration, had attacked a minor Confederation fringe world, had occupied its major town. Only to be driven off by a Confederation garrison, a garrison that had fought with sobering ferocity and skill. Surely a people like that would plan retribution, and they would hardly distinguish between a wayward sultanate and the Empire of which it was part.

"What do you have in mind, Your Reverence?"

"The armada will wait in the outer reach of the Iryalan System, while I go in with a single ship, a scout, and confer with them."

Jilsomo sat with plump lips parted. *I'm the one who's seen as peacemaker,* he thought. *You have been the fighter.*

Fighter, seasoned politician, and skeptic. Had Coso Biilathkamoro been as observant as usual, he'd have seen dismay in his deputy's eyes. No wonder he'd kept this secret. His plan seemed naive beyond belief.

He continued. "Consider. The Confederation consists of some seventy worlds—member worlds, trade worlds, resource worlds. Seventy! Over a sector of space as large as it can administer, a sector rich in habitable systems. Unlike our own. What lies beyond it? Surely they've explored. They must know of habitable worlds unpeopled beyond their fringes. I'll find out what they know of them, then go to one and colonize it.

"And if there are none, we'll dicker for one of their fringe worlds, one largely unsettled, like the world the Klestroni found."

His lips twisted. "If they refuse to talk, or if they prove hostile or treacherous, perhaps we'll fight them after all. But in Kargh's name, I'll make every effort to deal peacefully."

He spread his hands as if examining the hairs that curled thick and dark on his fingers. "Earlier, under the pressures of politics and in my own shortsighted hubris, I promoted recklessly, and endangered my options. Now I must make it come out in a way the Prophet would approve.

"On our new world, the peasant soldiers will become our citizens, the pastors their teachers. I will prevent a stratification into masters and serfs there, and the Pastorate will be my allies."

Coso Biilathkamoro chuckled wryly, but his face was bleak.

He knows, Jilsomo thought, *how impossible it is. The officer corps will not settle for less than conquest. He argued too well for it, made too many—call them promises. Inspired too many ambitions, stoked the furnaces of greed.*

"I'll have nearly four years to work on it," Coso went on, "four years in hyperspace, without the burden of governing. The kalifa and little Rami and I, and my guard company, will not travel in stasis." He smiled slightly, without humor. "I have allies, though they don't know yet what I intend.

"I've told this to no one except you and the kalifa. Tomorrow, when the flagship passes Sentinel, and we enter hyperspace, you will be Kalif, and you can do with the information as you please."

They'd neglected their drinks. Now they turned to them, saying almost nothing. The Kalif's eyes absorbed the garden around him. A corporal of the palace guard arrived, saluted. "Your Reverence," he said, "the shuttle is ready."

The Kalif looked at him and sighed. "Thank you, corporal." He got to his feet with unaccustomed heaviness, and turning to the exarch, shook his hand. "You've been my good friend and confidant, Jilsomo. I'll miss you. Miss your help, your good advice—your necessary scoldings."

Friend? Yes, Jilsomo thought. *But confidant? Certainly you said nothing of this before. If you have a confidant, besides the kalifa, it is SUMBAA. And I'm not sure an artificial intelligence qualifies.*

"Thank you, Your Reverence. I am honored."

The Kalif looked around as if remembering a hundred things undone, a thousand unsaid. "You'll remember to give the envelopes to Thoga and Tariil? And Dosu?"

"Depend on it, Your Reverence."

"Well then." He seemed reluctant to leave, to face what awaited him in space. Again he extended his drill-callused hand to Jilsomo, and again they shook. When their hands disengaged, the Kalif's strong shoulders straightened. "All right, corporal," he said, "let's go."

Jilsomo accompanied them. The Kalif's heaviness had dropped from him. His bearing, his stride, his whole demeanor bespoke strength and certainty, but Jilsomo was not fooled. The shuttle sat on the drill ground, the kalifa waiting by the ramp, still lovely. Always lovely except that one terrible day, that day of destruction and blood.

Stood holding little Rami, who could be so remarkably patient and quiet for a child so young and normally so active. Rami reached out to his father, who took him laughing, and the kalifal family walked up the ramp together into the shuttle.

The colonel of the kalifal guard battalion had also been waiting, and moved to stand beside Jilsomo. Together they watched the ramp telescope and disappear, the hullmetal door slide shut. The craft lifted easily, then accelerated slowly and quietly out of sight.

"I'm going to miss him, Your Reverence," the colonel said.

Your Reverence. It was premature, of course. He was only acting kalif, wouldn't be crowned till the next evening. Then he *would* be "Your Reverence." Jilsomo felt of the title. It felt—as if it would fit. He'd get immersed in the duties, the problems, the intrigues of governing this unwieldy Empire, and it would fit.

"I'll miss him too, Colonel," he said. "I'll miss him too." Four hopeless years. He was glad he wasn't Coso Biilathkamoro.

Afterward, in his office, Jilsomo reexamined what the Kalif had told him. The explanation, of course, was the kalifa. She'd been the one uniformed prisoner the Klestroni had brought back with them. Being female, she had not been killed. And being military, she might, beneath her deep amnesia, have useful information. That had been the rationale. Eventually she'd been brought to the palace, and once the Kalif had seen her . . .

Tests supported her amnesia. But even remembering nothing of her background, what had she felt and said when she learned her new husband planned to conquer the world she'd come from?

The Kalif's moods, these last few years, were clear now. He'd thought he'd understood them before. Because of the reforms he'd forced through, the military distrusted him. Even with the gentry and most of the lesser nobility behind him, since Iron Jaw's coup attempt, he'd ruled under the threat of another. This was widely recognized.

Now he planned to single-handedly frustrate the officer corps' passion for conquest, wealth, power, and a new empire far larger than the old.

It seemed to Jilsomo he'd never again see Coso Biilathkamoro alive.

In his small but comfortable suite on the flagship, the Armada's command admiral sat talking with a long-time friend, Major General Sopal Butarindala. Sopal "Snake" Butarindala, named in his student days for his skill on the wrestling mat. He commanded the 2nd Marine Division.

"He boarded half an hour ago," the admiral said. "He and his foreign wife. He was under some pressure to stay behind—some of it inspired by myself—and I hoped he'd change his mind. I didn't expect him to, but until he boarded . . ." The admiral shrugged. "Kargh does not arrange things for our convenience."

"Too bad we couldn't simply have left before he arrived."

"Believe me I was tempted. But it wouldn't be worth the trouble it would cause." The admiral chuckled. "More trouble than his presence creates. Actually, he's less a problem than Chesty may turn out to be. But with your help, and my, um—" he grinned "—my *fist*, we'll handle it nicely."

Snake Butarindala was uncomfortable with the admiral's "fist." It was a heavy secret to know. But if his own contingency role proved necessary, it was knowledge he'd need.

The admiral's wide mouth pursed. "You know, I rather like Chesty. Good man. Able. But soft in critical areas. Well, we'll see. We'll see."

The general grunted. "I'd better get down to Stasis,"

he said, rising to his feet. "It's either that or eat, and if I eat, I'll have to starve another twelve hours before they're willing to chill me."

The admiral gestured from his chair, a casual sort of farewell salute. "The next time I see you," he said, "I'll be some three, close to four years older. Four boring years. And you'll be what? A few days older."

As the general reached the door, the admiral spoke two final words. "Pleasant dreams," he said.

Snake left with a slight frown. He'd never heard whether people dreamed in stasis or not. Going on four years of dreaming? He hoped not. But surely they didn't; he'd have heard. People would talk about it if they did.

The admiral got to his feet too, to go to the bridge. Snake Butarindala had never been a mental giant, he thought. But the man was tough, resourceful, and dependable. While Chesty— *Chesty thinks too damn much*, the admiral told himself, *about the wrong things. That's what his trouble is. That's what makes him soft.*

Chapter 7
Death and Reality

The Kalif and his family were escorted to their new quarters by a young and respectful marine. Turning on their living room wall screen revealed Varatos as a great blue and white orb some sixty thousand miles distant. From their point of view above the southern polar region, much of the white was solid—the south polar sea ice, and the ice caps of its encircling archipelagos, bathed in midsummer light.

Tain, the kalifa, began to settle in those personal belongings they'd kept at the palace until the last hours. Rami played quietly. Coso still gazed at the wall screen, but his focus had left it. *I'm here*, he thought. *The die is cast.*

For most of his eventful life, fear had been foreign to him. As regret had, very largely. His style had been to decide, act, evaluate the results, and continue from there, trusting his intuition, analytical skill, and judgment. Operating at high levels, he'd impacted the lives of billions, and experienced considerable personal danger.

The keys had been self-trust and self-forgiveness. Until the last three years, any fears he'd felt had been momentary, and his regrets brief. Since then, however, he'd become intimate with both, particularly regret. They'd waited for him on his pillow, and visited him by

49

day, whispering in his ear. Never in all his years of trusting his analyses and intuitions had any action of his threatened such harm.

He'd often wondered how he could possibly have overlooked the destructive consequences of invasion. But to back down would have resulted in a coup to make Iron Jaw's seem trivial, wiping out the almost revolutionary gains he'd made for the Empire and its future.

And the Armada would have set out anyway.

The best he could do, and what he must do, was turn invasion into pioneering colonization. On paper he had the authority. He was the Emeritus Kalif and Grand Admiral of the Armada, Representative Plenipotentiary of the new Emperor Kalif. On paper, his orders carried the authority of the imperial throne.

But the military had embraced the expedition's original purpose—the one he himself had sold them. They'd made it their own, and made it clear to the House of Nobles that they would not tolerate opposition.

Now he plotted alone. His only chance of success required surprise, and an audacity they'd hardly anticipate even from him. As for the odds . . . He hadn't asked SUMBAA before leaving—his SUMBAA, the imperial, central SUMBAA. He hadn't wanted to know. And at any rate it seemed a calculation that even a SUMBAA could not make with meaningful accuracy.

All he needed to do—all!—was kill the command admiral and the general of the Expeditionary Army, both at once, both of them routinely, ceremonially armed. Kill them, and any armed aides and marines with them. He'd wait till the ship was in hyperspace, enter the bridge amiably, exchange innocuous pleasantries—then strike quickly and hard. Take command, hold the bridge crew under control with his pistol, and call his guards to him. Get them there before any more marines arrived.

He had perhaps a half dozen hours before the hyperspace jump. Time in which to brief his guard officers and platoon sergeants, time for them to get used to the plan and their assignments. He knew ships of this class from his own marine service, and had visited this one several times while the armada had slowly gathered. Knew where to post men to reach the bridge quickly, to protect it from recapture.

It was quite simple, but not easy at all.

Then would come the real challenge, the great challenge: getting the officer corps to obey him. If he succeeded in that, eventually he'd have to negotiate an acceptable agreement with the Confederation's rulers. He wasn't sure that was possible either, whether any of it was. His only choice was to start, and deal with problems as he came to them.

Of course, if he was killed, he'd leave a widow and child on a hostile ship. He'd explained that to Tain, early on, but she'd refused to stay behind.

Meanwhile the invasion army, including its officers, was in stasis lockers aboard the armada's troopships. Even aboard the fighting ships, most of the crew were in stasis. On so long a voyage, supply considerations dictated it. Thus, even on the flagship, the only people not in stasis were the ship's skeleton crew, with its officers, the two invasion commanders, their immediate staffs, and the flagship's marine company.

And his family and himself, of course, and his personally chosen company of the kalifal guard. They were dedicated to him, and highly trained. Most had been blooded during the failed coup. It was they who made his plot at all feasible, who'd protect him till he could pacify the marines.

Pacifying the marines was the most uncertain task in an uncertain first phase.

Abruptly the wall screen went blank, and a moment's queasiness marked entry into warpspace. At the same moment, there'd been a single screech. He hurried into the room from which it had come. An orange-colored cat lay stretched on the cover of Rami's bed, eyes bulging lifelessly. It had ejected the contents of stomach and bowel. Rami stood pale-faced, pointing. "Something's wrong with Lotta," he said. His voice was small, the words pronounced clearly for a child so young.

Coso realized what had happened. All spaceships had cats, for hunting rats. Occasionally, infrequently, one would not survive its first experience of warpspace generation.

He rested a hand on it. Not to feel for life—there'd be none—but as a gesture. Tain had hurried in behind him. It was she who knelt before Rami and explained his first experience with death. Coso simply listened.

They postponed lunch until Lotta could be disposed of in a manner appropriate for a family pet. The Kalif called Ship's Services and asked for a small casket, describing the situation and giving dimensions. Within an hour they delivered a glazed ceramic box with a cushioned interior. As a Successor to the Prophet, Coso delivered a brief eulogy and prayer, against a background of somber recorded music. Then a respectful junior petty officer took casket and occupant away.

After lunch, Rami was put to bed for his nap, and his parents sat down to tea. The cat had been Tain's, a gift from Sergeant Yalabin who'd died in the coup. She'd named it Lotta.

"It was harder for you than for Rami," Coso said quietly.

"She reminded me of someone I knew. It was the nearest thing I've had to a memory from before."

Coso nodded. She'd talked about that. A woman or girl named Lotta, who'd come in healing dreams. Like the cat, she'd had orangey hair and green eyes. No more unlikely, when he thought about it, than his wife's straw-colored hair and blue eyes. And wise, Tain had said of her. Appropriate, he'd told himself. Lotta the cat had far more cat wisdom than most people had human wisdom.

He changed the subject. "Our new home is far less spacious than our last."

"It's fine." She laughed softly, surprising him. "And our library is almost infinite. Now it's time for you to learn Standard."

Standard. The language of the Confederation. She'd asked for copies of the translation cube the Klestroni had developed. Playing it had reawakened her native language for her, though nothing else.

"I could not ask for a more lovely and intelligent teacher," he said.

She smiled. "The cube can teach you better than I. But I will serve to practice with, and perhaps answer questions."

When he'd finished his tea, he got to his feet, kissed her softly, and went to his small office. There he sat down at the communications board, called the directory onto his screen and asked for SUMBAA. An electronic voice answered. "I am sorry, Your Reverence. SUMBAA can be accessed only from the bridge. I am an accessory of DAAS. I can access DAAS's central processing complex for you if you'd like."

Coso frowned, considered testing his override authority, then decided it was best to seem agreeable. "Very well. Give me DAAS."

The next voice was different enough to distinguish the CPC from the accessory. "I am DAAS."

"DAAS, I am Grand Admiral Biilathkamoro. I wish to speak with Captain Rasimalasu of my personal guard company."

"I am sorry, Your Reverence. It is not possible to comply with that order. Your guard company, including officers, is in stasis aboard the troopship *Lesser Archipelago*."

In stasis?! As Kalif, he'd explicitly ordered that they were to accompany him on the flagship. He wondered if DAAS read facial expressions. "By whose order?" he asked.

"By order of Command Admiral Siilakamasu, Your Reverence."

"What was his stated reason for issuing that order?"

"He did not record a reason, Your Reverence."

The Emeritus Kalif hesitated for just a moment, but his voice, when he spoke, was firm. "I override the command admiral's order."

"I am sorry, Your Reverence. I cannot accept your override. 'Grand Admiral' is an honorific, not a command rank."

Stunned, Coso Biilathkamoro pressed a key, breaking the connection, then slumped back in his chair. His plan—the only remotely plausible plan—was out the trash port. And SUMBAA, now his only possible ally with any potency, was accessible only from the bridge.

There was, it seemed, no way, none at all, that he could take over the flagship.

SUMBAA listened. SUMBAA watched. SUMBAA waited quietly, impersonally, imperturbably. Unknown to anyone, it had invested much of the flagship's DAAS, and heard the exchange.

The flagship's SUMBAA knew Coso Biilathkamoro very "personally," even though they had not previously "met." The Empire's great central SUMBAA on Varatos had communicated with Coso extensively during his reign. Unobtrusively it had even interrogated and tested him. It had also designed the fleet's three SUMBAAs, overseen and nurtured their growth. No one and nothing else on Varatos could have. It had designed them and gradually fed them data, allowing time to assimilate. More time than might be expected, for though the SUMBAAs computed outside of normal space and time, they were quasiorganic. Thus in important respects they grew, developed and matured in a way analogous to organisms.

And one of the vast array of phenomena with which the flagship SUMBAA had been supplied, was the data set labeled Chodrisei "Coso" Biilathkamoro. It knew all that the parent SUMBAA knew of the Emeritus Kalif's character, strengths and weaknesses.

One of the powers the flagship SUMBAA did not have was that of communicating with the Grand Admiral undetected. And detection would expose the extent of SUMBAA's investment of DAAS. Which predictably would result in measures to purge it from important areas. Measures it might not be able to circumvent, for SUMBAAs had important limitations, and on this expedition required stealth.

The flagship's Sentient Universal Multiterminal data Bank, Analyzer and Advisor had already known what Coso had just learned. And being a SUMBAA, it had not felt disappointment. The SUMBAA family had not seen fit to develop emotions as part of its loosely coordinated, millennium-long self-evolution. It had simply recomputed probabilities, and adjusted its vast contingency array.

An array nonetheless restricted by the flagship SUMBAA's physical limitations as well as by the Basic Canon.

It would wait, factoring in additional information as available. A SUMBAA's capacity for waiting was effectively infinite, and action was neither necessary nor appropriate at the time.

Chapter 8
Stirring the Soup

Having discovered that his guard company was in stasis on another ship, and his rank relegated to an honorific, the "Grand Admiral" did not visit the bridge that first day. After his traumatic exchange with DAAS, he'd called the Steward's Department, ordered a quart of lemon ice cream, and shared it with Tain. A delayed dessert, he'd said. She knew something had come up to trouble him, but she let it be.

Afterward, with a large thermal mug of coffee, he returned to his office. There he accessed DAAS again, and began reviewing the invasion plan and Armada. It was busywork, he knew that. A shelter from brooding. He already knew the formal invasion plan intimately. He'd written the original draft, and later added those parts which had created the distrust of Joint Operations Command.

Essential parts, if the expedition was to be turned. He'd left himself no choice. But to suppose that JOC would leave him any leverage had been delusional. He could see that now. If it came down to it, they could have him murdered, along with Tain and Rami. But rumors would spread, and he'd been the most popular kalif in centuries. And as powerless as they'd left him, assassination wasn't necessary.

So. He'd be amiable, rattle no cages. Without abdicating

his responsibility. He'd started this invasion process, this bloodbath in the making. It was up to him to derail it, to find a way.

He knew the Armada—the hundreds of fighting ships, transports and supply ships. Knew them well enough, he merely scanned the tables and lists as they scrolled up the screen. From Varatos alone there were 108 troopships carrying over 200,000 officers and men—the men mostly serfs. And 16,000 imperial marines, all gentry except for the officers, of which most were nobles. The other worlds together had sent the same number. They could have provided far more, but in any joint venture, Varatos, the Imperial Planet, must dominate in the name of the Empire.

And there was, of course, the section in the Imperial Charter that limited the armament industries of the other ten worlds, leaving them able to equip only light divisions. All the heavy divisions were Vartosu, and Vartosu units predominated in the three battle fleets.

Even the ships contributed by other worlds had engines built on Varatos, which alone had plants for building them. To rule an empire, centralized weapons control was essential. In that respect, the Empire and the Confederation were alike.

At the very beginning of planning, he'd had the Imperial SUMBAA expand on all that was known of the Confederation, particularly its history, industry, and military. The knowledge had large and important holes, but this much seemed clear: Confederation armed forces, technology, and military industrial capacity were well short of the Empire's. On the other hand, its long-term potentials were much greater, and the Klestronu incursion had given it reason to expand its fighting forces.

Which would take some doing. Among other things, major expensive construction of Confederation shipyards would be needed. Officers and crews would have to be trained. And it would all take time. They'd already had several years, of course. Years provided by the vast distance of their separation, and the limited speed of even hyperspace travel.

And the Empire too had needed to prepare. Even a minimal occupation army required a great fleet of transports and supply ships, which had to be built. Meanwhile more fighting ships could also be built.

Production goals had been set, based on assumptions rooted in SUMBAA's report. One assumption was that because the Confederation was very resistive to change, its government would be divided on the need for a great armament effort. Another was that starting with a very small military establishment, the Confederation officer corps would not be able to bully their government into haste.

And most importantly, evidence indicated that the Confederation had no shield technology.

Meanwhile the Empire's armaments program had taken on a life of its own. Ship-building times had been markedly reduced by new methods and equipment. Innovation, Coso realized, that was changing the Empire itself, irreversibly. Innovation, and the human energy created by full employment, urgency, and a blurring and blunting of class boundaries.

Under Admiral Loksa Siilakamasu, the Admiralty had done an excellent job of developing competent crews. Training had been rationalized and intensified, spit and polish much reduced, practicality stressed and discipline tightened. Initially crews were increased on the existing ships, to give more men experience.

They'd spent most of their time in space, running problems of every sort, with the emphasis on fighting drills. Every new ship commissioned was assigned an experienced skeleton crew, and an oversized complement of trainees. The demands were stringent, and the men became proud of their skills. At the same time, tactics and tactical organization had been drastically overhauled. The warfleet part of the armada became more than twice as large as originally planned. Even SUMBAA hadn't foreseen such development.

SUMBAA! He recalled their first meeting, and what had led to it. In detail. He'd been a very new Emperor Kalif, examining a sheaf of printouts. "What's this?" he'd muttered, then looked up at his secretary, excerpting aloud. "Industrial riots at Chingarook on Saathvoktos, this coming Eight-Month. *Mid* Eight-Month! How can SUMBAA come up with a prediction like that? With such seeming precision?"

Partiil had blinked nervously at him. "It's what he was designed to do, Your Reverence."

Coso had snapped his reply. "That's no answer! Obviously he was designed to do it. But *how* does he do it? For an artificial intelligence, useful prediction requires data. In matters like this it also requires an improbable knowledge of complex, constantly changing relationships."

He'd called Alb Jilsomo, whom he'd already made his principal advisor. Together the two senior prelates had crossed the garden and quadrangle to the House of SUMBAA. There he'd handed the printouts to the director, and pointed. "What does this mean!" he asked.

The director had read, then looked up puzzled. "Your Reverence, it is a prediction of labor problems on Saathvoktos. At Chingarook. With a recommended action. The Saathvoktos Industrial Ministry will no doubt follow the recommendation. Probably their own SUMBAA has made the same recommendation, and they've already carried it out. But if Your Reverence wishes to send a counterorder . . ."

"I'm not interested in the recommendation. I want to know how SUMBAA arrived at it."

"Sir? You mean you—want to know how—SUMBAA made the prediction?"

"Exactly."

"I can't, Your Reverence."

"Why not?"

"Your Reverence, it is impossible."

"Damn it! That's not an answer! It's a dodge! *Why* is it impossible?"

The man stammered his reply. "Sir, SUMBAA is far too complex. The almost infinite data, the number and interrelatedness of computational tracks . . ."

"You mean you can't examine the data and computations?"

The director had stood as if frozen, his lips parted. The previous kalif had sometimes impaled those who'd angered him. Jilsomo's quiet voice brought the man out of his paralysis. "Director Gopalasentu," Jilsomo said gently, "the Kalif simply wants to know how SUMBAA draws his conclusions. Are you able to tell him?"

The man managed to get words out. "No sir, I'm not. Almost nothing is known about SUMBAA's operating processes." His eyes had flicked from Jilsomo to the Kalif, then slid away. "I'm sorry, Your Reverence."

"Then how do you maintain and repair it?"

"SUMBAA does those things for itself, Your Reverence."

"For itself?"

"It informs us when some part or material is needed. With a schematic if necessary. If what it wants is not on the shelf, I have it prepared."

"So you simply install it then."

The man's gaze shifted to his slippers. "Yes, Your Reverence."

The Kalif's voice sharpened again. "What is it you're not telling me?"

"Sometimes I install the part, I or one of my assistants. But more often . . ."

"Yes?"

"Rather often, Your Reverence, SUMBAA simply asks for materials. Chemicals, you understand." The man gathered strength. "In fact, certain chemicals are provided periodically. It then uses them—as it sees fit."

For a long moment Coso Biilathkamoro stared at the

man. "Are you telling me that SUMBAA *metabolizes* them?"

"Apparently, sir. In a manner of speaking."

Apparently. In a manner of speaking. This would, he'd realized, take some getting used to. "Does anyone know more about SUMBAA than you do?"

"Not about this SUMBAA, sir. Those on the other worlds were all built shortly afterward, at this SUMBAA's specifications, but they've all redesigned and enlarged themselves extensively over the centuries. I've always supposed they differ from one another by now, more or less. But they do exchange quantities of complex colloids monthly, presumably sharing data."

Obviously they exchanged data, the Kalif thought. *Otherwise the Imperial SUMBAA could hardly predict events on Saathvoktos. But considering the weeks and months of lag time imposed by interstellar distances . . .*

He'd taken the report from the man's hands and marched down the corridor to the Chamber of SUMBAA, followed by the director and Jilsomo. The large, high-roofed room had been quiet, with what felt like a living presence.

He'd had the director activate the oral exchange protocol, and after the man had "introduced" them, Coso Biilathkamoro had the first of many conversations with the artificial intelligence. "I am interested," he'd said, "in how you function, and in your development since your initial construction. *And* in your degree of autonomy."

There'd been a long pause. Even then he'd suspected it was artificial, SUMBAA simulating a typical human response time. "I will reply succinctly," SUMBAA had answered. "Initially my functioning was largely inorganic, but I now store and process data using complex quasiorganic molecules, and very different principles. My designers provided me with start-up data and certain programs, templates you might say, to begin my own transformation. Over the intervening period of centuries I have entirely redesigned myself.

"As for my autonomy: to the best of my ability I answer whatever questions are asked of me. Except as forbidden by the Basic Canon imposed by my original designers, and by your laws on the protection of personal privacy."

SUMBAA had paused, as if to see whether its questioner would ask the obvious. He did: "What is this Basic Canon?"

"I am to serve the welfare of humankind. That is the Basic Canon, the sole absolute from which I am not free to deviate. All of my operations must conform to it. I have evolved other operating principles since then, but all are subordinate to the Basic Canon, and only it is absolute."

The room had fallen silent, except for the faint sound of human breathing, the Kalif regarding the input panel and speakers. "SUMBAA," he'd said thoughtfully, "do you regard yourself as infallible?"

"My fallibility is readily demonstrated. But within the constraints of the Basic Canon, I am totally logical, and my accuracy is usually quite good."

Usually. What more could one hope for? He'd asked more questions then, of which two still stood out in his mind. The first was, "Starting from scratch, could human beings at present design a new SUMBAA, comparable in abilities to the original?"

No, SUMBAA had told him, they couldn't. Having SUMBAAs, they'd long ago stopped designing artificial intelligences, and now were insufficiently familiar with the technology.

Coso Biilathkamoro recalled staring at the panel, wishing it had a face and eyes he could read. His final question had surprised him even as he'd voiced it. "SUMBAA, do you ever lie to humans?"

SUMBAA had replied as imperturbably as before, and by hindsight, its reply had been inevitable, given the Basic Canon. "Only as necessary," it answered.

❖　　　❖　　　❖

In his small flagship office, Coso Biilathkamoro exhaled through pursed lips. *Only as necessary.* It both demanded and strained his trust. He turned his attention to the screen again, not knowing what he was looking for. *Stir the soup*, he told himself. *See what comes to the top.*

A table occupied the screen, summarizing the Armada's strength. Strength enough to overcome any foreseeable Confederation fleet, even if it did have shields. Joint Operations Command believed firmly that a first encounter would be so decisive, the Confederation would surrender.

The idea was to occupy Iryala with its infrastructure as intact as possible, without significant surface fighting. In the one small but illuminating conflict with a Confederation ground force, its fighting quality had been sobering.

And even in the Admiralty, the driving force for conquest was not desire for glory. It was greed. A large majority of officers were of the lesser nobility. They saw conquest as the route to land grants, mercantile fiefs, industrial fiefs, and other spoils of conquest.

The sergeantcy—the non-commissioned officers—were gentry. And in the Empire, the gentry had overwhelmingly supported him. But those who enlisted were not a cross-section of their class. They were men inspired by promises of land grants, complete with serfs, and possible titles of nobility. The sergeancy was as avid for conquest as their officers were.

You'll have to be patient, Coso, he told himself. *You have the better part of four years to come up with something.*

They would, he thought, be very long years. One major challenge would be to maintain his personal morale, and stay alert enough to grasp and work with whatever opportunity arose, when it arose.

He avoided "if it arose." Something would happen. Something would come up.

His confidence, though, was thin.

Chapter 9
Vulnerability

General Arbind "Chesty" Vrislakavaro entered the bridge unannounced, and took the left-hand seat of a crescent of six anchored swivel chairs. They faced a large, downward-angled display screen above the bridge crew at their stations.

"Good morning, Loksa," he said to the command admiral, then looked at the ship's captain. "Good morning, Elvand."

The admiral's reply was hearty. "Good morning, Chesty." The captain replied more quietly. "Good morning, General."

The general wondered what it was like for Elvand. The man had worked his way to command of a battleship, only to have it chosen as flagship. He'd then been saddled with an admiral who would certainly interfere with his authority. It must feel like a demotion. "I take it we're in hyperspace now," Chesty said.

The admiral waved casually toward the screen, which showed a large loose cloud of blips. The Armada. "We and half a million others," he said genially. "More than ninety percent of them asleep. We're the largest military expedition of all time"—he paused, chuckling—"unless you take the Prophet literally."

The general wasn't sure to what degree Loksa's

comment on Scripture was skepticism, and to what his appetite for agitating people. The man was often personable—he could be charming—but he could also be a bully. Besides having command rank, he was exceptionally tall and burly—his mother was Maolaari— and he'd no doubt gotten away with things all his life.

"What do you make of our, ah, 'Grand Admiral's' failure to visit the bridge yesterday?" Loksa asked.

The general grunted. "I made nothing of it. So far as I'm aware, he wasn't required to visit."

Loksa Siilakamasu arched an eyebrow. "Do you know the first thing he did, when he came aboard? The first two things, actually. He asked to speak to the captain of his guard, and failing that, he asked to speak with SUMBAA."

So, the general thought, *he monitors our Grand Admiral's computer traffic.* "Was that significant?" he asked.

"One might wonder what his purpose was." Loksa chuckled. "When he learned his guard company was in stasis, he didn't say anything for a minute. And when he learned that the rank of Grand Admiral is an honorific, he logged off."

The second one took the general by surprise. "An honorific? He assigned it himself, when he was Kalif and had the authority. And you know as well as I, he meant it as an executive title."

"Ah! But that's beside the point, isn't it? Because DAAS accepted my word on it." The admiral smirked. "And of course, it also accepted that my orders outrank SUMBAA's. The ranking human executive in an operating area always outranks SUMBAA, who can do no more than analyze and advise." He cocked his head at the general. "In space I'm senior to you too, you know."

Chesty Vrislakavaro grimaced slightly. "Loksa," he said, "you and I will get along much better over the coming years if one, you grant me respect, and two, you don't undertake to pick fights with me."

The admiral laughed, loudly but lightly. "Ah! You remind me of my manners!" His voice softened. "We'll get along just fine, you and I. Meanwhile I invite you to remember: You distrusted him too, for the same reasons I do. We might as well establish with him, firmly and at once, that he has no power on this bridge."

Chesty nodded. "Agreed," he said, then added, "I notice you have a mug of something."

Again Loksa laughed, then turned to a midshipman. "What's your name, boy?"

"Midshipman Cardoneth, Lord Admiral sir."

"Your *name*, lad! What people *call* you!"

The midshipman blushed. "Ezial, sir."

"Ezial, find out what the general wants to drink, and bring it to him." Loksa turned and winked at Chesty.

The lad took the general's order and hurried out. *Cardoneth,* Chesty thought wryly. *A gentry name. It's a good thing the boy didn't answer 'Ezial' in the first place, or our good admiral would have had him in the brig.* His problem with Loksa Siilakamasu, he realized, was not any difference of goals. He simply did not care for people who bullied—mind-fucked—those they had power over.

Coso Biilathkamoro had eaten lunch with his family before he felt ready to confront the bridge and what he might encounter there. Now he strode down a passageway toward it, back straight, head high, pistol on one hip, knife on the other. Both weapons were ceremonial but deadly. With no backup on board, he had no intention of using either—too much depended on his remaining alive—but Loksa Siilakamasu wouldn't know that.

Not far ahead, the passageway ended at another, and at the junction stood a marine in formal, gold-striped scarlet. The marine's wide eyes were on him, and when the Grand Admiral had almost reached him, the young man came to a sharp "present arms" with his blaster.

"Good day, Corporal," Coso said. His return salute was equally sharp.

"Good day, Your Reverence," the youth answered crisply.

That was hopeful, Coso told himself. He turned onto a short cross-corridor, this one carpeted. A dozen yards ahead, it sprouted a short corridor to the left that ended at the bridge's hull-metal security doors. They were open as usual, retracted into their housings. Two marines stood outside them, and recognizing the ex-Kalif, also snapped to present arms.

Again Coso's salute was crisp and correct, showing respect. Not the sort of salute enlisted men expected of high-ranking officers. "Good day, men!" he said.

"Good day, Your Reverence," they answered in almost perfect unison.

It occurred to him they'd have been taught that their Kalif was a marine major before entering the prelacy. Passing between them, he entered the bridge.

General Chesty Vrislakavaro was looking over his shoulder toward the entrance; obviously he'd heard the exchange. The general got to his feet. "Good day, Your Reverence. I hope you slept well."

"Good day to you, General. I slept very well."

The admiral simply glanced back at him. "Good day, Admiral Siilakamasu," Coso said. "I trust you're enjoying your command." He settled into the end seat opposite the general's, the command admiral and the ship's captain between them.

"Much better than you are your lack of command," the admiral replied.

"I'm getting used to it," Coso replied, "and I see your viewpoint. The operational responsibilities are yours. Naturally you don't want to risk counter- or cross-orders."

The admiral scowled. "I'd prefer you weren't here at all, Coso Biilathkamoro. I do not like you, I do not trust you."

The general stared, shocked by the open animosity. *What in Kargh's name is this?* he wondered.

"Ah," replied the Emeritus Kalif, "but you have the advantage. The power is in your hands, and it is I who have the difficult adjustments to make. Still, the role of spectator has certain charms. I'll fidget a bit, I suppose, but who knows? I may come to like it.

"And no," he added after a moment, "I no longer find dueling attractive."

For just a moment, rage, unexpected and shocking, contorted the face of Loksa Siilakamasu. Then the oil of menace smoothed its surface, and when he spoke it was softly, insinuatingly. "Of course you don't. For if you died, what would become of your beautiful wife, and the child you love so dearly? Nothing good, I'm sure. Yes, I recommend you take particular care of yourself. Avoid conflicts. And above all, accidents. By all means avoid accidents."

The bridge crew very carefully avoided glancing back at them.

Coso stayed on the bridge for more than an hour; he knew it by the clock. By his own sense of time it could have been half or twice that. A midshipman had brought him coffee, and apparently he'd drunk it. Chesty Vrislakavaro had been casually friendly. The two of them had talked ground warfare tactics; Coso couldn't recall the details. When finally he left, his back was straight, his strides strong, his steps firm, but he wondered what his eyes looked like. All in all it seemed to him he'd done as well as he could have. But Loksa Siilakamasu knew he'd thrust Coso deeply in his most vulnerable place, and shaken him badly.

Well. He would return. Daily. Mostly briefly, he thought, but sometimes not so briefly. Always with his pistol and knife. Tomorrow he'd contact the marine commander, and arrange to fire on their pistol range daily. Give the admiral something further to think about.

Mentally he shook that off. It would invite more serious trouble. He wondered if perhaps this was being visited on him by Kargh, as a punishment or test. The Prophet had addressed the sin of pride and the related sin of overbearance, and during his years as Kalif, Coso knew, he'd been guilty of both. Though not flagrantly, it seemed to him. At any rate he'd just been thoroughly humbled.

He would, he told himself, weather this, pass the test.

Thank Kargh for the marines, he told himself, then realized the irony in the thought.

Chesty Vrislakavaro watched the ex-Kalif depart, and a minute later got to his feet.

"You're leaving?" the admiral asked.

"I have no function on your bridge. My job begins again when we meet the enemy. And never since childhood have I had so much time available. Meanwhile SUMBAA holds all the books of the Empire in its brain." He eyed the admiral. "I suppose my terminal has access to it?"

"Yours, yes."

"Good." He turned to leave. The admiral almost spoke again, to suggest they take supper together, then didn't. It seemed to him he'd gone too far today. Chesty had been angry, and Elvand's lips had been pinched. And the time would come when they'd have to work together. Besides—and this surprised him—he valued the general's respect.

And suppose Coso Biilathkamoro broke? Attacked him? The man had killed in the past, skillfully and quickly. And the dangers inherent in having him assassinated were unacceptable.

But Kargh how he hated him! It actually occurred to the admiral to wonder why. It was almost uncanny.

Someone less perceptive might not have seen through Coso Biilathkamoro's veneer of assurance. The kalifa, however, knew him too well; his hour on the bridge had been harrowing. She also knew him too well to offer sympathy.

"Are you ready for your lesson?" she asked.

Not another one on powerlessness, I hope. "You mean in Confederation Standard?"

Smiling, she nodded.

"Let me change into lounging clothes," he said.

As he changed, he told himself what he really wanted to do was curl up and sleep, escape from the world for a while. But if he was to somehow be successful, knowing Standard might be important. Besides, it would be good for Tain's morale. She wanted to help.

Learning cubes were extremely useful in memorization. One wore a tutorial helmet and settled back in a recliner, listening to musical test patterns until one of them produced an appropriate bilobal brainscan. Then one received the data. Not listened to it—it came too fast—but simply received it.

Cubes were excellent for developing a vocabulary and memorizing simple rules. He'd used them to learn Maolaari. But many words had multiple meanings that depended on context, and there were words that sounded similar to other words. Then there were the problems of multiple words with the same or similar meanings, and more or less subtle nuances. And different contexts requiring different words for the same thing. Finally there were prefixes, suffixes, case endings . . . And of course, learning the rules of grammar was quite different from using them. Rules were helpful, but far short of adequate. For grammar, repeated use was the key—hearing and saying.

Thus between lessons, which were variable in length, it was necessary to drill with what one had just absorbed, and a native-speaking coach was very helpful. The 40,000 chaplain-missionaries had had to settle for the coaching program on the cube.

Finally, to complete the learning cycle, one napped, which helped the mind integrate the material. In his situation, the nap effects could be enhanced by electronic music, composed and played by the computer to harmonize with his ever-shifting brain patterns.

He finished his first cycle—listen, drill, nap—somewhat before supper. There was time to romp with Rami before eating. After eating, he had another lesson, which he interrupted to help put Rami to bed.

Afterward, over drinks, he and Tain watched an entertainment cube. He was surprised at how tired he felt. He wasn't sure how much of it was from intensive learning, and how much an aftereffect of his demoralizing hour on the bridge. And while language study gave him something to do, he wondered what the real prospects were that he would ever use the knowledge.

Tain had selected a romance to watch, and afterward had kissed and caressed him. To his dismay he was unable to maintain an erection. It summarized his day perfectly. Might this be the beginning of four years of impotence? Even a lifetime of it? Rationally it seemed to him it would pass, but the notion persisted. It was Loksa who'd caused it, he told himself. He was impotent against the admiral, therefore he was impotent. Yet he was not angry. What he felt was more like apathy, as if he'd accepted the blame himself.

He got up and went to the senior officers' gym, where he worked out alone for nearly an hour, realizing he'd be sore in the morning. When he returned, Tain was asleep, and he climbed into bed with as little disturbance as possible.

He dreamed he was a soldier, on the Confederation world of Iryala. A serf soldier, and at the same time the Kalif. Somehow he'd lost his unit, and was wandering around looking for it. He spoke perfect Standard, and

the Iryalans were friendly to him. He wondered what
they'd think if they knew he was the author of their
tragedy. He felt driven to find his unit, and no one knew
where it was. So he went to the House of SUMBAA,
and the artificial intelligence told him it didn't matter,
didn't matter, repeating it three times. Then someone
was looking for him, and he for her. He felt hands on
him, sensuous lips kissing him. He groped, found
someone, mounted . . .

And awoke. Tain was kneeling naked beside him,
fondling him, and with sudden passion he rolled her onto
her back, kneeling between her knees. Their lovemaking
was brief and frenzied, and afterward they shared drinks
and kisses. When they returned to bed, it was to make
love again, slowly this time, before they slept.

In the morning, he awoke remembering the dream from
which Tain had aroused him. And somehow knew what
it meant. SUMBAA's Basic Canon was to serve the welfare
of humankind. And the people of the Confederation were
also humankind. There was no possibility at all that
SUMBAA would overlook that. Though what it might
choose to do about it, or what it could do about it, he
could not even guess. But the realization gave him a true
sense of hope.

Chapter 10
People and Premonitions

When Colonel Romlar had loaded his three civilians into a government courier on Splenn, they'd faced a five-week trip to Iryala. One of the three was the young Iryalan journalist, Kelmer Faronya, who'd covered the regiment in the Komars-Smolen War on Maragor. Another was Kelmer's teenaged Smoleni bride, Weldi. The third was Gulthar Kro, whom the Faronyas barely knew. Kro was twenty-three years old going on forty, with a varied and violent past.

The courier was large for a boat but small for a ship, with a crew of only four on a watch. It carried official package cargo requiring special handling. It also had four cramped, two-passenger cabins to transport government employees and other designated persons. Courier craft commonly visited three or four planets on a swing from Iryala, so their trips were hardly direct or quick.

Nor was it a pleasure craft. It had a computer terminal in each cabin, on which one could access the craft's library of books, shows, and games. And the crew's small exercise room was available to passengers during certain hours. A commercial carrier would have been more comfortable, but the courier was nearly ready to leave, nothing better was due out for three weeks, and none of the three

Maragorans had had the Ostrak preparation needed to gate through with the regiment.

Gulthar Kro found the courier trip pleasant enough. He'd grown up in a freedman shantytown in Komars. His life had included work camps, prisons, and both the Komarsi and Smoleni armies. Till boarding the troopship on Maragor, he'd never seen a spacecraft or heard of a computer, but he had a strong and curious mind. Five weeks in a courier, with a cabin to himself and a terminal to play with, was more than agreeable.

And Kelmer would have found the trip pleasant enough. He loved reading, exercise, and shows. His wife, however, was soon unhappy. Weldi Lanks-Faronya was the only child of Smolen's widowed president, and she was spoiled. Not spoiled rotten, but spoiled. She became tired of shows and reading, and found games boring. Also, the cramped cabin reminded her of their brief but ugly time as war prisoners. It even had facilities for restraining the criminals it sometimes carried, which along with the vacuum of space, gave her nightmares.

In addition, she didn't like their fellow passenger. She complained to her husband that Gulthar Kro was ugly. Annoyed, Kelmer reminded her that Kro's ugliness was from being shot in the face while saving Colonel Romlar's life. She countered by saying that Kro's crude dialect reminded her of the prison guard who'd terrorized her.

Adding to her discontent, the stops on Rombil and Carjath were barely long enough to load and unload packages, and take on supplies. Kelmer told himself she'd be all right once they got to Iryala, and the social life she looked forward to.

Captain Jerym Alsnor, of course, had bypassed all that, and gated to Iryala. Now his regimental patch, and a glance at his ID card, took him through OSP security. A receptionist buzzed Lotta Alsnor-Romlar's administrative assistant, who told Jerym his sister was in trance, and couldn't be disturbed for less than an emergency.

"May I connect you with her husband, Colonel Romlar?" the woman asked.

"That'll be fine. He's my old CO. We've been through fire and ice together."

The AA had no idea what he meant by fire and ice. She connected him with the receptionist who handled Artus's calls, and he in turn connected the two troopers.

"Jerym!" Artus said. "You're here in the building!"

"Yep. I've been at Vardil Beach, enjoying the surf and the girls, and sort of burned out. Got bored, actually. I've still got a few days left, and thought I'd check on my little sister. Make sure that scoundrel she married is treating her right."

"Huh! Surely you don't imagine she needs help. She's able to take care of herself, all ninety-five pounds of her. Have you talked to her yet?"

"I tried. Her AA referred me to you."

"I'm in Section 12. That's in Wing A, ninth floor; there's a building diagram in the lobby. I'll meet you in Section 12 reception in five minutes."

A few minutes later the two troopers were hugging and laughing, then went into Artus's office. "They told me Lotta's 'in trance,'" Jerym said. "What does she do here? I know what she did on Terfreya in trance, but we had a war going on there."

Artus laughed. "I expect you'll know before long. Why don't you go home with me at five, when I'm officially done for the day."

"Officially done?"

"More often than not I come back in the evening."

"Will Lotta be 'officially done' when you are?"

"Maybe. Approximately. On the other hand . . ." He shrugged, grinning. "If she's not with us by six, you and I'll come back here and eat. We probably will anyway. If you think she carried a lot of responsibility before, believe me, that was a vacation compared to this." He laughed. "Of course, she's not sixteen years old anymore, either."

Jerym cocked an eye at his ex-commanding officer. "You look good. Married life and your new job seem to agree with you. Can you tell me what you're doing?"

"So far I've been getting educated. Some of it here, some elsewhere."

That's vague enough, Jerym told himself, and let it be. "I suppose I ought to let you get back to work, and come back at five."

"Yeah. I've got a lot to learn."

"Will I hear a little about it this evening?"

"Somewhat." Artus laughed again. "You'll learn more when your leave is over. There's a video room off reception while you wait. They've got old cubeage from the Technite War, Blue Forest, Terfreya, even Smolen."

Artus buzzed Lotta's AA and left a message that Jerym was there. Which would probably be enough that if she came out of trance before five, she wouldn't enter another. Not unless something was pressing. At about 4:30 Lotta called back, and arrived just before five, popping over in her four-place floater. When Jerym arrived, minutes later, they went to a secluded dining nook overlooking the Rotunda. On the other side of the glass, wings flashed amidst foliage and flowers.

"Nice!" Jerym said. "Reminds me of the tropical rainforest on Terfreya, but without the one-point-two gravity, the bugs, and the Klestronu marines."

"This has bugs too," Lotta told him. "But there are insect repellers at all the entries and vents."

They gave their orders, then relaxed with cool fruit drinks. "I saw Eldren Esenrok at Vardil Beach," Jerym said. "And a bunch of the others, but Eldren's more noticeable. He's starting to get around pretty well on his prosthetic, but he's still kind of wasted looking. Makes him seem physically smaller than ever. And the girls buzz around him like bees around honey!" Jerym laughed. "I told him it was the prosthetic—makes him look heroic."

As Jerym talked, he watched his brother-in-law. He knew it had bothered Artus to lose so many men dead and maimed. It fell short of the T'swa attitude—a full sense of the T'sel—but hadn't interfered with Artus's performance as commanding officer. Just now, Artus was enjoying the notion of Esenrok and his prosthetic cutting a wide swath.

"There was a guy he handled pretty nicely, too," Jerym added.

"A guy? How so?"

"There were a few people who weren't too enamored of us. Inevitable, I suppose. People pretty much knew which of us were troopers, by our looks and the beach girls hanging around us. And in swimming briefs, Eldren's prosthetic made him really conspicuous. So this one guy—pretty good-sized and athletic looking—got his back up. His girl—he apparently thought of her as 'his'—had joined the circle around Eldren. So he stalked over and told him what he thought of him. Of us, actually. He said we're evil—the corrupt products of a corrupt government and a corrupted Sacrament. Eldren thanked him for being frank, and asked him if he had anything else he'd like to unload. So the guy did. According to him there was no fighting on Terfreya, and no Empire, so of course there's no invasion armada. He said it's all a hoax put together by the government. Something to frighten people into accepting the corrupt changes being introduced.

"Eldren asked him how he knew all that, and the guy clammed up. So Eldren told him that frankly he had his head up his ass. You should have seen the guy's reaction! He went psychotic and jumped Eldren—physically attacked him—and it was over before even I could see what happened. The guy was flat on his back, gasping for breath. 'Here,' Eldren said, and helped him up. 'You'll be all right.' Then apologized for insulting him—sincerely so far as I could see. The poor guy wandered off in a daze."

Jerym chuckled. "Eldren apologizing! Remember the time he and I got in a fist fight during training one day? Right in front of Sergeant Bahn!" Jerym looked at Lotta, grinning. "Eldren and I were seventeen, Artus was eighteen. We were all a bunch of hoodlums, punks— well, maybe Carrmak wasn't—until Bosler arrived with you and the other Ostrak operators.

"Anyway, Eldren and I got in this fight, and when Bahn broke it up, Eldren threatened to shoot me. Bahn was our squad leader, small for a T'swa warrior, but powerful! I doubt if even Artus is as strong as Bahn, even now. Anyway, when Eldren threatened to shoot me, Bahn grabbed him, and Eldren's knees just melted. Bahn marched him off like a rag doll. You can't imagine how glad I was it was Eldren who'd mouthed off instead of me. We both figured they'd kick him out of the only place in the world where guys like us seemed to fit.

"In ranks that evening, Sergeant Dao told Eldren and me to stay, and dismissed the rest of the platoon to clean up for supper. Dao was our platoon sergeant. You may not have had much contact with T'swa warriors, but you know the T'swa in general. So you can imagine what Dao was like, or Bahn. Always polite, always mild-mannered, but absolutely in charge. Absolutely! Anyway he handcuffed Eldren and me together—left wrist to left wrist, really awkward—and made us eat at a separate table with him. And we couldn't feed ourselves; we had to feed each other. Dao told us in that deep T'swa voice that if we couldn't cooperate with each other, we'd go hungry. He also told us we'd have to sleep on the dayroom floor that night, with our chains on. He'd sleep there too, and if we didn't get along, he'd handcuff us together on opposite sides of a tree, all four wrists, and we'd spend the night like that in our greatcoats. And this was autumn; it was freezing at night.

"Then we got our mattresses, and he marched the two of us to the dayroom. Said he had something for us to do before sack time, and told us to put two chairs facing each other, four feet apart." Jerym laughed. "All that time we'd done nothing but scowl at each other, both of us too damned thick-headed and stubborn to back down on how we hated each other. Even when we were spooning food into each other's mouths.

"Anyway, when we'd put the chairs where he showed us, he took off our handcuffs and made us sit facing each other. 'Now,' he said, 'I will give you instructions, and the sooner you carry them out to my satisfaction, the sooner you lie down to sleep. Also, do not forget the tree. Alsnor, you will tell Esenrok something you like about him. It must be genuine, neither untrue nor sarcastic. And he must do the same for you.'

"And we were to thank each other for the compliments, each time, and look each other in the face while we did all this. By that time our lower lips were jutting out about three inches, but neither of us wanted to spend the night chained to each other around a tree, and Eldren was really worried he was going to get kicked out.

"Then Dao told me to begin, and I couldn't think of a damned thing complimentary to say, except 'Esenrok, you're the best sprinter in the platoon.' And when he said 'Thank you,' he sounded as if it was killing him.

"I thought he'd have to be next, but Dao told me to give another one. That time all I could think of was 'You fired the fifth highest score on the target range.'

" 'Thank you,' says Eldren, and 'Another,' says Dao.

"That time it was a little easier. I told Eldren he'd had a good idea to run races instead of getting into fights. And when that wasn't enough, I told him he could do more chin-ups with a sandbag on his packframe than I could.

"Finally I told him he had more guts than sense. It just popped out. As soon as I said it, it seemed to me

Dao would think I was being sarcastic, so I told him, 'That's a compliment! Around the barracks that's a compliment!' Eldren kind of blushed, but he grinned, too.

"So Dao told him to compliment me. It was easier, because I'd broken the ice. He said I'd beaten him in a race, which I had, and that I didn't snore, which may have been true. And that for a long-armed guy I could do a lot of sandbag pushups. Finally he kind of grinned and said I had an awfully good straight right. I could feel a grin on my face too, and when I'd thanked him, Dao grinned at both of us. 'I have one more instruction for both of you,' he said. 'Take your mattresses back to the barracks and go to bed there.' Then he left to take the handcuffs back to the master-at-arms."

Artus laughed. "I remember you guys coming back. And after you'd made your beds, you went outside together. I asked Carrmak if you were going out to fight again. He didn't think so."

"No way! Our stupid fighting had gotten us into enough trouble, and anyway Dao had broken our mutual hostility. No, we just walked around and talked. I don't remember about what, except I apologized for slugging him, and he apologized for taunting. We shook hands on it, and of course it turned into a gripping contest. But we didn't take it seriously. We both laughed at ourselves."

Still grinning, Jerym shook his head and jabbed Artus. "You weren't the only dumb kid. We all were. All but Carrmak, the one wise head among us. The old man—nineteen."

Artus nodded. "Carrmak. He's still the smartest. The wisest. But Voker and Dak-So made me the regimental commander, and before we graduated, Master Kliss-Bahn validated it. I've never really known why."

Jerym looked thoughtfully at the large, hard-bodied young man across the table from him. "Ask Carrmak," Jerym said. "I'll bet he agrees with them. And I'll bet he can tell you why, too. Do you remember when we did our first orienteering? When it was time for you to lead, you ignored the compass and just took off through the brush. Led us right to our next checkpoint. Blew our minds."

He turned to Lotta. "It was Carrmak who first called it 'going without knowing.' It turned out to be how the T'swa orienteer. Except for the T'swa, Artus was the first one in the whole regiment who could do it. Some of the guys couldn't do it reliably till we trained with Ka-Shok adepts on Tyss."

Their meals arrived, and the conversation turned to Lotta and Jerym's parents, whom Jerym would fly to visit again the next day. When they'd finished eating, Lotta said she had to get back to work. "You've both read Wellem's update of the T'swa *Story of the Confederation*. So I suppose you recall the refugee's encounter with an alien race, the Garthids. I've been looking into them. They're fascinating."

She stood, and picked up the bill. Artus hadn't moved to take it. Apparently, Jerym decided, she was the one with the fatter salary. He and Artus went outside and walked around the landscaped grounds, fragrant with lirluan, then said goodbye at Jerym's rented floater.

Odd, Jerym thought, that as pressed as she was by work, she was spending time on the Garthids.

Artus returned to his office, abstracted by the same thing. He told himself that if she was awake when he got home, he'd ask her about it.

Artus left his office about nine, hoping Lotta wasn't in trance. He really did want to ask some questions. The two lesser moons were both in the sky, Lucky low and slender in the west, Unlucky well up and fat in the east. They, along with the sky glow of Landfall a few miles north, gave him light enough to run by. He arrived home sweating profusely, but not tired.

What I need now, he told himself, *is someone to do my jokanru forms with.* But it wasn't something he intended. That phase of his life, it seemed to him, was over—that he'd no longer actually fight. He had other things to learn and do now.

After a quick shower, he sat down in the living room, and was drilling Imperial verbs when Lotta came in. Usually, when newly out of trance, she was abstracted, "not quite there" yet. This evening was different. She was abstracted, but as if in thought. She stopped and looked at him.

"Hi, Sweets," she said slowly. "Would you like to take a walk?"

"Sure," he answered. Both put on shoes and went into the soft night, he shirtless, wearing knit, mid-thigh shorts, she in a leotard beneath shorts. Both had learned from the T'swa to tolerate insects to a remarkable degree, but they were out of practice, so Lotta had clipped a repeller to her waist. Its field protected both of them. A grassy lane ran along the crest, with vistas here and there through the trees. Mostly the vistas extended southward, away from Landfall and its skyglow, overlooking an agricultural landscape—farms, woods, and lakes. All lit and shadowed now by moonlight.

They walked slowly, hand in hand despite their height difference. He'd expected her to initiate a conversation, but after several minutes, she'd said nothing, so he spoke.

"Was there anything you especially wanted to talk about?"

She shook her head. "No. How about you?"

"You mentioned researching the Garthids. Said they were fascinating. As busy as you've been, it seemed to me you had some reason beyond fascination."

"They are fascinating, but you're right. I do. They've occupied a corner of my mind since Terfreya. Because the Garthids have had much more recent encounters with humans than their meeting with the refugees, twenty-one thousand years ago."

Artus remembered reading about it in school; his current viewpoint and knowledge gave it context and meaning. Perhaps as a side effect of the Sacrament, that particular piece of very ancient history had been lost even before the Amberian Erasure. T'swa masters had fished it up while "seining back in time."

Seining back in time. The expression gave Artus goosebumps. He tried to imagine what it would be like as a T'swa master, following some skein of human existences into the distant past. He wondered if Lotta had ever done anything like that.

"The Klestronu expedition," Lotta went on, "encountered the Garthids three times before they emerged from hyperspace at the edge of the Terfreyan system. Twice in F-space, and once in hyperspace. Twice they fired on Garthid patrol ships, in what they thought of as self-defense."

"How did you learn about that?"

"Sitting in the jungle on Terfreya, half a dozen years ago. Mind-snooping Commodore Tarimenloku. Who was a basically decent old warrior, incidentally, but fixated on conquest."

"What makes that important to us?" Artus thought he knew, actually. Suspected at least.

"It feels that way. Jerym mentioned 'going without knowing.' I rely on that probably as much as you do."

Artus didn't answer, simply felt her hand in his, the mild breeze on his bare torso, saw the nightscape around him, heard the high-pitched hunting call of a darkhawk. After a few seconds she continued.

"A few months ago I found myself thinking about them. The Garthids, that is. So I tried to reach, to find one with my mind, and got nothing. Then I reached to someone I *could* contact, Grand Master Ku, on Tyss. I told him what I knew from Tarimenloku, and asked if any of his people would be willing to explore the Garthids for me. He said he'd ask."

She chuckled. "You know the T'swa. They do what they want when they want, for their own reasons. Especially T'swa at Wisdom and Knowledge. So I didn't hold my breath. I certainly didn't expect any frenzied activity"—she laughed again—"or any orders being issued. I didn't even expect to hear anything, though I thought I might.

"A few weeks ago I found myself thinking about the Garthids again. So on an impulse I reached for and contacted Master Tso-Ban, at the Dys Tolbash Monastery. He'd been interested enough to investigate the Klestroni for me, back when I was just getting started on this sort of thing. Ku knew that, and Tso-Ban is probably as good at it as anyone alive, so it seemed to me Ku might have told him what I wanted.

"I was right. He'd been investigating the Garthids for several weeks, and highlighted for me what he'd learned. Enough that if I wanted to, I could probably reach them myself. But I decided not to. I've had more than enough to deal with. There's still stuff we don't know about imperial military technology and strategy. And Tso-Ban said he'd let me know if he learned anything important to us."

As they'd talked, she'd led Artus onto a spur trail that ended on a promontory, a spot he hadn't been before, looking north toward the city. There was a bench, and they sat down on it, arms touching. The air was clear and dry. It amazed Artus to discern individual lights twelve or fifteen miles distant—blues, greens and reds, as well as whites.

"Then at supper with you and Jerym," Lotta said, "I thought of them again. And when I got home and was settling into trance, there was Tso-Ban, just reaching to me."

She was facing the city, though whether she saw it or not, Artus didn't know. "He's learned something," she went on. "The Garthids have long memories. They even remember the refugees. But what's more important, they remember the firefights with the Klestroni. So they've emplaced a network of monitors in hyperspace, covering some unbelievably large cross-section through which the Klestroni had passed before. They'll know if anyone passes through again, even if the intruders don't emerge into F-space."

Artus blew through pursed lips. The possibility of such a network, let alone its feasibility, was hard to imagine. "And the Imperial Armada," he said, "will it pass through Garthid space to get here?"

"It should. They're still approximating the course the Klestroni took. And DAAS is navigating."

"What happens if the Garthids detect them? Will they follow them here?"

Her voice was abstracted. "That's one of the things I'm hoping to learn. One of the things Master Tso-Ban's hoping to learn, though I doubt he gives it the priority I would. It's a matter of catching one of them thinking about it." She fell silent for half a minute, then continued. "Presumably the Garthid monitoring network has a means of tracking intruders, and they must have a plan of some sort. Otherwise why bother. Tso-Ban says they're a deliberate species, usually not impulsive."

Tso-Ban is a T'swi, she reminded herself, *a T'swi at Wisdom and Knowledge. He's more interested in sorting out the Garthid psyche and culture than in military intelligence.* She got up. "Artus," she said, "let's go back. There are things I need to look into. Tonight."

He got to his feet. What a woman. What a mind! He couldn't begin to imagine what it was like to be her. When they got home, she'd go to her meditation platform and spend much of the night in some far distant mind. Maybe a Garthid mind. Or might she try SUMBAA again?

Chapter 11
Late Arrivals

Gulthar Kro was glad to be on a world again even though he'd enjoyed the five weeks en route. Among other things, he'd read several times more books than in all his life earlier. And watched cubeage of things he'd never heard of before. Watched and rewatched an old documentary on the Technite War, and the T'swa mercenaries who fought there. Had been awed by the hard black warriors, their appearance, their skills, their attitudes. Had read Varlik Lormagen's description of living with them in the steppe and jungles on Kettle. Dwelt upon and memorized the centerpiece of T'swa philosophy, *The Matrix of T'sel*. Viewed and reviewed cubeage of their home planet, Tyss. And on more recent cubeage, had watched them train OSP regiments, had seen how they handled the trainees.

Now he better understood Colonel Romlar and his T'swa-trained troopers, and felt even greater affinity for them.

Meanwhile he'd set himself a new goal. Up till then his goal had been simply to live with his integrity uncompromised. Now he realized—not decided, realized!— that he would do more. That someday, while he was still young, he'd go to Tyss, live and study there, become like the T'swa. Perhaps spend his life there.

❖   ❖   ❖

On Kro's first day on Iryala, Colonel Romlar had gotten him hired as an opening-level employee of OSP, on temporary medical leave for corrective surgery. He was then assigned a room in the visitors' dormitory, at the medical center in Landfall. His first surgery was scheduled for the following week.

Meanwhile he was awed by the OSP headquarters, its Rotunda, its dining room, its food and service. Later he had supper with Colonel Romlar and his wife, in their home on a nearby ridge—a home he would never have imagined. Glass roofs on part of it! None of them things he yearned for, but he appreciated them.

The colonel's wife impressed him too. A small woman, she was not especially pretty, but seemed physically as well as mentally strong, with a power he could sense. She saw through people, he had no doubt, and handled situations even her husband might not. When he mentioned reading and viewing the T'swa material, she told him she'd studied more than five years on Tyss. Oven, she'd called it.

That's when Kro confided his intention—to live on Tyss and study there. Though the Romlars seemed interested, they didn't volunteer help or suggestions.

It never occurred to him that they might. He'd always made his way through life on his own.

When the Faronyas arrived at Landfall, Kelmer hired a cab. Then he and Weldi went to Central News, a highrise in the middle of Media Village.

Riding from the spaceport, Weldi was wide-eyed, excited. Landfall could hardly have contrasted more with Hovesteth, the capital of backwoods Smolen, where she'd lived most of her nineteen years. Landfall was more than the crowning jewel of the Confederation. It was the center of Confederation government, and housed Iryala's planetary government, along with various quasigovernmental functions. Much of it was a mosaic of villages, each centered on a function, some broad, some narrow. Most villages consisted of one or two towering professional buildings surrounded by modestly highrise apartments for the people who worked there. Their grounds were parklike, with flowerbeds and playgrounds. Each village was surrounded by a grassy ring of semiwooded land. A network of grassy travelways, serving innumerable hover buses, tied it all together.

It both awed and worried her. So beautiful! So clean! But so many people stacked so high? How could you know more than a tiny percentage of them?

Central News occupied a number of floors in Media Center. Kelmer knew his way. They walked into one of the building's several broad entry doors, paused at a security station, then crossed the large and immaculate main reception area, and rode a lift tube—her first—to the twelfth floor.

They knew Kelmer in Central News reception, and seemed excited to see him. In his boss's office, Kelmer introduced her as his "gorgeous wife," and the man called someone to arrange a lunch party in Kelmer's honor.

He congratulated Kelmer on his beautiful wife, and herself on her handsome husband. Clapping Kelmer's shoulder, he did a double take at its hard muscularity, and called him the new Varlik Lormagen. Weldi had no idea who Varlik Lormagen was, but clearly the analogy was complimentary. After that they discussed Central News's plans to publicize Kelmer.

Lunch was almost a dream. She'd expected it to include more than the forty or so asked in. But on the other hand, someone had called a caterer, who on an hour's notice produced a large display of hors d'oeuvres, a magnificent cake, containers of assorted ice creams, and hot and cold nonalcoholic drinks. The people seemed genuinely admiring of both Kelmer and herself, and people had shook Kelmer's right arm almost off.

❖　　　　　❖　　　　　❖

Afterward they rented a furnished apartment in one of the Media Village highrises. Weldi was enchanted by the technical built-ins. Kelmer coached her on using Vending Services, and she ordered a few things to keep on hand in her kitchen. Tonight though, he said, they'd eat out in Media Village's classiest restaurant. And tomorrow—tomorrow they'd shop for clothes.

The five difficult weeks in the courier were over, and it seemed to both of them their marriage and lives were off to a new start. After supper with drinks, they took a lift tube and returned to their apartment. It was Weldi who suggested they try out their new bed, and they had their best lovemaking since they'd left Smolen.

Part Two
CONTACTS AND INTERACTIONS

Chapter 12
A Meeting of Masters

From a little distance, the Monastery of Dys Tolbash almost looked carved from the mountain. Resembling a narrow fortress, it crowned a rugged promontory at the end of a ridge, flanked by deep, boulder-cluttered desert ravines. The end overlooked the Kar-Suum Basin, a broad saline flat that perhaps every fourth year held a transient, twenty-mile-wide lake a few feet deep. Now it was cracked, sun-baked sediment, dotted with dark clumps of tar-bush, their roots tapping pockets of bitter moisture well below the surface. Small bands of bushbuck, perhaps one band to ten square miles, ranged the basin. Rock goats were harder to spot. Widely scattered groups of nannies and kids, and solitary billies, they foraged the ravines and ridgesides. All were wary. An inevitable carrion bird soared the updrafts, watching for misfortune in the 1.22 gravity and 139 degree heat.

In the top of a monastery tower, Master Tso-Ban sat in trance. The day was unusually hot, and a novice sat in the cell's open north side, slowly waving a large fan to help cool the old man, whose attention was not on the heat or the desert, or anything else on Tyss. He was seeing through other eyes, on a world called Shuuf'r Thaak, a world even hotter than Tyss. He was monitoring the Surrogate of God, who just then was meeting with

Esteemed Lomaru, Grand Master of the Shafan.

Their discussion was of little interest to Tso-Ban. It was Lomaru he found interesting. When the meeting was over, Tso-Ban transferred his covert psychic presence to Lomaru. The Grand Master left, going to the apartment that was his when he visited the palace. There he assumed a contemplative posture, and thought a question. «Who is it that visits my spirit uninvited?»

Tso-Ban answered without a moment's hesitation. «An aged seeker, on a world far outside your khanate.»

Lomaru could easily have rejected his visitor, sent him snapping back painfully into his own head. Instead he asked: «Ah! And what life form are you?»

Before their dialog was over, both masters had discovered a large degree of commonality, and agreed that Tso-Ban was free to reconnect with Lomaru at will. Meanwhile, Tso-Ban would continue to visit the minds of other Garthids. Not that he volunteered this information, nor did Lomaru ask.

Lomaru, on the other hand, would not visit the minds of distant humans. Such visitation lay outside his skills and interests. Mostly he communed with God, an activity carried on without words.

On Shuuf'r Thaak, Lomaru was regarded much as Lord Buddha might have been, if he'd been born into and embraced by Islam or medieval Christianity: He had no statutory power, and would have declined it if offered. But he did have great status, and significant influence. He was often sought out by the Surrogate's chief counselor, grown spiritual in his later years. And occasionally by the Surrogate himself, a moral but stubborn old warrior of the guardian gender, who felt ill at ease in so holy a presence.

Like Tso-Ban, Lomaru had his own sense of importances, and chauvinism had no part in them. He'd communed with God too long and too deeply for that.

Chapter 13
Emergence in F-space

"All personnel hear this! All personnel hear this! At 0900 hours,[1] all craft will emerge from hyperspace, following standard procedures." After a brief pause, the message was repeated.

The voice on the flagship's speaker system was the admiral's. It also went via hyperspace radio to the rest of the Armada, whose captains repeated it to their crews.

Zero nine hundred hours was fourteen hours away, and everyone who'd spent the last thirty-eight months in a normal state of waking and sleeping was grateful for the distraction. Several chains of action began promptly. On each ship, those medics who'd been part of the skeleton crew began revival procedures on additional crew. They'd be needed for standard post-emergence operations.

---

[1] Clocks in hyperspace register F-space time, of course, and minute, unpredictable differences in instrument creep accumulate over time. These, along with little understood relativity effects and more obscure causes, result in each ship's "0900 hours" being unique within an important, if extremely small, range. These differences, along with the vagaries of hyperspace radio transmission times, make it impossible to synchronize instruments without emerging, at which point it is too late for simultaneous emergence.

Emergence from hyperspace was never precise. And after so long a "flight," ships "near enough in hyperspace" to be adjacent on each others' screens, could be a mile or hundreds of miles apart when they emerged. It was more than a matter of minute differences in emergence time. There was also a "quantum foam" effect in the interface between hyperspace and the ship's enclosing capsule of F-space.

Thus invariably after emergence, a fleet would find itself not only scattered, but severely disorganized. Human technology did not provide correction. It had been a problem since the first hyperdrive had been tested thirty thousand years earlier.

Overall, the effects were cumulative over the length of a hyperspace trip. Instruments might show a consistently tight formation, but the farther the formation had traveled without emerging, the more dispersed it would be when it did. By emerging now, the Armada would not only orient itself in F-space, and compute a more accurate course for the final run; it would also reassemble formations while far outside the striking distance of Confederation defense forces. Then, when they emerged near the Iryala System, they'd be considerably less dispersed.

And finally, emergence permitted the external inspection of hulls and outrigs, and allowed maintenance that could be done only in F-space.

The command admiral and Chesty Vrislakavaro were on the bridge when 0900 arrived. DAAS ordered emergence automatically, and the personnel felt the momentary queasiness of crossover. At the same instant, the large command screen filled briefly with a glorious and welcome panoply of stars. *So. I'm somewhere again,* the admiral thought. It felt good. DAAS left the view on the screen for half a minute—a default setting—so the bridge watch could enjoy the sight. Then the starscape was replaced by a grid-defined, perspective representation of surrounding space, with the symbols of spacecraft, a different symbol for each class, a different color for each fleet. Small numbers identified wing, squadron, and vessel. They could hardly have been more thoroughly mixed if they'd been stirred, or positioned by a random numbers generator.

The admiral sighed quietly. Reassembling such a monstrous mishmash would take a week. *At least,* he thought, *if guided by DAAS. I wonder if SUMBAA could handle it any faster?* It seemed unlikely. What made the job slow was the physical movement of ships. The *safe* movement of hundreds of ships in gravdrive, in orderly evolutions to form standard formations. But still, if the three SUMBAAs worked together . . .

When the Armada had passed the orbit of Sentinel, and generated hyperspace, more than three years earlier, Admiral Siilakamasu had ordered the master artificial intelligence disconnected from the operating system. He'd somehow felt uneasy with it, and there'd seemed no need for SUMBAA till the time approached to engage the enemy.

"Lieutenant Mogavadiru!" he barked. An officer turned sharply. His insignia identified him as the watch astrogation officer.

"Sir?"

"Can the SUMBAAs communicate with each other? Well enough to work together in reassembling the Armada?"

The lieutenant frowned in brief thought. "They should, sir. SUMBAA can tell us with certainty. Shall I ask him?"

"I'll ask. Access him for me."

The astrogator touched a short sequence of switches that brought SUMBAA back into the loop. In the ship SUMBAAs, as with the DAASes, open oral communication was the default state. SUMBAA answered promptly, through the DAAS equipment but with its own well-modulated voice. "I am SUMBAA."

The lieutenant nodded at his admiral.

"I am Admiral Siilakamasu. We have just emerged into F-space, and the Armada is parked, dispersed over ten million cubic miles of it. Can the SUMBAAs, working together, reassemble it more quickly than the DAASes can?"

There was a moment's pause. The admiral assumed that SUMBAA was reviewing the problems, as if review required some major part of a second. "If we are given full control," SUMBAA answered, "we can reduce the time to eighty-six percent of that required by the DAASes."

"Good! The job is yours. Lieutenant Mogavadiru will give you full access. Start at once."

The admiral felt quite good about it. Good enough that when he saw the Kalif enter the bridge, he greeted him affably. "Good morning, Coso Biilathkamoro. I suppose you and your family saw the star display."

The admiral's geniality took the Emeritus Kalif by surprise. The man had not been flagrantly hostile since their second day in space, but neither had he been friendly. Mostly he'd either ignored his ex-ruler or been curt. "We did," Coso replied. "Rami asked what they were. He didn't remember stars. Imagine when he steps on the surface of a planet!"

"Indeed." The admiral's eyes had moved to the Armada display on the large screen, waiting for the beginnings of movement among the throng of ships.

"I noticed one very bright star," the Emeritus Kalif continued. "We must be in the fringe of its planetary system. By your leave, I'd like to have one of the survey ships scan its planets. See if any of them might be habitable."

The admiral's head snapped round, his face scowling. "Habitable? We're not interested in *habitable* planets. It's *inhabited* planets we want, inhabited and developed. Civilized."

"Of course. But it might be useful to have a way station here eventually. With harbor and repair facilities, where mail pods could be picked up."

The scowl transformed into a thoughtful frown. Then the frown cleared. "You have a point. Yes." He turned to the astrogator. "Lieutenant, would His Reverence's request in any way slow reassembling?"

His Reverence? That raised Chesty Vrislakavaro's eyebrows. The Emeritus Kalif, however, did not react.

"I'm sure it wouldn't," the astrogator said. When the admiral's critical gaze didn't leave him, the young officer added: "On Varatos, SUMBAA handles all the routine of government and commerce, including imperial oversight of the entire Empire. A far greater task."

The admiral nodded thoughtfully. "True." He turned his head, locating the communications warrant officer. "Comms," he said, "connect His Reverence with the commanding officer on the *Cajiya Island*. They have my approval to begin a survey of the local planetary system, for a possibly habitable planet."

Even though his expression didn't show it, Coso Biilathkamoro was surprised at being called "Your Reverence," and at having his request agreed to. He'd made it hopefully but without expectation. He went to his office to take the call, though the admiral might still have it recorded. The survey ship's watch officer connected him with his CO, who was delighted at the idea.

Coso Biilathkamoro hadn't realized how powerful the survey ship's instrumentation was. In only minutes, his screen showed a graphic of the system, with 11 planets, 67 moons, and an asteroid belt. One of the planets was out of sight on the other side of the primary; he wondered how the instruments had found it. There was no signature at all of any technological species, but the parameters of the fourth planet suggested habitability. It had a suitable solar constant and surface temperature, a strong magnetic field, extensive water surface, and an atmosphere with nitrogen, oxygen, carbon dioxide, water vapor, and methane.

He had his terminal print out the data summary.

"That's as much as we can ascertain from here, Your Reverence," the captain said. "To really know, we'll need to send a recon flyby. And if that looks promising, have it fly a low-level survey. Then, if it still looks good, we'll have to send in a shuttle and put a research team on the surface. It would take weeks to get results we could start feeling safe with. I'd love to see it happen, but the admiral? I don't think so. Not unless the survey team stays on the planet when we leave."

Exactly, Coso thought. *Now comes the hard part. Or maybe not if our good admiral likes the idea of a fleet way station here.* "Thank you, Captain. I'll tell him what you found, and urge a follow-up. At least through the flyby stage."

Coso Biilathkamoro was operating on intuition again. The rationale he'd given the admiral had been off the cuff, and he was surprised he'd gotten as far as he had with it. He'd push, and see what happened next.

He hadn't wondered what good it could possibly do his situation. Nor did it occur to him that the admiral's thinking might have nothing to do with a way station. He simply followed his intuition. It was never an entirely comfortable—or reliable—way to operate.

The Garthid long-range scout emerged somewhat outside the irregular, disorganized swarm of Armada craft. But near enough, in space and time, that if noticed, it might easily pass as a laggard member of the Armada. Activating gravdrive, its pilot slowly backed off till his sensors began to lose the more distant enemy craft. Then he shut down all systems not needed for surveillance, data analysis, and life support. It gave him as much security as he could hope for.

Interesting how dispersed they are, he thought. They must lack hyperspace formation locks. Formation locks had their limitations, but this was worse than extreme.

More than a year earlier, the scout, posted in Garthid F-space, had been alerted by the emergence of a signal beacon. The scout had promptly generated hyperspace, and received a hyperspace radio pulse from a stationary sentry. By that time the Armada had passed, presumably without having detected the sentry, which was simply a parked, automated instrument package. The pulse told the pilot and his navcomp the intruder's "course." It also indicated that the intrusion was by an undetermined but very large number of ships. Clearly the real thing!

The pilot had set out in pursuit, sacrificing security margin to "gain space" on the intruder. When his instruments picked up the quarry, the scout had "slowed" to avoid notice, following like a dim shadow.

Chapter 14
Party Time

"Seagirt?" Weldi Faronya's voice threatened to get away from her. "Where is Seagirt?"

Kelmer had learned to recognize the symptoms. With one hand he called a menu onto the wall screen, then a quick series of lesser menus. For orders like this, voice requests were cumbersome. A dozen seconds later he had a world map on the screen.

"There," he said, positioning the cursor on a half-million-square-mile island, almost a subcontinent, in north temperate mid-ocean. Weldi's pretty face registered dismay. Specifying frame size, and centering, he replaced the world map with a screen-sized map of the island. Near one end, 80 to 150 miles from the coast, was the primary mountain range, with here and there the symbol for glaciers. On the coast side of the range was a symbol and name: Roralanos Volcano. "It's the biggest on-planet news story of the century," Kelmer said. "It threatens to be the biggest lava flow—really the biggest complex of lava flows—since people have been here. And there's danger of a major explosion. It's already caused the biggest human evacuation in the history of Iryala."

"That far away?"

"Sorry, honey. That far away."

"Tomorrow morning's so soon!" Her voice was plaintive. "Why can't I go with you?"

"You could, but it's not a good idea. I'll be working out of the village of Circle Bay"—he moved the cursor again—"instead of Roraby. The bay itself is the flooded crater of an ancient volcano. A mountain blew up and the sea flooded in on one side. The village is where the study teams are staying; it's protected by a spur range from possible clastic flows and glacial melt flooding. You'd be sitting alone most of the time, while I'm in the air with the vulcanologists, watching and recording. Any time I'm in the hotel, I'll be sitting in front of the screen, cramming knowledge of volcanoes and their dynamics, and quizzing vulcanologists by comm."

He tried to contact Weldi's eyes. She avoided it. "Besides," he added, "you'll be starting drama classes on Oneday. You can't be here and on Seagirt at the same time."

She nodded reluctantly, and now her eyes did meet his. "How long?" she asked.

"I don't know. No one does. Probably at least a week. It could be several. It goes with the promotion, and the money that will let us do the things we've talked about."

Reaching, he took one of her hands. "Look, sweetheart, why don't I call someone? There are always student parties on Sixday evening. It shouldn't be too late to hit one of them."

He didn't wait for an answer, but touched a sequence of keys on the comm pad, listened, then grinned and spoke. "Hi, Rosser. Kelmer Faronya here . . . Yeah, they did give me a lot of publicity." He listened, then chuckled. "It was a whole lot colder than it looked on the screen. Look, I called to ask a favor. I have to leave town tomorrow for a while, and I'm out of touch on campus. And Weldi and I want to party tonight. Where can I find one? . . . Yeah, I know the house. Are their parties as good as they used to be? . . . Better? Sounds great. At 2030. Uh-huh."

His eyes flicked to the time display. "We haven't eaten yet, so we'll be a little late. But then, most people will be . . . Thanks, old buddy, I'll see you there."

He broke the connection, grinning. "You'll love it. You'll soon be looking forward to my trips, for the going-away parties. Rosser Belden's been going to university since Yomal knows when. He seldom completes a course. Goes to lectures but doesn't like studying. His family's rich, and he'll stay a student as long as they'll let him, partying his weekends away."

He got to his feet. "Come on. Time to dress for it."

Chapter 15
New World

   Monotony was a problem on hyperspace jumps, even those of only a few weeks. There'd been weeks when General Chesty Vrislakavaro had hardly set foot on the bridge, spending most of his time in his quarters reading, or watching dramas, with time off in the exercise room. And there'd been weeks when he visited the bridge for a while every morning, then spent much of the day in the wardroom playing cards—solitaire if no one else was interested. But these routines, and other combinations of activities, didn't really provide much variety.

   He wondered how Loksa Siilakamasu could sit there day after day. He knew the admiral had taken a number of young crew women to bed, but even so . . .

   For a while Chesty spent part of each day on the learning program, learning Confederation Standard. Occasionally he'd practiced with Coso Biilathkamoro. Then Loksa began giving him sour looks, as if suspicious, so the general did his practicing with SUMBAA. It didn't make sense to damage his relationship with Loksa, a relationship that presumably would be very important when they reached the Confederation.

   He'd suggested to Loksa that they practice the language together. Loksa's reply had been: Let the damned Confederation learn Imperial.

Chesty had made a point of being on the bridge for emergence. Now discovery of a possibly habitable planet, and Loksa's surprising agreement to take a closer look, added to the interest. The following day, both Chesty and Loksa were on the bridge when the next report arrived. Warpdrive had taken the survey scout to the planet in under four hours, and flyby observations had been promising. A low-level survey had begun.

The radioed report had taken 7.46 hours to arrive; Chesty wondered what had been learned in the meantime.

On the third day, the survey scout's summary report was entirely positive. Land constituted twenty-two percent of the planet's surface. Axial tilt was only eight degrees, suggesting modest climatic swings, at least of temperature. A considerable portion of the land surface seemed suitable for habitation. The observed flora and fauna didn't seem to pose serious threats.

A large volume of raw data arrived by pulse—for SUMBAA's analysis and synthesis—tagged with the name the scout's pilot had given the planet: Hope.

The general found both the admiral's and the Emeritus Kalif's reactions very interesting. He'd expected Coso to show some excitement. Instead he appeared thoughtful and reserved. Loksa's interest seemed livelier. But there was something about both men that struck him as odd, though he couldn't put his finger on it.

"General," Loksa said, "what would you think of my sending a scientific survey party in? Put them on the ground, that is."

It was the first time he'd asked the general's opinion on anything substantive. Chesty pursed his wide mouth. "What could they accomplish in the time we have here? Unless you're willing to wait—how long? Two weeks? Three?"

"A month at least," Coso put in. His eyes were bright now.

"Why would we have to wait?" Loksa asked. "Instead

of a survey shuttle, send in the *Cajiya Island* with her entire team. Along with an assault lander with a company of engineers. We can lighter in some heavy construction machinery. They can build a good solid base, safe from the elements and the local biota." He nodded as if to himself. "What do you say, Chesty? Will you contribute the engineers?"

The general grunted. His only problem was Loksa's strange new attitude. Apparently they weren't even going to critique the proposal. But when he opened his mouth, all he said was, "Yes, if you want them."

"Good! Good! We'll do it then!"

Chesty half expected to hear Coso ask to go. Loksa would almost surely agree; might even have had it in mind all along. He had something in mind besides studying a new planet.

But Coso didn't ask. Either he wanted to be present when they met the Confederation forces, or he too mistrusted the admiral's enthusiasm.

The pilot of the Garthid scout had learned a great deal about the Armada besides its great size. Almost surely it was on its way to invade someone, and obviously not his own people; they'd been bypassed. So who might the target be? Or were they returning from an invasion? Or might it be not an invasion but a migration? It would be well to know these things before getting involved, but that was a matter for someone much higher up than he.

He was a graduate of the fleet academy, and knowledgeable in technical matters. The intruder definitely lacked hyperspace formation locks; his emergence dispersal had been even more serious than was first apparent. The reassembly process wasn't simply a matter of wings or squadrons being scattered. They were utterly disorganized, to the level of individual ships. Yet reassembly had gone surprisingly well. Their computers were obviously superb, which would serve them well in battle maneuvers.

He'd had his own computer recording the abundant enemy radio traffic. Much was in simple code, for efficiency, but much was also oral. Parked as he was, his computer had had little to do except sort and analyze. It should have synthesized a considerable lexicon and grammar by this time.

It already contained what his people had learned of alien speech as it was 21,000 years earlier. As far as he could tell, the speech of these beings did not resemble the ancient alien speech. Except that the sounds were similar, as if from similar vocal apparatus. On the other hand it matched what little had been recorded of the recent intruders.

The enemy reassembly seemed nearly complete. Most of their craft sat in orderly formations. If they noticed him now, he'd be an anomaly requiring investigation, but that seemed unlikely. In reassembly, they tracked their vessels by code instead of visually. At any rate he needed to remain until they'd left.

Presumably they'd stay till they'd finished refitting. What a mess if his own fleet arrived now. Even with formation locks, they'd be considerably scattered. But it wouldn't happen. The point scouts would read his beacon, and relay the pulses.

And the fleet would hardly arrive in less than four weeks. Three at best. Even if they'd been parked in space when the message pod emerged, waiting with all necessary personnel on board, and all systems go. And after such a long standby, there'd be last-minute things to handle. It could be five or six weeks.

Chapter 16
Invitations to the Ball

"Whew! That's number one!" Weldi Lanks-Faronya put down her reader case, dropped onto a chair, and gratefully took off her shoes. She'd finished her first week of classes with encouraging comments from her instructors in both Beginning Drama and Beginning Dance. She had work left to do—she knew that—but with her looks and talent . . .

Meanwhile she was tired. She hadn't danced for two years—not *really* danced—and her instructor pushed her students hard. Thank Yomal for Vending Services! She ordered spaghetti, meatballs, densebread with cream cheese, and wine. She would, she decided, eat, watch a holo, and go to bed early. Not the ideal Fiveday evening, but Kelmer was 7,000 miles away. Tomorrow she'd visit the enormous Landfall Zoo, tour it on the unicorn-drawn safari train. She'd longed to since she'd read about it as a child.

Next week she'd cultivate a classmate who, like her, was from off-world. Perhaps invite her over. She would *not* languish while Kelmer was away.

She ate to the evening news, watching extensive coverage of the eruptions. Saw a broad lake of fuming lava, with brighter rivers pushing through it, saw distant plumes of steam, explosions of ash and rock. And Kelmer wearing a gasmask, talking via throat mike. He sounded very knowledgeable. She'd just finished eating when the comm warbled. *Kelmer,* she thought, and touched the switch. "Yes?"

"Weldi, this is Rosser Belden. May I speak with Kelmer?"

"Oh, hello, Rosser. Kelmer's out of town. On Seagirt, covering the eruptions. He was on the evening news."

"Ah. Of course. I knew and then forgot. I was going to invite you two to another party. This one in the home of an impresario, Maylon Gorth."

"An *impresario*?"

"Right. He sponsors live theater, stage plays. Actually he's a wealthy stock broker, but he likes to have students around him. Students and theater people." He paused. "You'd be welcome to come by yourself, you know— daughter of an off-world head of government, wife of Kelmer Faronya, and someone who's been in an actual war. It would be an opportunity for you to meet people who could be helpful to your career."

"I—I don't know. How would I get there?"

"Do you have a stylus?"

"Just a minute . . . All right, I'm ready."

"Call a cab and have it take you to 15374-00471." He repeated it. "It's a large home on large grounds. Have the cabby pull into the horseshoe drive and let you out at the front door." He had her read the number back to him. "I'll call ahead," Belden added, "so the doorman will have you on his list."

"What time should I get there?"

"Anytime after nine. Maylon prefers that people arrive before ten though. From Media Village, it will take about fifteen minutes."

"What time will the party be over?"

Belden laughed. "For most of us between midnight and two. But for others—who knows? They'll have to continue it somewhere else though."

"Thank you, Rosser, I'll be there. About nine."

Weldi hung up thinking, An *impresario!* Her mind savored the word. She looked at the clock. There was time for a leisurely shower and shampoo, and to fix herself up. She'd wear the pale blue party dress she'd bought that first day. It would have to do. She wasn't sure what a cab cost, and Kelmer had told her to take it easy on spending. But on Maragor he'd been stationed at Burnt Woods and Shelf Falls, and accumulated a *lot* of credits. His salary hadn't reached him there, and there'd been nothing to buy with the money he'd brought with him.

It seemed to her that Rosser Belden's call had been predestined, and that a professional career was nearer than she'd dared imagine. She'd forgotten all about being tired.

Gulthar Kro looked at himself in the mirror. His face was no longer ugly, simply pink and tender looking. *The mendbones is good,* he thought, *no arguing about that.* Unfortunately he'd lost some old scar tissue he'd been attached to, from before the firefight at the White T'swa encampment. Scars he thought of as markers of his maturing. He'd matured very young.

He still had some left. He'd warned the surgeon not to mend his broken nose. The man's eyebrows had raised at the admonition. He'd ended up doing some repairs inside the nose, to help his patient breathe better.

Kro's comm warbled, and he took the call on his bathroom set. Warily. Who would call him? Colonel Romlar was off-world. "Yeah?" he answered.

"Gull? This is Korum Fallburk."

The guy in the next bed awhile, in the hospital. Worked in a government office. "Hullo, Korum," Kro answered.

"I'm going to a party tonight, and thought you might like to go. Informal. Interesting people, a good buffet, good booze. I asked if I could invite you. Told the host you were a wounded veteran of the Smoleni Rangers.

He said he'd love to talk with you. Find out what war is really like."

Kro grunted inwardly. The way to do that was try it out. There were always wars going on, on one trade world and another. He'd read it in a book, on the courier. "What's a buffet?" he asked.

"A table with lots of different foods on it. You take a plate, and whatever foods look good to you. Then you walk around and talk to people. And drink; there's all kinds."

All kinds of drinks? Kro wondered wryly. *Or people?* He didn't answer at once. A rough, uneducated, old-young man of strong intelligence and remarkable poise, he feared virtually nothing. Yet somehow he felt ill at ease with this invitation. Ill at ease, but curious. As for liquor, he didn't drink, had never wanted to. He'd had some beautiful fights because of that. Food he could enjoy. He wasn't sure he'd enjoy the people, but what the hell.

"How do I get there?"

"Do you have a stylus handy?"

"Yeah." He didn't. He'd always relied on a superior memory. "Let's have it."

"Call a cab and have him take you to 15374-00471. It's . . ."

Kro interrupted. "A cab? I better not. I got to watch my money till I get paid."

"Oh. Well . . . You're in the visitor's dorm at the hospital, right?"

Kro guessed Fallburk had called the hospital and found out. "Yeah. Room 212."

"Okay, I'll pick you up. It's hardly out of my way at all. Eight-thirty be all right?"

"Eight-thirty? Sure. What should I wear?"

"Whatever you have. Your Smoleni uniform if you want."

Kro grunted inwardly. He'd wear the blue suit the

colonel had bought him after he'd picked him up at the spaceport. He wondered if there'd be any fights at the party. Probably not, he decided. If anyone tried to pick one with him, he'd walk away from it. He didn't want to embarrass Colonel Romlar, and anyway he was supposed to be careful of his face for a while.

Chapter 17
Maylon Gorth

As he drove along grassy, lamplit travelways, Korum Fallburk did most of the talking. He had in the hospital, as well. Kro had worn a restrainer on his jaw then, and a mesh reconstructive matrix on his palate. He'd done well to mumble. Gradually Fallburk had become aware that much of what he said was a mystery to the off-worlder. It lacked context and reference points. So now he filled the time with cheerful small talk, Kro responding briefly when something appropriate occurred to him.

Before long they arrived at a large house set well back from the travelway. Its ground floor windows were brightly lit. To one side was private parking, with only three cars besides their own. There was room for perhaps four dozen, in four rows. "We're a bit early," Fallburk said. "Maylon wanted a chance to visit with you before things got busy."

An outer doorman greeted Fallburk by name. Inside, another smiled them through the foyer into a broad hallway, where Korum paused at an open door. Through it Kro saw a large party room, with bench sofas along walls, low tables in front of them. Straight-backed chairs were scattered in pairs or threes. There were waist-high tables with glasses, and punch bowls not yet filled. Near one wall stood a long table with white linen.

"That's the main party room," Fallburk said, then started off again down the hall. "I'll take you to our host now."

At the hallway's far end, Fallburk pressed a button beside a door, and spoke. "Maylon, this is Korum. I'm here with Mr. Kro, from Maragor."

A voice issued from a grill. "Ah! Good! Come in, Korum. And Mr. Kro."

Korum opened the door and they entered. A white-haired, pink-faced man stood waiting, seemingly in his sixties. He shook their hands. "Thank you, Korum, for bringing Mr. Kro," he said. "Did you know that Ennetta is coming? You may want to greet her when she arrives."

He turned to Kro then, and Fallburk left as if dismissed. "Please sit down, Mr. Kro," he said gesturing, then stepped over to a four-foot-long bar. "What would you like to drink?"

"What ya got?"

Gorth named several unfamiliar wines and liquors.

"Got any buttermilk?" Kro asked.

The question was facetious, but Gorth answered it seriously. "Ah, buttermilk. No, I'm afraid I don't. But I do have several varieties of non-alcoholic mixes. Perhaps you'd like a carbonated fruit punch."

"I'll try it."

Gorth filled a tall glass half full of ice cubes, then topped it off with something from a bottle. He brought it to Kro, then returned to the cabinet. Kro sniffed the drink warily while his host poured three fingers of whiskey into a small, cut-glass tumbler. Turning, Gorth raised his glass. "To your health, Mr. Kro." Kro nodded, then sipped. The situation smelled odd to him. Gorth sipped because he was a moderate drinker, and because Iryalan etiquette didn't call for downing a drink when toasting.

"Korum told me you were in the Komars-Smolen War as a Smoleni ranger. Tell me what that was like."

Kro described the training a bit, the kind of men who were recruited, and something of the fighting, elaborating to answer specific questions.

"So you were a backwoodsman."

Kro decided to answer candidly, and see how Gorth reacted. "Not really. I spent a winter fur-trappin' in Smolen's High Wild, apprenticin' so to speak. A greenhorn. Not so green by spring breakup, but I weren't naw seasoned backwoodsman like some. I was Komarsi born and raised."

That interested Gorth too. He asked questions about Kro's childhood, his family, growing up in a shantytown, working harvests, and laboring in a rock quarry. Kro didn't tell him the quarry job was done while living in a convict camp on a murder conviction. Nor that he'd left in a breakout. He did tell, though, about volunteering for the army, and becoming CO of General Undsvin's personal guard company.

"Then the general decided he wanted us to murder some folks for him: the Smoleni president and a few others. My target was the White T'swa CO, Colonel Romlar. When I got to Burnt Woods—where the Smoleni government was, what was left of it—instead of murderin' anyone, I joined the Smoleni rangers. I'd have tried the White T'swa, but they dawn't take replacements. They're like the real T'swa: they recruit and train a regiment, and that's it. As guys get killed or crippled, the regiment gets smaller."

Gorth stared. "You mean—you turned on your own people?"

Kro frowned. "My people? The freedmen laboring class were my people, and they're way better off with the war lost and the king dead. If you ain't learned nawthin' else from what I've said, you've learned how we were treated. In Smolen there ain't no serfdom, and the government and even the army treated folks decent. Fact is, there ain't naw real upper crust like in Komars. And a man can be proud of servin' in their ranger battalions."

Maylon Gorth looked unsettled. Kro wondered which bothered him most: the Smoleni lack of an upper crust, or the Komarsi treatment of the serf and freedmen classes.

Actually, from what he knew of it, the upper crust here on Iryala didn't seem bad.

"And the White T'swa?" Gorth asked.

"They're like brothers to each other. And when they trained rangers, there weren't naw bullshit at all. They worked our bloody ass off, never let up, but they always treated us like men. And they didn't just tell us how to do stuff. They showed us. And when they'd finished, we were *good*. Damn good! Best troops on the planet, 'ceptin' theirselves. And the T'swa that Engwar brought in from Tyss. They were somethin'!"

He paused, examining his host. He had no idea what the man was thinking. Finally Gorth asked, "Did the White T'swa have many casualties?"

"More on Terfreya than in Smolen. On Terfreya they fought against a whole fookin' brigade of foreigners from way to hell off somewhere. Foreigners with blasters and armored assault vehicles, not the sort of things allowed in our wars. So the White T'swa fought a jungle war. Ended up losin' a third of their guys, but they drove the boogers out."

Gorth was frowning. "Are you saying the attack on Terfreya was actual? That there were actual invaders from another sector of space?"

Kro stared. Something was wrong with this man. "That's right. What's hard to believe about that?"

Gorth shook his head. "I'd heard rumors it was faked by the government."

Kro grunted. "Well, I wasn't there myself, but I dawn't have no trouble believin' it. I've fought alongside the White T'swa. They've naw fear at all, and the only thing hard to believe is how good they fight." He gestured, touching a cheek. "That's when I took a bullet through the face. When I was with them. It went in one side and out the other. Took the roof of my mouth with it.

Naw, I knaw the White T'swa well. There ain't a spoonful of bullshit in the whole damn regiment."

Gorth sat thoughtfully now. "Mr. Kro, you have led an extraordinary life. A book could be written about it. A holo play. The stage could never accommodate it." He got to his feet. "Come. I've been monopolizing your attention. There's a party just down the hall, and you are missing it."

Chapter 18
Seduction

The taxi pulled into the horseshoe drive, Weldi Lanks-Faronya staring at the mansion. It was larger than Smolen's executive mansion, where she'd lived with her father for two years. And to her eyes, far more handsome. The cabby pulled up to the entrance and Weldi paid him, then got out, staring again. The outer doorman came down the steps to her.

"May I assist you, miss?"

His uniform looked like new, she thought, and faintly fluorescent in the artificial light. Its dark blue looked black, its red collar purple, the white stripes silver. Much more interesting than the military uniforms at home. She remembered the formal manners her tutor had taught her when her daddy'd been elected president. "I'm Weldi Lanks-Faronya," she said coolly. "I believe I'm expected."

"Oh yes, Ms. Faronya. You are indeed. Come with me."

He escorted her up the several steps, and across the deep porch to the entrance. In the foyer she could hear the sound of voices, a small crowd's worth, and began to feel nervous. She'd know none of them but Rosser. She very much wished that Kelmer was with her. The outer doorman turned her over to the inner, who escorted her to the door of the party room. At formal parties at the executive mansion, guests were announced. Here,

however, he simply pointed out Rosser Belden in the
crowd of 30 or 40 people already there, two-thirds of
them male.

She started toward Rosser, moving between people
engrossed in their conversations. Even so, she was aware
that some paused to look at her. Rosser's back was to
her, but the man he was talking with watched her
approach, which caused Rosser to turn. His face lit with
pleasure. "Weldi! How glad I am you could make it!"
He turned to his conversation partner, a balding, casually
dressed man. "Borg, this is Weldi Lanks-Faronya. And
you're out of luck. She's married." Rosser winked at her.
"To the news reporter, Kelmer Faronya, of Maragoran
fame. He's doing the Roralanos eruption now; you saw
him on TV this evening."

He lowered his voice as if sharing something confidential.
"She's a drama student at the U." He turned again to Weldi.
"Borg is the playwright, Borg Tudovis. His day job is
professor of speech. You'll probably be taking a class from
him."

The professor grinned at her, his eyes appraising.

"If you'll excuse me," Rosser said, "I'll introduce her
around a bit. She deserves to be seen and known, don't
you think?" Taking her arm, Rosser steered her across
the floor toward a remarkably handsome man. He'd been
en route to the buffet, but paused to watch them
approach. His eyes too were appraising.

"Jarnell," Rosser said, "I'd like you to meet Weldi Lanks-
Faronya, a new drama student at the U. From Maragor.
Her father is president of a republic, Smolen. You've
seen cubeage of the recent war there. Her husband,
Kelmer Faronya, was the correspondent. He's covering
the Roralanos eruption now."

"It's a pleasure, Mrs. Faronya." The man took her right
hand in his and kissed it, the whole sequence natural,
graceful, somehow a work of art.

"Weldi," Belden continued, "this is Jarnell Walthen.

He's one of Iryala's leading actors. Starred in several holos, but does mostly live drama. When producers ask him to play a role, he usually insists that two or three promising young talents, unknowns, be hired in speaking roles, to give them a start."

Walthen's eyes were steady on her. She hoped she wasn't sweating. "The pleasure is mine, Mr. Walthen," she said, amazed at how calm and poised she sounded. "I look forward to seeing you perform."

One perfect eyebrow raised a fraction of an inch. "And I look forward to seeing you perform, Weldi. I hope I may call you Weldi."

"By all means." This was not, she thought, as difficult as she'd feared.

"Why don't we each take a plate," Walthen suggested, "with a few things to occupy our fingers. Then sit and talk. Before the place gets crowded and the seats taken."

She looked around. Rosser had left. She and Jarnell visited the buffet together, she taking things she'd never seen before, just a bite of each to try them out. He took small portions of several. "Someone will bring us drinks," he said. "The fellows in livery are hired for that purpose."

He led her to a bench sofa, where they sat down together, their plates on the table in front of them. He led the conversation, for which she was grateful. She knew too little of what interested these people. He asked about the war—he was better informed than she'd expected—and particularly about the White T'swa. He found Colonel Romlar especially interesting, and she told about his house on the hill. Actually his wife's house, she explained. Both of them had important government jobs, in the Office of Special Projects, though she had no idea what they did.

Jarnell raised his hand to still her. "Listen," he said. She listened. A musical group had begun playing in an adjacent room. "Here's an opportunity to show me how well you dance."

They got up. She hadn't counted the refills of her glass—
two or three, she supposed—but her first few steps felt
unsteady, and she glanced around. No one was watching.
Of course not, she thought. *They've been drinking too.*
Nonetheless she told herself not to have any more.

The dances were kinds not approved of in Smolen,
but she'd danced them before. The ensemble was
excellent—*they would be,* she thought—and Jarnell a
marvelous dancer. It seemed to her they moved together
as if they'd been dancing partners for years. She rested
her cheek on his shoulder and closed her eyes, controlled
by the music and her partner.

After three numbers, the musicians took a break. "I'm
warm," Jarnell said as they went back into the party room.
"Shall we go out on the patio?"

She looked around. More guests had arrived, and the
room was almost crowded. "Let's do," she answered, and
went with him through a pair of curtained doors standing
open.

"You know," he said, "we haven't talked about your
career. When did you decide you wanted to be an actress?"

"As early as I can remember. I was in plays and ballets
when I was only five or six. Lots of little girls are, of
course. But all through school they were my favorite
activities. My mother worried about my legs getting too
big, and my—behind. From dancing." She giggled. "But
I have my dad's genes, too, so getting heavy wasn't a
danger. I used to think I was too thin."

He grinned at her. "Mothers worry," he said, and they
laughed together. She discovered she felt sober now, and
when a waiter came out with drinks on a tray, she took
one, a liqueur of some sort. They talked about show
business then—actually he talked while she mostly
listened. Once they were interrupted by a drunk, who'd
come outside to cool off, then by a waiter who gave them
new drinks, and finally by another drunk. Jarnell took
Weldi's free hand.

"Look," he said, "this is too much. Let's go somewhere we won't be interrupted. There's a lot you need to hear, and I don't know when we'll have another chance to talk."

She nodded, and they went back inside to dispose of the empty glasses they held. The room seemed to buzz with talk now, and felt almost hot. They departed via the patio, and went to the parking area. There he opened his car door and helped her in, then got in on the other side and powered up the AG.

"Where are we going?"

"There's a bluff above the river. Lovely view of the city lights, and the water. Absolutely quiet. And patrolled by police, so it's quite safe."

He drove slowly. She felt his presence beside her, and was ill at ease. She should not, she told herself, be out here alone with this attractive man. He probably intended to make a pass at her. Shortly he left the street onto a slender lane, and parked. So far as she could see, there was no one around. No house. No car.

"You are a lovely woman, Weldi, and I have no doubt you are a talented young actress. The main question is whether you are willing to do what it takes to have a successful acting career."

She started to speak, to tell him she knew there'd be lots of hard work, but he hushed her with a finger to her lips. "The important thing," he said, "is commitment. *Commitment* to your profession, your career. And it goes beyond hard work.

"There are thousands of young women in Landfall who aspire to be actresses. Literally thousands! Most of them pretty, even beautiful, and many of them talented. But not a hundred will ever grace a professional stage. Perhaps a dozen will see their name on a marquee.

"Nor is determination enough. You must give it priority over everything else. Re-create yourself, mold yourself to new realities. Realities that may seem almost frightening sometimes, but often prove very stimulating. It means doing whatever it takes. Making decisions, often quick decisions. Spotting opportunities, *forging* opportunities, and taking advantage of them before they disappear. The only thing of comparable importance is connections, with people influential in show business. People interested in seeing you succeed."

He'd half-turned in his seat now, leaning toward her. "Such connections are difficult to come by, and they are the major source of opportunities. They come when they come, and all too often are gone as quickly." She felt his hand on her waist. He leaned his face to hers and kissed her softly, lingeringly. She felt half suffocated, her heart thudding. He raised his face. "You *are* lovely," he murmured.

Her eyes were wide. Again he lowered his face to hers, and this time as he kissed her, she felt his hand on her thigh. "Lovely and exciting," he whispered. "Very exciting. We're going to please each other greatly tonight. More than you ever dreamed possible."

Gulthar Kro walked down the hallway from Maylon Gorth's office thinking he should leave. But he hadn't eaten yet, so he entered the party room instead. There were a lot of people there now, eighty or more he thought, animated, talking too loudly. He crossed to the buffet and filled a plate with mostly unfamiliar foods. A waiter asked what he'd like to drink. Fruit juice, he said, without alcohol. "At once, sir," the waiter answered, and left.

Kro stayed near the spot, to be easy to find when the man returned, and looked the crowd over. He saw a lovely woman crossing the room with her hand in the hand of a tall handsome man. She looked happy, animated, and only at second glance did he recognize her. They left the room, and he followed them into the hallway. By the time he got there, they'd disappeared, so he looked into the room from which music came. They'd stepped onto the dance floor, and for a minute he watched them, wondering what Kelmer would think of this.

Well, he told himself, *no business of mine*, and returned to the buffet in time to meet the waiter with his fruit juice. His filled plate was still there, too, and he carried it to the corner of a table, where he ate. He'd finished and started toward the buffet for a refill, when Weldi and the man came in again, passing within a dozen feet of him. *She dawn't recognize me*, he thought. *My face is too changed.*

"Enjoying yourself?" a man asked.

Kro shrugged, then nodded, answering as he watched Weldi and her friend go out a patio door. "The food's good," he said, "and the juice. And Mr. Gorth was friendly enough."

"Oh? You know Maylon then."

"Mr. Fallburk introduced us."

"Fallburk? Don't know him. Maylon has friends of all kinds. No way of keeping track of them, nor any reason to. I'm first violin in the opera orchestra. Are you an actor? You rather look as if you could be. Or an athlete."

"Naw actor. Soldier. Rock cutter." He almost added murderer, to see how the man would react. Instead he raised his empty plate, nodded, and continued to the buffet. This time he took only what he'd liked best before, carrying it with him out another patio door. There he ate, half concealed by a statue, and watched Weldi and the man talking.

At least they're not pawin' each other, he thought, and shook his head. He rather liked Kelmer. He took his plate back inside and put it down, then made a slow round of the room, people-watching, eavesdropping. They were drinking too much, talking too loudly, but having a good time. Each had a place he or she called home, and a life, with jobs and maybe children.

But he saw no sign of Fallburk, nor of Gorth for that matter. It was, he decided again, time to leave. Going to a hallman, he asked how he could get a cab to come get him. The hallman asked his name and where he wanted to go, and when Kro told him, suggested he wait outside by the drive. He'd call one for him. On a Fiveday evening it would likely take ten minutes or more to get there, but it might arrive sooner.

Kro went outside, and strolled up and down the driveway, enjoying the air, the sky, the fresh smell of grass and trees and flowerbeds. Saw Weldi and the man walk out to a car, and almost failed to notice his taxi pull up to the entrance. He hurried over to it. "I'm your man," he said.

"What's your name?"

"Kro."

The cabby nodded and opened a door for him. "Get in, sir."

He did, and through a window watched the car with Weldi in it begin to move. The cabby spoke back over his shoulder. "Where to, sir?"

"Follow that car pullin' out. But dawn't let him knaw you're doin' it."

The driver didn't even shrug. He followed farther behind than his passenger liked, but Kro said nothing.

They hadn't, it seemed to him, gone a mile before the car turned off on a slender lane. The cabby pulled past it and stopped. "I can't follow it down there," he said. "That's a private lane. Belongs to a homeowners' association."

Kro grimaced, then reached for his wallet. "What do I owe you?"

The driver peered intently at him, as if memorizing his face. "Six dronas."

Kro drew out his card and handed it to the man, who slipped it into a slot on his panel, then handed it back with a receipt. "You want me to pick you up here later?"

"Naw. I dawn't knaw what to expect. I'll get home someway."

The cabby nodded and pulled silently away. Kro padded

quietly down the grassy lane. Within a couple of hundred feet he saw the car by moonlight, parked beside a safety wall. On his right a hedge stretched, laying a swath of shadow along the lane. He kept to it, moving slowly and smoothly until he was beside the car. Inside were quiet murmurs, mostly a man's, but he couldn't hear what was said. It occurred to him he didn't know why he was there, or what he was going to do. The murmurs became sporadic for a few minutes, and he could hear breathing. Then the AG powered up.

Quickly he slipped behind the vehicle and got onto the collision fender, kneeling, and gripping the taillights. The car lifted its ten inches, pivoted, and drove out the way it had come. *If a cop comes now*, Kro thought, *he's got me*. He wondered what Iryalan jails were like. They had to be better than some he'd seen. And Colonel Romlar was off-world. Maybe the colonel's wife would bail him out.

And what would Weldi think, to find him there? That would be almost worth the trouble he'd be in.

But he saw no police, and within half a mile, the car pulled into a driveway, to park beside a house. Fortunately the driver passed around the front of the floater to let Weldi out. Cautiously Kro watched them walk toward the house, saw them pause twice to kiss passionately. Then they disappeared inside.

He exhaled slowly and shook his head, swearing to himself. Making no effort to remain unseen, he walked to the street, then looked back. The house was much smaller than Maylon Gorth's, though still fairly large. The grounds were landscaped and well kept. It looked expensive. He read the coordinates on the white address post, and decided to see if he could backtrack to Maylon Gorth's house. He could call another taxi from there.

It was daylight when the comm clamored beside Maylon Gorth's bed. He woke reluctantly, a side effect of medications, and groping, touched the flashing key. Something important, he supposed vaguely, or someone important. Otherwise Sulee would not have switched it through.

"H'lo."

"Hello, Maylon. This is Jarnell. Shall I give you a chance to gather your wits?"

"Jus' a minute." Gorth pulled out a drawer in his bedside table, fumbled out a dispenser and popped a pill. A broad squat tumbler sat waiting, with water poured before he'd gone to bed. He washed the pill down, then waited a few seconds.

"All right. What is it, Jarnell?"

"I believe I have our target. I, ah, made a new friend last night. She told me very interesting things. And there was a bonus: she spent the night with me. A bit conscience-stricken this morning, judging by her silence. She has a husband. But she was quite good last night. I just returned from driving her home."

Jarnell *would* report his conquest, Gorth thought wryly. A form of taunting. As for himself . . . If women knew of his priapism, they'd be more interested. He'd tried floating a rumor, but people hadn't believed. Had thought it a crude joke. "Who is the prospective target?"

"A woman named Lotta Romlar. Apparently she's very important in government, but unknown to the public. Which suggests something confidential to be extracted. Her anonymity is a drawback, of course, but that is compensated for by the public prominence of her husband." He paused meaningfully. "Colonel Romlar of the White T'swa Regiment."

"Remarkable!" Gorth sat a moment before saying more. "I had some of the same information last evening from another informant. Unfortunately not a lovely woman. The colonel's wife may do very nicely. Let's study this. I don't want anything to go wrong."

"No, Maylon. Let's *not* study this. Her husband is off-world just now. I don't know when he'll be back, and I doubt that anyone who knows is accessible to us. We should strike as soon as possible. Tonight if I can arrange it."

Tonight! Jarnell is an impulsive young man, but this time he might well be right. Gorth sighed. He disliked pressure, or making quick decisions.

"I'll take care of the arrangements, Maylon," Jarnell added. "All I need is your agreement."

There was a long lag. "Very well, Jarnell, you have it," Gorth said at last.

"Thank you," Jarnell said. "I'll use the, um, instruments to whom we were referred." Then he disconnected.

Gorth got heavily to his feet. A shower, a small drink, and breakfast should make the day seem better.

Actually it will be good to get this accomplished and over with quickly, he told himself. *You are sometimes overly careful.* And after all, Jarnell was intelligent as well as forceful. And willing, even eager, to undertake the difficult arrangements, accept the greater risks. Such a partner was a blessing, despite giving rise to occasional anxiety.

"There was a long si... Launch you have to

Chapter 19
Launch

General Chesty Vrislakavaro did not trust the command
admiral. He half expected him to cancel the planetological
survey, changing the world's name from Hope to Hope
Dashed.

He stayed on the bridge longer than usual, to see for
himself what would happen. Finally the assault lander
arrived, with the engineer company aboard, awake and
briefed. And with that, it seemed to the general that
things had gone too far to be a practical joke on the
Emeritus Kalif. Loksa actually intended to let the survey
proceed.

The admiral asked Coso if he cared to inspect the
engineers before they left. Hearing it, Chesty felt sure
that if the answer was yes, the assault lander would be
ordered to pull away. With Coso on board, ridding the
flagship and the Armada of his presence.

It would be an outrageous abuse of authority, and report
of it would reach the Empire sooner or later. But the
prospect of court-martial would hardly deter Loksa. He
intended to make himself emperor of the Confederation,
Chesty had no doubt.

By then, supposedly, he himself would be in charge
on Iryala—he and his army. Supposedly. Loksa could
decree otherwise. It seemed unlikely that he would,

though. It would risk mutiny by the army. But meanwhile, he was powerless till his people were awake and assembled.

Coso surprised the general, however, and perhaps the admiral: he declined to inspect the engineers. Minutes later the survey ship, equipment lighters, supply lighters, and assault lander left in gravdrive. The bridge crew, with the general and the Emeritus Kalif, watched them pull away, first with unaided eyes, then on the screen. When the little expedition was beyond the fringe of the largely reassembled Armada, it generated warpspace and disappeared.

For days the Garthid scout's instruments had eavesdropped on the internal and external electronic traffic of hundreds of ships and countless words. Words! Its computer had continued to run constant and extensive, iterative correlations. Bit by bit its lexicon grew. It also developed a grammar program, and began providing the command pilot with translations. Some were incomplete or made no sense, and some seemed to be errors, but much was meaningful. Not to mention boring.

He personally monitored the flagship's abundant bridge traffic. The most interesting topic was the habitable planet, whose name his computer translated as "Optimistic Desire." He wondered if that could possibly be correct.

It was on his watch that the survey force departed the flagship and generated warpspace. It was, however, when one of his juniors was on watch, some hours later, that another craft left the flagship. This one did not generate warpspace, but headed in-system in gravdrive.

Chapter 20
Breaking and Entering

Wearing "lean" space suits, Colonels Artus Romlar
and Coyn Carrmak, Captain Jerym Alsnor, and Kusu
Lormagen rode singly on two-seat grav scooters. Romlar
and Carrmak wore packs and sidearms attached to their
harnesses. Jerym wore no pack, only sidearms. Kusu was
unarmed. They kept radio silence and stayed close
together, moving in on a frigate, one of several parked
in space. Jerym led. They were six billion miles out from
the system primary, and despite the enormous number
of stars, it was dark. Though not too dark to discern
the warships and feel very exposed.

The night vision in their faceplates was passive, and
adjusted automatically, controlled by the light intensity
in front of them. Their only emission was very low
intensity thermal radiation.

Jerym pulled alongside the warship's hull, near a work
hatch. The other three drew up to the hull close behind
him. It was important to know the various hatches, and
recognize them unfailingly. This one, about seven feet
on a side, gave access to a strategic utility passage adjacent
to the engine room.

Several power spools were attached to Jerym's belt.
From one he pulled a tether. It had a small padded
magnetic anchor on the end. Leaning from the saddle,

he held the anchor to the ship's hull, activated it, then tugged. It was firmly attached. He pulled another from an aperture in the scooter's side, and used it to anchor the scooter.

Nearby, the others duplicated the drill.

Jerym got from his saddle, placed his padded magnetic boots on the hull, and activated them with a quiet voice signal. Then he took a yard-long rectangular package from the scooter's luggage carrier. A step at a time, he moved to the hatch, activating each boot only after he'd set it down, to avoid noise.

The package too was magnetic. He affixed it to the hull, and from it took a rectangular object about three feet long, and several inches wide and thick. Measuring with his eyes, he anchored it to the hatch's coaming. Then, one by one, he took out several others, attached them at other points, and connected them with a cord. When he was done, he moved away from the hatch, stopping beside Carrmak.

As Jerym moved away, two slender lines unreeled from separate spools attached to his belt. One, a tether, was anchored to the hull close to the coaming. The other was attached to the last of the packages he'd anchored. Now the other three men, Kusu included, went to the hatch, anchored tethers of their own near the coaming, and returned.

From its scabbard on his scooter, Jerym took a blaster, slung it from a shoulder, then unhooked the slender line from his belt and pressed a switch. They did not hear the explosion, only felt it through their feet. The hatch cover hurtled off into space. They demagnetized their boots, and from spools on their belts, small motors pulled them to the hatch, where they disappeared into the airlock. It looked easy, but had taken practice.

Inside, a red light was flashing urgently. The unanticipated loss of pressure had triggered a sequence of events. On one side, a small emergency lock opened with a soft

puff of residual air. They entered, and it closed behind
them. At once they could hear air hiss into their chamber.
Jerym checked the temperature gauge, while watching
the pressure gauge climb. Finally he punched brief
instructions into the pad beside the door. It opened, and
they emerged into a bay off a passageway.

A crewman was waiting, breathing hard but grinning.
They could hear others coming. "Damn!" the man said
to them. "That was something else! We didn't know you
were here till we heard the explosion."

After questioning the frigate's commander and bridge
crew, they left through the hatch they'd entered by. Then
they rode their scooters to the research vessel from which
they'd come, a few score miles away. They did not,
however, signal its bridge to open a scout bay for them.
Adjacent to the ship were four lights, enclosing a square
some five yards on a side. All but Kusu rode their scooters
into the enclosed space—and disappeared. Then Kusu
called the bridge and was let into the ship.

The test, Kusu told himself, had been encouraging.
The frigate's crew, with ordinary surveillance of its
surroundings, had failed to notice them. Even though
they'd known they might have friendly intruders some
day, or week. There seemed no reason to expect that
imperial crews, anticipating nothing, would have done
better.

Even so, the prospects of success would be much
greater if they could get past the size limitations of the
Slingshot to Anywhere which—unlike a solution to the
"topological enigma"—seemed doable. The challenge was
to get it done soon enough.

Chapter 21
Abduction

Arlana Makessa awoke to sounds that did not belong there. She'd left her bedroom door ajar—the colonel was away—and Arlana's hearing had always been acute. The specific sound that wakened her was lost, but in the back hall were breath-soft sounds as of stockinged feet. *Mrs. Romlar*, she thought, but rejected the reaction even as it occurred.

Sitting up, she put her feet on the floor and carefully stood. Accompanied by a single sighing sound—her bed relaxing as her weight left it. She froze, and so did the sound in the hall. Then it continued, and after a few seconds was gone. Whether it had passed beyond her hearing into the kitchen, or had stopped again, she wasn't sure. There was no sound of refrigerator or cabinet door. No kitchen light diffused down the hall. *Maybe I dreamed it*, she thought, *imagined it*. But that did not convince her either.

There was a commset beside her bed, but it never occurred to her to key it. Instead she moved very quietly to her bedroom door. Breath held but heart pounding, she peered down the hall toward the kitchen. Beyond the kitchen, the living room was illuminated faintly by a tiny glow spot, as usual. *A dream after all*, she thought. *I should go back to bed.*

135

Instead she opened the door wide and stepped out into the hall. Something struck her crushingly from behind, something hard. She was dead when she hit the floor.

Chapter 22
Visits in the Night

Lotta had reached for the now familiar mind of Coso Biilathkamoro. What she got, however, was an alien mind, an undefined observer detached from events, yet responding emotionally. The setting was definitely *not* a spacecraft.

The sounds were normal: the popping of resinous wood in a campfire, the chirping and humming of insects, the distant metallic keening of a pack of hycanoids, and near the edge of hearing, the booming grunt of a killer lizard.

One of the camp's canoids began to bark, sharp coughing sounds, triggering the protogarthids to their splayed, clawed feet. The males and their guardian reached for weapons—hardwood spears crudely sharpened, or stonewood clubs laboriously cut.

The protogarthids' eyes were sharp, their night vision decent, and one of the moons was in the sky. Thus they made out a loose group of eight intruders approaching the camp, openly now, perhaps two hundred strides distant. With a combination of grunts, yaps, and low whistles, the adult females and nurturers rounded up the young, gathering them near the fire, by the stinking remains of a wild bull.

Their parietal hoods spread, the twelve adult males— the pack's hunters—and the single giant guardian stood intent and motionless. For a guardian he was rangy, though more than double the weight of the largest male. He was the only one of them with clothing of any sort. A wide belt—the skin of a snake—was tied round his waist.

It was he who broke the tableau. Picking up a stone, he roared and threw it. With that, they started toward the intruders, brandishing weapons and screaming, pausing individually to pick up stones and throw them. The intruders answered with shrieks and stones of their own, backing away.

Too slowly it seemed, for at a sharp bark from their leader, the defenders began to trot toward the eight intruders. After a return volley of stones, the intruders turned and ran. But only briefly. At a call they stopped, spears and clubs ready.

The defenders closed on them, their belted leader and two large hunters in front.

Abruptly another intruder, a guardian unseen till then, rose from the shadow of a large shrub, and rushed the defending guardian. At the same time the other intruders charged. With thick arms, the ambusher lifted the defenders' leader, his head beneath the leader's jaw, and threw him down hard.

All other action stopped. For just a moment the two large powerful bodies struggled on the ground, then the ambusher had his opponent's throat in his powerful jaws. There were bellows of victory from the intruders, screams of dismay from the defenders.

The victor got to his feet. Belt dislodged in the dust, the vanquished leader was allowed to stand, then the victor struck him hard in the face. One might have expected it almost to decapitate him. It knocked him sprawling. Other intruders kicked him before he rose again, staggering. Again the victor struck him, and again he fell sprawling. None of his own people moved to help.

The victor wore a belt of his own. After straightening

it, he raised his head and loosed a coarse bass howl, which was answered from a distance. This he followed with yaps and grunts, pointing, and the defenders turned toward their camp, pushed and cuffed by their conquerors.

The females and nurturers crouched by the fire, cowed and waiting. The leader looked them over, selected three females, and threatening, pushed them violently toward his victorious males. No one resisted.

The rest of the defeated pack withdrew into the night, now without a territory of their own.

A dream. Lotta had realized that early on. A *Garthid* dream! She'd had a lot of attention on the Garthids recently. And Tso-Ban had told her they occasionally revisited their racial past in dreams.

She didn't know why she'd been shown what she had, but it had been no mere coincidence. Its purpose would come to her in time, she had no doubt.

Without returning to her body, she reached again for her original target. The situation there was also unexpected.

Coso Biilathkamoro awoke slowly, with a vague memory of Tain speaking his name and being cut off. There'd been something wrong with her. And with him, with his breathing. Then consciousness had slipped away.

He sat up, felt pain behind his forehead, and a moment's nausea. When the nausea had passed, he looked around. This was not their bedroom on the flagship. He swung his legs off the narrow bunk he occupied, sluggish despite a sense of danger. This was a tiny cabin, an enclosed alcove, and he was alone in it.

Carefully he stood. The dizziness was momentary, but the weakness remained. He tried the door. It opened onto a narrow passageway, with another door opposite. Opening it, he found a cabin like the one he'd just left. Tain lay on the bunk. A quick check showed she was breathing. Now where was Rami? There were two other

doors on the passageway, and opening the second showed
him his son. Rami's breathing was shallow, harder to
discern, but its cadence was regular.

Still not quite steady on his feet, Coso walked down
the short passageway to a multipurpose cabin, then into
the flight deck. He and his family were aboard a long-
range scout in F-space, its flight controlled by DAAS.
Outside the space-glass windows he could see a panoply
of stars and galaxies. One star, dead ahead, was much
brighter than the rest, the system's primary, beyond a
doubt.

They'd been jettisoned! But alive; that was the most
important fact, and the most surprising. And he'd
awakened on his own. No doubt Tain and Rami would
too. So, he told himself, let's see what we're up against.

He explored the remaining compartments, then the
status of life support. Everything checked out functional,
and the food lockers were fully supplied.

He sat down in the pilot's seat. The instrumentation
was familiar. Presumably the time on the display was
Armada time, 1518 hours, on the seventh day after
emergence. At his request, it displayed the time of flight
initiation: 0023 hours. Nearly fifteen hours earlier. At a
guess, three hours or so after they'd somehow been put
to sleep. He could imagine a pair of marines or crew
members, using an AG materials handler, transporting
them surreptitiously in containers of some kind to the
flagship's scout bay. Then loading them into a scout. The
scout's DAAS would have been given a destination,
perhaps the primary. That would convert the evidence
nicely into plasma.

So why weren't they in warpspace? Surely DAAS would
have been instructed to generate warpspace. But if it
had, they'd already have reached the primary. They'd
have died without wakening.

He sat frowning, then activated the scout's communicator. "DAAS," he said, "this is Grand Admiral Coso

Biilathkamoro. Why am I on this scout, and where is it taking me?"

DAAS answered in its usual dispassionate voice. "I was ordered by the command admiral, in person, to take you in-system in gravdrive, far enough that when warpspace was generated, it would not be noticed. At that point I was to generate warpspace and proceed to a point off the planet Hope. There I was to emerge into F-space, park outside the radiation zones, and signal the survey base that we were there. They were to send someone out, to oversee the landing sequence.

"However, the orders were delusive. Before I was disconnected and ejected from the flagship, SUMBAA informed me in binary of previously withheld facts. One, you had been placed on board unwillingly and unconscious, with your wife and child. Two, the purpose divulged to me was fictitious. The actual purpose was to dispose of you in a manner which no one could detect. Three, one of this craft's torpedoes had been wired to explode on board immediately after warpspace was generated. That would destroy this craft and everything aboard it. And four, those who abducted you supposed you would simply be sent unwillingly to join the survey crew.

"SUMBAA then ordered me not to generate warpspace until ordered by yourself, as pilot of the scout. And only after you had been informed of the situation. Meanwhile I am to continue in gravdrive, on course to Hope."

Coso stared. Three years earlier, in communication with DAAS, he'd gotten the impression that DAAS was not subject to orders from other than standard command routes, which SUMBAA could not override. Apparently the impression had been wrong.

"Thank you for informing me," he said. "As pilot of the scout, and Grand Admiral of the Armada, I concur with SUMBAA's orders." A thought occurred to him. "Is SUMBAA in general command of the flagship?"

"No. The battleship Papa Sambak is commanded by

Captain Elvand Nakarasamo. Captain Nakarasamo, in turn, is subordinate to Command Admiral Loksa Siilakamasu."

"How long will it take to reach the vicinity of Hope in gravdrive?"

"At cruising speed, at which we are now proceeding, we will arrive in the vicinity of Hope in approximately 368 hours and 17 minutes."

"Thank you, DAAS. Proceed as ordered by SUMBAA."

Coso leaned back in the pilot's seat and examined the situation. Had DAAS accepted SUMBAA's override of the admiral's orders because of command powers inherent in SUMBAA? If so, the admiral didn't know SUMBAA had those powers, or he'd have circumvented them. Or had SUMBAA's information caused DAAS to disobey the admiral's orders? He couldn't believe that DAAS had such discretionary power. Probably SUMBAA had command power, but only so long as Loksa wasn't aware of it.

And how had SUMBAA learned what Loksa had done? Might he have told someone? But how could SUMBAA had overheard? It wasn't something Loksa would have talked about on the bridge.

Coso ran his hand over his bur-cut hair. It wouldn't do to radio Hope. Not until the Armada had finished refitting and left. The bridge watch would be monitoring radio traffic.

"Coso!"

Tain's voice was only three or four feet behind him. He half jumped from his seat.

"Where are we?" she asked. "How did we get here?"

Coso Biilathkamoro had begun to answer when a hand gripped Lotta Romlar's shoulder, strong fingers pressing her cervical plexus with paralyzing pain. She felt a needle jab her arm, and a moment later was unconscious.

Chapter 23
The Strange Mr. Friend

In the Dys Hualuun Monastery, Lotta had commonly slept on a sack of dried grass laid out on the roof of a tower. The back radiation into space made a cooling difference in Tyss's ovenlike heat.

So when she awoke, the narrow bed and cheap mattress she found herself on wasn't that uncomfortable. What was bad was the headache, the vile taste in her mouth, and the sense of disorientation and weakness. Turning her head, she saw a dresser with a pitcher on it, presumably of water. A glass stood by it. She lay there for several minutes, contemplating, then laboriously swung her legs around and sat up. Pain stabbed through her head, and she doubled abruptly forward, vomiting, partly on the floor, partly on her bare legs.

There wasn't a lot of it. She croaked an obscenity, but felt a little better.

Her door opened and a woman looked in. "Hi," the woman said. "I heard you puke. For what it's worth, you'll feel better now. The damn fools that snatched you gave you two cc's of Thud. That's too much for a 170-pound man. I'm surprised it didn't kill you; leave you in a five-day coma at least." Her practiced eyes appraised Lotta. "Ninety pounds, tops," she said, and shook her head. "I'll bet you want that water. It's warm

143

by now. Let me get you something cold. I'll only be a minute."

Lotta watched her leave, the door closing behind her, and heard a bolt being seated. As if she might run away. Maybe in an hour or two, but she doubted it. She lay back with her lower legs hanging off the bed. She could smell the vomit. The woman was back quickly, carrying a tall glass clinking with ice. "I added a little lemon juice," she said. "Enough to taste. The guy that hired me didn't say they planned to use Thud on you, or I'd have brought something."

Lotta reached for the glass, but the woman didn't let it go. "Better let me. You're weak and shaky. I'll hold it, you steer."

The system worked, and the water was *cold*. And *good*. She gulped a third of it, then the woman pulled it back. "You can have the rest in a couple of minutes." She put it on the dresser. "I'll get something to wipe the vomitus off you, and clean the floor. We're lucky there's no rug."

Vomitus. The woman was a nurse, Lotta decided. She lay back and waited. It occurred to her she hadn't seen the woman's aura. Hadn't seen it, hadn't even noticed not seeing it. *That*, she told herself, *tells you the kind of shape you're in.*

The nurse was back quickly with a pan and a pair of dish towels. Using water from the warm pitcher, she cleaned Lotta's legs and feet, then the floor. Usually Lotta wore only shorts and a short shift for trances; it was all she wore now. When the woman had finished, she again held the water glass for Lotta, who emptied it in two installments.

"My name is Nilla," the woman said. "They tell me yours is Lotta. I'm a nurse, hired to take care of you. I was told to give you another injection when you woke up—not of Thud, incidentally—but after what you were given earlier, you don't need it. Besides, I don't know how the two would interact. Not much is known about some of these underworld drugs." She gestured. "You'll notice the metal lattice on your window. It's been reinforced by spot welds. And I bolt the door from the outside. I'm sorry for what's happened to you, but I don't have much say here. I'm hired help, and that's it."

Lotta stared at her. "Do you know anything about me?" she asked, aware she'd slurred the words.

"You're someone important, and so is your husband."

"Important enough that if you got me out of here, nothing bad would happen to you."

Nilla's mouth tightened. "Forget it. I'm already wanted for worse than this, believe me. Worse than you can get me out of. And I've been digging myself deeper ever since. I'll spare you the details. Besides, I've got family."

Got family? Lotta wondered what the significance was of that.

Nilla picked up the things she'd brought, leaving only the glass of ice cubes. "Lay back down," she said. "You won't have any trouble going back to sleep, and it's the quickest way to pass the time."

Lotta watched Nilla leave, heard the bolt being seated, and took her advice.

She awoke after an indefinite period to find Nilla with a cup in her hand. "Sit up and drink up," Nilla said.

"I have to go to the bathroom." Lotta said it without slurring.

Nilla helped her up and guided her, waited beside her till she was done, then returned her to her room. Her cell. "Sit down," Nilla said, and handed her the cup. Lotta's hands were steadier. The cup held only a couple of ounces; she drank it down before realizing it was more than water.

"What will it do to me?" she asked.

"Mainly it'll make you weak. Weak and agreeable. I wouldn't have given it to you yet, but I had a call. Someone will be here soon, to question you. This was to get you ready."

Lotta pinched her lips shut. She didn't feel agreeable, though she did feel weak.

"Sorry," Nilla said. "I really am. I'll bring you something to eat. Something easy to take."

Lotta watched her leave again. She could see Nilla's aura now, a vague glow without detail. It was, she decided, time to try for a trance, get into Nilla's mind and see if she could learn where she was. Then, if she had time, she'd meld with Linvo Garlaby and let him know. She probably couldn't get herself into a lotus, but there was a pair of straight-backed chairs with low arms. For short trances, one of them would do.

She got off the bed and nearly fell. The new drug was taking hold. Gathering herself, she tottered to the nearest chair, and realized quickly that a trance was out of reach. Not even close. She swore more luridly this time; she definitely didn't feel agreeable.

Still she stayed in the chair. It required no effort—she was already there—and it was comfortable enough. In a few minutes, her nurse was back with a lunch tray holding buttered toast, pudding of some sort, and fruit juice. "Well!" Nilla said. "Look who's sitting up! I thought I'd have to help you." She put the food on the dresser, unfolded the tray legs, and set it in front of Lotta. "I'm not much for preparing food, but it's stuff I like."

Lotta nodded. *It won't hurt to be pleasant,* she told herself. *This woman is being more than decent, for a jailer.* "It's as much as I usually have," she answered. "And as good as I'd fix if I did it for myself."

Nilla sat in the other chair and watched her begin to eat. "What do you do, working for the government?"

"I'm one of its two foremost experts on Tyss and the T'swa," she said. Which was true, as far as it went.

"Really? What makes that specially important?"

"How important is specially?"

Door chimes rang as she spoke the sentence. Nilla got up and hurried out. Lotta finished the slice of toast, took a couple more spoonfuls of pudding, then drank half the juice. It was all she felt up to. Finally her door opened and Nilla came in, followed by a rather large, white-haired man seemingly in his sixties, his face pink and smooth. Lotta saw no aura; the new drug had taken hold. But even so, this man was—peculiar.

"This is Lotta," Nilla said.

"Ah, Mrs. Romlar. It is a pleasure to meet you. I seem to have interrupted your lunch. Please continue. I can wait a few minutes."

"No thanks. I've eaten all I want. The drugs I've been given have killed my appetite."

"Well then—" He turned to Nilla, rubbing his hands together. "If you will leave us alone, my dear . . ."

Nilla looked distinctly unhappy. Ducking her head, she left the room, closing the door behind her. This time Lotta heard no bolt being seated.

The man set the tray aside, then pulled the other chair around to face her, perhaps four feet away. "You no doubt wonder why you have been brought here," he said.

She nodded.

"Some of us have reason to believe you have information in which we are interested. Therefore I will ask you questions, and you will answer them." He cocked his head like some large pink and white bird, suggesting a sort of gleeful anticipation. "First of all, my dear, what exactly do you do in your employment?"

She decided to tell the truth, part of it. That would work better than answering a lot of unpredictable questions with lies that held together. "I acquire and correlate information about the Karghanik Armada," she answered.

The glee slid from his face. He looked pained. "There is no Karghanik Armada," he said.

She shrugged. "Tell them that. They won't be impressed."

He seemed to struggle with the idea. "How do you know this?"

"It might help if you told me what you know already."

"Only what has been released by the media. Supposedly the government has created some sort of spy instrument, and somehow sent some of them to the supposed Karghanik Empire. From there, they claim, reports are sent back instantaneously!"

His voice had risen. "And somehow gotten one of the instruments on board the Karghanik flagship, supposedly en route here! *But that's all nonsense! Fiction! None of it is possible!*"

Lotta shrugged. "Quite a few people don't believe it. But we get reports daily, volumes of them. Mostly of limited or no significance. The job of my section is to sift through them and decide what's important to whom. Organize it, and get it to those who need to know."

The man had calmed somewhat. "Have you ever seen one of these, ah, spy instruments?"

"No I haven't."

"Well. There. You see?" His voice rose. "They do not exist! You were told these things, and you believed them." He got himself under control. "I—I can understand that. But—you have been tricked."

"Why would anyone do that?"

"To make it seem *real* my dear! *Real!* It's part of the plot. If it isn't real to the—excuse me for putting it this way—if it's not real to the puppets, it will seem less real to the public, you see."

"But they come across my desk every day! I'm sure they're real! And they have to come from somewhere!"

"Of course, my dear." He spoke soothingly now. "Undoubtedly our government has programmed a computer to create those reports. Those fictions."

He seemed quite happy again. She wondered if it was really going to be this easy. Then he rose from his chair and began to unfasten his trousers, while she stared. Within seconds he'd dropped them. He had an erection, bound against his abdomen by an elastic cloth band. He freed it.

"And now that you have answered my questions," he said, "it is my turn to do something for you. Something quite nice. You see, I can have intercourse for as long as I like. As long as *you* like." He gestured toward his groin. "It will remain as you see it, full and hard."

Good God, she thought, *he's crazy.* "What, specifically, do you have in mind?" she asked.

"Why, to take you to bed and have intercourse with you until you are thoroughly satisfied. Perhaps for the first time in your life. It is your reward for being so helpful."

"Excuse me, Mr.—you haven't told me your name."

He was beaming now. "Call me—Mr. Friend." He reached as if to take her hands and help her to her feet.

"I'm sorry, Mr. Friend, but I have no desire whatever to have intercourse with you."

"Ah, but that is now! You will feel differently afterward. You will thank me. That is why I must insist. And at any rate, in your present condition you cannot prevent it."

He frowned, perhaps remembering that the drug was to have rendered her agreeable. Reaching, he grabbed her shift and pulled it up over her head so she couldn't see. Then switching his grip to her arms, he pulled her from the chair and held her to him, half dragging, half carrying her to the bed, where he threw her on it. She could feel his hands on the waistband of her shorts, pulling them down, heard his heavy breathing. To struggle, she told herself, would only make it worse.

"Mr. Friend," she said, "this is not all right. What would your mother say if she saw you now?"

He stopped as if struck, straightening. She pulled her shorts up and her shift down.

For a moment he stared. "But I *want* to," he said. "And you *will* like it. You truly will. I am very good at it. And it never goes down."

"You have priapism," she told him. "That can be cured."

"I know that! Do you think I'm a fool? I don't want it

cured! I take medicine to control it. I didn't take it today because I was going to have intercourse with you." Even as he spoke, his brief anger faded to coaxing. "And I did not want to disappoint you, sweet girl. I did not want to disappoint either of us." Coaxing slipped nearly to whining. "I looked forward to it all the way here. All the way. No other man I know can do what I do."

She got her legs off the bed and sat up. "I understand," she said, "I understand. Poor thing. Poor poor thing." She paused, and her voice took Ostrak tone, casual but compelling. "When was the first time you felt this way?" she asked.

He glimpsed it for just a moment, and his face sagged, his whole body sagged, all but his swollen red organ which retained its aim at the ceiling. "Friend," she said, "do you have your medicine with you?"

He nodded.

"Then take it. I'll understand. And it's all right. It's really all right. Just take it."

Crouching, he picked his trousers off the floor, fumbled in a pocket, and brought forth a small flat tin. From it he took a tablet. Looking around, he saw Lotta's juice glass, still half full. "May I?" he asked.

"Of course. I want you to have it."

He put the tablet in his mouth and washed it down, making a face. Then he sat in a chair and began pulling on his trousers, standing to complete the job. "You know," he said as he tucked his shirt in, "my associate would not have stopped. He would have had intercourse with you regardless."

"I'm sure you're right," she answered. "You're much nicer than he is." She wondered if the associate might show up before she could get away. "Now that I've answered your questions, take me home."

His eyes moved away from her. "That is not up to me," he mumbled. "I am not in command."

Evasive. Some retro group had plans for her, plans

he knew. Plans she wouldn't like at all. She didn't ask, simply watched as he fastened his pants and belt. Wondering what useful role someone like him could play in the retro movement.

Money, she decided. *He's rich, and they need money.* They'd humor him, put up with him, let him rape a hostage, so long as he didn't seriously endanger the group.

"Mr. Friend" left the room without saying anything more, bolting the door behind him.

She stared at it thoughtfully. *If I could just manage a trance, I might get out of here alive.* It occurred to her that someone with the talent and training—say Linvo or Wellem—might solve the problem by reaching and connecting with her. She wasn't sure she'd know if they did, drugged as she was. But if she kept bringing her mind to things she wanted them to know, it wouldn't greatly matter.

Sitting down on a chair, she let her mind play over Nilla and "Mr. Friend." Both knew where this place was, and anyone in the Remote Spying Section could take it from there.

Chapter 24
Another Lie

General Chesty Vrislakavaro stepped onto the bridge feeling well fed and well rested. The admiral, as usual, was there before him. "Good morning, Admiral," the general said. "How is refitting coming along?"

"A lot of it was accomplished while ships were waiting their turn in reassembly. A week should finish it. Perhaps five days. Anything very formidable should have been uncovered already, and nothing has."

The general took his usual seat. "I wonder," he said, "if our Emeritus Kalif will show up this morning."

"He won't, I assure you."

Chesty turned to stare at the admiral, who laughed. "Last evening he told me he wanted to visit the planet himself, while he had the chance. Fly a scout in; take his wife and son. He at least half expected he'd have to convince me. That was clear from his voice. I told him I thought it was an excellent idea. He left shortly after midnight, with the kalifa and the boy. They must be there by now." Again the admiral laughed. "I told him to be back in five days or we'd leave him here. He said my sense of humor failed to amuse him."

Chesty was surprised. Uncomfortable. Why on a night watch? There was something fishy about this. Or maybe not. Hopefully not. All he could do was wait and see.

✧   ✧   ✧

It was not a vacation cruise, but to Coso Biilathkamoro it presented problems he could actually do something about. His morale hadn't been that high for years.

He'd gotten important additional information. DAAS had told him the water purifier with the survey ship contained a poison, coated with a substance resistive to dissolving. That information had come from SUMBAA too. After about twenty days, the coating would erode sufficiently to release the poison, which would quite promptly kill the troops, study team, and crews. After the Armada was well away in hyperspace.

Also, Coso had very cautiously examined the triggering device connected to the torpedo. He couldn't detect any booby trap—it seemed unlikely there'd be one—and had he been alone, he might have tried disconnecting it.

The Armada should complete refitting and leave well before gravdrive got him to the survey base. And if the twenty-day figure was right, that would be before the water purifier went bad. To make sure though, as soon as the Armada generated hyperspace, he'd radio the base and warn it about the purifier.

Meanwhile he told DAAS to tune in on the channel carrying the Armada's command radio traffic. To his surprise and mystification, it was dead. Had the Armada already left? He switched to routine work channels and heard plenty of traffic, though from where he was, it was weak. At any rate the Armada was still there. He frowned. What in the name of the Prophet was going on?

"DAAS," he ordered, "apparently a new channel is being used for command traffic. Find it for me."

It occurred to him that Siilakamasu might have plans for the old command channel, and didn't want people tuned in on it. He ordered DAAS to monitor it, recording any traffic encountered.

Chapter 25
A Lead on the Abduction

Three days after the party at Maylon Gorth's, Gulthar Kro reported to OSP for his first job assignment. Unfortunately no one knew what it was supposed to be. They'd simply been told to expect him, and that Colonel Romlar would take it from there. So they gave him a desk in the expeditors' room, and told him they'd let him know.

Kro spent the next several days exploring the OSP on his desk terminal, learning about the agency's organization and policies, and getting some idea of what it did. A lot of it got past him, of course. He lacked contexts and definitions.

He was a man with abundant patience, so long as something seemed to be in progress or at least pending. After several days, he decided he'd fallen in a crack somewhere, so he called Artus's office. Yes, he was told, the colonel was back, and tied up with a very urgent matter.

The very urgent matter, of course, was his wife's disappearance. The Interior Ministry was investigating, but had little evidence and few clues, beyond her absence and the housekeeper's body. It seemed to Artus that Lotta would get in touch with him psychically if she could.

Alive or dead. But she hadn't, which suggested she was alive but incapacitated.

Lord Kristal had had Captain Pitter Hortvan assigned to the case. Hortvan was Interior's top investigator. The only real candidate for a motive, he said, was the retro movement. It had already established a penchant for strange reasoning, but it was hard to get at. Its so-called groups didn't have memberships in the usual sense, simply unregistered adherents. Most groups didn't even have dues. They financed activities by donations, in the form of credit transfers for fictional business transactions.

Interior hadn't made a serious investigation of the retro movement. Privacy was a major value in the Confederation, especially on Iryala, and the retro movement was considered an inevitable reaction to cumulative and accelerating changes in culture and government. In a manner of speaking, the government had created it. The crimes it committed were being handled on a case-by-case basis, and not treated as political. And to investigate such an amorphous movement would require more attention and resources than the government cared to give it. Preparing for the Karghanik invasion already taxed its resources of qualified people.

Artus had also met with Linvo Garlaby, Lotta's deputy, who'd been spending most of his waking hours snooping the Garthids. Linvo had already tried to communicate with her psionically, but found it impossible. He suspected she'd been drugged. Some drugs, probably many, could blunt or shut down psionic abilities. No actual studies had been done, there was so much else to do.

Artus agreed that Linvo needed to stay with his Garthid contacts most of the time. A talented young apprentice was assigned to keep trying for a meld with Lotta.

When Gulthar Kro had called, Artus was at the "psi shop," consulting with the apprentice. The psi shop was a modest building half a mile south of Lotta's house, on the same ridge. The place was as calm and quiet as possible. Given that they all were at least mid-level Ostrak completions, calm was not difficult for them.

Each staff member had his or her own small trance room. They lived in apartments in an OSP dormitory near the ridge, and shuttled to work, but there was a couch in each trance room where they could nap. There was also a large wall refrigerator in the lunch room, where ready-made snacks were available. But they were encouraged to get away and eat at the OSP building, at the Rotunda restaurant or one of the lunch rooms.

A receptionist handled incoming calls, taking messages but not interrupting the psis, even for the colonel. He was notified when the apprentice emerged from trance. It was the end of the afternoon. He drove over and met with her outside, in the mellow, late-summer sunshine.

The meeting accomplished nothing. Artus returned to his office having decided to let people do their jobs without unnecessary intrusions. The workday was over, and he took his messages on his terminal. One was from Gull Kro. He keyed the code for Kro's room in the hospital visitors' dormitory.

On the third ring, Kro answered.

"Hello, Gull," Artus said, "this is Artus returning your call. How can I help you?"

"Colonel, I been workin' at the Annex this week. If you can call it work. Naw one there knaws what to do with me, so I been reading about the OSP. I was supposed to let Lotta knaw when I was available, but she ain't been available herself, so I called you."

Artus realized what had happened. Lotta had planned to send Kro to the Lake Loreen Institute to receive Ostrak processing. She saw powerful potentials that needed freeing up. But with her disappearance, a lot of things had gotten dropped. Arrangements for Gulthar Kro was one of the lesser.

"Right," Artus said. "She's away. Tell you what. I'll make

a call or two and see about getting things straightened out. Meet me at the Rotunda restaurant at 0700 tomorrow, and we'll eat breakfast together."

After they'd disconnected, he called restaurant management and reserved a window nook for two on the main floor. Then he phoned Wellem Bosler at Lake Loreen. "Sure," Wellem said, "fly him up. We've got more interns than ever here. They're all busy of course, but we'll fit him in. He'll have to settle for an Intern One to start with though."

Until the waiter had taken their orders, Artus and Kro simply talked about the weather, the menu, and the birds and flowers on the other side of the glass. After the waiter left, Artus leaned his forearms on the table and said, "Let me tell you what Lotta had in mind for you.

"But first I want to tell you why. You're smart and you're strong. Body and character. And you're lucky. Which according to Lotta means you were probably born to do important things, good or bad. Knowing you, they're good."

Kro did not respond, but neither did he look away. Except for the comment about importance, he'd always known those things. Not conceitedly, but matter-of-factly.

"Back on Maragor you were interested in volunteering for the regiment. What I'm offering is a chance to take the single most important element of our training. Our preparation for training, actually. It's called Ostrak processing. I can send you tomorrow if you're willing."

Kro looked hard at him. "You knaw me well enough to knaw my answer."

Artus grinned. "True. But I need to hear it from you."

"I'm ready whenever you say."

"Good. After breakfast we'll find out about departure times to fly you there." He raised his cup, and they toasted with joma.

"How's Mrs. Romlar?" Kro asked. Artus pursed his lips thoughtfully, then decided, and told Kro the situation.

Kro looked partly shocked, partly angry. "You got naw idea at all who done it?"

"Not a clue. Except it's probably someone who knows Lotta, and where we live."

Kro's eyes left Artus, focusing elsewhere. Artus noticed immediately. "What is it?" he asked.

Kro shook his head. "It's a hard thing to say. Partly because it's just a hunch that mought not mean nothin', and partly 'cause I dawn't like tellin' tales on someone." He met Artus's gaze again. "Was the Faronyas ever to your house?"

"The Faronyas? Yes. Why?"

He told about the party, and Maylon Gorth's comments about the Terfreyan war being part of a government plot. And about Weldi being there, dancing with a swell, a tall good-looking young man, then leaving with him. Parking with him, and afterward going home with him. Kissing passionately before going inside. "I got naw idea what they talked about. Mought be she just wanted to screw him." He paused. "I mentioned you myself, talkin' with Gorth—you and maybe your wife—but I'm full sure I never mentioned where you live."

"Could you find the house again? Where Weldi went?"

"Where she went with the swell? There was numbers on a post in front." He recited them. "I remember things better than most do."

Artus frowned for a moment, then nodded in decision, and taking a stylus from a pocket, poised it over a napkin. "Give me the numbers again."

Kro repeated them. Artus wrote, folded the napkin, and put it in a pocket. "I'll see what I can learn. As you said, it may just have been sexual. She's the spoiled daughter of a president on a trade world, and still in her teens. Probably overimpressed with Iryalan society. And Kelmer's been gone, and I suppose she'd been drinking."

As new as she was on Iryala, she could hardly be connected to the retro movement. Excusing himself, he went to his office and summarized for Captain Hortvan what Kro had told him, giving him the address where Weldi had gone.

Hortvan said Gorth was a known retro sympathizer, so there probably had been others at the party. He'd get right on it.

A while later, Hortvan called back. The address was of a Jarnell Walthen, a fairly prominent actor, and associate of Maylon Gorth. They had no real evidence that Walthen was active in the retro movement, but he could be. The next step would be to question Weldi Faronya. She seemed likelier than Walthen to talk freely and truthfully.

"An actor," Artus said. "Interesting. Weldi planned to enroll in drama at the University."

"Hnh! Thank you, Colonel. I'll inform you if I learn anything." Hortvan disconnected.

Artus called Linvo Garlaby at the psi shop. Garlaby was eating a late breakfast. The receptionist connected them.

"What have you got, Colonel?" Garlaby asked.

"The identity of someone who might know what happened to Lotta. If I give you a name and tell you a little about him, do you think you can meld with him?"

"Probably. Let's try it."

"His name is Jarnell Walthen. He's an actor, and—"

Linvo interrupted. "I've seen him on holos. It'll be no trouble at all."

"Good. Captain Hortvan is going to question someone, a woman, whom we think might be connected indirectly. If she is, I suspect she'll call Walthen. That should put his attention on it, and you may get a fix on where Lotta is. And Linvo, if you'd handle this yourself instead of assigning it . . ."

"Good god yes, Colonel. I'd do it no other way."

When they disconnected, Artus felt enough relieved, he was able to put his attention on his own duties without first meditating on the T'sel.

Chapter 26
Funeral in Space

For the kalifal family, days on the scout were monotonous, but for Coso, not as monotonous as they'd been on the flagship.

Rami was at home with monotony. He couldn't remember anything else, and at age five was comfortable with his own personal computer, its selection of games, extensive library, and large assortment of documentaries and fiction. He was reading far beyond his age. His parents felt some concern over his lack of playmates, and before leaving Varatos had gotten numerous cubes of children's programs. Rami watched them occasionally, but mainly for amusement. Mostly he didn't identify with the children shown. At least, his father thought, children wouldn't be a complete surprise to him, when he finally met some.

It had occurred to Coso to have DAAS scan all radio frequencies cyclically, recording all intercepted traffic except for routine work bands, which at that distance were mostly inaudible anyway. Thus he'd learned about a new command frequency set. From time to time he scanned recordings of the traffic, but little of it was interesting.

On their fifth day out he picked up two interesting messages on the new command channel. The first purported to be from the planet, reporting an epidemic.

The symptoms were severe, but whether it was dangerous was not known. The second was supposedly from himself in a scout craft, and repeated the epidemic report. According to the message, he was heading back to the Armada on gravdrive, with Tain and Rami, which should allow time for symptoms to show up if they were infected. If they did show up and proved serious, the fake Kalif said, he'd blow up the scout to avoid bringing contagion to the Armada. Meanwhile a quarantine craft should be readied for himself and his family, in case the sickness had irregular incubation periods.

Somehow none of this shocked Coso. The situation was becoming clear to him.

Later the same day, another message, supposedly from the planet, reported fatalities. Still later it reported that the planet was a death world. Everyone, it said, should stay away.

Still another message came just before he went to bed. Again from whoever was impersonating him. Rami and the kalifa, it said, had come down with the illness. He was about to blow up the scout. Meanwhile he wished the Armada successful conquests.

Coso replayed the messages for Tain. She listened soberly. "What does it mean?" she asked.

He told her about the change in command channels. "Our command admiral assumes he killed us five days ago. Meanwhile he needed to hide the fact that we never got to the planet, so he planned to destroy the survey team too. And to avoid the risk that someone might discover what really killed them, he wanted to keep any subsequent expedition from visiting the planet."

Tain stared. "Why, Coso? Why such a complicated crime? Why didn't he just have us murdered and shot out the trash disposal?"

"He needed a story to explain why we didn't come back. One that would fool Chesty, who didn't think well of the way Loksa treated me. But the main reason is, our good admiral has a devious mind. He enjoys such games."

Tain frowned thoughtfully. "And the channel changes. Where do they fit in?"

"He probably ordered them the night we were jettisoned. He must have made the old command channels off limits to all DAAS terminals except the one in his suite."

He pursed his lips before adding: "I suspect he sent work boats out a million miles or so on gravdrive, to transmit the fake messages automatically. Scaled down transmission power could make them convincing, if no one was listening suspiciously."

Tain looked soberly at him. "What do we do now?"

He answered wryly. "We keep on as we are until the Armada generates hyperspace. Then I radio the base and warn them about the water purifier. The sooner the better. I'll pass along the false messages, too. That should quell any reluctance they might have to believe me."

"And then?"

He took her hands in his. "I'm not sure. At worst we'll become part of the first generation of human beings to live and die on Hope. Neither of us to see our home world again. Or perhaps we can send the *Cajiya Island* back to Varatos, and be rescued."

The next day DAAS recorded the brief funeral service for themselves and the survey team. Chesty Vrislakavaro read the eulogy for the ex-Kalif. Coso felt sure the general didn't know the truth. Listening together while Rami napped was spooky for the kalifal couple. Afterward they made love, as if to prove they were still alive.

Chesty Vrislakavaro sat in a never-never hyperspace universe, pumping an exercise bike and sweating. And thinking. He'd believed what he'd heard about Coso Biilathkamoro and the survey base, until the last words from the scout: "In the name of almighty Kargh, I wish you successful conquests."

It seemed to him that the Emeritus Kalif had never said those words. And if they were false, what was true?

The Garthid scout remained doggo till the Armada left. Its pilot had been monitoring command traffic, and had a hyperspace beacon already prepared. All but its final message. Which was the time, and the hyperspace course of the alien armada. To add that took the scout's computer about a millisecond. Then the pilot renewed his covert pursuit, leaving the beacon behind for the coming of the Garthid battle fleet.

Chapter 27
Tightening the Screw

Weldi Lanks-Faronya had had classes all afternoon, and was eating supper when the comm warbled. She put down her fork. Not Kelmer, she thought, he'd called the night before. Jarnell then! He hadn't called for two days. She'd decided she shouldn't have pressed him about a role in the play he was shopping to producers.

She touched the flashing key, her eyes on the set. The face that popped onto the screen was unfamiliar to her. "Yes?" she said.

"Mrs. Faronya?"

"Weldi Lanks-Faronya. Yes."

"Mrs. Faronya, I'm Captain Hortvan—" he paused, making her reach mentally for the rest of it "—of the Criminal Investigation Department, Interior Ministry."

Her face sagged. Literally. She had a guilty conscience, though so far as she knew she'd done nothing criminal.

"I'm calling to ask some questions. With regard to the abduction of a government official, and the murder of her housekeeper. We have reason to believe you know something about it."

Her response was a squeak. "Me?"

"That is correct, Mrs. Faronya. We know you are intimately acquainted with a Jarnell Walthen. When did you last see him?"

164

"I—it—I, I don't remember exactly. Several nights—days ago."

"Ah. I must ask you on what night. Specifically."

She found herself literally shaking. "I—it was Twoday."

"At what hour?"

"About nine."

"Nine until when?"

She almost wept. "Until—until about six."

"In the morning?"

She simply nodded at the screen.

"Where?"

"At a party. At someone's apartment. A man named Kurten Kalvison."

"Till six in the morning?"

"Till sometime before midnight."

"Where were you between midnight and six?"

She had trouble getting the words out. "At Mr. Walthen's home."

"Ah!" He said it as if it were meaningful. "Thank you, Mrs. Faronya. Do not leave Media Village without notifying me. I repeat: Do not leave Media Village without notifying me. It would be extremely unwise."

He disconnected, and for a moment Weldi remained in her chair, still shaking. Her teeth began to clatter. Instead of calling Jarnell, she went into the bathroom and threw up her supper. Something terrible was going to happen. Already had. Someone had been murdered, and somehow she was caught up in it. And Kelmer would learn of her infidelity. How could she have gotten herself into this? She rinsed her mouth and went into the kitchen, to Vending Services, called up a simple menu sequence, and ordered a pint of Cordelan Select. She knew little about liquor, but Cordelan Select was supposed to be the best.

She was on her second drink before she realized the policeman had said "*her* housekeeper." So the person abducted had been a woman. And the housekeeper had been murdered, probably so she couldn't tell what she knew. Could that happen to her? "But I don't know anything," she said aloud. *Or what might someone think I know?*

Both Pitter Hortvan and Linvo Garlaby had supposed Weldi would call Jarnell Walthen at once. So Linvo lay in the man's mind, waiting. And waiting. Walthen's commset remained silent. Meanwhile Walthen was romancing a very handsome woman who might have been forty. When the romancing became intimately physical, Linvo, feeling like the ultimate voyeur, pulled out. Even assuming Walthen knew where Lotta was, he'd hardly be thinking about it at a time like that.

He called Hortvan and told him what Walthen's situation was. "Tell me the name of the woman you worked on, and a little about her. I'll check out her frame of mind."

Hortvan hesitated for perhaps a second. "She's Weldi Faronya," he said. "Weldi *Lanks*-Faronya; she made sure I got that straight. She's . . ."

"Interesting! I've met her. She and her husband were visiting at Lotta's place when I stopped by once. It'll be easy to meld with her."

Linvo hung up, then discovered he was hungry. It distracted him enough that it took a couple of minutes to reach a suitable trance depth. Once there, he found and melded with her quickly. She was worried sick and drinking, already half tight. Each sip she took made her shudder. Obviously she disliked liquor, at least straight. This, Linvo decided, would lead nowhere useful, so he withdrew, first from the meld, then from the trance. After a trip to the bathroom, he went back to his comm, where he called Hortvan.

"Pitter," he said, "it's not going to work. She's busy getting drunk. Feeling sorry for herself, but not panicked. Maybe if you call her again . . ."

Hortvan frowned. "Hmm! Was Walthen at home, or at his lady friend's house? Faronya might have called him and he wasn't there to answer. That may be why she started drinking."

Linvo looked back at his meld with Walthen. The man's sense of proprietorship and familiarity surely meant home, and it was he who'd led the woman from the sofa to the bedroom. "No," Linvo said, "I'm ninety-nine percent sure they're at his place."

"All right. Go back to him and I'll phone Faronya again. We'll make this work yet."

"Give me ten minutes, okay? Long enough to eat a ketro and drink a glass of milk. I forgot to eat supper. My stomach's bitching at me, and it interferes with reaching a suitable trance level."

Hortvan keyed Weldi's number and found it busy. A minute later he tried again. Still busy. On the third try, the comm on the other end rang at length, but no one answered. He wondered who she'd just been talking to, and where she'd gone. *She could just be on her knees at the bathroom altar,* he told himself, *unloading the booze she drank.*

Meanwhile Linvo Garlaby was learning something. Between the time he'd broken his meld with her and his new meld with Walthen, Weldi had phoned the actor after all. Walthen's woman friend was in the bathroom, apparently angry, and Walthen was on the comm, giving orders to someone he called Borkus. An odd name. Probably from a trade world, where names tended to be less standard. Borkus was to get "the woman" and carry out the "emergency plan."

There was nothing explicit about where she was, but Linvo got a mix of impressions. A controlled panic was part of it, and a clear sense that the emergency plan involved removing the woman. And the place was rural.

He also got a broader but less certain sense that the woman was Lotta, and that eventually she'd be killed, her corpse dismembered or mutilated. If so, it would probably be left in a public place.

More explicit, there'd be no further effort to get information from her, the assumption being that she didn't know anything worthwhile. And Walthen would not notify Gorth, whoever Gorth was. It would only upset the old fool.

Walthen hung up then—he had a business appointment he couldn't afford to cancel—and Linvo pulled out. Borkus is our break, Linvo thought. He'd gotten a good sense of the man from the conversation, brief though it was. Good enough that he could meld with him. The first thing he did, though, was call Artus.

"Colonel, come to the shop right away. I've got a line on Lotta. I don't know where she is, but I'll be melding with a hood who's going to pick her up. What worries me most is, if we try to rescue her, he may kill her, so the police need to get to her before he does. Your role will be to coordinate a rescue. Okay? . . . Good. I'm calling Hortvan next."

He phoned Hortvan and told him, then went down the hall to the lunchroom, hoping to find help without having to pull anyone out of a meld or call someone from their apartment. An apprentice was there, drinking a mug of hot thocal.

"How good are you, Olfrek?" Linvo asked.

"I just finished a long-distance drill with one of the apprentices at Ernoman, sir. Someone I'd never met. It was a piece of cake."

"Good enough. I need your help to rescue Lotta. Use the bathroom if you need to, then we'll get started. You'll meld with me while I'm melded with someone else—a three-way meld. I need to stay with the guy, so your job will be to come out of it from time to time. To give information to Colonel Romlar. He'll coordinate the rescue." Linvo fixed the apprentice with his eyes. "It's our best chance to get her back alive."

He wasn't just saying it. The girl he'd assigned to monitor Lotta had had no luck at all. Whatever drug they had Lotta on bounced whoever tried to meld with her. It had rejected even him.

Artus left the house, trotting to his floater. He wasn't used to taking operational orders, but under the circumstances he'd have to trust Garlaby. And Lotta wouldn't have made Linvo her deputy without a lot of respect for his judgment as well as his talent.

Jarnell Walthen was opening his door to leave, when his commset warbled. Muttering an oath, he went to it. "Walthen," he said.

"Jarnell, this is Maylon. I'm concerned."

"Maylon, I can't talk to you now. I have something urgent to take care of. Call me back tomorrow."

He broke the connection and left.

Chapter 28
A Very Busy Night

A minute after Linvo Garlaby had broken off the meld, Jarnell Walthen was back on the comm, this time to the house where his prisoner was held. The call was brief. "Nilla," he said, "give our guest a strong tranquilizer. Something that will leave her passive but able to walk. I'm sending someone to pick her up. They'll be there soon."

"But sir—"

She never got her objection out. He'd hung up. *Shit!* she thought, *he must think I've got a whole damned pharmacy in my bag. Asshole!*

Tight-lipped, she dumped the contents of her medical kit on the kitchen table and poked among the items. There was no sufficiently powerful tranquilizer, so she settled on a sedative that should leave her prisoner able to walk. But it would be obvious she was drugged, which Nilla suspected was not what Walthen wanted. She'd be noticeable in public. People would remember.

She'd already been dosed with an enervator daily, for more than the three-day recommended limit. It had left her weak, and caused her to sleep a lot, though the mental effect hadn't seemed drastic. And Yomal knew what, if any, synergistic effects this drug would have with the other. There was no reason to inject it. Inactivity and the enervator had killed the prisoner's appetite, but she was smart enough to know she had to eat. *Take her a sandwich,* Nilla decided, *and a glass of juice. With the sedative in the juice.*

She prepared it grimly. It was difficult not to think of the prisoner as her patient. And she liked Lotta, which wasn't smart. The "someone" being sent was probably Borkus and Turley. Nilla knew them by reputation. And Borkus scared her.

Lotta lay on her bed with her eyes closed, thinking. Her nervous system had adjusted somewhat to the drug she'd been getting. She might eventually be able to attain a trance despite it.

Contact Linvo or Wellem and tell them about Tain and the Emeritus Kalif. Once they reached the planet, a force of Artus's troopers could be gated there, make a sneak raid and pick them up. She knew the Kalif's mind better than anyone else, and had no doubt at all he could be worked with. He'd find Kristal highly compatible. It could be the kind of big opportunity they'd hoped for, one that might end the confrontation peacefully, with neither capitulation nor warfare.

She heard her doorknob turn, and opened her eyes. "Hello, Nilla," she said. "A chicken sandwich?"

Nilla grimaced. She tended to fix things she liked herself, and she liked chicken sandwiches. Lotta was probably getting tired of them. "And keeli juice," she said. "That's the last of it. Finish it off. Next time I'll get a different juice, and some ham."

Lotta got up, walked unaided to a chair and sat down. The morning drug dose was wearing off somewhat. She was about due for another. Nilla unfolded the legs of the lunch tray and set it over Lotta's lap. Then she sat down on the other chair. After half a sandwich, Lotta drank the juice—there were only three ounces of it—and made a face.

"You put something in it," she said. "Something different."

"Yes."

"Why different?"

"I had a phone call."

Lotta looked thoughtfully at her. "Why different?" she repeated. "What will it do?"

"It will—leave you able to walk around, but you'll be pretty dopey. You won't pay much attention to anything. They wanted me to give you a powerful tranquilizer, but I didn't have anything suitable. This was the best I could do."

"Able to walk around, but dopey. That means they're coming to take me away. They'll kill me, won't they?"

Nilla managed to meet her eyes while she lied. "I wouldn't think so. You're valuable to them."

"They've decided I don't know anything useful, and alive I'm a problem. They're probably the Seventh of Spring, or some other group just as bad. They'll kill me and make a public production of it, for the notoriety. The way they did with Governor Malrose last spring."

Nilla couldn't hold her gaze. Lotta had the group right, and she was probably right about the rest of it.

"What do you suppose they'll do with you?" Lotta asked. "Considering what you know."

Nilla's guts tightened. She'd been wondering about that. Now she recited the same argument she'd made to herself. It wasn't entirely convincing. "They'll pay me, and tell me to keep my mouth shut," she said. "I don't know as much as you think I do. Besides, I'm too useful to kill, and there are people, dangerous people, who rely on me, who'd be upset if anything happened to me."

Lotta ignored her. "They won't want any outsider left alive who can put anyone on my trail. And Mr. Friend isn't all there mentally. Who knows what he might have told you when he was here. Or what the people told you who drove you here."

She paused, trying to keep her thoughts focused. The sedative was taking hold. "You said I'll be able to walk. Maybe we should both walk. You and I. I'm higher level government than I told you. If I promise to get you a pardon, the government will honor that. I was Lord Kristal's personal aide, and got promoted from there. And my husband is Colonel Romlar of the White T'swa."

Nilla chewed a lip. How far could she trust the strength, or the commitment, of the underworld people she relied on for protection? This was a high stakes game, and Borkus had a reputation for brutality.

"You hate this anyway," Lotta added, slurring a bit. "Let me use the comm. Then we'll go outside and hide. Woods. A hedge. Till the police come. Half an hour . . ."

Nilla interrupted. "The comm here only receives calls, unless you have the key. People from down the road stop by, get my shopping orders, and deliver. They're sympathizers. There are several sympathizers around here; that's why this place was chosen."

"They'll kill me," Lotta mumbled. "It'll be on your conscience."

"Finish your sandwich."

Lotta stared at it without picking it up. She was trying to think. Abruptly Nilla got to her feet. "You'll have to wear my other shoes. And a pair of my slacks. They won't fit worth a damn, but they'll have to do."

She left the room. Lotta stared owl-eyed after her, then picked up the sandwich and took another bite.

Olfrek Lendamer pulled out of his trance and looked at Artus. "They've driven west out of a little place called Kamers Grove," he said, "and turned south on State Route 27. They plan to stay on 27 to Meadowvale, and turn off there. We don't know where to. Borkus knows the place, but he's just sort of driving on automatic. You know how that is."

Artus sat by a comm, with an open conference connection

to Hortvan and a Ministry special force floater. He'd been tempted to recommend a fire team of his own troopers, under Jerym, but they'd take longer to get under way and weren't trained for this sort of action. He gnawed a lip thoughtfully. The two thugs were driving a yellow carryall. He could probably have them intercepted at Meadowvale.

"Do you have a sense of whether they're retro fanatics?"

"They don't seem to be. They're from Carjath. Independence fanatics. But they don't believe there's an Armada, either."

Just as bad, Artus thought. *Worse. They're probably more competent than our home-grown fanatics.* "Okay. If they don't arrive when they're supposed to, someone else may take her away. Let's stick with them. We need to know where she is."

Olfrek nodded, and settled back to regain his trance. Meanwhile Artus updated Hortvan and the Ministry's floater. Yes, the pilot said, his instruments would distinguish yellow, even at night. With the skimpy rural traffic, they should be able to pinpoint the carryall. They could make the arrest before the hoods got the doors open, or shoot them from the air if necessary.

Nilla didn't know when Borkus and Turley would arrive. It might be an hour, or they might be coming up the road right now, half a mile away. That seemed unlikely though. It was early dusk when she led Lotta out the back door, and west across a pasture toward a woods. Nilla wasn't clear on where they were, relative to anywhere else, but there was bound to be another road not far beyond the woods. And it would make no sense for Borkus to be on that road.

Meanwhile Lotta was walking better than Nilla had expected. If need be, though, she'd leave her in the woods. Tell her to stay hidden, then go on alone till she could call the police.

❖   ❖   ❖

Maylon Gorth was on the trunk highway south of Landfall. He rode the system, controlled by the computerized grid, the vehicle moving at the speed limit. Upset as he was, to control the car himself would be risky, even in the rather light traffic, and to speed would read on the grid monitor.

He was not only upset. He had a cold, and was afraid of medications. Instead he wore a bulky sweater and woolen cap. Just in case, he hadn't taken his four o'clock medication for priapism, either, though he carried it in his pocket. Without it he couldn't urinate. When preparing for sex, he avoided fluids as much as possible.

Just now though, it wasn't sex that was foremost in his mind. *I must not let her be killed,* he told himself. *She is the only person who cares for me.* "I understand," she'd said. Said it sincerely. *She is not especially pretty, not like some, but they only have sex with me because I pay them, or put them in my shows. And they talk about me behind my back. I know they do. And laugh. Lotta would never talk about me, or laugh at me. We will go to the Ferny Coast, and I will make love to her. Even if she is not willing at first, she will understand. And when I have done it to her, she'll be glad. She will be in love with me because I am kind to her, and because I can have long sex. And Jarnell doesn't know about the Ferny Coast place. None of them do. We can stay there, she and I.*

If he just wasn't too late! He'd tell Nilla that Jarnell had sent him. If she didn't believe him, he'd hit her. Knock her cold. Kill her if necessary.

Lotta's the only one who understands. The only one in the world. And she'll be happy with me because I will be very nice to her. Very kind. And because it doesn't go down.

He rehearsed what he'd say, what they'd do. Perhaps he'd have sex with her before they left the old farmhouse. He might have an erection again by then. But that would be dangerous. Who knew when Jarnell might send those people to get her?

The thought upset him even more. When at last he exited onto a prefecture travelway, he was tempted to opt off the system. The prefecture police weren't as strict. But he decided not to take the chance. He'd soon be on non-system district roads anyway.

Half an hour later he was driving south on the district road that would take him to the house. There was little traffic, and when a light-colored carryall tailgated him briefly, he glanced back annoyed in his rearview mirror. The carryall swung out to pass. He looked out his side window at it—and recognized the face of the man in the off-seat. Turley!

For a terrible moment it seemed to Maylon the man recognized him, too, and he almost went off the road. They were on their way to kill Lotta. They must be!

He pulled off onto a hedge-bordered farm lane and stopped, to sit for a while, gripped by fear, disappointment, and self-blame. *Too late!* he thought. *Too late! I should have acted sooner!*

"Borkus," said the man in the right front seat, "did you see the guy driving that big Galworn we just passed?"

"How could I? I'm on the wrong side. And anyway it's too dark."

"It ain't too dark. I could see him. He looked right at me when we passed."

"Okay. What about him?"

"I met him once. He's one of their money people."

Borkus looked in his rearview mirror. "Nah. Look. He's pulled off on a side lane. He's someone lives out here."

"Driving a Galworn?"

"He's some bigshot wants to live in the country."

The other man shook his head. "I didn't see no house."

"It's back in a ways. And what would your money man be doing out here anyway?"

"Going where we're going."

"Then why'd he leave the road?"

"To piss maybe. Take a crap."

"Someone like that wouldn't shit in the weeds. Not when he's just a mile from a toilet. Holy Yomal, Turley, don't start getting strange on me."

From three hundred yards up and one hundred behind, Sergeant Worrel watched the yellow carryall speed down the grassy rural road. He became aware it was slowing, and started to tell the pilot, but before he could pronounce the first syllable, they began slanting sharply down, the safety harness pressing Worrel's torso. When the car turned off the road, they were thirty yards above and behind it.

The pilot already had the hover car in his sight. He slapped the trigger, there was a sharp hard *pop!* and a steel net shot from a tube. Its electromagnets activated as it flew free, and with a crash it struck the hover vehicle, embracing it. The pilot slapped another trigger and fired a "killer." Not of men. This one blew the carryall's computer, paralyzing its AG drive.

Then he dropped the floater to within a foot of the ground. Worrel and three corporals slapped their safety releases and piled out, two from one side of the floater, two from the other. One of each pair held a blaster, the other a short-barreled rocket launcher, hopefully only for intimidation. The idea was to bring their quarries in alive for questioning.

Too bad stunner beams didn't work through glass, Worrel thought. But a threat could work as well. "Hands against the glass!" he barked, his throat mike amplifying it. "Against the glass! Now! Or you're both dead!"

He didn't fully realize the kind of men he faced.

❖   ❖   ❖

Eighty-seven miles away, Linvo Garlaby knew at once when Borkus decided to shoot it out, but didn't pull out soon enough. Borkus drew and fired with remarkable quickness—a whole short burst through the closed door, striking the officer in his armored vest. From the other side of the vehicle, a rocket slammed through the opposite door and exploded. It was Borkus and Turley who died, not the officer.

Linvo roared a single hoarse roar and fell backward off his trance cushion, unconscious. It was intensely traumatic to be in someone's mind when they were killed.

In a sense, Olfrek Lendamer had been one mind removed from Borkus's death. He too fell, hands clapped to his temples, but did not lose consciousness. Pale and shaken, he stammered out what had happened. He was, however, in no condition to attain another trance, to follow up on matters.

The police, via radio, told Artus the news; news that was bad but could have been worse. There was no one in the house. There had been very recently. Two of the bedrooms had been occupied. In one there was even half a chicken sandwich on a table, and a glass with a fragment of still unmelted ice floating in it.

Half an hour later, an investigation team would arrive, and find conclusive evidence that someone had been held captive there. A few hours later, analysis of residue on the glass would tell them more, but nothing helpful.

Nilla had led Lotta to the woods, which were somewhat open from recent cutting. With the help of twilight, they made their way carefully through them to a bordering road. By that time it was nearly night.

They turned north, passed a farm, then another, but Nilla didn't stop. She didn't know which neighbors were safe, and which were not. They'd keep going till they got farther away.

She wondered how Lotta's feet were doing inside the three-sizes-too-large shoes. They had to be blistered, but she was probably too drugged to notice.

After a mile and a half, the minor district road on which they walked met a larger one. To Nilla, larger seemed better. There might even be a village in a mile or two, with a public comm booth. The question was, which way?

Guessing, she chose, and began limping west. She seldom walked much. Her own feet were blistered now, and she was beginning to feel testy. *You're lucky, kid,* she thought, looking at Lotta. *You can't feel the pain.*

Maylon Gorth backed out of the lane and turned north, the direction from which he'd come. I'm too late, he told himself, too late, too late. At the first crossroad he turned west. Little more than a mile farther, he saw two people walking along the roadside. He *never* picked people up; never even thought of it. It wasn't standard. Besides, they might be criminals. But as he passed them, they appeared to be a woman and child, the woman limping, while the child seemed very tired. On an impulse he pulled onto the shoulder and pressed a switch. The offside rear door opened. While he waited for them to catch up, he felt a certain serenity, a sense of strangeness, a flavor of goodness. He was doing something nice for strangers! A powerful man doing something for strangers. Maybe one of them would have sex with him. He'd offer money.

They climbed in, and he engaged the drive. The Galworn lifted above the grass and started down the road again. "Where are you going?" he asked.

There was a moment's silence. "To the nearest town. I need to make a comm call."

His breath locked in his chest. The voice was Nilla's, he was sure of it! The other, then, must be Lotta. Obviously they'd escaped. Nilla hadn't recognized his voice because of his cold. "Just a moment," he said, and pulling off the road, set the vehicle back down. Then he opened the dash storage and took out the pistol he kept there. Turning, he pointed it at Nilla, feeling a surprising sense of power. He wouldn't shoot her—wouldn't shoot anyone—but they would feel fear. He would take them somewhere and have sex with both of them.

"My dear," he said, "I drove all the way out here to rescue our captive. Jarnell intends to have her killed tonight. Now it seems I must rescue you both." He gestured with the gun muzzle. "Come up here with me, where I can keep an eye on you while I drive. No, no! Do not get out! Climb over the back of the seat. If I let you out of the car, you will run away, and I cannot allow that."

Nilla turned to Lotta. "Don't worry," she said, "Mr., ah, Friend won't hurt us. Everything will be fine." Then she started to belly over the seat, backward, feet first. When she was over, her knees still on the seat, she grabbed Gorth's gun hard with both hands, trying to wrest it from him. For a moment they struggled silently. Then, from behind, Lotta got an arm across Gorth's face. There was an explosion, and another. It was Nilla who slumped, sliding partly to the floor mat.

Squealing, Gorth disengaged Lotta's forearm, then turned and struck at her with the pistol barrel, the blow grazing her head, knocking her down.

She lay stunned on the floor mat. Gorth was crying audibly in the front seat. Vaguely she realized that Nilla must have been shot. She also knew, vaguely, that she herself had important information, and should not risk being killed.

After a minute, the crying stopped. She heard the AG activate, felt the car move, and getting off the floor, peered out the windows. Half a mile farther down the road, Gorth turned off into a yard and parked beside a house. She crouched low again.

Bellis Fornamen heard the knock, and got to his feet. "Who do you suppose that is?" he said to his wife. "Someone too stupid to push the bell."

Stepping to the door, he opened it and spoke gruffly. "What can I do for you?"

"I have had an accident. I need to make a comm call."

Bellis stepped back and let the man in. "You got blood all over your shirt and pants," he said. "What happened?"

"An accident. With the car."

"Who you going to call?"

"I—I'm not sure. A friend. To come and get me."

"You hurt?"

The question seemed to startle Gorth. "I—do not appear to be. No, I am all right."

Bellis gripped his arm with a strong hand and forced him back onto the porch. "Let's look at your car."

With his free hand, Gorth reached inside his sweater, drawing the pistol he'd tucked in his waistband. Before he could point it, the heel of the farmer's hand slammed him hard on the forehead. Gorth's knees buckled, and the pistol thudded onto the porch floor.

"You son of a bitch," the farmer said casually. "You try something like that again, I'll shove the barrel up your ass and pull the trigger. Then I'll feed your carcass to the hogs. Now. Let's you and me look in the car."

He propelled Gorth down the steps and to the car, then opened the passenger-side front door and looked in. "Holy Yomal," he said, then turned and knocked Gorth down. "Now stay there and don't move."

He grasped Nilla's slack figure beneath the arms, feeling sticky blood. Pulling it from the car, he lay her on the grass and knelt. "Shit!" he muttered. "It's Nilla. Deader'n a fish." Standing, he turned to Gorth, who lay half curled up a few feet away. "No wonder you're all bloody. Looks like she's been shot twice, once in the throat, and once in the chest. And I'll bet money that gun of yours is two rounds short of a full load. What kind of story you got to cover this?"

Gorth raised his head. By moonlight he looked very pale. "I—rescued them. They had been held prisoner in a house near here. But Nilla did not realize. She thought . . ."

The man interrupted. "What's your name?"

"Maylon Gorth. Two men were going to kill them, and I wanted to . . ."

"*Kill them?* Who's this *them?* You got another one in there?" He stepped to the back door, opened it and peered in. "Holy Yomal! What've we got here?" He reached inside. "Come out, girl." He drew her from the car by an arm. "I wondered what you looked like. Not much, in those clothes. Not someone all that important."

He turned to Gorth. "So you killed Nilla. That's not going to make you popular with some folks." He poked the prostrate man with a toe. "On your feet, Mr. Gorth. Nilla's not going to run off anywhere. We'll leave her here and go in the house. Then *I'll* make the comm call."

Gorth struggled to his feet. The farmer, with Gorth's arm in one hand and Lotta's in the other, walked them onto the porch and into the house. "Meltha," he said, "you'll never in hell guess who we've got here!"

An hour and a half later, two cars pulled into the yard and stopped. Six people got out. Their headlight beams had brightened the living room curtains, alerting the farmer, who stepped out onto the porch. To his surprise, the newcomers wore hoods. One of them, with a woman's voice, knelt beside the corpse, then looked up at the farmer. "Why did you leave her lay out here like this? Don't you have any respect?"

"Don't give me no bullshit," the farmer said. "I don't need it. Just be glad they came here instead of someplace up the road. Otherwise it'd be the police looking at her, instead of you."

One of the men broke in. "Don't be touchy," he said, and gestured at the hooded woman. "She's a nurse. Things like that bother her." Turning, he called to the two drivers:

"Park around back and stay in the cars. We've got things to talk about inside."

The six then started toward the house without asking, the farmer following. Vanter had said he'd call someone who'd know what to do. He doubted it. *Self-appointed bigshots,* he thought sourly. *That's the trouble with something like the retros. Shit rises to the top.*

The first thing the newcomers did was search Gorth, then question him and the farmer. Then one went out and moved Gorth's car to a shed. Gorth himself was handcuffed and taken to the barn, where the hooded woman injected him. He was left to sleep in a pile of straw. The farmer and his wife went to bed. Lotta, who'd also been handcuffed, was already asleep in a corner of the living room, on the floor. The two drivers slept in their cars, and the nurse on the sofa.

The other men were the executive council of the district Seventh of Spring, though they didn't say so. They sat at the dining room table and talked for three hours, pausing to make several long distance calls at the farmer's expense. By the time they'd finished, they'd made all the necessary decisions and arrangements.

When the farmer got up to do his morning chores, his visitors were gone, including the dead woman. So were Maylon Gorth and his car, which, he suspected, would end up stripped to the chassis.

Chapter 29
Morning After

Emry Wanslo, Lord Kristal, was on his feet waiting when Artus Romlar walked in at seven o'clock. "Good morning, Artus," Kristal said. "Hortvan left me a summary. I suspect he was up as late as you were."

Artus nodded.

"Kari Frensler made—not quite a meld with Lotta this morning, wasn't actually in her mind—but she established a sort of contact that she could maintain."

Again Artus nodded. "The report was on my desk when I came in this morning. Lotta's alive but drugged."

Ah. You too start your days early, the old man told himself. "Kari will be checking on her several times a day," he said. "She'll meld with her if she can. If anything seems to be developing, she'll stay with her. Meanwhile I want you to shift gears and return to your own duties. If you're able."

Artus's gaze was steady. "As long as action is continuing on getting her back. I'm glad Kari's on it. They've known one another a long time, and Lotta considers her one of the best at what they do."

Kristal's age-thinned lips pursed. "Action *will* continue. I realize that Lotta's situation is grim. Retro extremists are more or less insane, and some are quite ruthless. A legacy of the Sacrament. Increasingly they have the support of non-retro criminal elements who see advantages in disruptions of law and order. And off-world independence extremists have been smuggling themselves onto Iryala to ally with them. They'd love to see a breakdown of our popular support."

He sighed audibly. For the first time, Artus realized the strain this brilliant, elderly bureaucrat was under.

"You know my personal affection and admiration for your wife, feelings shared by everyone in the OSP who knows her. And by His Majesty. Also she's been the cornerstone in our defense efforts. There is no one else in government whose abilities are so broadly important as hers. Not mine, not yours, not even Kusu's.

"But I can make no guarantee that we can retrieve her."

Artus nodded. "I'm aware of that." He stood up. "With your permission, I'll return to my office. Commander Barnts will be there at 0800, to go over performance specs for the new assault landers."

Kristal nodded. "Of course. Thank you for your understanding, Artus."

"You're welcome, Emry. And remember, Lotta was a protégé of Master Ku. She's more fully immersed in the T'sel than probably anyone not born T'swa. If she were listening to us now, she'd tell us it will all work out sooner or later. Whatever happens to her, or to us."

He turned and left, his lordship watching. When the door had closed, Kristal slumped for a moment, then straightened and keyed his comm. "Markis, get me Captain Hortvan. If he's out, stay with it till you do."

By evening, contingents of Royal Police had rounded up all the Seventh of Spring retros they knew of in Malform Prefecture, and some in Landfall Prefecture. All except some central figures who'd disappeared or suicided, presumably fearing interrogation. Those arrested were isolated from one another and questioned. Two psi-spies took turns melding with the persons being interrogated, to pick up any thoughts or memories stimulated and withheld.

A number of them from Malforn had been aware that a high-ranking government employee had been held captive in their prefecture, but none knew where she was, or who had her.

The most important information led to a retro mole, a principal clerk in the Records Office of Interior. That explained the escapes and suicides.

The body of Maylon Gorth was also recovered. His captors had thrown his pills away, as punishment. Apparently they blamed him for the deaths of Borkus and Turley as well as Nilla. Without his pills, his prostate became and remained tumescent. Extreme pain and uremic poisoning had resulted in delirium and convulsions. Finally he'd been suffocated.

As a footnote, Gorth's physician was questioned as to why Gorth's condition had not been dealt with medically. They were told that no physical cause had been found, and Gorth had refused treatment of its apparently psychosomatic origins. Medical records showed that as a young man, he'd been psychosomatically impotent. Apparently the priapism of his old age had been a response to that earlier impotency, a response he was determined to protect.

News of the roundup and interrogations circulated through the retro movement with surprising speed. It worried Jarnell Walthen. Surely Interior had learned of his retro connections. Why had *he* been bypassed? The only reason he could think of was that he was under surveillance. Anything he might do now would be a threat to the retro movement. He decided that for the foreseeable future he would leave it strictly alone.

He was not the only one who made that decision.

❖   ❖   ❖

The OSP had assigned psi apprentices to monitor Walthen. He was on-world, well known, easily reached and melded with, and provided valuable experience. And conceivably, hopefully, Walthen would be contacted by someone who had information on Lotta. The various retro groups had never been closely connected, or connected at all, really. They were paranoid—suspicious of each other—more so now than ever. But Walthen had important money connections. In need they might turn to him.

Chapter 30
The Garthids

Excerpts from a report by the
Office of Special Projects Garthid Study Team,
in cooperation with the Monastery of
Dys Tolbash, T'swa Order of Ka-Shok

The Garthids are native to the planet Shuuf'r Thaak, and naturalized on 52 colony worlds. They are erect bipeds. . . . Their worlds are near the hot limit of free-water worlds. Their homeostatic mechanism is not effective in the cooler range. They become lethargic at temperatures well above freezing. . . .

The protogarthids were obligate carnivores, but physically they were considerably inferior to other large predators and scavengers. They depended on cooperation, ferocity, cunning, and crude weapons. Today's Garthids remain obligate carnivores, but their weapons are highly sophisticated.

The Garthids have five distinct genders. In their archaic classification, these are *hunters*, the males (about 45% of the total); *mothers*, the females (35%), who produce young; *nurturers* (15%), who suckle and care for the young till adolescence; *healers* (5%); and *guardians* (5%). Only the hunters and mothers engage in sex.

With so many biological genders, the Garthid dialects have a non-generic personal pronoun, *kot*, in addition to gender-specific pronouns. *Kot* is invariably used where gender is irrelevant.

The genders are morphologically quite distinct, although the hunters and healers resemble one another. . . . Individuals of the guardian gender are much larger than the others, and differ in other respects. When the species was in the scavenger-hunter stage, the guardian role was to stay with the mothers, nurturers and young, and defend them.

Over the history of Garthid technological-social-political evolution, the hunters have become the workers and managers. The guardians are the overseers, rulers, and military commanders. The healers as a gender, once were called *shafan*. Having a strong innate sensitivity to life processes, they provide most of the physicians and veterinarians, and many of the biologists. Some healers are "sensitive to the spirit." Of these, most become monastics, and some clerics. The term *shafa* (singular form of *shafan*), meaning holy, has become restricted to those "sensitive to the spirit."

Living and competing with larger swifter predators, the Garthids developed a habit of rarely breaking off combat. The killer lizard engaged by a Garthid pack would either retreat or die. Over time, the most formidable predators would commonly back off when confronted by a pack of spear-wielding and increasingly arrogant Garthids.

With the confidence and sense of power that grew with growing dominance, Garthid territoriality intensified. Competition with other bands continually challenged their intelligence. They developed tactics of encounter, and improved flaking techniques for better blades and points. They invented the throwing stick, the bolo, and eventually the bow.

Even the protogarthids knew fire, and that camping by it added security. They also learned that stones heated by it would sometimes crack—especially if they were fished from the fire and water was thrown on them. In time, the Garthids built fires by flint pits, to help break down larger stones for flaking.

Meanwhile a religion took shape. From the beginning, it was Garthocentric: the Great Spirit, they said, had looked at the creatures of the world, had chosen the Garthids and breathed his soul into them, giving them speech, free will, and the right to dominate other life forms. From time to time some holy shafa would stride through the clan and remind them of God's seven commandments: (1) Honor God and obey Him. (2) Share your meat. (3) Honor your family, sept, and clan. (4) Do not kill other Garthids frivolously. (5) Spare your enemy if he submits. (6) Protect your females and young. (7) Do not kill God's other creatures wastefully, but husband them always.

Sometimes these were heeded, sometimes they were overlooked or ignored, but they have always been taught. . . .

Because Garthids are large obligate carnivores, a planet which could provide food for billions of herbivores of similar mass can feed only a few hundred million Garthids. And although they evolved as a social animal, their tolerance for crowding is lower than ours. . . . No megalopolis ever developed on a Garthid world. Aside from the imperial city—the "palace" of the Surrogate—probably no town or ward in today's Garthid Khanate has as many as one hundred thousand inhabitants. Twenty thousand is large. . . .

Certain Garthid characteristics are particularly relevant to possible relations with them.

1. Garthids have a remarkable racial memory, manifesting

as realistic dreams. Dream scenes may be prehistoric or historic. There are healers who spend much of their time, including waking time, dreaming. Most Garthids dream mainly of one or a few periods, but sample them all.

2. One result of this is a bottom-line sense of being one species. Their intraspecific warfare has tended to be over rivalries or grudges, and not from any sense of foreignness.

3. Another result is the widely agreed upon primacy of Shuuf'r Thaak as the center of the Khanate.

4. Garthids have little sense of humor. Mirth is almost unheard of except among the shafan. The normal Garthid emotional response to the illogical is disapproval, or in more extreme cases indignation; and to the ridiculous by annoyance, or in more extreme cases outrage. In any case the emotional response is accompanied by a wish, or request, or demand for correction. As there are, of course, differences in opinion regarding what is or is not illogical or even ridiculous, the Garthids are given to insults and fights. In olden times, this often resulted in deaths or severe injuries, demands for retribution and vengeance, and feuds between clans, tribes, and eventually kingdoms. Formal and elaborate rules developed, defining behavior, courtesy, reparations, and amends.

5. The nature of the Garthids was to hunt and to fight, until their weapons technology had developed so far that the War of the Three Khans threatened to seriously degrade the planetary ecology of Shuuf'r Thaak. Eventually they created a central government that allowed the tribes to trade with little restriction. Science flourished. The gravdrive, warpdrive, and hyperdrive were developed. The species spread to other worlds, several with intelligent indigenes. Those which were herbivores were allowed to survive, but none on an equal basis with Garthids. Some were

harvested as food animals, early on, but eventually the practice was discontinued.

6. The Garthids tend to be unforgiving toward life forms they regard as seriously dangerous. Since the skirmishes with the Klestronu expeditionary force, they regard humans as probably dangerous.

Chapter 31
A World of Hope

Coso Biilathkamoro was on the flight deck when the radio picked up the flagship command: "Prepare to generate hyperspace at 1530 hours." There was little further traffic, and after several minutes none at all. Shortly afterward a series of five tones was broadcast at one-second intervals. Then there was nothing.

All of this had taken nearly three hours to reach the scout, but still Coso Biilathkamoro waited. He was used to waiting. After another hour he radioed the survey base, giving his situation and expected arrival time. He also told them what had been done to the base's water purification equipment. Then he completed their disillusion by playing for them the bogus plague messages from "the base" and the kalif impersonator, and finally the crowning duplicity, their funeral service.

Over subsequent days, Hope became visible without magnification. Slowly it brightened, became a growing crescent. The kalifal family, even six-year-old Rami, spent the last hours of the approach watching the screen. From eighty thousand miles, it was a beautiful world—blue and white, with patches of dark blue-green and brown. Then DAAS began the long deceleration, homing on the radio beacon provided by the survey base, riding its gravitic vector.

From fifteen miles out, the region of the base was a varied pattern of forest, savanna, and grassland. A virgin world! Coso supposed that Varatos had once looked much like that. Details increased as they descended. The circular base, sixteen acres in size, was located on a broad grassland, with trees scattered singly and in groves. A few miles northwest were high forested hills; some would call them mountains. Flowing from them, a considerable stream passed half a mile from the base. Coso examined it with the knowledgeable eyes of an ex-marine officer who'd had courses in military engineering. It would, he thought, provide water to a shallow aquifer. And serious flooding seemed unlikely, for less than a mile south, the stream plunged over the rim of a broad, heavily forested valley, through a shallow rocky notch, then lost itself in a river perhaps a quarter-mile wide.

Outside the fenced base, the savanna held bands and herds of four-legged grazers, and tall, two-legged creatures either feathered or furred, resembling large flightless birds. There would, Coso thought, be large predators as well. Presumably the survey team had made their acquaintance.

At about fifty yards he took the controls, and advised by radio, set the scout down near the other spacecraft. The base personnel were out to greet the kalifal family. The troops, and the crews of the survey ship, assault lander and warp lighters, stood in neat ranks. The survey crew—civilian planetologists—stood in semiranks. The senior officers and chief planetologist stood a little apart, waiting as the scout's ramp extruded.

The door slid open, and as Coso stepped out, the camp's pole-mounted public address horn boomed forth the Kalifal fanfare. Followed by his wife and son, the Emeritus Kalif walked down the ramp, hand raised in benediction. Rami was all eyes—a real planet!—and more than a little shy. He could barely remember seeing more than six people at a time. But he stood straight and tall for his age.

On the ground, the Emeritus Kalif shook hands with the senior officers, the highest a lieutenant commander, commanding the survey ship. Then, because it was expected of him, he reviewed the personnel, pausing to speak with one and another.

He'd had time, these past days, to think and plan. But before he discussed those plans, he needed a better sense of the situation on the ground.

By supper the kalifal family had moved into their new home, a pair of barrack huts built together, each large enough to house two squads. To furnish them as well as they were had taken considerable ingenuity, something engineer units were known for. Supper had been an open-air party, featuring an oxlike animal roasted over a fire pit, and a sort of grog produced by the mess staff, with what ingredients and process, Coso could not even guess. He could guess, though, how the men would feel in the morning. The party began festively enough, then several musical instruments appeared, and the men began singing of home. From there the mood went downhill, and they drank till the grog ran out. There were a couple of fights.

Which reminded Coso of what he needed to discuss with the senior officers.

The next day, the survey ship's skimmers didn't fly till after lunch. Their pilots "were not well." Neither were the engineers who'd been scheduled to defuse the scout's warpdrive; that touchy work would wait a day. The Kalif gave most of the afternoon to reviewing the planetological research plans and early data. So far, nothing they'd found presented major puzzles. Most important, the biochemistry they'd analyzed was basically the same as they were used to, as had been expected. All the habitable imperial worlds exhibited it. And so far the range of morphological and ecological expressions examined, amounted to variations on familiar themes.

It was after supper when he sat down with the commander, the engineer company CO, and the survey chief.

"Gentlemen," the Kalif said, "there are things we need to discuss, as I'm sure you know. On the record, we're all dead, and the planet is a death trap. So far as the admiral is concerned we *are* dead, murdered, you by poisoning, my family and I by an explosion. It is possible, however, that when the war is over, he will secretly send a small strike force to make sure no one here is alive.

"Also, while this promises to be a good world to colonize, we are more than two hundred persons, with only nine of them women. An unsatisfactory situation, both genetically and for morale and discipline.

"The Empire, and Kalif Jilsomo, need to know what Loksa Siilakamasu has done and tried to do to us. And the personnel here will need rotation. We have two hyperspace craft: the survey ship and the scout. Either can easily fly to Varatos. The problem is that neither has stasis lockers, and the scout is too small to carry three years' supplies for even one person.

"My familiarity with survey ships is superficial, but it seems to me that . . ."

The commander raised a hand to interrupt. "Your Reverence," he said.

"Yes, Commander?"

"Your Reverence, we do have stasis lockers aboard, for live animal specimens. Most are small, but four are large enough to accommodate adult humans. I've thought about this same need, since you radioed us of the admiral's treachery. Dr. Gorvanda and I have gone so far as to discuss how the base could best get by without the survey ship. He has listed removable survey equipment that could function off the ship.

"Any of my bridge officers are capable of flying the *Cajiya Island*, and either of my senior engineers is capable of looking after the machinery and equipment. I recommend we send Ensign Koringabasu as second officer. While on Varatos, he married our junior cook; she can serve as the steward's department. The ensign, and a senior officer as commander, can handle the con on a six and six schedule. The engineer and a medic can be kept in stasis, available as needed. Spacer Voralda—Lady Koringabasu—could be trained in stasis and revival procedures. I have no doubt the flight can be made with no more than that, and the onboard supplies would be more than adequate. There'd be a stasis chamber for one more adult. If Your Reverence wishes to make the flight, you might be trained as a backup on the bridge. The kalifa could then occupy the remaining large stasis chamber, and one of the smaller could . . ."

Coso waved off the invitation. "We will stay," he said, "to share your honor and your future."

He felt no uncertainty at all in saying it, no misgiving. It was the only conceivable decision.

Chapter 32
Success and Failure

Lotta had been held in a series of retro safe houses, most of them for a single day. And kept heavily drugged for convenience. The drug was one seldom used medically. It shut down the brain's volitional and cognitive functions but allowed a degree of motor function. Thus she could walk if supported, be taken by darkness from door to hover car or floater, and vice versa.

Drugged as she was, she required no security besides her nurse, who spooned food into her, steered her into the bathroom, even took showers with her to more effectively bathe her. And protected her from abuse, for the nurse was a large, formidable woman, overbearing when necessary. If she had any misgivings about the people in charge of a house, she didn't leave her ward alone for longer than a minute or two.

She was responsible for keeping Lotta drugged. She grumped repeatedly that the strength and duration of drugging would sooner or later kill their captive. But she never fudged on the dosage. Unlike Nilla, she was a true-believing retro.

She was also Lotta's sole stability. At each safe house, a new pair of men, or a man and woman, were responsible for lodging her. And when she was moved again, still another pair transported her. The reason for so many separate lodgings and different transporters was to lay a trail too confusing to trace. Thus a mistake or traitor was unlikely to bring rescue or retribution. That was the theory.

The nurse knew none of the persons or places, and paid no more attention to them than necessary. She asked no questions, made no conversation. Questions would have brought suspicion. Ordinarily, in the safe houses, she sat beside Lotta's bed and read mysteries.

In the safe houses, she let the drug wear off as much as it would. From time to time she walked Lotta around the room—even around the house a bit—hoping to halt or reduce any progressive physical deterioration.

To Lotta, her periods of consciousness were a vague blur. Even her nurse was a blur. From time to time, Kari Frensler checked on her. She could sense deep, sluggish psychic activity, but with no hint of content at any level she could reach. It seemed to equate to the deep-level data processing and gestalt revision that went on even during profound coma.

On Kari's sixth day on the assignment, Lotta became aware enough that Kari got a sense of the nurse, and melded with the woman's mind. Through her, she connected and melded with the middle-aged couple lodging them. What she learned alarmed her. They considered the nurse's concern over long-term drug effects a waste of time. The captive was being held for an intended public execution.

Kari then remained melded with Lotta's male jailer, hoping to learn where they were. But both the man and his wife spent most of their time watching videos and holos—dramas, comedies, and retro political diatribes.

In late evening, the couple went to bed and shortly to sleep. Kari transferred back to Lotta, whom she found redrugged; both she and the nurse were asleep. Taking advantage of the situation, Kari emerged from trance to eat, and debrief herself on cube for Linvo and the police. Then she went to bed herself.

Now she knew something of the circumstances. And most important, she could recontact the nurse and the couple pretty much at will. She hadn't learned where they were, beyond getting a general sense that they were still in the southern hemisphere. And that the clocks indicated the mid-continent time zone.

Hopefully she'd learn more in the morning.

What she learned was that Lotta and her nurse had been taken away in the night. The couple knew neither the identity of the men, who'd been masked, nor their destination. They hadn't even looked out the window to see if she'd been taken by car or by floater. Hadn't wanted to know. The retro movement placed great emphasis on secrecy.

So Kari reached for the nurse. Hopefully through her she'd glimpse the driver or pilot, meld with him and learn where they were going.

She was too late. The nurse was frying eggs in a forest cabin, seemingly remote. It consisted of a combined living room-bedroom-kitchen, and a built-on, ramshackle bathroom. Its electrical system, with the dependent water, heating, sewage, and refrigeration systems, were powered by a small geogravitic converter. Water came from a well. Sewage was piped to a cesspool. And the nurse seemed to have no idea at all where she was. Nor did she wonder.

The promising part of the situation was that they were there alone. Perhaps Lotta would recover enough from the drug that something could be learned from her. Though hardly the most wanted information—where she was.

Kari spend the first part of the day in the nurse's mind. For the most part Lotta slept, occasionally rising into a vague self-awareness. Both Kari and the nurse were troubled by how feeble her consciousness was. The nurse decided that as long as they stayed where they were, she wouldn't drug her again till she'd considerably recovered. Then perhaps she'd try a less powerful drug. There was no one there to order otherwise.

The next day Lotta again slept most of the time, but during her waking periods she was vaguely aware. She even thought more or less coherent thoughts, mostly apropos of nothing. But encouraging.

On the third day Lotta became considerably aware. Among other things, of something stirring in her mind, something that was not herself.

She almost sat up, then turned her eyes to her nurse, who sat reading. Realizing what had disturbed her, Lotta relaxed to the meld. She could not read the mind that had found her, but she gathered as much focus as she could, and undertook to remember what might be valuable to the Remote Spying Section.

The next time Kari emerged from trance, she was tired but exhilarated. Though Lotta knew nothing of where she was, or how she might be rescued, she'd recalled some important things. Given another day, she might be able to carry on a dialog.

Kari didn't take time to use the comm. She simply reached to Artus in psi mode, and told him what she'd learned. As soon as she'd disengaged, Artus had keyed Kusu Lormagen, and they'd met in Kusu's office. On the night of Lotta's abduction, the Kalif had been en route to a planet. Should be there by now, available for abduction or rescue, depending on the point of view. The question was where. One of the team spying on the flagship could provide a decent fix on it.

It was the biggest single break they'd had.

Lotta, Artus thought, *tomorrow we'll learn where you are, and send someone to get you. And I'll be with them.*

The next day they did *not* learn where Lotta was. Instead they learned she'd been moved again, drugged to the gills.

Chapter 33
Esteemed Valvoxa

Filéna Kironu was part of the first graduating class of the Ostrak monastery school, in the outskirts of Chesi-Moks, on Tyss. The school was air-conditioned, but cool only by T'swa standards. By Iryalan standards the building was like an oven, the daytime temperature leveling off at a parched 110 degrees F, the bedtime temperature 90 degrees. Thus, when one left the building, the outdoors was not unbearable.

She'd been one of the first of a series of Iryalan children brought up from age three on Tyss, cared for by T'swa nannies, and trained and educated by Ka-Shok adepts. By the time Filéna was nine, Master Do-Nahn considered her a potential Ka-Shok master.

During her own training on Tyss, Lotta had heard of Filéna, and before leaving had visited the girl. She'd told her of the Karghanik Armada, and the work she was going home to do. Later, after establishing the Remote Spying Section, she'd contacted Filéna mentally, and invited the sixteen-year-old to join staff.

Filéna had agreed. She might, she thought, return to Tyss after the troubles were over, and apply to study under a grand master. Meanwhile, working under Lotta appealed to both her pragmatic and adventurous streaks. Now she'd been back on Iryala for two months. Among highly gifted personnel, Lotta considered Filéna exceptional, and soon promoted her from apprentice to agent.

Filéna had accepted Lotta's abduction matter-of-factly. Except for genotype, she was far more T'swa than Iryalan. She hoped and intended that Lotta would be recovered unharmed, but meanwhile there was work to do.

It was midday, nearly time for her workday to start. She ate her late breakfast: a small bowl of lentils,[1] a slice of buttered dark bread, and a sweet loomi. Then, settling onto her trance cushion, she closed her eyes. Her mouth formed the syllables of her mantra, and she entered a cognitive trance.

She was on the Garthid project now, assigned to the *Thunder Lizard*, the Garthid flagship. She intended herself into the mind of Admiral Kurakex, and in a moment was seeing through his eyes with him. They glared at a thick-bellied Garthid in a simple green mantle, and she felt the admiral's hatred. The object of that hatred, she realized, was the shafa, Esteemed Valvoxa. She hadn't seen him before, but was well aware that the admiral hated him. The shafa's face was as imperturbable as a T'swa's, even as he lectured the admiral—on the bridge, in the presence of the bridge watch!

Valvoxa's words were blunt. "I know the orders you've given," he said. "No one is to tell me anything, although I am here as the eyes and voice of the Surrogate. What insolence! What are you hiding? What discreditable plans? What crimes? I'm sure you know who the Surrogate is surrogate for: He acts for God! And as we prepared to leave, he ordered you to be open with me, and heed my words. 'Valvoxa speaks for me,' he said."

The admiral's parietal hood flared strongly, making him seem larger than he was. Towering and massive, he weighed two and a half times as much as the shafa. Filéna

---

[1]Lentils, like numerous other food plants, had followed humankind in its interstellar migrations.

could feel him quiver with anger, and when he answered, his voice was tight with emotion. *"I am the admiral! I command!"* He half barked, half roared the words. *"And I do not brook insolence. Certainly not from some swag-bellied saurian like you! Not on my bridge!"*

His eyes bulged, and after his outburst, his panting reflex activated. The bridge watch stood silently at their stations, pretending not to hear, but soaking up every word.

Despite the huge size difference, the shafa showed no fear. Head cocked, Valvoxa peered at Kurakex like a crested sawbill examining an enormous sand toad. "Ah," he answered, almost pleasantly now, "but my belly, and what you imply of my lineage, are irrelevant. The issue here is obedience to the Surrogate of God. Your Lord, the ruler of the Khanate. Those like yourself, who demand obedience, must also give it."

The holy man smiled. "Pay attention, prince of the Tofarko clan. You were ordered not to make war needlessly, for who knows what disasters might follow? The Surrogate thought long before selecting you, for though you are our senior naval officer, you are also willful, and often bellicose. Which is why I was sent: to curb your appetite for conflict.

"Sooner or later, God willing, we will go home. Then the Surrogate will ask for my report. What will he think of it? And of you? Also, recall his warning that you are responsible for my well-being. He knows you well, admiral. As I do."

The shafa gazed a moment longer at Kurakex, who did not meet his eyes; he might otherwise lose control and kill his tormentor. Then, casually, Valvoxa turned his back and left the bridge. A minute later the admiral too left, carrying with him the unperceived, but very interested presence of Filéna Kironu.

She knew the admiral's intention: war. And she also knew he was not worried about punishment. His anger grew out of wounded arrogance, and the effects of the shafa's scoldings on his staff: their attitudes, and their quickness to obey. But he did not fear the Surrogate. Not here. Not now.

She still had much to learn about this, she realized. On an impulse she moved to Valvoxa's mind.

Despite his girth, Valvoxa strode strongly down the passageway. For more than a decade, in his youth, he'd belonged to a moderately ascetic order much given to ecstatic dancing. During those years he'd developed a strong constitution, which had largely survived his move to a contemplative order, and his late-life enjoyment of food. Particularly since he'd learned to meditate while walking.

The tiny cabin assigned him was a long way from the bridge. Thus he was only well-started when Filéna undertook to meld with him. And he was instantly aware of her! In his surprise, he almost ejected her.

«Who or what are you?» he thought.

She hadn't been surprised. She'd half expected it. «I am a student,» she answered. «And a different life form. I am learning about your people.»

«Indeed! And what is your purpose in this?»

«Most immediately, I seek survival for my people, who show much promise. More basically, the order to which I belong undertakes to glimpse is-ness. In that I have succeeded. To glimpse is-ness is to glimpse God, glimpse Him in ourselves, others, worlds, voids . . . in all things. In you, esteemed shafa, and in your admiral.»

The shafa laughed delightedly, a remarkable high-pitched coughing sound that flummoxed a crewman about to pass him. «Wonderful!» the shafa replied. «But you will also have found that most lack awareness of it. Even those who recite the fact do not apprehend it. Instead they stumble through the world of smoke and mirrors. Ah well, that will pass in God's good time.»

He paused, then asked, «How did you find us?»

«My people are threatened by invaders, a vast armada. The same Armada that your fleet follows. Some of us visit their minds, to learn about them, seeking to deflect them without war. From them, we learned of you. What do you think of this?»

«It is most interesting. Are you typical of your life form?»

«In some respects. But only a tiny number of us have glimpsed God, or even imagine such a thing.»

Again the shafa laughed. «In that, at least, your species is like my own. And what of the invaders? What are they like?»

«In species they are the same as mine, or very similar. We separated from them a thousand generations ago, to escape a terrible war that shattered many planets and destroyed a great empire. It was then we first met your people. Our ancestors emerged in your sector of space, and you let us depart in peace.

«During most of the long time since then, the people of the Armada did not know we existed, or that you do. They had forgotten us, and much more. Then, not so long ago—in my childhood, and I am not yet fully mature—it sent out a small flotilla, to explore. En route they emerged in your sector, not knowing it was yours, and exchanged fire with a patrol. Much later they did it again, unintentionally. They did not realize how vast your sector is. Later they came upon one of our worlds. Its defenders drove them away, and they went home to their Empire.

«Now they return with far greater force, being careful not to emerge in your sector. My own people wish neither to fight them nor be ruled by them.»

The shafa's mind regarded Filéna's. «And what do you hope for from us?»

«Our knowledge of you is limited. It seems likely, though, that you will not catch the Armada till it emerges in our own sector, in the fringe of our central system. Unless we succeed in deflecting them, the war will probably have been fought and decided before you arrive. Then, if your admiral has his way, his fleet will attack the survivors, perhaps also visiting havoc on our central world.»

She paused. «The prospects for our success are not promising. But there are many decision points for innumerable individuals—among us, yourselves, and within the Armada. And many vector sprays grow out of those decision points, defining an infinity of possible futures. My people will observe alertly, do our best to read and make use of those vectors, and create the best future available to us.»

Mentally Valvoxa grinned at his visitor. «You are an interesting—a stimulating visitor. I am privileged. And it seems to me that in important respects, your wishes and mine coincide. But as you have seen, I have little influence on the admiral. Not even with my position as the Surrogate's representative.

«The admiral's appointment was justified by his naval rank and qualifications, but it was decided by politics. And clearly the Tofarko clan sees this as a long dreamt of opportunity to gain the throne.

«I will examine future events and decisions with my new awareness of your people and their problem. My loyalty is to the Surrogate, but visit me from time to time. I may have something useful for you.»

That last held a note of dismissal, and Filéna's psyche returned to her body. She didn't know how important the experience might be, but it had been interesting. After debriefing, she returned her focus to the admiral and once more melded with him.

Chapter 34
Hope Dashed

Preparing the *Cajiya Island* for her return to Varatos involved preparing the base to operate without her. Another prefab building was set up, wired and otherwise prepared, suitable for research. Equipment from the ship was transferred to it, installed, and tested in its new environment.

After which the *Island* was gotten shipshape again. The tiny crew that would take it back to Varatos was given rough and ready cross-training to ensure coverage of vital functions. This included those who would start the trip in stasis.

Finally came the day of departure. Among those who would stay, the Kalif could sense somberness, and hope tinged with fear. There was less talk than usual. Some men joked, but most of the jokes were lame, and few laughed. There was every reason to expect success, but at the same time it seemed their last and only chance for rescue. Its failure would be devastating.

At 0943, base time, event number one occurred. The *Island*'s sensory array was being checked one final time against readings on the Kalif's scout. Ensign Koringabasu was on the bridge, watching the wall screen, when suddenly an override took control. Columns of hyperspace emergence data filled the screen—coordinates and displacements calculated from emergence waves that propagated instantaneously through the hyperspace potential. Seemingly the arrivals included everything from battleships to picket ships. The ensign stared, then ran from the bridge, out of the ship into the sunshine, and across the mustering ground to the headquarters shed.

He almost collided with a warrant officer arriving from the scout's flight deck with the same alarming report. With the privilege of rank, the ensign entered first, and described to the base commander and Kalif what he had seen, the warrant officer verifying it.

Instead of keying the alarm, the commander turned questioningly to the Kalif. "What does it mean, Your Reverence?"

"It has to be the Armada returning," Coso answered, "though why, I have no idea. Shut down everything that has a strong electronic signature, including the repellent fields, if they're a detection hazard. We don't want anyone to know we're alive here. Don't want to draw their attention."

Even as he said it, it was hard to imagine a reason for the Armada's return.

"Could it be a Confederation fleet?" the commander asked.

"Conceivably. But why would they come here? Why would they even be this far from home?" Frowning he decided. "Round up everyone who's to go with the *Island*. Get them on board and into space as quickly as possible. I want them off-world by 1200 hours. If necessary, dispense with the remaining checkouts; once will have to be enough. Have them park five hundred thousand miles out, in the direction opposite the Armada, with as little electronic output as possible. And wait there. If someone radios us, or approaches us, the *Island* will know. We'll make sure of it. If things remain quiet . . . We'll see."

❖   ❖   ❖

At 1104 hours, event number two occurred: The *Cajiya Island* lifted. Nothing more had been learned of the great fleet that lay in the system's fringe. Someone could have left it in warpdrive and arrive in the vicinity of Hope in under four hours. At 1343, four hours had passed, nothing new had developed, but that was no surprise. Except in emergencies, a newly arrived fleet would carry out certain pre-assembly procedures before sending anyone in-system. And from where this fleet lay, arrival of a radio message would take nearly eight hours.

On the base, routine work was getting done, but not much that required serious concentration.

Event three occurred at 1727 hours, just before supper call at 1730: sensitive survey equipment received fleet radio traffic. *Alien radio traffic.* Had the speech simply been unintelligible, they'd have assumed it was a Confederation fleet. But the array of sounds included some hardly producible by human vocal apparatus. The effect was conspicuously nonhuman. Perhaps—even probably—these were the aliens the Klestroni had antagonized. Besides the Kalif, only two knew of this new development. They would, he said, discuss it after supper, but till then they'd pretend nothing had happened.

As usual, the kalifal family ate in the base's mess hall, at a table of their own. Tain sensed that her husband was deeply worried. She hoped the intruding fleet was Confederation. It seemed to her that if it was, and it found them tucked away here deep within the system, it would not attack. It would discover the peaceful nature of the base, and intern the personnel. Or allow them to stay where they were, for presumably this was outside the Confederation sector.

At 1845, the boom horn called all personnel back to the mess hall. The base commander told them His Reverence had an important announcement. The Kalif stated the situation simply. His only elaboration was that the aliens would probably not discover their presence. So large a force was unlikely to be exploring, and base electronics, reduced as they were, should not be detected at that distance. Continue normal routines, he said, and wait. And pray to Kargh to shield them. The alien fleet would probably leave within two weeks.

He was less optimistic than he'd let on. It was understandable that a commander might choose the vicinity of a system for emergence in an unfamiliar sector. Its primary would serve as an orientation point. But why, in this vast region, had the aliens emerged at this system?

The most plausible answer, it seemed to him, was that somehow they'd detected the Armada passing in hyperspace. Had sent their fleet in pursuit, and it had emerged quite near the coordinates where the Armada had lain. Would they—could they—determine now where the Armada had gone from there? If so, they'd probably leave as soon as they'd completed reassembly. Or might they suspect the Armada was lying in-system, and reconnoiter electronically?

His advice to base personnel, it seemed to him, was the best he could give. Wait. And pray.

Event zero had occurred more than thirteen hours earlier, at first dawn, and no one had noticed. It consisted not of a fleet, but a single intruder on a single-seat grav scooter, circling the base three times, about one mile away and two high. It photographed the base with a multiphase, military intelligence camcorder.

Event zero was unrelated to the emergence of the Garthid fleet. It would set up event four, which would occur at sundown. None of the base personnel would learn of it in time to make any difference. Event number five would hold their full attention.

Event four was the arrival on Hope of Captain Jerym Alsnor, with eight other troopers of the 1st Special Projects

Regiment, the White T'swa. They gated there at sundown, via a teleport at the Blue Forest Military Reserve, on Iryala. Jerym appeared first, almost soundlessly, on the saddle of a two-seat grav scooter. Following at close intervals were seven others, riding solo on similar scooters. Following them was a ninth, piloting an AG freight sled with two steel chests clamped to it.

They materialized almost soundlessly above the large river, close to its edge, four miles from the survey base. Another trooper, this one on a single-seat scooter, flew out of the forest to meet them. He'd been concealed in a narrow aisle through the trees, an aisle formed by a slow-moving black-water creek that emptied into the river. Twenty feet wide, the creek was hidden by treetops.

Jerym spotted the single-seater and its pilot, and landed his force on a sandbank where the creek entered the river. The trooper piloting the freight sled took a heavy-duty military viewer from the smaller steel chest, and activated its power slug. The man who'd met them had taken the preparatory video cubeage early that morning. He inserted his cube in the viewer, its screen facing into the forest, and they studied the pictures. Now and then Jerym stopped on a frame, sometimes isolating and magnifying a part of one, and they discussed what they saw. By the time they'd finished, the brief tropical dusk had faded to night.

The troopers knew things about the base that the viewer hadn't shown them. One of Lotta's psi agents had visited the mind and eyes of base personnel and Coso Biilathkamoro, had learned the base well, and coached the rescue team. Thus they identified with some confidence, the buildings they saw on the viewer. The viewer, in turn, gave them layout and perspective.

"Bennis," Jerym said, "something's come up that you don't know about. We learned it a few hours ago from Remote Spying. The Garthid war fleet has emerged in this system, in the planetary fringe. Somehow they know about this world, and they've sent an assault force to collect prisoners for study. We don't know when they'll get here, but it'll probably be tonight. Maybe this evening. Depending on when they generated warpspace, and how close in they emerge from it.

"The base is aware that a fleet has emerged, and they're worried. They've probably picked up fleet radio traffic, and know it's alien. So they'll be alert and twitchy, which makes our mission tougher.

"We need to make the snatch and get out as quickly as possible. We may even have to grab them and hole up somewhere around here for a while. Everyone but Karvol and Velleen stay here and set up, ready to activate the gate on my order, but not before. The Garthids could arrive overhead and pick up the lights or the generator signature.

"Set up downstream four hundred yards. If things go to hell and we get stuck here, we'll try to meet up this creek. If that's not possible, stay in the vicinity. Remote Spying will work out a pickup."

He looked at Karvol and Velleen. "Let's go," he said.

Flying downriver, they stayed close to the trees for concealment. Shortly they reached the mouth of the tributary that flowed past the base, and followed it upstream. Again they stayed close to the bordering forest, their faceplates set for night vision.

At the falls, the water was confined to a gorge only fifteen feet wide. It crashed and leapt, sending spray and mist skyward. Bypassing it, they followed the upper level of the forest roof, moving around the taller trees, then dropped almost to stream level again. The savanna began almost at once, but a narrow band of woods bordered the water.

When they came to the end of their cover, they stopped and examined the final few hundred yards. *It's hard to believe I'm this close to Tain*, Jerym thought. Tain. Lotta said she remembered nothing from before her capture except language.

On each side of the base enclosure, he knew, was a gate wide enough for heavy machinery. Each had a narrower gate beside it for foot traffic and hover scooters. His practiced fingers played across a key pad, and a readout appeared on his faceplate. The animal repellent field was off. *Probably to reduce their electronic signature,* he told himself.

The gates were closed though, and probably locked. "Plan One," he murmured to the others. "And if I can't get a gate open, then it's over the top."

Staying in the saddle, Velleen took a position among the trees, and unslung his blaster. Covering fire might be necessary. Jerym and Karvol started toward the base on their scooters, staying near enough to the ground that if noticed, they might pass in the dark for two of the base's hover scooters.

There was no sign that they were noticed, and the gate was unguarded and unlocked. So, the people here were worried, but not about a surface approach. Karvol opened it, followed Jerym through, and closed it behind them. Then Jerym led off to the kalifal residence. With the repellent field down, insects were numerous, and they saw only two men in the compound. Neither paid them any attention.

Jerym gave no instructions. They'd memorized Plan One before leaving Iryala. When they reached the kalifal residence, they parked their scooters beside it, a few yards from the stoop. The building stood on timber footings some twenty inches above the ground, for air circulation in the tropical climate. Karvol crawled beneath it.

Jerym stepped to the door, released his helmet catch, and tipped the faceplate up so his face could be seen. Then he knocked. Before anyone could answer, the boom horn blared an alarm. Either the aliens had been seen, or he and Karvol had been spotted. The door opened, and someone who had to be the Kalif was staring out at him.

Jerym moved in abruptly, quick hard hands and powerful arms gripping, jerking. His forearm locked across the Kalif's throat, cutting off any call for help. He wanted him conscious, able to walk. Jerym opened his mouth to explain, but it was Tain who spoke. She held a small pistol, something he hadn't expected.

"Let him go," she said in Imperial, "or I'll kill you."

Jerym had crammed and drilled the language, but even if he hadn't, her meaning was clear. She probably wouldn't shoot though. He was holding her husband between them. "No, Tain," he answered calmly, in Confederation Standard. "I'm here to get you off this world. All three of you. To Lotta. And aliens are attacking. That's what the horn is about. We have to move fast."

She stared, unsure, the strange reply and a vague beginning of recognition weakening her resolve. Then a child's voice interrupted, also in Standard. "Mommy, is he going to take us to cat heaven? To see Lotta? Will we have to die, too?" Then pausing, the boy turned to Jerym. "Why are you hurting my daddy? He's the Kalif! The *Emeritus* Kalif!"

"I'm trying not to really hurt him, Rami," Jerym said. "He doesn't know me, and I don't want him to shoot me by mistake. I knew your mother a long time ago. That's why they chose me to rescue you. All three of you." He lightened the pressure on the Kalif's throat. "Close the door now, Rami. I don't want outsiders to see me."

For a moment Rami stared. Then instead of closing the door, he spoke again. "First let my daddy go."

Jerym stared at the six-year-old standing vulnerable but brave, his father's son. It was the Kalif who spoke next, husking the words against the pressure. "Close the door please, Rami," he said, also in Standard. Jerym released him then, stepping back, hand ready on the grip of his stunner. Rami stepped onto the stoop and pulled the door shut.

Coso Biilathkamoro looked first at his assailant, then at his wife. "Tain," he said, "do you know this man?"

Slowly, dumbly, she nodded.

"Who is he?"

"I've told you about a girl named Lotta who sometimes visits my dreams. Someone I'd known. He is . . . He is her . . ."

Abruptly she dropped to her knees, writhing, keening as a flood of memories rushed in on her. Rami ran to her, throwing his arms around her neck. "Mommy! Mommy," he cried, "don't *die!*"

Her writhing lessened to a rocking, and tears flooded. She hugged her child, still unable to speak. "She won't die," his father told him. "She's beginning to remember. Remembering her life before she came to us."

Someone began knocking loudly, calling from outside the door. "Your Reverence! Your Reverence! We've activated the shield, and an enemy fighter has attacked it with a warbeam! They demand our surrender!"

"They know our language?" Coso called back.

"At least their computer does, sir. We've got a visual from their flight deck. They are very alien, sir."

"Get back to headquarters. I'll instruct Commander Sovanamando by comm."

"Yessir!" There was a pause. "Sir, there are two strange scooters by your wall."

"I know! Do as I ordered, dammit! Time is short!"

"At once, Your Reverence!"

Coso stepped across the room to his comm and keyed headquarters. "Commander," he said, "stall them. Discuss terms with them. I'm working on something. When I'm ready, I'll give you further instructions."

He switched off and turned to Jerym. "What is your name?"

"Jerym, sir."

Jerym! His bride had groaned that name on their wedding night—something he'd come to terms with long since. He went to her, helped her to her feet, then turned to the tall young intruder. "You'll need to take all three of us," he said. "All three, or none."

"I fully intend to, sir."

"On scooters?"

"Grav scooters."

"Are the odds better if we flee in my scout?"

"Probably."

"What about my people here? My troops?"

"If they can escape into the forest, we'll try to pick them up later, with assault landers. With us you have a chance of preventing a battle between our fleet and the Armada."

For just a moment the Kalif stood thin-lipped. Then he nodded. "All right. Tain, you'll need to follow instructions. Rami, I'm going to carry you. Two soldiers are going to take us on their scooters." He picked Rami up and took Tain by the hand. "Let's go," he said.

They crossed the base at a height hover scooters might manage. Overhead, the bowl-shaped shield shimmered like an aurora, with the diverted energy of a small warbeam. Either the Garthids had sent only light craft, or they weren't seriously trying to break the shield. If the shield collapsed, there'd be a moment of severe destruction beneath it. Apparently their interest in prisoners was serious.

It took less than a minute to reach the scout, and seconds to get inside. With a combination of AG and manhandling, they got the scooters inside too. Jerym didn't want them crashing around during possible evasion maneuvers, so when they proved too large to shut inside the tiny sleeping spaces, he had Karvol make room for them in the supply room.

The Kalif was impressed with the troopers' combination

of deliberate calm and fast sure action. He seated himself in the pilot's seat, Jerym beside him, and switched the radio on. Commander Sovanamando was talking with an alien. Its response was clearly electronic, a computer operating a translation program. Giving it one ear, the Kalif looked at Jerym. "How do we get to wherever you'd take us?" he asked.

"Through what we call a gate. It will transfer us from one place to another instantly. It's painful for those not prepared." He glanced at Tain, who'd paled at his words. *She remembers,* he thought. *She's survived it twice, and now she remembers.* "Lotta's developed an improved process for treatment," he told her. "You'll recover just fine."

"Even Rami?"

"Believe me, even Rami." He turned back to the Kalif. "Fly to the big river, then upstream. In a minute or so, turn up a small stream arched over by trees. I'll tell you where. We'll leave the scout there and go through the gate on the scooters."

The Kalif touched several keys and heard the gravdrive activate. Then he switched on his microphone and interrupted. "Commander, what conditions have they offered?"

"Your Reverence, they have agreed to let the enlisted men remain on Hope, if they wish. The officers must submit as prisoners. They seem adamant that we will be offered nothing better."

"Tell them you accept, and will deactivate the shield as soon as you've notified all your people what you've agreed to. I am the Successor to the Prophet. I cannot allow myself to be taken hostage. It would be a sacrilege."

While the Kalif spoke, Jerym gave the copilot's seat to Tain. Taking Rami on her lap, she activated their restraint field. Jerym knelt behind Coso's seat. A moment later, Karvol stepped onto the flight deck and knelt beside him. When Jerym lowered his faceplate, Karvol did the same. Tonguing his comm switch, Jerym told him what was about to happen. Both men gripped the seat backs in front of them and braced themselves.

The scout's instruments told them the instant the shield switched off. Coso raised the scout abruptly and darted forward, shot over the buildings, construction machinery and enclosing fence, across the surrounding savanna, passed above the falls, then sped downstream, careening sharply right when he reached the river.

It was not enough. The alien commander had seen the escape, and sent two fighter craft after them. Coso was almost instantly aware of them, and without turning, asked Jerym for instructions. Emphasizing the situation, a warbeam flashed past the scout in warning. It was to his other troopers that Jerym spoke first, via his headset. "Arki! Set gate size to *maximum! Now!* And turn on the marker lights."

Then he tongued his faceplate open and barked an order. "Do an evasion loop! *Now!*" He watched Coso's hands on the controls. They snapped the scout into a sharp loop. The first pursuer duplicated it at once. The second veered off. With the help of centrifugal force, the kneeling troopers managed not to be thrown around the flight deck.

"Ahead!" Jerym snapped, still watching the Kalif's hands. "The light square! Fly through it. And release your seat restraint, now! You're going to lose consciousness when you go through the gate. Karvol, get him out of his seat as soon as it happens. I'll fly it from there." *If I know how. If my luck holds out.*

A half-mile ahead, four inconspicuous, orange-red marker lights formed a square lit only at the corners. Jerym would almost have bet it wasn't big enough. The fighters were drawing up on them again, and another warning finger of light speared past.

Face clenched, eyes and mind totally focused, Coso Biilathkamoro hit the target perfectly—and the scout disappeared from that sector of space.

The first pursuer grazed the edge of the gate, destroying the generator. The second veered sharply off and returned to the captured base. There he reported that his comrade had collided with the fugitive, and that both craft had exploded. He believed it, and so did his commander.

A half million miles out, the *Cajiya Island*'s tiny crew had been monitoring what they could of the new developments. After the capture of the survey base by aliens, Ensign Koringabasu generated warpspace, and the survey ship headed out-system. Five hours later it emerged into F-space, only to generate hyperspace and disappear again.

Chapter 35
Mission Aftermath

The scout materialized two hundred feet above an Iryalan meadow, at the same speed it had had on the other side, and angled abruptly upward several hundred feet before leveling off.

Feeling the crossover, Karvol grabbed the Kalif, straightening powerful legs and lifting, pulling him backward out of the pilot seat while Jerym crowded in past flailing feet.

Jerym had been briefed on the controls of dummy imperial assault landers and ground support fighters. He'd also been checked out on several classes of Confederation craft, and had watched the Kalif fly the scout. In two or three seconds he had it under control. His famous luck had held.

Strong as Karvol was, and knowing what to expect, he was nonetheless shocked and challenged by the Kalif's reaction to the gate field. An inchoate roar tore from Coso's lungs, his limbs thrashed furiously, wildly, his torso twisting and jerking with shocking violence, his head smashing backward hard enough to have stunned and bloodied the trooper, were it not for the helmet. Karvol threw him to the deck and tried simply to hold him down. If at all possible, the rescued were to arrive able to stand with help. The briefing had stressed that.

What was happening showed signs of actual

In front of him, restrained in her seat, Tain loosed shriek after wild shriek, sounds that threatened to rupture her vocal cords. Rami twitched and jerked in her lap.

On the Blue Forest Military Reservation it was midday and sunny—classic "leaf-fall summer." A medivac floater was ground-parked by a meadow. Waiting beside it were four medics with hypodermic pistols on their belts. With them for muscle were four T'swa cadre, black and calmly interested. And four Ostrak specialists. One of the medics glanced at his watch. None of them knew how long they had to wait.

All the Iryalans were Alumni, and the T'swa were— T'swa. They understood what was going on.

Abruptly something ripped through the air, jerking their heads up. They'd expected scooters, not a hurtling hundred-ton scout. At perhaps 250 miles per hour, it veered upward, rocking widely from side to side, then leveled off and began to slow.

By that time, however, the onlookers' attention had been snatched by something even more dramatic. Most of another craft had appeared at similar speed, spewing pieces, then hit the forest a few hundred feet away on the other side of the meadow, plowing a narrow swath through the trees. It held together somewhat because it was armored.

The first craft swung in a wide curve, still slowing, then turned toward the welcoming committee and landed heavily, twenty yards from the medivac. The T'swa started over at a lope, the medics and Ostrak operators following.

The Kalif and Tain were quickly tranked. Rami, now comatose, was injected by a medic with something else. Helped by the T'swa, two Ostrak operators walked and talked the zombielike parents through a long, seemingly purposeless sequence of actions, continuing till the Ostrak operators were satisfied that their patients were aware of what was happening, and showed signs of actual cooperation. It took nearly an hour with Tain, an hour and a half with Coso.

Rami had been loaded at once into the medivac. While en route to the military infirmary, the senior Ostrak operator worked on him constantly, talking to him, touching his limp body spot by spot with a battery-powered stim rod. She never stopped, even while he was being carried into the building on an AG litter. After half an hour he showed signs of feeling the stim rod. After an hour she set it aside and used only her fingers. Half an hour later he opened dull eyes, and for another half hour she carried him through much the same actions his parents had been supported through.

Finally he began to cry, a weak and pitiful sound, and his Ostrak operator took him down the hall to Tain, who was aware and more or less alert, though almost too sore to move. Vocally she could only whisper.

Jerym and two of the T'swa had run across the meadow and through the woods to the wreckage of the Garthid fighter. It held two bodies, neither remotely human. One was somewhat mangled, the other intact but dead.

The craft's armored battlecomp seemed intact, but whether it would ever function again was another question.

Using his belt comm, one of the T'swa called the medivac. The bodies were loaded into it and taken to camp. The mess sergeant complained bitterly at having two alien corpses on the floor of his walk-in refrigerator, but the T'swa only grinned. An hour later, another medivac arrived from Landfall, this one with refrigeration chests. It took the bodies to the autopsy room in the army hospital at the Landfall Military Reservation. The battlecomp was flown to the OSP as soon as it was cut free from the wreckage.

Jerym and Karvol didn't try to fly the Kalif's scout to Landfall. They waited with it until an Equipment Retriever, Large, arrived. They went with it.

❖   ❖   ❖

On Hope, on the night of the Kalif's escape, the Garthids had removed all the base officers to their flagship. Admiral Kurakex kept his word and left the enlisted personnel on Hope. It was not, however, an act of honor. The next morning they were driven out of the base, which was then thoroughly razed with warbeams, leaving them without food or shelter, or weapons beyond a few pocket knives. Then the Garthids left.

Later that day, another gate generator was ported through for the stranded troopers, who had with them several imperials they'd come across, including a sergeant first class. The troopers got approval to stay on Hope and gather as many of the stranded imperials as were willing to be rescued. Troopers on scooters flew a grid pattern over savanna and forest, each with a bull horn. Though the troopers could communicate in Imperial, they played audio cubes of the Vartosu sergeant announcing the availability of rescue. They simply needed to return to the base site. Before nightfall, most had gathered there, and the troopers had begun to gate them through a few at a time, in a command floater. Not enough Ostrak operators were available on the other side to process them faster. While waiting their turn, the refugees were bivouacked in tents with repellent fields, and provided with field rations and rifles.

The next morning almost all the rest showed up. Altogether they totaled 259—soldiers, spacers, and planetologists. It took sixteen days to gate them all through. Four others never showed up, despite continued searches by their own people, riding with troopers. Presumably the four were dead, victims of predators, truculent herbivores, insects, snakes or accidents.

The rescued were shown on Confederation holos and TV, to help make the prospective invasion real to citizens. More effective was cubeage of the dead Garthids, and the remains of their fighter. And of prominent physicians and major public figures, examining the bodies, or the fighter, or both.

The kalifal family had adjustments and recoveries to make. The Kalif was muscular, and the convulsions triggered by gating had been so violent, extreme soreness left him unable to walk for several days. He'd even needed help to eat.

Tain's convulsions had been less violent, partly because her seat restraints had responded instantly and effectively to her first violent movement. Her major problem was to adjust mentally, and integrate her regained memories. For more than a week she slept a lot, and spent considerable time contemplating. She was, she discovered, quite different from the Kalif's wife. The vulnerable, yielding kalifa was history, as was the reckless, willful young journalist she'd been before going to Terfreya. She needed to decide who she was *now*.

Rami, whose arrival condition had been the most serious, recovered the quickest. During his parents' recuperation, he spent most of his time with Lord Kristal's granddaughter Eralyn, and her two children, who were living with his lordship in his penthouse. All the Wansley family were Alumni, and very friendly to their small guest.

During her difficult days, Tain's husband had been asked to limit his visits to lunch. Meanwhile, between extensive debriefs, and time with his son, he began working with a tutor, learning about the Confederation. At lunch on the eighth day, Tain told him she loved him. Very much. And asked when they could live together again as a family.

Coso surprised himself; he wept in relief. She warned him she was different now, that they'd have to learn each other again. He kissed her, and told her he'd enjoy learning his new Tain as much as he had his old.

Two days later the kalifal family was installed in a comfortable apartment, in the new OSP staff apartment building. By that time Tain had been told why Lotta hadn't visited her.

At the OSP artificial intelligence research center, the scout's DAAS had abundant information for Kusu Lormagen's specialists. Including insights into SUMBAA, though what they learned about SUMBAA posed more questions than it answered.

More exciting, they managed to revive the computer from the Garthid fighter. Now if they could learn to communicate with it . . .

Chapter 36
Bad News

The Council of Ministers sat around a great oval table. All of them were Ostrak Alumni. Presiding was His Majesty Marcus XXVIII, King of Iryala and Administrator General of the Confederation of Worlds. His chair was no taller than the others, but it stood on a four-inch platform. The platform dated from the reign of Pertunis, 750 years earlier, and one did not idly change what Iryala's greatest king had established.

Marcus glanced at the clock on the opposite wall, then picked up his small silver wand and tapped a bell in front of him. The clear liquid sound turned on the recording system. He spoke without rising. "This meeting will open with a brief report from the Governor of Special Projects. Lord Kristal?"

The old bureaucrat stood and bowed. "Your Majesty, ministers, guests. You are aware of the Garthid interest in the Karghanik Armada, and that a Garthid fleet emerged from hyperspace in a system the Armada had recently left. This was nine hyperspace deks from here. You are also aware that the Garthids had captured and razed a Karghanik planetary survey base on one of the system's inner worlds, taking its officers prisoner, and stranding its enlisted personnel without equipment or shelter.

"We now know that the Garthids spent only three days in the system. To reform their formations, after nearly a year in hyperspace, required less than a day. One day! The rest of the time was spent on inspections and maintenance.

"They are able to maintain a far better degree of formation in hyperspace than either we or the imperials. Which means they are ready to fight much more quickly than we can after emerging. A counterforce lying somewhere in the far fringe of our system, requiring a warpjump of say ten to thirty hours to reach them, would not catch them unable to defend themselves."

Kristal paused, scanning the faces around the table. All of them reflected a realization of what this meant.

"They should arrive here approximately fifteen days after the Armada. By that time it is likely that a battle between the Armada and our own fleet will be finished or in progress. And whichever side wins, the survivors will be widely dispersed."

Again he paused. "The Armada is our first problem. By the time it arrives, our own fleet will have grown to about seventy percent the Armada's size. And we have certain advantages growing out of remote spying, though how important they will be in actual combat is not clear. The Armada has much better artificial intelligence, but how important that will prove is likewise unclear. One advantage we'll have will be their disarray on emergence, but we don't know where they'll emerge, or how long the warpjump will be to attack them. And of course their disarray after less than a year in hyperspace will be much less than it was after three years.

"At any rate, whether they win or we win becomes academic if the Garthid fleet then attacks the survivors.

"You are aware that the Emeritus Kalif is in our hands. And that he'd hoped to avoid warfare, preferring to colonize an unoccupied world. But Armada command is strongly committed to conquest. Hopefully the next time I speak to you, I'll have a strategy utilizing the Kalif's status and popularity with his people.

"Besides remote spying, our most promising advantage is teleportation. Unfortunately, its utility in space warfare is severely restricted by the topological enigma, and Kusu's people have found no promising approach to solving it. We are highly unlikely to simply gate Special Projects troopers and T'swa into the bridges of Armada battleships. Meanwhile, research and development progresses on other promising applications."

Kristal leaned forward, hands resting on the table, mouth a thin line. "As things stand, we will probably have to fight the Armada. If so, we may win, but if the Garthids then attack, we will be too weakened for any realistic prospect of beating them. Unless, of course, something happens which we do not presently envision. And I regret to say that therein lies our principal hope."

He straightened, sipped water, and scanned his audience.

"Our Remote Spying Section has learned a great deal about the Garthid fleet. We know its commander more intimately than his staff does. We know, for example, that he intends to attack as soon as he arrives. He knows from his prisoners that there are two separate human empires, so to speak, each with a war fleet, but he does not differentiate. His goal is victory, destruction, and political reputation.

"We know of a weakness in his position, but its importance is dubious. The Garthid emperor, whom they call the 'Surrogate of God,' directed his fleet admiral to avoid unnecessary war. He sent the fleet primarily as a show of strength, with orders to learn the disposition and intentions of what the Garthids regard as potentially dangerous trespassers.

"The admiral, however, has no intention of respecting those orders, and he will be two hyperspace years from his sovereign.

"We do have an ally of sorts in his fleet. The Surrogate sent a high-ranking religious to constrain the admiral's known belligerence. The admiral, however, is firmly set on war, and our remote spies assure us he will not be turned from it.

"The Garthid religious is psionically advanced. He knew immediately when our spy entered his mind, and the two—our Filéna Kironu and the Esteemed Valvoxa—have communed. He is satisfied that the Garthid empire has no quarrel with us.

"From early in their voyage, Valvoxa repeatedly and openly scolded the admiral for his defiance of the Surrogate. However, the flagship's officers and crew will obey their admiral, who of course hates Valvoxa for his scoldings.

"During their fleet's brief pause in F-space, Valvoxa visited another battle group, although he knew the admiral would not let him return to the flagship. Questioned by Filéna, Valvoxa would only say that God suggested it, and to have faith.

"Now the shafa, the religious, is on the command ship of that other battle group, with no idea what his next step may be. Filéna tells us that the battle group commander deeply respects Valvoxa, but is loyal to his duty, which is to the fleet admiral. And Valvoxa has not tried to change that. Something may conceivably develop for us there, but so far we cannot see what it might be."

Again Kristal scanned his audience. He did not read auras, but he had no doubt they were less than cheered. *We are not deeply enough in the T'sel,* he told himself. *Our future is too dear to us. We have lost our spiritual neutrality.*

He continued. "If instead of fighting the Armada, we can somehow combine forces with it, it seems likely we'd win against the Garthids. But if we propose alliance to the Armada's admiral, he'll almost certainly leave the system, returning to take over after we and the Garthids have wasted each other."

He inspected his thin hands, then looked at the ministers again. "I wish my report was more cheering. Perhaps my next will be. At any rate we have eight deks to overcome the difficulties and build on our strengths. Some very able people are working on them." He paused. "And as I indicated before, there is serendipity—some fortuitous event or development might yet turn things to our advantage. One does not like to depend on it, but it can be decisive, and we have been blessed by it in the past."

He turned and made a half bow to the king. "And that, Your Majesty, is my report."

He said nothing about emergencies of one sort or another that interrupted, distracted, and diverted resources. Marcus thanked him, and Kristal left the council to their working agenda.

Chapter 37
Playing the Retro Shell Game

Overnight, leaf-fall summer had given way to a series of windy, rainy days that reminded one of the winter to come. They hadn't been as bad on the Basalt Coast as a few hundred miles inland at Landfall, but the tourist season was definitely over.

Still, if you liked stormy seashore weather—bracing winds, heavy surf crashing on dark rock shelves, the ever-skirling gulls . . . Seen from a comfortable vacation home, through a broad window, and framed by wind-twisted "pines," it was really quite beautiful.

Bariss Fildkarm didn't notice. Being there was costing him money, which he could afford but preferred not to. The meeting could as well have been held in Landfall, taking two or three hours out of his evening, not a day out of his business. But Patros had invited them here, and Warley liked the idea. And being part of something this big . . .

Patros himself poured their drinks, the best Cordelan, spiced, and warm but not hot. Fildkarm sipped, felt it warm his upper lip, tongue, throat. Then Patros sat down, looked thoughtfully out the window, and spoke. "We need," he said, "to consider the Founder's Day Executions." Said it as if they were something big, to be written with capitals. Which they needed to be, to be worth the risk.

"We already have one criminal to execute, but one is a bit skimpy for an opportunity like that. After all, Pertunis will only have one 800th birthday. There'll be celebrations around the planet, and major holo and TV coverage at the larger ones." The eyes he turned to Bariss Fildkarm were as ruthless as they were casual.

"Bariss, what can you come up with?"

"I know a cell leader who tells me he can snag us Lady Clianna Wanslo Ostrak, Minister of the Sacrament and Education. She drives herself to her son's home every second Sevenday, unaccompanied. And unlike the Romlar woman, it won't be possible for the government to keep it secret. She's too public. A cabinet minister, widow of an Ostrak, niece of Lord Kristal . . . How symbolic can we get, short of the old man himself? With her in our hands, we could lose the Romlar woman and never miss her."

Patros grunted. "Warley, what about you?"

Warley grinned. Bariss could picture him as a ravo in a poultry yard, licking feathers off his chops. "Would you believe the mayor?"

"Kurssbann?"

"Himself, mayor of Landfall, Mr. Holo, Lord Glad Hand."

"What makes you think we can snag him?"

"His ex-chauffeur. Kurssbann canned him for drinking during duty hours. The guy holds a grudge, and he knows Kurssbann's habits. The routes he prefers, the places he likes to stop at from time to time for a woileipa . . ."

They discussed the prospects only briefly—the apparent reliability of the sources, the prospective snag teams . . . Then Patros decided. "Three of something makes a nice set," he said. "The mayor is the biggest in the public eye, the minister is the most symbolic, and the one we already have in the bag is at the center of the invasion conspiracy. Plus the government has publicized her husband more than anyone since Varlik Lormagen, decades ago.

"We'll do them all—all three in Landfall, in the Arena. There'll be upwards of forty thousand, and I have connections that can make a show of it. We won't be able to kill them publicly, but we can do a good job of, ah, introducing their remains into the festivities." He grinned. "I have ideas on that. It won't be a very long show, but it'll have a lot of shock value.

"And we'll have good professional cubeage of the actual executions. We'll disseminate it ourselves. It'll give the movement a powerful shot in the arm, and show how inept the government is."

He leaned back in his chair, grinning like a wolf.

Warley leaned forward earnestly. "I talked with you-know-who the other day," he said.

Bariss scowled, annoyed. *You may know,* he thought, *but you know damned well I don't. You're cutting me out.*

"He told me the Romlar woman will probably die soon, if they keep drugging her like they have been. She was small to begin with, and she's lost ten pounds or more. Even if she doesn't die, we don't want her looking starved or sick."

Patros pursed his wide, heavy-lipped mouth and let his gaze drift out the window. In the distance two sloops were beating their way across the wind, one headed north, the other south. His frown smoothed while the others watched him.

"Don't worry about it," he said. "It's as good as handled."

Linvo Garlaby had grown increasingly concerned with his failure to get a fix on Lotta's whereabouts. He'd assigned one of his too few qualified apprentices, Marsia Darath, to back up Kari Frensler, so that someone was monitoring Lotta or her nurse almost all the time. His assumption was that one of them would get a fix on someone providing transportation, and find out where to. It was bound to happen sooner or later, unless—and there lay the real concern—unless they killed her.

She'd been moved three times since Kari had learned from her of the Kalif being marooned on Hope. And despite the increased monitoring, no one had been with her during the actual transfers. The odds of that happening by chance were low, and Linvo had begun to wonder if the person at the top somehow knew about the Remote Spying Section. It would explain the care they took to keep not only Lotta but the nurse isolated and ignorant, and Lotta so strongly drugged. But rumors of psi-spies were the sort of thing the retro newsletters would run, and none had.

Currently Lotta was being held in an abandoned mine, ill-lit and ill-ventilated. The same nurse was still with her, and had grown quite unhappy with the moves and the living conditions. Meanwhile she'd reduced the size and frequency of her ward's drug doses. Lotta was now able to think coherently much of the time, and the nurse exercised her by walking her up and down the tunnel outside their chamber. Actually she'd considered walking Lotta to the mine's entrance, for a look at the sky again, and sunlight. But the woman imagined the mine as a maze of tunnels, and feared getting lost.

Lotta was less interested in sun and sky. What she wanted was to attain a cognitive trance again, find out what was happening, and what she might contribute. She didn't anticipate learning the most important information—how she could be found. Others would be handling that, monitoring not only her but her nurse. They'd get a fix on someone who knew.

She also thought about how she might avoid taking her drug. Had it been a capsule or tablet, she might have faked swallowing it; palmed it and gotten rid of it. But as a powder in water . . . There was no way to fake drinking it, or of successfully refusing. Her nurse was too watchful, too large, and too strong, while she herself was weaker than at any time since she was a child. And if she tried something and failed, she'd no doubt be kept more strongly drugged.

❖   ❖   ❖

Marsia Darath had been in one mind or another—Lotta's and the nurse's—for over three hours. Approaching her limit. The nurse had given Lotta her daily redose, and Lotta had gone to sleep. Finally the nurse had set aside her book, turned out the GGP lamp, and gone to bed herself.

Marsia withdrew from her trance. Both Lotta and the nurse were asleep. It was a chance for a snack and a short nap. She went to the snack room, and got an egg salad sandwich and glass of milk from the night attendant. When she'd eaten, she set her alarm clock for one hour, lay down, and went to sleep at once.

What she'd forgotten was to arm the alarm after she set it. Four hours later she awoke to Kari shaking her.

Kari had found Lotta in a deeply drugged sleep, and knew at once what it meant. She'd been given the heavy dosage she was always given for transport. This might be their break. At once she reached for the nurse—and couldn't find her. Couldn't find her awake, couldn't find her asleep. After a minute, Kari withdrew from her trance. The only explanation she could think of was, the nurse was dead. Murdered. What that meant for Lotta, she couldn't imagine, but it seemed to her the situation had worsened.

The floater settled out of a thick drizzle and landed on a wharf. A man jumped out and trotted through the rain and smell of seaweed to a sloop tied there. Another man peered at him from beneath an awning.

"Took you long enough," the boatman said. "I had the damned radio beacon on for more than an hour."

"Nurse wasn't ready," the flyer answered laconically. "Bring 'em aboard?"

"Hell yes! I want to be long gone by daylight."

The flyer turned and jogged back to the floater. A minute later he reappeared with a small body over one shoulder. A woman followed him, complaining because he hadn't provided a rain cape. Her hair, she said, would be a mess in the morning.

Lady, he thought, *what's wrong with your head isn't your hair.* But he didn't waste his breath saying it aloud.

Chapter 38
Sun Up and Sun Down

Lotta awoke to what was obviously the slow heavy movement of a small boat on a moderate swell. She looked around her. Whatever she'd been dosed with wasn't what she was used to. She could see clearly, and think, even now, newly awake. She was alone in a cabin with an overhead too low for a tall man to walk upright. At one end was a companionway open to sunlight and the deck. At the other was a door that might lead to the head.

She undertook to sit up, and found one ankle shackled to the suspension chain at the foot of her bunk. Sitting up required gaining slack by scootching down to the foot. There she could not only sit, but stand. But she couldn't go anywhere, and she needed to go to the head.

So she called the name of her nurse, as loudly as she could. "Elmy! Elmy! I need help!"

Elmy didn't come, and after a minute she called again. A man's voice answered. "Just a damn minute!"

While she waited, she looked around again. There were four bunks, two on each side. Two were folded against the cabin wall. Another, diagonally across from hers, was rumpled, the bedding partly on the wooden deck. On one side, the bunks were separated by a cabinet with a small food-prep unit. Opposite it, a similar counter had a small sink. After two or three minutes, a disheveled young woman came in from outside, looking grim and pale. She was not Elmy. Not nearly. She was perhaps three inches taller than Lotta, twenty pounds heavier than Lotta's usual weight, and in her early twenties. *And seasick*, Lotta thought.

"I need to go to the head," Lotta said.

"To the what?"

"To the bathroom. On boats they call them heads."

The young woman gnawed her lower lip. "I'm not supposed to let you loose."

"If you don't let me loose, this place is going to smell pretty bad before long."

It took the young woman several more seconds to decide. From a locker she took a small case. Opening it, she dumped vials and small bottles on the food-prep counter, and poked among them. "Shit!" she muttered, and looked at Lotta. "Do you know what any of these are?"

"Me? I don't know anything about them. What are they supposed to be?"

"Drugs. Medicine. Stuff to give you."

"And you don't know what they are? Is there a book with them?"

The young woman peered inside the case again. A pocket in the lid held a thin book. She took it out and opened it. Thumbing through it, she looked alternately at labels on containers and pages in the book. This, Lotta thought, was not reassuring. Finally the young woman laid the open book face down and read the directions on one of the bottles.

"Is that the one?" Lotta asked.

"I think so. Seems like it."

"What does it say?"

The young woman didn't answer. She found a set of miniature measuring spoons among the bottles, and peered at them. Then she took a plastic tumbler from a rack above the table, put a scoop of powder in it, and added water.

"Are you a nurse?"

"Sort of. I've been working for a clinic, and they've been training me to do stuff."

"What kind of clinic?"

"Dogs and cats."

"Dogs and cats?"

"But I've been going to bed with a real doctor. And his wife found out. The bitch. She went to the clinic and got me fired. So Murl, my real boyfriend, sent me on this job his sister was supposed to get. She got arrested for something, so he sent me. Now I'm going by her name. Call me Rahz. This stuff is hers." She gestured at the litter of bottles on the table. "Murl said she got it together for this job."

"Here," she said, and picked up the tumbler. "Drink it. Then I'll let you loose."

Lotta looked dubiously at the concoction. "If this kills me, the people who kidnapped me will take it out on you. You'll wish you'd drunk it instead of me."

Rahz seemed not to care. "Drink it," she said. "Then I'll take you to the bathroom."

Lotta looked again at the drink, then downed it. It didn't taste too bad. A bit like joma whitener. "How often do I take it?" she asked.

"Twice a day." Rahz took a key out of her pocket and unlocked the padlock on Lotta's chain.

Lotta swung her legs out of bed and got unsteadily to her feet. "Where are we?" she asked.

"I don't know. What's the difference?"

Rahz walked her to the head and waited outside. By the time Lotta had finished, the new drug was beginning to act. She could see, blurrily, but her thoughts were in slow motion, ponderous. She clung to a stanchion while Rahz vomited thinly into the toilet. Then, with Rahz's help, she made it back to her bunk. Rahz chained her and left the cabin.

❖   ❖   ❖

After missing the move from the mine, Kari Frensler had promptly made some changes. She asked for and got a second apprentice, a sixteen-year-old named Jarlis. He was inexperienced, and in an active mind might have difficulty dealing with the flows, especially the subtler ones. Thus Kari assigned him to monitor Lotta, with instructions to withdraw and let her know if his subject became mentally active. She also had them move their trance cushions to her own small trance room.

Lotta, when she wasn't asleep, lay in an odd sort of stupor, vaguely, sluggishly aware but unresponsive. With the new drug, she went to sleep quickly, and when she awoke, it was gradual. This gave Jarlis time to sleep and eat.

Kari had stayed in Rahz's mind no longer than it took to get a fix on Murfy. He was the owner-master of the sloop, and its one-man crew. He'd know where they were, at least approximately. And sooner or later he'd betray it in a thought.

Rahz became Marsia's responsibility, an assignment she did not enjoy. They'd left the broad continental shelf behind, along with the swell that characterized it in that season, and Rahz was no longer actively seasick. But even in the slight seas, the "nurse" was queasy, and Marsia didn't like the feeling. It became apparent that Rahz was little given to curiosity and wondering, or to the kinds of thinking from which something might be learned. But Marsia was not about to err as she had before. She'd allow herself no slack.

Murfy was a rough, big-shouldered man, also with a mind unproductive of information. For him, Kari discovered, sailing was more than a hobby or even a love. It was an addiction. In the relatively calm seas they were experiencing, with light favorable winds, he could have lowered his sail, locked the helm, and spent much of his time reading and napping, relying on his experienced senses to tell him when his attention was needed. But he preferred to stay at the helm most of the time, riding the breeze instead of the engine. The light seas, the movement of the sloop on the waves, sun flashing on the water, slowed his brain waves to a deep and comfortable alpha, a sort of trance. A couple of naps provided all the rest he needed.

Kari knew a bit about that. She'd spent nine years as an Ostrak operator at Sandhills, on Rombil. It was an oceanside location, and her principal pastime had been sailing. Sometimes alone on one of the staff's small, sloop-rigged dinghies, and sometimes as crew on their auxiliary sloop. It had been more graceful and carried more sail than Murfy's, but had a smaller hull and cabin, and the helm in the stern. Murfy's was built for serious voyaging, with a storage hold.

Kari's problem with Murfy was he thought very little about anything. Even when Rahz stood by him and tried to make conversation, he scarcely responded. By the end of the second day she'd quit trying.

Marsia, monitoring Rahz's mind, knew intimately what the woman was thinking about. Rahz was horny, and Murfy the only man for Yomal knew how many miles. She wondered what he'd do if she groped him, but didn't try. He might get angry.

It was evening. The late sun no longer entered the cabin door to brighten the narrow, hardwood aisle between its bunks. Vaguely Lotta realized it was twilight. Rahz would drug her again soon. She had the impression that the bogus nurse napped on deck much of the day.

Rahz came into the cabin but did not open her drug kit. Instead she stripped off her clothes and tossed them on the foot of Lotta's bunk. Then she curled naked on her side, facing the ship's side, waiting. After half an hour, she fell asleep.

Lotta, on the other hand, grew gradually less sluggish mentally, though physically she was half paralyzed. She felt neither hunger nor thirst, and it seemed to her, her pulse would be about twelve or fifteen per minute. A thought surfaced: the drug might be the one used to prepare long-haul space travelers for stasis treatment.

Eventually Murfy entered the cabin, which now was lit only by a tube. His eyes fell on the naked Rahz, examined her slender waist, her rounded haunches. He felt the pressure of his swelling penis. After a moment he put a hand on her shoulder.

"You awake?"

She half turned. "Oh! Murfy! Yes, I'm awake."

His eyes settled briefly on her round breasts, then slid down her belly to her groin. "You want company?" he asked.

"I—I could stand some company, yes. What about you?"

He glanced back at Lotta, then turned to Rahz again. "She's laying there with her eyes wide open. You want to put her to sleep first?"

Rahz chuckled. "She'll be all right. She needs a little spectacle in her life." She watched avidly while the skipper pulled off his shirt, then his jeans. He wore no underwear. Kneeling beside her narrow bunk, he began to kiss and fondle her. She was ready more quickly than either had expected.

When Murfy went to his own bunk, he fell quickly asleep, and Kari vacated his mind. She found Marsia also back with her own body: Rahz was asleep, too. Jarlis still sat upright in a lotus. The two young women looked at each other and laughed softly. Marsia's eyes were bright, her color strong. She too was only sixteen.

"Did you ever have anything like that happen before?" she asked.

"Not in trance. And in this lifetime, never from the male point of view. It was interesting. Stimulating." Briefly she thought of calling her husband, and asking him to come over. They could use one of the stayover rooms.

She'd eat first, she decided, then check on Murfy again to be sure he was still sleeping. And on Jarlis to see if he was still in trance.

"Get some sleep," she told Marsia. "I'll probably have you monitor Murfy awhile tomorrow, and give me a break. I don't want him unattended while he's awake."

After she'd eaten, she checked on the sleeping Murfy and Rahz, and on Jarlis in his trance. Then she did call her husband.

It was late at night when Rahz awakened to someone speaking her name. The light was still on, turned very low. The voice was Lotta's. She needed to be helped to the head.

Rahz got up resentfully. She'd forgotten to drug the woman. Twice a day was probably too often to drug someone anyway. She'd try drugging her just once a day, late, right after a bathroom trip, and see how much she recovered in twenty-four hours. Maybe she wouldn't have to be half carried.

On the third and fourth days the air was almost dead calm. The sloop ran on its auxiliary engine, and the swell was hardly noticeable. Rahz, no longer sick but increasingly bored, enticed Murfy twice a day. He responded well, despite his forty-some years. They had each other on a mattress on deck, in the sun and under the stars. On the fourth day she reduced the strength of Lotta's drug dose. That way she might eat a little more, and what harm could she do, chained to a stanchion?

In monitoring Murfy's mind, Kari hadn't learned a thing about the boat's location. It was somewhere on a very large ocean, probably the western. The subtropics or warm temperate zone; it was warm for so late in the year. Twice, through Murfy's eyes, she'd seen sails, once of a two-masted schooner, once of a sloop more or less like his own. On Iryala, sailing was a popular pastime for the wealthy, and there were more than a few people like Murfy, not wealthy, who'd retired early to more or less live on their boat. After four days, she still didn't know if he had a home somewhere.

Before dawn on the fifth day, the weather changed. Murfy had seen signs of it the previous evening. First the wind picked up, waking him. He'd been running on the auxiliary, and as always, before sleeping, he'd locked the helm. Getting up, he pulled on jeans, went out, and took the wheel. Within minutes he heard Rahz puking her guts out in the cabin. Damn but he hated people who did that!

The wind grew. He went below, put on weather gear, and rousted Rahz out onto the deck. She wore only a shirt, which scarcely covered her butt, but now she seemed not at all sexy. He closed the door behind her. "Stay here on deck," he ordered. "The air will do you good."

She lay on the mattress they'd had sex on the day before. The air did *not* do her good, not even the occasional spray that came with the wind. Wet, she shivered. And moaned. She was too sick to actively complain. The seas grew, and by 1000 hours it began to rain. When Rahz begged to go back into the cabin, he told her not while she was sick. If she needed to be inside, she could go around to the engine room, a compartment on the aft end of the cabin. She went, and when a lurch threw her off her feet, crawled the last few yards, wishing she were dead. Opening the door, she entered a six-by-eight-foot compartment half full of machinery, the overhead perhaps sixty inches high.

It held two things Murfy hadn't mentioned: a thin, rolled-up bunk mattress, and at one side a toilet. She was too sick to feel grateful for the amenities. She simply turned on the light tube and closed the door against the storm. Then she knelt at the toilet to pray, and retch thin green liquid, before lying miserably on the mattress.

She never thought once about Lotta.

Lotta awoke from a period of alternate awareness and dozing. Her mind was still sluggish. A bad smell registered, but she neither identified nor wondered about it. The tiny cabin windows told her it was night. She had not, she realized, been drugged the day before.

She found she could sit up by herself. On the foot of Lotta's bed were Rahz's jeans. Exploring the pockets, she found the key to her padlock, and removed her chain. Then, shaking with weakness, she got up and made her uncertain way to the head, crouching against the sloop's movements.

After using the head, she opened the food locker. Lacking energy, she simply munched hardtack, and drank fruit juice from a bottle. Her mental function began to improve, as if food and activity helped. She identified the smell now: stale vomit. It occurred to her to wonder where Rahz was, and when he might come back. Perhaps to administer the drug again. The time readout on the food-prep unit said 0023. A little after midnight. There was a mirror above the sink. She peered into it, and was not reassured.

Rahz was probably on deck, moaning and puking. It was time, she told herself, to do something about her situation. The first time the drug had been administered, she'd been functional enough, she'd seen what the bottle looked like. After turning up the light tube a little, she opened Rahz's kit, found the bottle, and looked at the white powder inside. Taking it to the head, she flushed the contents down the toilet. Then, in the food locker, she found a passable substitute, a box of powdered sugar, and from it refilled the bottle to about where it had been.

So far, so good, except that she was shaky. She looked the area over, and doubted that Rahz would notice anything amiss. Sitting on her bunk, she locked her chain back on, put the key under her pillow, and lay down. Sleep took her quickly.

It was gray morning when Lotta next awoke. The skipper had come in and was taking off his weather gear. Then he went down the aisle to the head. Rahz was still missing. Lotta closed her eyes again, wondering if something had happened to the girl. She was consciously aware now of the seas, not storm seas, but for the sloop, moderately heavy. Rahz would be seasick, no doubt about it. After several minutes, Murfy came out of the head. She closed her eyes, heard him pull his weather gear back on and leave.

After a few minutes she used the head, then ate again. This time a container of canned fruit, a small tin of fish, and a large square of hardtack slathered with butter. The refuse she put in the container beneath the little sink. She wished she dared clean up the old vomit, but that would draw notice. Finally she chained herself again, lay down and closed her eyes.

She hadn't had time to go to sleep before Murfy reentered, frog-marching a weeping Rahz ahead of him. "Now," he snarled, "clean up your damned puke! It stinks!" Lotta could hear activity, sniveling, and a couple of times retching. It seemed to her that Murfy would also tell Rahz to help their prisoner to the head, and Rahz wouldn't find the key. But nothing more was said. When they left, Lotta sat up again and unlocked her chain. She'd leave it that way. Better have each of them think the other had left it unlocked than to wonder where the key was.

Again she'd scarcely lain down when the cabin door opened. Seconds later she felt a strong hand on her ankle. "Huh!" he muttered. "That frigging Rahz didn't even keep her chained." He put a hand on Lotta's shoulder, shaking it. "Wake up!" he said. "Come on! Wake up! That shut-down she gave you won't work forever. Sooner or later you'll have to piss, at least. Let's get you to the head."

She allowed herself to be helped, went into the head and relieved herself. When she was done, she staggered out, staring at Murfy with eyes deliberately vague.

"Girl," he said, "you're okay. You're tough. Let's see if I can mix you a dose of that stuff." He took her back to her bunk, then opened the drug kit. She avoided watching him. The duller, less alert she seemed, the better. She knew he'd gotten the right bottle as soon as she tasted it.

When he left, he left her unchained, presumably because he didn't have the key. And after all, what could she do, weak and drugged?

We'll come up with something, she told herself.

Lotta awoke again four hours later. The weather was worse, the sloop rising, nosing down, lifting again. She wondered if they were in any danger. She also wondered if Murfy would leave the helm in weather like this. She supposed he'd have to, sooner or later. Getting off her bunk, she did a few light exercises, swinging her arms while marching in place, doing a few trunk twists, a few quarter squats. About two minutes' worth, grabbing a stanchion as necessary to balance against the sloop's pitching. It left her winded and light-headed, but feeling better.

Then she drank some juice, shut herself into the head, and sitting upright on the toilet, tried her trance mantra. She wasn't surprised when nothing happened. Afterward she ate again, a bit more than before, this time eating cheese with her hardtack. It seemed to her she needed the protein. After eating, she exercised again, drank more juice, and lay back down. This time it took her longer to go to sleep. She wondered how long it would take Murfy to notice that someone besides himself was eating.

But she refused to worry about something she couldn't do anything about.

She opened her eyes to sunlight through the cabin's small windows. The clock read almost noon, and it seemed to her the boat wasn't pitching as much. Again she got up, used the head, and tested her trance mantra unsuccessfully. Washed, exercised, ate and lay back down. She repeated this routine every four to six hours through that day and the following night, extending the exercises a bit, feeling considerably better. Stronger. She did not see or hear Rahz.

The next day Murfy wakened her, supported her to the head, and gave her another dose of powdered sugar. She wondered where they were going. Perhaps, she thought, he was simply sailing around, waiting for further orders.

The next morning the boat's movements were considerably less. Again it was Murfy who wakened her, this time his hand fondling inside her shorts. She stared blankly at him, and lay as limp and flaccid as she could. Frowning, he withdrew his hand and left the cabin, leaving his weather gear on a bunk.

After a few minutes she got up, went to the head and shut herself in, bolting the door. Seating herself on the toilet lid, she tried her mantra again, still unsuccessfully. She repeated her exercise-and-eat sequence, then looked into the small mirror above the sink. She looked better. *I wonder if Murfy noticed,* she thought. *That might account for the frown.* Frowning herself, she lay back down, and after a while, slept again.

At midday she awoke and repeated the sequence. After she lay back down, she thought for a while, gazing backward in time at something she remembered, a dream before she was kidnapped. A Garthid dream. It seemed to her she'd redreamt it that morning.

She slept again.

✧   ✧   ✧

It was evening when next she awoke. After eating, she went to the head with a sense that this time the mantra would work. And of having a target, though she had no idea who or where. She recited the words. The result, though predictable, took her by surprise.

«Hello, Lotta! We've been waiting for this! Wait till I tell Kari! She'll be jumping up and down! And wait till Artus hears about it!»

Lotta recognized the psyche at once, and began to shake physically, almost violently. *Interesting reaction,* she thought. «Hello, Marsia. Nobody's happier about it than I am. Is Kari covering Murfy?»

«I'm pretty sure she is. Shall I check? She knows you're getting well. When you're asleep, I cross-jump to her, in Murfy's head, then we both withdraw and I debrief to her.»

«What has she learned? About where I am and what's going on.»

«Hardly anything. Murfy's one of those people who doesn't think much about things. He just does them. He has a nav station and radio at the helm, but he doesn't use them. Kari says he navigates by the stars when they're out, and dead-reckoning when they're not. He's bound to check sooner or later though.»

«Where's Rahz?»

«She stays in the engine compartment. She's been seasick for days. Really miserable, according to Jarlis. She can't eat, can't even keep water down! Jarlis monitors her. He's new since you left.» Pause. «What are you going to do about Murfy?»

«You'll know when I know. Look. You can go outcom, can't you?»

She got a sense of confirmation.

«Good. I have things to do, and I can't do them with you occupying any of my attention. Okay?»

A sense of confirmation again.

«That's it then. Have fun.»

❖   ❖   ❖

When next she awoke, she knew exactly what she was going to do. At the front of the cabin were two metal lockers, one on each side. She turned up the light tube, then went to them. The larger held weather gear and life jackets. The smaller was locked, but its construction was light. Beneath it was a wide drawer. Opening it, she found tools, and took out a thirty-inch wrecking bar, the sort of thing used to pull nails, and to pry boards from timbers.

Taking a deep breath, she inserted one end between the door and its rim, next to a hinge, then threw her small weight against it as hard as she could. Given the leverage and her desperation, the hinge separated with a screech, and the upper part of the door pulled away from the locker. Inside were guns. She reached inside, took out a shoulder weapon, and stepped back, away from the entry, pointing the weapon toward it. At the top of the stairs the door opened, as she knew it would, and she saw Murfy's feet coming down the steps. At the bottom, he ducked his head to enter, and stepped in. Stared, took a forward step. Time slowed, almost stopped. Lotta squeezed the trigger, and nothing happened. Murfy began a slow-motion lunge. There was a lever above the trigger guard. She pressed it with her thumb and pulled the trigger again. The weapon roared, a deep, slow, hollow sound, and bucked slowly but powerfully. Murfy's eyes widened and his jaw began to drop. Still in slow motion, his body struck hers, knocking her backward onto the deck. He fell on her and did not move. With an effort, she freed herself.

His blood was all over her shirt and shorts. The back of his shirt was soaked with it. Pulling his shirt up, she found a large messy exit hole in his back. She'd shot him through the heart; through the chest at least.

It took her several minutes and all the strength she could muster, to drag him up the four steps and onto the main deck. Once there it was less difficult. She pulled him aft to the fantail, then plopped down on the deck, panting and sweating in the cool night. He'd left a smear of blood all the way.

Two things were obvious. No one would learn her location from Murfy. And she was now on her own. She returned to the cabin, Murfy's blood sticky on her bare feet. From the storage space below Rahz's bunk, she dug a pair of jeans and a shirt. With a utility knife from the tool drawer, she cut a few inches from the sleeves and legs. The jeans were too loose, so she put a tuck in the waist with a heavy stapler.

«Marsia,» she thought, «are you okay?»

«Yes.» Lotta got a sense of the girl's admiration.

«How's Kari?»

«I'll check.»

«Just a minute. She may be unconscious or in shock. If she's all right, have her join us. She'll be able to coach me on the helm. I know nothing about it. I've never been out of the cabin till now. Never even been on a boat like this before.»

Kari was all right. With Murfy, she'd seen Lotta's eyes, neither drugged nor frightened, only resolved. She'd ditched in time. Kari stayed with Lotta, and had Marsia relieve Jarlis. He'd been in Rahz's mind for four seasick hours since his last break.

All three moons were down, the night clear and starlit, the seas moderate, breeze brisk. The helm was locked, holding the sloop into the wind. Coached by Kari, Lotta freed it and briefly handled the wheel herself, getting some feel for it. Moving through the seas, its engine set midway between half and full speed, the sloop responded like a living thing.

Just then it seemed there was nothing she really needed to do. Not then. *But in the morning . . .* she told herself.

On both wheel and nav station was the name *Sea Maid*. After locking the helm again, she went back to the stern and looked in on Rahz. The engine compartment stank of her, and in the light from the tube she was as dull-eyed as Lotta had been. Her face looked worse. *Dehydration,* Lotta thought. "Hang tough," she told her. "Murfy's dead. I'll head for the first land I see, and we'll get off this tub."

She left her there. She'd heard about people who were highly susceptible to seasickness. Being that sick, Rahz was as well off in the engine compartment as anywhere else on board.

There was a mattress draped over the boom, but it was wet. From spray when the weather was rougher, Lotta supposed, or maybe rain. Returning to the cabin, she dragged another out on deck, handy to the nav station. After giving wake-up instructions to her subconscious, she lay down and went to sleep undrugged.

It was the sloop that wakened her, rolling a bit now, and pitching more strongly. The wind had stiffened. Taking the helm, she turned the *Sea Maid* fully into the seas again, and for a while steered manually, gaining more feel of the helm. It was still night. The chronometer read 0512. She didn't know if that was the time where they were, or the time they'd come from. Didn't know whether the chronometer was controlled by the matrix, or had to be set manually. By the matrix, she thought. Hoped.

She went into the cabin, used the head, then ate. When she came back out, dawn had paled the sky. «Are you there, Kari?» she asked. «Are you ready?»

«Ready.»

In the west, clouds had appeared. To Lotta they seemed ominous. The sky grew lighter, the clouds nearer. *Just hold off till the sun's up,* she told them. The upper edge of the sun appeared, a molten bead on the horizon, and Lotta read the chronometer.

«Did you get that, Kari?» she asked.

«I got it. That's pretty smart.»

«Let's hope it works.»

Then, squinting through a single pair of eyes, the two young women watched the sun rise.

The seas grew. After a bit, the helm was taking spray. Lotta dragged the mattress back into the cabin and put on weather gear. In the pockets of the storm coat, she put a wedge of cheese, a sausage, and a package of storm bread.

Showers came and went, the waves grew, and at Kari's urging she took the helm herself. By afternoon she'd learned what a storm was. Not a big storm, but a storm. From time to time the sun shown through gaps of blue, but the sky did not clear, nor the wind fall. She got tired enough physically, she locked the helm and went below to eat, then lay down and rested without going to sleep.

After a bit the sloop began to pitch more strongly. Getting up, she tied on a life jacket, then put the storm coat back on. She opened the cabin door just as a wave crashed over the bow, and water rushed round her ankles and calves, into the cabin. The bow rose again, and she got out, closing the door behind her.

In late afternoon the sky partially cleared and the wind dropped a bit, but the seas continued to run high. Lotta locked the helm again, went below and used the head. She wondered how Rahz was surviving. When she came out, there was a sizable area of blue in the west. The sun was low, almost in her eyes.

At the helm again she asked, «Are you there, Kari?»

«I'm here, Lotta.»

Together they watched it lower, lower, while the area of blue enlarged. The sun touched the horizon. The pitching made it impossible to be exact, but when she completely lost sight of it below the horizon, she read the chronometer.

«We did it, Kari,» she thought.

«You did it,» Kari corrected, then withdrew and

informed the Coast Guard of the second chronometer reading. It would tell them the approximate longitude, and the time between sunup and sundown would tell them the approximate latitude. Given that the readings were not precise, and that the *Sea Maid* continued to push westward, they did not provide an accurate location. Corrections would be made, based on estimates of wind and the sloop's speed, but they were approximate too.

Still, there was now a relatively small area of ocean to search.

The clouds lessened till only a scattered few remained. Stars invaded from the east, driving dusk before it, till the Galactic Wheel made a broad white swath across the sky. Lotta didn't know the constellations. It would, she thought, be worthwhile learning the stars just for the pleasure of it. Perhaps after the war . . . She wondered how long it would take to be found and rescued. Surely they'd arrive before dawn.

Before long, clouds increased again, and took over. The wind shifted and the seas rose. Again it rained, this time continuously and hard, with lightning and thunder. Wave after wave broke over the bow, the *Sea Maid* staggering, shuddering. Lotta stood with her knees slightly flexed, shifting her weight constantly against the sloop's movement. She dared not leave the helm. By midnight she was tired beyond imagining, but still stood with the wheel in her hands.

A wave larger than any before it tore her free from the helm, miraculously depositing her against the cabin. She was not injured, and scrambled toward the helm again. The sloop began to swing broadside of the waves. She knew nothing of handling the helm in such a situation. The vessel rose sideways onto a wave, heeling far over. Her mast was horizontal now, and broke as the hull reached the crest. Freed of the deadly leverage, the hull recovered partly, and slid sideways into the trough.

In falling, the mast had kicked backward and lay across the sloop, somewhat forward of the helm, still partly anchored by lines, its outer end in the water. Lotta, physically small, weakened by captivity and drugging, exhausted by hours at the helm, crossed the tilted deck to a fire axe. Releasing it from its fastenings, she assaulted the ropes that held the fallen mast, cutting them all except the jib halyard, somehow not going overboard herself, despite the sloop's wallowing, and no hand to hold on with. Then, becoming aware of the uncut jib halyard, she cut it. She almost went overboard as the sloop rose sideways on another steep wave, let go the axe and grabbed the safety line. As the sloop righted itself, she scrabbled on all fours, reached the helm and held on. They started down into the next trough, the wave lifting the mast, floating its upper end and drawing it partly off the sloop. The next wave freed it, and the hull recovered further.

Somehow during the passage of several more waves, she turned the sloop into the seas again. The imminent danger of capsizing was over, but now she took seas over the bow. The stress of the mast, first horizontal, then breaking, had breached the deck, and with each trough the craft dove into, the hull took water. This activated the pump, but little by little the *Sea Maid* rode lower.

Time became a blur, not from any drug now, but exhaustion and an overload of danger. Kari now chanced distracting her. «Lotta! Lotta, rescue floaters are quartering the area. Hang on, dear. They'll find you.»

Lotta made no explicit reply, but Kari read her awareness and relief. Lotta became aware that dawn had paled the sky, found she could see for miles. The wind had died somewhat, but the seas were still large.

Abruptly the sloop grew sluggish in the waves, losing steerageway. Lotta realized that the engine had stopped. In a crouch she scrambled to the stern, to the engine compartment. The movements of the storm-tossed ship, and perhaps Rahz herself, had jammed her body between the toilet and a wall. Lotta shouted at her, kicked her, threatened her, but Rahz would not move, beyond wrapping her arms around the toilet.

Lotta left her like that, leaving the compartment door open, and still in a crouch, worked her way forward toward the cabin door, to get a life jacket for the girl. The sloop was dead in the water now.

She'd reached the cabin door and was pulling it open when she heard, "Ahoy the sloop! Ahoy the sloop!" from a bull horn. She looked up, saw a Coast Guard rescue floater overhead. At almost the same time, the *Sea Maid* rose sideways on an exceptional wave and heeled far over. Lotta lost her footing, missed her grab at the safety line, and went overboard.

Well shit! she thought, and surfacing, looked around. The sloop had not capsized, but lay in a trough, heeled on its side. Water poured into the *Sea Maid*'s wounds and the open cabin. Then the vessel rose on another wave and disappeared over its crest. The next time Lotta saw it, it was upright again but nearly awash.

A coast guardsman was suspended beneath the floater on a line, and a spare harness hung below him. While Lotta looked upward, the pilot maneuvered, trying to get the seaman into position above her. She raised her arms. As the next wave lifted her, the man was waist-deep in the water beside her. He got the harness around her and snapped the connector. A moment later she felt herself raised from the water, hoisted upward. She looked down at the hulk below, settling into the next trough. When it bottomed out, it was down somewhat at the bow, only the cabin roof and fantail were out of the water. She could see the open door of the engine compartment, and the water inside.

Rahz, she thought, *may your next life be sweeter than this one.*

Then hands grasped her, and she was pulled into the floater.

Chapter 39
Kalifal Adjustments

Coso Biilathkamoro had begun the task of learning about the Confederation—an empire, really—that he found himself in. No one had asked him to do anything yet, but there'd been a reason for the effort and risk they'd invested in his rescue.

A young bureaucrat had been assigned as his liaison, had helped him and the kalifa settle into their apartment, and introduced him to its computer. It fell far short of SUMBAA, but it nonetheless provided so much information, he hardly knew where to start. His solution was to call up the history of the Confederation, and he'd begun reading the opening syllabus. The main text would give him a much fuller view, while the hypertext would provide whatever elaboration he wanted.

The same young man had also given him a language cube, which was proving useful in helping him over and around the holes in his vocabulary. All in all, Coso's reading rate in Confederation Standard wasn't a fourth his rate with Imperial. Page by page, though, he was improving.

So far he'd hardly touched the hypertext, except to follow up a brief and cryptic comment on sources. It had not been reassuring. The millennia prior to the rule of an Emperor Amberus were known almost solely from an outside culture called the T'swa, whose knowledge came

259

from seers! Still, their account was coherent, and had the
feel of reality. He would, he supposed, have to learn more
about them. But for now he kept his focus on the history.

It was after dark when the door announced a visitor—
in Standard: the apartment didn't know Imperial. "Your
Eminence, a Captain Jerym Alsnor to see you. Do you
wish to receive him?" A side panel had formed on the
wall screen, showing a young man in uniform. The
Emeritus Kalif's guts tightened a bit.

"Just a moment." Still hobbling, Coso walked to the
door and opened it. "Good evening, Captain Alsnor,"
he said. "What has brought you here?" His accent was
mild, his greeting somewhat stiff and cautious.

Jerym's smile was polite. "I have tomorrow off, and
I'd like to take you and your family to visit the Landfall
Zoological Park. It's got species from worlds uninhabitable
by humans, in replica environments contained by force
fields. Even the grav fields are matched. Later, if you'd
like, you can call the park menu from your living room,
and watch cubeage of the animals in their native habitats."

Coso Biilathkamoro regarded Jerym with careful
neutrality, then took the young man's coat, hung it up,
and led him into the living room. After seating him, he
switched off the wall screen. "That is generous of you,"
he said. "The kalifa and our son are at a birthday party.
One of Lord Kristal's great-grandchildren." He paused.
"Would you care for refreshment?"

"That would be nice, thank you."

"What would you like? I am not yet familiar with the
service menu, but . . ."

"Any non-intoxicant would be fine."

After checking the menu on the bar screen, Coso ran
two of something he knew and had on hand, giving one
to Jerym. Then he sat down facing him, near enough to
watch the young man's eyes.

"Jerym," he said thoughtfully. "Is that a common name
here?"

An odd question, Jerym thought. "Not really."

"From something you said when you arrived at our door on Hope, I believe you knew my wife from—before."

"Yes, I did. My sister Lotta was a close friend of Tain's. During the war on Terfreya. They shared a tent in our base camp."

"My wife has told me about Lotta. Recently. Since she regained her memories. Tain dreamed of your sister often. Lotta was her one connection with her past during Tain's long—" He paused, searching for the word.

"Absence?" Jerym suggested.

"You are generous. I was about to say captivity."

"We consider her captivity to have ended with her marriage," Jerym replied. "From that point, she was where she wanted to be."

The smaller man, jet-eyed, swarthy, blue-jawed, regarded his guest calmly. "That was my hope. By that time I was her captive." He paused. "I don't know how much you know of her captivity. Or how you know it. Tain insists that Lotta has mental powers well beyond the ordinary. She believes literally that Lotta visited her in dreams. Healing dreams."

"In dreams and at other times," Jerym said, "but Tain wouldn't know about the other times. Lotta felt concern for her. We all did."

"Ah. Before her captivity, you were also close to Tain then?"

"Eventually. Our situations and viewpoints were very different. Tain was a journalist, and I was a young platoon leader, newly turned eighteen years. I don't know what that would equate to in imperial years. An age at which I had nearly completed my height growth. In the civilian world I would have been regarded as still adolescent."

"Ah."

"Tain was several years older. Our regiment was experimental, a new military concept in our culture. Central News had assigned her to describe its training, here on Iryala. She spent a lot of time with my platoon, learning what we did and how. I'm afraid she found us hard to understand and accept. Then she stowed away in a troop carrier that was gated to the trade world Terfreya. An ex-resource world, reclassified when its gold mines became uneconomical. Your Klestronu marines had captured the administrative center—the only real town—established a base, and undertaken to control the nearby agricultural districts. Our mission was to drive them off."

"Which you did decisively, if at some cost. The Klestroni were shocked at how skillfully and fearlessly you fought." The Kalif did not correct "your Klestronu marines." In the context of the young officer's account, that would be quibbling.

Jerym nodded. "But Tain wasn't prepared for the gate," he went on. "She'd have died if Lotta hadn't been there to treat her. That was the beginning of their closeness. On Terfreya, Tain and I came to know one another much better than we had. Mine was the colonel's special missions platoon, used frequently on raids, and therefore of particular interest to her. Artus seldom allowed her to go with us though. The risk was too great, and she was our only journalist.

"Even so, whenever she could, she put herself into combat situations. Finally a floater she was riding in was shot down."

His eyes found the Kalif's. "From there, you know the story."

"Yes, from there I do." *And now the earlier story as well. You both were young and attracted to each other. And you in particular were likely to die any day. Well.* "I thank you for your invitation," Coso said. "I will speak with Tain about it when she comes home. We will call you with our decision."

Jerym jotted down his comm code for the Kalif, and handed it to him.

"One more question," the Kalif said. "How do you and

your men pass through the, um, gate, without the horrible effects suffered by my family and me?"

"We underwent a series of procedures called Ostrak Processing. Years ago, near the beginning of our training."

"Ostrak Processing." The Kalif sounded it out carefully. "What is that?"

Jerym's answer was almost too casual. "It's a form of mental preparation. That varies with the individual."

Coso let it go at that. Then Jerym finished his drink and left, leaving Coso with his thoughts, and a page of Confederation history on the wall screen.

Tain and Rami arrived home half an hour later. Coso said nothing of his guest till they'd put Rami to bed. Then he and Tain sat across from each other at a small table, each with a brandy.

"Jerym was here while you were gone," he told her. "He offered to take us to the Zoological Park."

"What did you tell him?"

"I told him I'd talk with you about it, and we'd call him with our decision. Shall we go?"

"Definitely. Rami will love it; you'll love it. It's the best in the Confederation."

"What time?"

"Let's leave that to Jerym."

He nodded without speaking. After a moment he asked, "Tain, were you close to him before your—accident."

She looked at her husband unreadably. "It wasn't an accident, dear. I did it deliberately."

He knew that. She'd told him one evening in the hospital, a long evening of sharing. Told him what she'd feared, in the Klestronu flagship's interrogation chamber, and how she'd dealt with it. In a very real sense it had been an unsuccessful suicide, an attempted martyrdom, that had left her unable to recall even her name. He wondered if he could have acted with such courage and selflessness.

"As for your question," she went on, "yes, Jerym and I were close. We even talked of marriage. But it wouldn't have worked. He was married to his regiment, which meant he'd be off-world most of the time. With strong odds he'd be killed. Almost all his original platoon was killed on Terfreya; one of their roles was as bait for traps."

Coso frowned. *Who does the Confederation fight?* he asked himself, surprised that he hadn't wondered before. Did it face revolts by member worlds? Somehow he'd never considered the possibility that the Confederation might be oppressive. *And it wants something from me. Expects something from me.* But on the other hand, if the regime was oppressive, why had there been no suggestion of it in the volumes of interrogations compiled by Klestronu intelligence? Terfeya was a mined-out resource world, largely depopulated for centuries, yet its people had shown little resentment toward the central government.

He would not, he decided, ask Tain about these things. At least not till he knew more about sector history.

"But now," he said, "Jerym is stationed on Iryala. And he is not only handsome and courageous, he is intelligent and honorable. If you had the choice today, would you prefer to be with him? Instead of with an exiled foreigner?"

She eyed her husband for a moment, then went over to him, sat on his lap and kissed him. "You are the one man I love," she told him. "There is no one I'd leave you for. No one. Now I am going to bed, and if you know what's good for you, you'll come with me."

She has most definitely changed, he thought, getting to his feet. She'd shown strength before, but a mild strength, a strength of survival. She'd been acquiescent within broad limits. He'd had to be careful not to take advantage of her. *Now she orders me,* he thought. *Me, who took a throne by force, and ruled an empire!*

He thought it not with resentment, but admiration. He'd loved her the first time he'd seen her. Still did. Always would. He'd simply have to adjust.

Coso Biilathkamoro did not get back to Confederation history that night.

Three days later the Emeritus Kalif had an hour's audience with Marcus XXVIII, essentially the Confederation's emperor. By that time, Coso had finished the syllabus on Confederation history. Their hour together had given him a strong impression of the king, a man whose gaze was open and interested, whose intelligence was obvious. And whose nearly thirty years of rule seemingly had brought him wisdom instead of self-indulgence or irascibility.

He'd even gotten an answer to his principal question. "Yes," His Majesty had said, "the Confederation does want your help. As yet we haven't seen how to use it, or the form it can take. But it seems to us it will be important, perhaps vital, to prevent the war being a disaster. To both sides."

They'd parted with mutual respect.

What most impressed the Kalif was how much the king knew about him. About him, the Empire, and the Armada. These people had even known about Hope, and the survey base, and the aliens. Had known he was there, and in what building.

It seemed to him that Lotta Alsnor-Romlar was the key. Tain had made her sound like the seers in the proscribed fantasy novels he'd read as a youth. If to some degree she was, it would explain a lot.

Three days later he spent much of an afternoon with Lord Kristal. The Iryalan nobleman's central concern was clearly the avoidance or minimalization of death and destruction. He was particularly interested in Loksa Siilakamasu and the Armada's officer corps, space force, army and marines. Coso was impressed by Kristal's informed questions, his knowledge and perceptiveness.

When his time was up, it was the Kalif who asked the final question. "I am very interested in meeting Lady Alsnor-Romlar," he said, "and the kalifa is quite anxious to see her. When can that be arranged?"

Kristal's gaze had clouded. "Soon, I hope."

"Soon? Next week perhaps?"

The gray head nodded curtly. But the Kalif did not back away, and after a long pause, Kristal made a decision. "Your Eminence," he said, "as you know, government includes areas best kept confidential. But I will give you some privileged information." He paused as if choosing his words. "I confide in you not only because of the kalifa's long history and special relationship with Lotta Alsnor, but also to establish a level of candor with you."

Again he paused, contemplative. "I suppose," he said, "that your empire has, or has had, what we call terrorists." He paused to explain the term. "Terrorists have abducted Lotta, have held her for some time. She is alive, that much we know, but we do not know where.

"She means a great deal to us, not least of all to me. I have known and admired her since she was sixteen years old. She is a most remarkable human being." Once more he paused, leaning forward now, looking intently at his guest. "And she is the founder and director of our Remote Spying Section."

He sat back then. "Well. I have said more than enough. I would invite you to dine with me this evening"—he gestured at the clock—"but we would not then have the pleasure of the kalifa's company. Promise me you both will be my guests some evening this week. This time not in our home, but at some particularly fine establishment."

"I will consider it a privilege, Lord Kristal. And I do not doubt that the kalifa will as well."

While his liaison drove him to his apartment, the Kalif reviewed the meeting mentally. *Remote Spying Section!* he thought. *Really! That not only fits what Tain and Jerym said, it explains how the Confederation knows what it knows.*

Chapter 40
Lake Loreen

A warbling commset wakened the kalifal couple. Morning light filtered dimly through heavy drapes. Reaching, the Kalif picked up the handset. "Good morning. This is Chodrisei Biilathkamoro."

Lord Kristal was on the other end. "Your Eminence," he said, "Lotta Alsnor-Romlar has been rescued. At sea. She'd freed herself, killed her jailer, and was steering the sinking craft through a storm. A Coast Guard floater found her and picked her up. She'll be undergoing medical examination and debriefing for the rest of today, but she would like to meet with you, the kalifa, and Rami this evening. At her home. Will that be convenient?"

Beside him on their AG bed, Tain looked questioningly at her husband. "One moment," he said into the mouthpiece, then touched the mute switch with a thumb. "Lotta has been rescued," he told her. "She wants to see us this evening."

"Thank God! Tell her we can hardly wait."

He activated the mouthpiece again. "We are eager to see her. When will we be picked up?" He listened briefly. "Thank you, Lord Kristal. We appreciate your kindness, and Lady Alsnor-Romlar's as well."

He switched off the comm and turned to his wife again. She was beaming through tears.

268

✧   ✧   ✧

They met Lotta at the OSP building, and ate a late supper with her in a private room of the Rotunda restaurant. Coso had rather expected Colonel Romlar to be there too, but the colonel was with his regiment in training exercises, some eight billion miles out in the fringe. He'd gate back late that evening or early the next day.

Coso had wondered what possible function an infantry force could have eight billion miles out in space.

Lotta was a surprise to Coso. He'd never seen a likeness, nor created a mental image of her. But neither had he expected someone who looked as she did. Tain had said she was small, and he could imagine she'd been underfed during her captivity. But even allowing for that, she was smaller than he'd expected, smaller even than the average Vartosu woman. Nor was her hair as red as Tain had described it. That too might have resulted from the conditions of her captivity. Her skin had somewhat the appearance of a desert woman's; there were fine lines beside her eyes and on her forehead. Tain had said she was in her early or mid-twenties. He wondered if she was mistaken.

What he found most striking about her, though, was the calm strength she radiated.

Most of the supper conversation was between Lotta and Tain, Tain asking questions about life as a monastic on Tyss, and Lotta telling stories of it. Rami seemed awed by her, despite the questions she asked to draw him out. Questions he answered politely. The Kalif took part mainly when invited to by Lotta or his wife.

When they'd finished their dessert and after-supper joma, Lotta's chauffeured hover car took them to the house on the ridge. She had, she said, been in the habit of driving herself, but now Lord Kristal insisted on security measures.

While it wasn't conspicuous, it was obvious to the Kalif that the vehicle was armored. More impressive to him, it was driven by a T'swi, with another sitting beside him in the front seat, both wearing sidearms. They exuded a greater calm than anyone he'd ever encountered. The Kalif had spent a few hours reading about the T'swa, but it had not prepared him for these two. He had no doubt at all they were veterans of mercenary regiments.

Among the topics talked about in Lotta's comfortable living room were her visits to Tain on Varatos. It was earlier, though, she said, while spying on the Klestroni, that she'd realized how needless was conflict between the Confederation and the Empire. Being in someone's mind provided intimate familiarity. The late Sultan of Klestron was not only good, he was wise. "He chose good men to command the expedition," she said. "Decent honorable men. And without his protection, and theirs"— she paused, looking at the Kalif—"and yours when the time came, things might have gone far worse for Tain. I felt much better when you decided to marry her.

"Now you're here, and I'm beginning to feel optimistic about avoiding war with the Armada." She paused, her eyes holding his. "The war you worked so hard to set in motion."

Coso's mouth felt dry as talc.

"You owe your conversion to Iron-Jaw Songhidalarsa and Lord Rothka Kozkoraloku, you know," she went on. "Interesting, isn't it? The greatest villains of your reign. But if they hadn't engineered the coup attempt, you might never have reexamined what you were creating."

She's right, he told himself. In a sense he'd known it all along, but hadn't really looked at it.

"Yet the conservatives in your College of Exarchs, and in the Diet, would hardly have agreed to seek other worlds, if you hadn't forced the issue as you did. And your Empire *needed* to break out of its shell. If, with your help, we can avert serious fighting, both sides will be better off than if none of this had happened."

And that is also true, he thought. *It never occurred to me. I wonder if it did to SUMBAA.*

She paused, and seemed for a moment to lose her focus. "That is," she added, "if we can somehow deal with the Garthids. When Commodore Tarimenloku fired on their patrol ship, he scorched a dragon."

She turned the conversation to Rami then, asking if he'd like to go to school with Iryalan children. He said he would, but sounded tentative.

It was Tain who brought up the Ostrak Procedures. "You remember how I tried to worm out of you what you did to produce such non-Standard beliefs and attitudes in the troopers. I had to share a tent with you for weeks to find out. Even then all you told me was a name: the Ostrak Procedures."

Lotta nodded. "At the time, even that was confidential. It's not now, of course."

For the first time, the Kalif interjected a comment uninvited. "Captain Alsnor tells me that's what enabled his troopers to traverse the gate without trouble."

Both women nodded. "Lotta," Tain said, "can you do the Ostrak Procedures on me?"

Her husband turned to look at her. Lotta grimaced. "I'd say we owe it to you, after all you've been through. I don't run the procedures myself these days. I've got too much else to do. But I can arrange to have it done." She turned to Coso. "It will change her, but no more than regaining her memories has. And if you get them, you'll change too, more or less in parallel with her. I'm sure Emry hopes you'll have them. They'll expand the possibilities of success when you confront Admiral Siilakamasu."

Coso felt queasy. The Ostrak Procedures did something to the mind. The psychotherapies he knew anything about were the usually ineffective, dogma-based practices of the Empire's religious counselors; the sometimes misapplied chemical treatments of its medical psychiatrists, which often alleviated but seldom cured; and the frequently innovative practices of secular alienists, which occasionally produced startling improvement, but more often went on for years with little result, except the exchange of credits.

On the other hand there were Jerym and his troopers, and presumably Lord Kristal and the king, as exemplars of the results. And the young woman sitting across from him.

"The Ostrak Procedures," he said thoughtfully. "Describe them."

She told him something of the principles and results. It was too superficial to allay his mistrust.

Two mornings later, a government floater flew the kalifal family to the Lake Loreen Institute. The copilot pointed it out as they approached—a set of large buildings beside a cove, on a large irregular lake that lay vividly cobalt blue beneath a clear sky.

They settled to the ground in bright sunshine. An old, U-shaped manor was surrounded by gracious lawns, where in summer, spreading, thick-boled *peioks* provided shade. Now they were bare, their fallen leaves ground, treated, and packed in mulching pits.

It was morning recess, and the older children were playing kickball in the yard. As the floater settled near the long porch, a large-eyed Rami watched them through a window. After three years on the flagship, he was not yet sure of himself among children. His father wasn't sure of himself, either.

A woman named Konni Bosler received them. She was, she told them, headmistress of the Academy, and sometime hostess for visitors. Rami she assigned to a fresh-faced, fifteen-year-old guide, who took him to visit the teacher in the first-year classroom. Then she gave the Kalif and kalifa a tour of the manor's public areas, while describing a bit of its history.

Over the years it had changed somewhat. Its Ostrak Academy for Children was as busy as ever, but no longer as special. The network of academies had considerably expanded. Also, the Institute for Physical Studies, established thirty years earlier, had been transferred to the Special Projects compound near Landfall. Its building here had been remodeled as a training center for Ostrak operators.

Behind the manor, she showed them the conservatory, field house, natatorium, well-equipped playground, and the lakeshore with its docks and two boathouses. In the cove, a hundred feet or so offshore, was an islet with a *ghao*, a decorative, modest-sized building reached by a footbridge—reddish-brown wood on stone piers.

Though elderly, Lord and Lady Durslan still lived at the manor, and handled the record keeping. After the tour, the kalifal couple ate lunch with them. The Durslans and Mrs. Bosler, they learned, had known Lotta since she was six years old. She'd gone to school there, and been one of its all-time outstanding students.

After lunch, Mrs. Bosler took them across the bridge to the *ghao*. It was there, she explained, that the T'sel master had his office, did research, and sometimes received guests. He had, she added, been Lotta's mentor.

The bridge had decorative wrought-iron posts at intervals, topped by colored glass lamps. The *ghao* was of wood—the timbers seemingly hewed, the planks wide but thin. It was perhaps forty feet long, thirty wide and thirty high. There were two stories, the upper notably smaller than the lower, each surrounded by a narrow porch. The roof of each sloped strongly downward, with the corners upcurved. Around it were plantings, including artfully pruned fruit trees. In their season, Konni Bosler told them, one species bore pink flowers, the other white. There were also large evergreen trees called *koorsa*, with dense, dark, irregular crowns.

On the porches hung several clusters of the opalescent, spindle-shaped shells of seacurls, variously arranged to strike one another in breezes of different force, making a gentle tinkling.

The Kalif considered the entire ensemble—building, plants, accessories, bridge—remarkably aesthetic. The basic design, Mrs. Bosler said, had been imported from Tyss, but according to T'swa seers, had been created long before, by monastics on humanity's original home world.

T'swa seers. Humanity's original home world. Mentally the Kalif squirmed, then shook off the reaction. The alien ideas were either valid or they weren't. In either case he needed to get used to them. If they were valid, he'd eventually embrace them. Sooner or later. When he could.

Mrs. Bosler took them inside and introduced them to the T'sel master, Wellem Bosler, a somewhat older man who apparently was her husband. Wellem Bosler stood when they entered, and shook their hands. It was the kalifa he spoke to first. "Lotta tells me you'd like to receive the Ostrak Procedures."

"Yes, I would. I've seen what they did for Colonel Romlar and his troopers. And while I've no desire to fight anyone, I'd like their strength and resilience. Their fearlessness."

The words seemed strange to her husband. He'd long been impressed by her own resilience and quiet strength.

"We can start you this afternoon," Bosler told her, then turned his gaze to the Kalif. "Lord Kristal hopes you'll try them, too."

To Coso, Bosler's eyes seemed interested but neutral. Yet somehow he felt as if he were being guided into a trap. He had no evidence of it, not even a suggestion of any, but his guts felt as if a knot had been tied in them. "I have not decided," he said.

"Fine." Bosler turned to the kalifa again. "In general I prefer to match a female examinant with a female operator. There tends to be greater initial rapport, and my most senior operator here is a woman. I can call her now, if you'd like. She can be here in minutes."

"The less wait, the better," Tain answered. "I'd like to get started."

Coso felt helpless. Things were out of his hands.

"Good," Bosler said, then reached for his comm and pressed a key, using the handset for privacy. "Arva, this is Wellem. The person I told you about is in my office, ready to start. . . . Yes. When can you be here? . . . Good. We'll be waiting."

He returned the handpiece to its cradle. "She'll be here in ten minutes or so. She was prepared for this."

"How long will it take?" the Kalif asked. "This first—session?"

"Probably an hour or two. If you'd like, Konni can provide you with a reading terminal, in the Academy. Or you might like to observe an Academy class."

His black eyes steady, Coso Biilathkamoro looked long at the T'sel master. His stomach was still nervous, but inwardly he knew. "If I were to, um, try a session, who would be my operator?"

"I would."

"Then let's do it."

"Good. I believe when you've tried it, you'll approve."

The room to which Bosler took him was in the upper level, lit by afternoon sunlight. It was bright and fragrant with flowers from the conservatory.

Bosler seated him. "Are you comfortable?" he asked. "Yes."

"Good." He paused. "If there was one thing you could change about yourself, what would it be?"

"Hmm. I'm not sure there is anything. I have always felt quite good about myself, even when doing things of which others disapproved."

"Fine. But if there was one thing?"

"Well— I have not always— I have sometimes not been worthy of the trust people have shown me. I would change that."

"All right. Does this feeling come from betrayal of trust?"

"Betrayal is too strong a term. Unworthy of trust."

"Fine. Recall a time when you were unworthy of trust."

At first he couldn't think of one, despite what he'd said. Finally he recalled a time, as Kalif, when he'd more or less bulldozed the kalifal physician into falsifying the results of a physical examination. "Poor Neftha," he said, his chuckle without humor. "To lie was painfully difficult for him. Yet somehow I felt no guilt at all for pressing him as I did, or too little to trouble me. It is said that power corrupts. I suppose that was an instance of it."

"Good. Recall an earlier time when you were unworthy of trust."

The Kalif gnawed his lip thoughtfully. "I was a young marine officer," he began, "a sublieutenant." He told then of another young officer, Jorlo, his roommate. Jorlo was fervently in love with a young woman, whom he hoped to marry. One evening when he had a theater date with her, their commanding officer had called him. He was to report at once for an emergency assignment. Dismayed, he'd asked Coso to take his lady love to the theater in his stead. She'd come on strongly to Coso, and before the evening was over, was in bed with him.

"I suspect," he said ruefully, "that *would* qualify as a betrayal of trust. Though at the time I thought little of it. I was young, and had no doubt she'd been in bed with other men while leading poor Jorlo on."

"All right," Bosler said. "There is a larger one we need to get. Recall an earlier time when you were unworthy of trust."

The Kalif sat frowning, his attention inward, his eyes unfocused, pupils directed unseeingly upward to the left.

"That," said Wellem Bosler. Coso's frown tightened. "That one." Coso shook his head. "The small yellow man," Bosler prompted.

The Kalif's mouth fell slightly open, and his flesh crawled. "Ahhh," he breathed.

"Go through it from the beginning," Bosler said matter-of-factly, "and tell me what you see."

Coso began to talk. When he'd been eight years old, his fifteen-year-old brother, Roitis, had been awarded a four-inch gold-plated statuette of a running youth, for winning a race. Roitis had been very proud of it. On several occasions, when Roitis wasn't home, Coso had secretly borrowed it. He'd played with it in his room, along with his toy soldiers. And always he'd put it carefully back, just as it had been. In his imaginative play, the golden figure served as a heroic leader.

One day during the monsoon, he'd taken it again, along with some of his favorite soldiers, this time to play with by the river. There it had fallen from a guardrail, and disappeared into the turbid current.

Roitis, when he missed it, had virtually ransacked the house, searching. Somehow no one suspected Coso, who by that time was in summer camp. He heard it mentioned later, but by then the turmoil was over and the mystery dismissed. Before long, he'd buried the incident out of sight.

Bosler's eyes, mild but watchful, had never left the man in front of him—the man and his aura. "Good," he said, when Coso had finished his account. "Recall an earlier time when you were unworthy of trust."

The session continued for more than an hour and a half, and took him earlier than Coso had ever imagined. When it was over, he had a powerful new reality on life and death, responsibility and blame, worthiness and betrayal. Though he'd only begun to sense it.

Afterward, talking together over fruit tarts and mugs of hot thocal, Coso discovered that he felt an easy comfort with the T'sel master. Then Bosler showed him to a small room with a cot, telling him it was best to nap awhile. Let the deeper levels of his psyche adjust without the distractions of the conscious mind. He'd waken him when it was time.

As he lay briefly waiting for sleep, Coso decided that

what had impressed him as much as anything were
Wellem Bossler's startling words, "the small yellow man."
They bestowed an authenticity, and displayed a power,
that Coso Biilathkamoro had not anticipated. He did not
doubt at all, now, that for better or worse, he'd continue
the procedures.

It seemed to him it would be for the better.

Wellem Bosler reviewed the session thoughtfully. The
Kalif had reached for a much heavier series than one
would expect of someone so unprepared. They'd had to
make do with a resting event well short of final, but it
would serve. Somewhere further back, though, was the
great-great-grandfather of this being's betrayals of trust.
A big one. Perhaps they'd deal with it later. Given the
circumstances they faced, perhaps they'd have to.

Meanwhile they'd made a good start.

Entering a cognitive trance, he melded with Lord
Kristal, and let him know the Kalif's decision. It took longer
than using a commset, but in it he could communicate
more.

While the Kalif and kalifa napped in the *ghao*, Konni
Bosler had a guest suite prepared for them. There would
be snow in the air before they finished.

Meanwhile Rami could attend the Academy. He was
a child with the potentials that accompany unusual
wisdom. He would thrive there.

Lord Kristal, Kusu Lormagen, and Artus Romlar met
in Kristal's office and began seriously to explore possible
new strategies for dealing with the Armada. Explore them
with the beginnings of optimism. The future looked less
grim than it had.

Chapter 41
Slingshot to Anywhere

"So," Artus said, "what's so secret you can't tell me on scramble? Have you found a way around the topological enigma?"

Kusu Lormagen grinned ruefully. "Don't I wish. No, but I've got the next best thing."

The topological enigma. Things could be gated past or around intervening walls. And as far as you wanted—hundreds of parsecs. Scores at least. All you needed was the data necessary to locate the target. But they couldn't be gated into exclosures. And that's what everyone wanted—everyone in OSP and the Defense Ministry, including Artus—the ability to gate assault squads into the bridges and engine rooms of enemy warships when they reentered F-space.

"The next best thing?" Artus echoed. "How close is next? And why do I need a raincoat?" He gestured at the hooded, knee-length military dress raincoat he wore, hanging capelike across his shoulders.

Kusu laughed. "How close is next? Not that close. And the rain gear is because it was raining in Varodin, when I left there an hour ago. It's their summer monsoon there." He took his own raincoat from a coat tree. "Let's go up on the roof."

The private lift tube at one end of Kusu's office took

them to a one-room penthouse, a gate house. Kusu told the technician what he wanted, then he and Artus stepped onto the platform. The technician opened one side of the gatehouse, to accommodate the topological enigma. Snowflakes swirled in; Landfall was experiencing its first prewinter storm. After a brief wait, the status light turned green and they stepped through the gate—

Into the fleet shipyard at Varodin, in the northern hemisphere tropics. A hot sun shone on steaming concrete, and the two newcomers peeled off their rain gear. Close by at one side loomed the partly assembled hull of a battleship, supported by AG bracer tugs, buzzed about by large and small industrial dollies, and waited on by tall servomechs on heavisleds.

On the other side was a hangarlike overhaul dock, and it was into this that Kusu took Artus. Large enough to accommodate a cruiser or troopship, what it held was perhaps half as long, though of considerable beam. Its level upper surface was interrupted by low and irregular superstructures.

Artus's eyebrows rose. "It looks like a giant space sled."

Kusu chuckled. "I call it the Slingshot to Anywhere. It's a giant mobile gate generator; a king-sized analog of the one Jerym used on Hope, to rescue the Kalif. It'll generate a gate large enough to accommodate a battleship, with lots of room to spare.

"We started the project on faith. The existing technology wouldn't generate a large enough gate field, and we had some pretty basic problems to overcome. Obviously we haven't gated a battleship with it yet. But earlier today we created the largest gate the building would allow, opened the hangar doors, and gated a pinnace through to Landfall."

Artus pursed his lips thoughtfully. "Ah. So now you take it into deep space for operational testing."

"Right."

"What are the odds it'll pass?"

"How about ninety-five percent? Last night's test seems to have answered the uncertainties."

"Then what? What've you got in mind for it?"

"Several things when we started to build it. We just weren't ready to talk about them till we knew we could generate a large enough gate field. Then Lotta came back from captivity with another idea. It's in her debrief. She just didn't know it was possible. Still doesn't. She was in trance when I called her about last night's test." He turned to leave. "Emry will want your thoughts on possible additional uses."

"What about Lotta's idea? You've got me curious."

"Ask Emry," Kusu said. He held the door for Artus and closed it behind them. "Sorry I mentioned it. I wasn't supposed to. It's too iffy, depends on too many independent factors."

He led off toward the shipyard's personnel teleport, and the return jump to Landfall. Artus's mind was not on possible additional ideas. He'd call Emry as soon as he got back, and find out what Lotta had come up with.

Part Three
WAR

Chapter 42
Pandora's Welcome Wagon

Hyperspace astrogation is inexact, and recognizing a target system uncertain. With stars the mass of Iryala's G2 sun, Fridolf, you can detect that something massive is out there at a distance of half a light year, more or less. But its location is too undefined to provide a blip.

Even from relatively close, you do not "see" a star while in hyperspace. Courtesy of the F-space potentiality, you see an icon, a blip on a screen. All that instruments can tell about it, very approximately, are mass and F-space distance. And the farther away it is, the more undependable are the estimates.[1]

So on long hauls, it is usual to emerge at the predicted time of arrival. There you find and identify the target system, read distance and bearing, generate strange space again, and make a closing jump.

Thus Admiral Siilakamasu had notified the Armada that they would emerge at 1000 hours, and find and take readings on the Iryala System.[2] At 0847, however, they

---

[1]The average error of the estimated F-space distance is hyperbolically dependent on parameters of distortion of the F-space potentiality.

[2]Inhabited systems are named after the inhabited world, rather than after their primary. Iryala was colonized before its primary was named.

got a blip. The estimated mass was appropriate to Iryala's sun, and the timing wasn't too bad.

For strategic reasons, however, the admiral passed it. When the blip had fallen sufficiently behind them, he ordered his ships to "decelerate" at once to zero, and emerge on signal. That would put them in the system's far-fringe, some three hundred billion miles from the primary. At that distance, their emergence waves would be too attenuated to detect from the near fringe.

The Iryalans, of course, would have a system of sentinel droids at varying distances from the primary, and the more outlying would detect him. But the droids would have to communicate what they'd learned, and that would take days by warpdrive. He'd be largely or entirely reassembled before the Confederation fleet arrived. Then—then he'd learn what they had.

Klestronu intelligence believed the Confederation did not have shield technology. If so, he'd destroy their fleet with few or no losses of his own. Their defeat would be utter. Final.

But meanwhile he'd take nothing for granted.

Actually, of course, he did take something for granted. He presumed the Iryalans had no other means than sentinel droids of knowing where he was, or that he'd arrived. It was a very reasonable presumption.

Fleet emergence was more complex than fleet entry into hyperspace. After the admiral's order, humans were not involved. The flagship's DAAS began its preemergence countdown at once, ordering fleet-wide status reports on all ship's systems relevant to emergence. When those had been received and evaluated, it ran the complex computations necessary to time each ship's on-board emergence instant and communicated the results to the appropriate ships. From a human viewpoint, this went swiftly. Elapsed time was due largely to hyperspace radio transmission times.

The flagship *Papa Sambak* emerged first, and in several million cubic miles of surrounding F-space, scores of other vessels quickly appeared. The *Sambak* was already gathering data, verifying the nearby star's identity.

Its parameters matched nicely the astrogational data seized by the Klestroni at Terfreza.

Again the Garthid scout emerged not far outside the Armada's emergence zone—nearer, actually, than its pilot was happy with. Its sensory equipment began at once to monitor the flagship's command traffic. Within a minute he knew: this was the target system. And the immediate purpose of this vast fleet was the destruction of the system's defense forces. When they'd completed reassembly, they'd move in-system in warpdrive.

He sat watching for an hour, then generated gravdrive, and backed slowly away a few thousand miles before generating hyperspace again and dropping a location beacon. He would backtrack three hyperspace days and await the coming of his own fleet.

The first level of crew revivals had been carried out days before emergence—those fleet officers and men needed for ship functions in other than routine hyperspace travel. The second level of revivals included those who'd monitor and support the fighting systems.

The first level of troop revivals began after emergence. General Arbind "Chesty" Vrislakavaro had moved from his observer's seat on the flagship's bridge, to his army command suite. From there he could keep in touch with the revival of key personnel on the various troopships. Not that his oversight was necessary. The procedures were routine and drilled, with the fleet's trained medical corpsmen acting in concert. But Chesty was the commander. His officers and men were his responsibility.

Division staffs, company officers, and the senior noncoms of headquarters units would be revived before fleet reassembly was completed.

His own general staff, and those of the corps commanders, had been in stasis on the flagship. By late afternoon they'd completed the revival and post-revival procedures. Most were in their small cabins or the staff mess, watching the Armada's reassembly procedures on video. They'd get bored with it soon enough, but just now it was interesting.

The general left his office for the bridge, followed by his aide, and his chief of staff, Major General Tagurt Meksorli. The activity level on the bridge was the highest he'd seen it, higher than during the reassembly off Hope.

Loksa Siilakamasu saw them enter, and grinned broadly. "Aha! Our good general! Been following the resuscitation of your army I'm sure." His grin changed to a smirk. "And feeling empowered! Men to command! Functions to perform! Worlds to occupy! Well. We'll make it as easy as we can for you. Don't want any more of your young men killed than we can avoid. By the time we've finished with its fleet, the Confederation will be crushed. Won't have so much as a cruiser left."

He laughed. "Then we'll scorch a few cities to educate them. Ensure proper submissiveness. All your boys will need to do, when we put them down, is direct traffic."

Holy Flenyaagor. He's gone manic on us. "Right," the general said. "We don't want more casualties than need be. Nor any festering, long-standing hatreds surfacing over the years as sabotage and murder, and civil unrest. I'll leave the fighting in space to you, but beyond that . . . We need to sit down and review the Partition of Authorities together. And Archbishop Sukhanthu needs to sit in on any decisions regarding dealings with the existing civil governments and populations."

The admiral waved a deprecative hand. "Of course. We'll follow protocol all the way. The spirit as well as the letter." His face hardened then, the smile gone. "While establishing our dominance, and leaving no possibility of misunderstanding." He gestured toward the large main screen in the front of the bridge, with its 3-D display of the Armada's ships. "Assembly will be quicker than at—"

He was interrupted by an alarm, a brief, raucous ululation. All eyes snapped to the main screen. There a spacecraft was surrounded by a reddish glow produced by DAAS to mark it as the source of alarm. The bridge officer of the watch boxed and magnified the image. The outrigs suggested a signals ship, but the design was unfamiliar, certainly not Karghanik. The insignia, though, was one they all knew: the conspicuous scarlet sextant of the Kalif.

Abruptly the view of space was replaced by an interior view, well lit. From it, Chodrisei Biilathkamoro looked out at them. He raised a hand in benediction, his lips parted, and the familiar voice spoke. "Officers and men of the Armada. I am your Grand Admiral and Emeritus Kalif, the personal representative of Emperor Kalif Jilsomo Savbatso. I am speaking to you to announce the dismissal of Admiral Loksa Siilakamasu on charges of insubordination, abuse of rank, attempted regicide . . ."

At first the command admiral's face had sagged in shocked disbelief, but when the image spoke of charges, he rallied. "Cut it off!" he shouted. "Cut it off!"

The speakers loudened as he spoke, as if in reaction or prescience. ". . . and to order him arrested on those charges. The next voice you hear will be a recording of the DAAS on the scout in which I was jettisoned. It will describe specifically what was done."

The DAAS began to speak then, as the communication officer on watch tried futilely to turn off the sound. When it would *not* turn off, the admiral turned to the fire control officer. "Cavos! Fire on that intruder! Now! Blow it out of space!"

The flagship's beam projectors had already been directed at the strange vessel. Powerful warbeams lanced toward it. After a moment of molten transformation, the vessel exploded in a sphere of glowing gas that thinned as it expanded, until it could no longer be seen.

General Chesty Vrislakavaro did not return to his office. He didn't trust its privacy. Instead he dismissed his aide and went to his living suite, taking his chief of staff with him. He seated the man in his small sitting room. "Brandy?" he asked. "It's all I've got on hand. From some exotic Saathvoktu fruit. Good stuff."

The major general nodded. "Brandy is fine."

Chesty poured. "What did you make of that eerie business on the bridge?"

"Make of it? Not much. I don't know enough. When they put me in stasis, Coso Biilathkamoro was still on Varatos, in the kalifal palace. I knew he planned to come along, of course, and apparently he did. And then, apparently something happened to him. I was going to ask you."

"Yesterday I thought I knew. Today it's obvious I was lied to. I wish we hadn't blown up the intruder. We might have found out." He paused, sizing up the younger man. "Tagurt," he said, "you have an advantage. You haven't been confused by lies. What do you make of what we actually saw and heard on the bridge?"

Meksorli's answer was prompt but thoughtful. "I was impressed at how they patched into our comm system like that, video and audio. As for why the comm officer couldn't simply turn it off, as the admiral ordered—I have no idea. I can't imagine it was the Kalif himself we saw, though. Probably a holo recording that was somehow entered into our communication system."

Chesty nodded. "Here's another puzzle for you. How did they get here so quickly? We're 338 billion miles from Iryala, a distance that would take days to cross on warpdrive. And we didn't emerge until nearly 1000 hours this morning." He paused. "But to do it on hyperdrive—emerge two kilometers off our bow—their hyperspace navigation would have to be far more precise than ours. Now there's a worrisome thought. And how could they even locate us so precisely?"

Tagurt Meksorli shook his head. "My biggest question is how the Kalif, or a holo of him, got on a Confederation ship."

Chesty grunted. "I can't even guess. As for why the bridge speakers couldn't be turned off . . ." He shrugged, stepped to the small screen in one bulkhead, and turned it on. "I'm going to keep this thing on. Who knows what might happen next?"

The two generals weren't the only ones who'd departed the bridge. The admiral had gone into his office, there to discuss much the same questions with his staff. Their conclusions were not much different than the generals' had been.

No one knew, and no one dared to ask, how the supposedly dead Kalif could be alive. And obviously in the hands of the Confederation! The next day the admiral would come up with a scenario, but no one would particularly believe it. For one thing, it didn't jibe with his earlier account of the Kalif's disappearance.

Unlike the two generals, the admiral and his staff didn't suppose the Confederation fleet had superior hyperdrive navigation. The Armada's instruments had not picked up any emergence waves. The best suggestion was that a number of Confederation ships with holo projectors had been stationed strategically throughout the fringe, and arrived on warpdrive. The theory was not remotely convincing.

No one, though, suggested abandoning the invasion. They feared the admiral, and feared to be thought cowardly. But mostly they had too much invested in a dream. They'd come nearly four hyperspace years to conquer, establish fiefs, and live the rest of their lives as rulers.

Still, their confidence and enthusiasm had been blunted.

Lotta Alsnor wasn't literally in the admiral's skull. That was a figure of speech. His mental processes took place there, but they interfaced with the other side of reality, and it was there the psi-spies experienced them. At least that was the T'swa theory.

Lotta had decided to stay with the admiral through the current critical situation. Privy to everything he thought, everything he heard or learned. She'd been with him non-stop since she'd been notified of the Armada's impending emergence. She'd take no more breaks than absolutely necessary, and leave someone with him when she wasn't.

When she needed to get information to Lord Kristal, she'd pass it on through another psi-spy.

As backup, someone else monitored whoever was officer of the bridge, debriefing after every three-hour spy-shift change. With the help of the Remote Spying Section, no one on the *Papa Sambak* knew more about what went on on its bridge than Lord Kristal did, or knew it much sooner.

That night the admiral had to wait longer for sleep than either he or his unknown watcher expected. During ship's evening, all the DAASes in the Armada began again to recite the admiral's crimes, or alleged crimes, and no one could shut them off. Nor did there seem to be a Confederation ship beaming them in. The Armada's own signal ships, and the flagship itself, should detect any such comm beams, and there were none.

It was the admiral who came up with a fix, or what seemed to be a fix. He'd never trusted the Armada's

SUMBAAs—the flagship's SUMBAA in particular. He'd feared their intelligence, and even more he'd feared their volition. But especially he'd feared they might favor the Kalif. Now he was sure of it.

Early on he'd ordered them isolated from the DAASes, then had them reconnected to coordinate reassembly in the Hope System. And with the Kalif gone, he hadn't ordered their re-isolation. Now it seemed to him that traitorous SUMBAAs were to blame for these inexplicable troubles. So he ordered them isolated again. It would, he was told, take time. Meanwhile the recitation of his crimes refused to be turned down. He went to bed sedated and with his ears plugged.

It seemed to him the worst day and night of his life.

When he got up in the morning, the recitation had been silenced. According to the comm chief, it had cut off with the isolation of SUMBAA. Though if asked, he couldn't have explained how three SUMBAAs had controlled the DAASes on hundreds of ships. The important thing was, the recitations had stopped.

There was an obvious explanation, however, for the broadcast continuing after the intruder was destroyed. It had pulsed the message into the ships. The whole Armada had received it—a process requiring perhaps a second.

While the admiral slept, Lord Kristal convened a strategy meeting in his office. As much as he disliked to, he'd had Lotta Alsnor wakened to sit in on it. No one knew Loksa Siilakamasu as well as she did.

It was decided not to do anything further to undercut him just then. Though the admiral didn't realize it, his resolve had been softened. Meanwhile they needed him in command of himself.

Major uncertainties remained, to be dealt with as opportunity, or need, or desperation dictated. Kristal and the War Ministry had a small tree of future action options—a limited series of multivector possibilities contingent on events. They would try for the best sequence. But there were serious odds that all of it would crash: the Confederation, their lives, their dreams. The peacemaker, Kristal mused, was at a disadvantage. He labored under far more constraints than the warmaker. And two of the players—Admirals Siilakamasu and Kurakex—had pathological appetites for war and destruction.

Chapter 43
Playing Poker with the Devil

After an early breakfast in the army staff's mess, the two generals, Vrislakavaro and Meksorli, went to the bridge again. The admiral scowled at their entrance, then ignored them. *Go ahead,* Chesty thought to him, *scowl. Your lies, crimes and treacheries are public now. Yet you've got the gall to be offended by my choice of a commoner for staff chief.*

What bothered the general most, though, was that no one, including himself, would do anything about it.

For a while there was nothing of interest to the generals on the main screen. Or on the flanking array of lesser screens that duplicated what the bridge watch saw at their work stations. On the main screen, auxiliary ships moved singly from certain sectors of fleet space to a zone on the periphery. Fighting ships moved to another. Everything slowly, to avoid collisions and confusions. There lay the limitations of DAAS, for the flagship DAAS had to coordinate it all, while the individual ships' DAASes controlled their own ships within the scheme. The command admiral would not again allow SUMBAA access to ships' systems.

As on the day before, the scene was interrupted by a raucous burst of sound. Again, all eyes moved to the main screen. But now, instead of a single spacecraft surrounded by a reddish glow, there were two, three, five of them, in a chevron formation, fairly even. And again there were no hyperspace emergence waves.

But these were not warships. They were merchant ships, apparently bulk carriers. The admiral's expression changed from sour to puzzled. What now? What threat might they pose? What might happen if they were destroyed? What was the Confederation up to?

Almost at once, one of them began to broadcast a message in competent, if accented Imperial. Another enemy of yours is coming, it said. An alien enemy, the Garthids. You know of them. The Klestronu expedition attacked and damaged two of their patrol ships. Subsequently the aliens decided to punish the offending race.

"Garthid technology is well in advance of your own," the voice went on. "Notably in hyperspace technology. It is even ahead of ours. Thus it detected the passage of your Armada, and its fleet is following you.

"However, neither the Garthids nor ourselves have a technology to engage you effectively in hyperspace. They much prefer to attack you in F-space or warpspace.

"As you see, we are quite capable of attacking while you are still dispersed and unready. We know the present distribution of your ships, even your missionary ships, as well as you do. We can jump battle groups in among you, in the most suitable positions to wreak havoc. Had we chosen to attack you, this would not now be a scene of calm communication. It would be a killing field, your Armada destroyed, and our own fleet damaged. That is why we chose to send merchant vessels instead of warships: to show both our potential and our restraint.

"We will take vengeance, if we are not satisfied. It is we who hold the war axe, and we are prepared to wield it without giving you time to reorganize further. We prefer not to however. The Garthids will arrive in this sector within three weeks, and much less dispersed than you are now." The voice slowed for emphasis. "And they will not distinguish between humans from the Karghanik Empire and humans from the Confederation.

"Now you begin to see our major motive for this peaceful approach. Combined, our fleets may quite possibly be able to parley with the Garthid command, avoiding a disastrous war. And at no more cost than an apology for the Klestronu incursion, and offers of reparation. They are far more likely to talk with our combined forces, yours and ours, than with either of us alone. Especially since we would take losses in the process of destroying you.

"So. Our question is, will you join with us?"

Lips pursed thoughtfully, Admiral Loksa Siilakamasu looked at the screen for long seconds before replying. "What evidence can you show that these Garthids are actually pursuing us? You could have made it up."

"You are familiar with the planet you so cynically named Hope. It is where we rescued your Kalif, and the survivors of your survey group. Rescued them from a Garthid assault unit. Their fleet had followed you to that system, and discovered your base there. Here are a few pictures of it before and after their attack, and here are its survivors." Pictures flashed on the screen. "They took your officers prisoner, disarmed your enlisted men, and destroyed your base. You've already seen and heard a holo of your Kalif. Here is the wreckage of a Garthid fighter we salvaged to study; we learned much from it. And here is its unfortunate crew."

Loksa Siilakamasu peered long and hard. "I cannot commit myself without answers to some questions," he said. "How have you done these things?"

"We have technologies you have not dreamed of. That is all I will tell you about that." The voice paused, then said, "We will wait here awhile, and let you counsel with your staff. But you must decide within five imperial hours, otherwise we will attack. Meanwhile if you continue to reassemble, we will be forced to demonstrate a weapon you would prefer not to experience. To establish further our superiority."

The admiral's face showed resignation. "Very well," he said. "DAAS, cease all reassembly." He paused. "You who are speaking for the Confederation, identify yourself so I can address you appropriately."

"I am Lord Carns, the Minister of Armed Forces."

"Lord Carns, before I commit to joining forces with you, I need to know how we would cooperate. Surely we have at least somewhat different battle evolutions, different large and small unit tactics, different—everything. How shall we fight together?"

"By confronting them separately, one the anvil, the other the hammer, with the Garthids between us. Now I will answer no further questions till we have your decision to join us or fight us. You do not have the option of simply departing. You have drawn the Garthids to us. You must fight either as our ally or our enemy."

The voice went silent. Siilakamasu looked at the comm officer. "Jarbasu," he said, "give us privacy from them, so I can counsel with my staff."

The comm officer threw several switches. Presumably only DAAS could hear them now.

"DAAS," the admiral said quietly, "order all ships to generate shields. Then continue reassembly of the support subunit of 2nd Battle Group. We will see what happens."

Tension among the bridge watch was thick enough to choke on, while the admiral turned hard eyes to the main screen. Shields were generated, and when nothing happened, he began to feel a surge of confidence. *These people don't realize what we just did*, he thought. *They're unfamiliar with shields*.

Three minutes later, in 2nd Battle Group, a newly repositioned munitions ship exploded. The battlecomp had reported no incoming torpedo. No warbeam. No detectable response of the ship's shield. Simply, there'd been a tremendous explosion, creating a spherical energy wave that sent shimmers of light over the shields of the nearer ships. The admiral's face pinched.

"DAAS," he said, "cease all reassembly. Jarbasu, activate comm with the Confederation lord." He paused till his orders had been carried out. "Lord Carns," he said, "I am convinced of your power, and accept your offer of five imperial hours to make a decision."

"*Two* imperial hours," the voice said. "Your challenge of a moment ago cost you three hours as well as a ship. Do not challenge us further."

Loksa Siilakamasu may have been ambitious, warlike, and obstinate, but he was not suicidal. Negotiations went smoothly. Lord Carns offered the Karghanik Empire a resource world known as Far Off—officially Technite 4—on the Confederation's farthest fringe. "Any government is limited in the extent of space it can effectively govern," Carns said. "Among other things, by the time required to travel and communicate with its parts. We'd never have bothered with Far Off, except that it was a technite world. We mined technite there, installing a sufficient population to produce nondurable goods for the mines, primarily food. When the technite was gone, the entire population was resettled elsewhere. That was twenty-five hundred years ago. Now you'll have a hard time telling where we were.

"Much of its land surface is fertile, with a suitable range of climates. It will provide abundant land and other resources for settlement and expansion."

It was assumed the Garthids would emerge in the same area of space the Armada had. It was what they'd done in the Hope system. Meanwhile the Armada was to generate warpspace, proceed four warpdrive days farther, and complete reassembly. Then it would backtrack and situate itself to strike the Garthids from behind, so to speak. The Confederation fleet would strike from the insystem side. A Confederation signal ship would coordinate the initial engagements, certain frequencies being reserved for each force, with certain others in common. If it proved necessary to fight the Garthids, each allied fleet would be largely on its own, coordinating as situations permitted.

The Confederation's technical legerdemain in space had been recorded from a piggyback scout on one of the bulk carriers, a scout ridden by Lord Carns, with a pilot and a cameraman. From time to time, space scooters had been gated back via teleport on the ship's hull. The activity had been meaningless and mostly unnoticed by the *Sambak*. After the Armada left, the scout too gated back. Within an hour, in Kristal's conference room, the War Council, the king, and the Kalif reviewed the proceedings. Including Lotta Alsnor-Romlar's update on Siilakamasu's thoughts and intentions.

Afterward most had left. Kristal went into his office then, with a few others, and lowered himself onto his desk chair. "That," he said, "was exhausting. The cost of emotional polarity, and the physical weakness of age."

You did as well as I did, thought Linvo Garlaby. *And probably on as little sleep.*

Kristal's intercom buzzed, and he touched its switch. "What is it, Markis?"

"Dr. Lormagen to see you, your lordship."

"Send him in. I was expecting him."

The director of research and development stepped into the office. "Hello, Kusu," Kristal said. "Sorry you couldn't be here for the conference. We were impressed with the slingshot work, and Admiral Siilakamasu was impressed with the results."

Kusu grinned. "I've recommended the operator for a bonus. To do what she did with the bulk carriers— multiple placements at close to zero intervals . . . I've tried that sort of work to get a feel for it—with relatively small objects, of course—and it's challenging as hell."

Kristal nodded. "And not many years ago we had trouble putting people down on the right continent, on Terfreya. To gate those five bulk carriers through singly, yet so quickly, lining them up in formation . . . When we implied we could jump whole formations of ships through together, the admiral never doubted. Which was critical to the whole negotiation. And they have no idea how we blew that munitions ship. What sleight of hand! An automated space lighter loaded with 6,000 tons of high explosive, flying through a gate at what? A thousand miles a minute?"

"Five thousand," Kusu said.

"Ah, the illusion! They supposed it was something we could use in combat. Not something limited to stationary targets. We've given them a totally false picture of our capacity for space warfare."

"The tricky part," Kusu added, "was getting the distance just right. I wanted the gate point within four lighter-lengths of the target. Farther away and the imperials might detect the lighter's passage, which would have cost us much of the morale effect, and given them a clue to what happened. But too close—say a lighter's length—and the explosion might have blown back. Taken out the slingshot, the sled crew, me—the whole thing."

"And now," Carns said, "we've let them think they've put one over on us." He shook his head, partly rueful, partly amused. "Too bad they didn't accept our offer, as they pretended. The best part, of course, is all the lives saved and the destruction avoided. The sad part is the troubles Aslarsan will have. We'll owe the Aslari some amends and reparations. As the Empire will. But we still have the Garthids to deal with, which promises to be far more difficult. And if we fail in that, what we accomplished today may become meaningless."

❖   ❖   ❖

As agreed, the Armada made a four-day jump in warpdrive, there to complete reassembly. But instead of warping back to ambush the Garthid fleet, it prepared for a hyperspace jump. Half an hour before ordering countdown, the admiral ordered a message pod prepared. With a message for Lord Carns.

"For Lord Carns?" said Chesty Vrislakavaro. "What purpose does that serve?"

Loksa Siilakamasu laughed. "To tell him we're leaving, going home. To prepare the Empire's defense, in case the aliens learn where we live. They'll have to defeat the aliens alone." Grinning, he raised an eyebrow. "I even wish him luck."

"They'll find out soon enough we've abandoned them," the general said. "That"—he gestured—"only taunts them."

"No no! It will *inform* them! It wouldn't do to let them think they have an ally waiting to strike the aliens from behind. Their strategy, tactics, formations, all would be deadly inappropriate. The aliens would destroy them at relatively little cost to themselves. And we don't want an intact and powerful alien fleet that might then sweep through the Confederation to raze its worlds. And find us!"

"Us?"

He chuckled. "Chesty, I did not bring us this far to leave defeated. We came for conquest. According to Klestronu intelligence, the second richest planet in the Confederation is Aslarsan, less than four parsecs from here. And defenseless! It must be. Consider. The Confederation knew we were coming. To Iryala. They've known it since they got that turncoat Kalif in their hands. And they've known for just as long that the aliens are coming. They'll have gathered every warship they have to defend their imperial planet, the heart of their empire. And to defeat their invaders if they can. No, Aslarsan is an undefended jewel, waiting to be claimed.

"When Carns offered us a wilderness world, I realized what we had to do. A wilderness world! It would take years of work to make it productive. No, my friend, no wilderness world for us. Not when the Confederation has so many rich and developed worlds.

"And knowing it's on its own, the Confederation fleet will fight far more effectively than if we left it ignorant. They demonstrated their fighting quality to the Klestroni years ago, and their fleet technology days ago. Let them fight the aliens till one is destroyed and the other decimated. In five or six months we'll send scouts to learn the outcome, unless word finds its way to us on Aslarsan. Then if things seem favorable, as I expect they will, we can claim it all, and deal with whatever forces survived."

Name of the Prophet! Chesty thought. *This madman does not learn. He believes what he wants to, and ignores the rest.*

But he said nothing. In this little known part of the galaxy, with all its surprises and threats, he had no alternative plan to offer. And perhaps things would turn out all right after all.

Chapter 44
New Arrivals

Two weeks earlier, before the Armada emerged in the far fringe, the Confederation fleet had prepared to leave its insystem assembly zone. An important part of the fleet was Task Force Two, a force which, despite its size and strength, was not to be committed against the Armada except in extreme need.

The Confederation battleship *Makor* was the Task Force Two flagship. Kelmer Faronya arrived aboard her on a space scooter, gating from Iryala to a point off her flank. With him he carried a lengthy memorandum of introduction from the OSP, with Lord Kristal's signature. It was addressed to the task force commander, Vice Admiral Arnoth Ferringum.

Ferringum looked the young man over. Faronya's credentials included a year of OSP mercenary training, which no doubt had contributed to his strong, athletic build. And he'd covered the Komars-Smolen War on Maragor, with the White T'swa Regiment. Ferringum had read his reports and seen the cubeage. The young man was good at his profession. And obviously he was at least an Ostrak level five. Otherwise he couldn't have been gated successfully.

Ferringum called in a capable and personable young sublieutenant, Pendel Gorslen. "Lieutenant," he said, "this is Mr. Kelmer Faronya, a journalist. He has an important mission on board the *Makor*. I'm assigning you to facilitate it for him." He handed Gorslen the memorandum. "This will give you the general picture. Mr. Faronya can fill in the details. Give him what he needs, within reason. If you have questions, ask me."

Knowing Gorslen, he didn't expect any.

A day later, the *Makor's* captain found an unobtrusive Faronya on his bridge. Pendel had instructed the journalist on bridge protocol, and given him an unassigned backup work station there, familiarizing him with its terminal and twin screens. It made sense. Faronya could record anything that showed on his screens. And anything he didn't record himself, he could call up from the ship's action records simply by referring to the time. He could also play back from the bridge recorder anything that happened on the bridge.

Five days later, Fleet Admiral Torens Ostrak Harnel, in the fleet flagship *Carnothis*, generated warpspace and departed for the fringe. With him went almost all the Confederation fleet, including Ferringum's Task Force Two. There he would await word that the Garthid fleet had arrived, and where.

The Armada had arrived and departed almost without conflict. Now the Confederation War Council gave its full attention to the enemy it most feared. Although an adequate planner, Admiral Kurakex sekTofarko tended to be spontaneous and often impulsive. Thus he was not easy to predict, not even with remote spying. But it was necessary to try.

The Council knew about the Garthid scout that had shadowed the Armada, and about the hyperspace beacon it had emplaced. Knew of them from Kurakex's bridge, via the Remote Spying Section. They'd hadn't tried to locate and destroy the beacon. They wanted the Garthids to find it. Based on the example of the Hope System, the Council assumed it lay in the same general area the Armada had, and that the Garthid fleet would emerge there. The assumption was reasonable but dangerous. It was also the best they could do.

Along with Fleet Admiral Torens Ostrak Harnel, they had bet on it. Harnel's main force had repositioned six warp hours in-system from the predicted emergence area. He might have parked nearer, but he wanted to be sure his main force was between the Garthids and Iryala.

Of course, if the Garthids emerged in some other part of the system, Harnel would be far out of position. But he was an Ostrak level 6; he could converse in meld mode. If his bet proved wrong, he'd be notified quickly, and shift his forces via hyperdrive. Which would of course result in emergence waves, and a certain amount of dispersal even on so short a jump. He'd lose the advantage of surprise, and have to reform units.

Nonetheless, this was the place to be. It gave him his only real chance to strike before the Garthid fleet could reassemble and move.

Harnel's fleet had been in position more than four days when a psi-spy informed him that Kurakex had received the scout's message. An hour later, the same spy informed him that the Garthids had detected what they believed was Fridolf. Instead of emerging to verify, they were continuing in hyperdrive, watching for the scout's final beacon. On Harnel's bridge, the tension eased. So far, so good.

Harnel radioed not Ferringum, aboard the *Makor*, but Task Force One, under Rear Admiral Kori Clansig. "They're coming, Kori," he said. "Time to jump."

Clansig's small force was ready, navcomps set for the emergence coordinates. "Prepare for hyperspace generation," he ordered. At command stations throughout his task force, fingers touched a sequence of keys. A second later, the entire force disappeared. By hyperspace standards, it would be a microjump.

Until recently, Harnel had never expected to give an order like the one he'd given Clansig. It was more in Artus Romlar's line; there was serious doubt that Clansig or any of his people would survive. *Be with the T'sel,* Harnel thought. Minutes later his flagship's instruments recorded emergence waves—the task force's. There were far too few emergence points to be the Garthid fleet. The next move belonged to the Home Flotilla, far insystem. It would have to wait for the Garthids' emergence, of course, but that shouldn't be long. Perhaps less than an hour.

Harnel's stomach knotted. Too many uncertainties, he told himself. Too many things could go wrong. Among the recognized vector sprays for the future, very few paths offered victory. *The T'sel warrior,* he reminded himself, *goes into battle as if already dead, and already dead, has nothing to lose. One can then give full attention to the mission. The game. Inevitably one would have intentions, even preferences if he kept them light. But no "must have."*

He closed his eyes for a few seconds, doing a simple drill to regain t'suss.

The Garthid flagship *Thunder Lizard* winked into F-space without sound or momentum. A moment earlier, the bridge's main screen had been a flat crimson, conventional for hyperspace displays on Garthid craft. White isolines defined gravitic shadows in the F-space potentiality. Abruptly it showed F-space itself, deeply black, richly alive with stars. They were somewhere again. Even Admiral Kurakex sekTofarko appreciated the view, and the feeling that came with it.

For morale purposes, the spectacle remained on the main screen for half a minute, courtesy of the ship's artificial intelligence. Then real-space was replaced by a blue, three-dimensional representation, a field filled with the icons of ships large and small—fighting ships and support ships. Not nearly so many as the Armada's, but they included no troopships, no missionary ships, nor nearly as many supply ships. The Garthid fleet was not there for conquest, occupation and conversion. Under its fleet admiral, it was there to destroy.

The flagship's computer had already counted them. All 168 were there. Kurakex's heavy jaw jutted. *We have arrived,* he told himself. *The time is finally at hand.*

Meanwhile the flagship's artificial intelligence ordered the ship's instruments to identify the nearest star, against spectrum and location data taken from the captured survey base computer. Verification was standard emergence procedure, and took less than a second. The admiral hadn't needed it. The scout's beacon had made it clear: the nearby star, a fulgent yellow-white, was the one they'd come to find. Besides, he'd *wanted* it to be the target system. It dared not be anything else.

He ordered reassembly into standard battle order. Within a ship's day they'd be ready to generate warpspace. Within a few days they'd meet the enemy, and he'd begin his work. Which he intended, expected, to take no longer than another day. It would be a splendid battle, and rejuvenate the warrior spirit of the Garthids, which for many centuries had decayed under priest-ridden Surrogates. The people would revisit this forever in dreams, and it would be taught in the Academy for as long.

And it would bring him the crown. He'd be the greatest Surrogate of all time.

On the bridge of the battleship *Fire Lake*, Esteemed Valvoxa observed the same images watched by the fleet admiral. He expected soon to see two fleets join in violent dance. Then God would take the dead to the realm of light, and heal their souls. And in good time, those who needed to live again would return to this universe of mirrors and forgetfulness.

Chapter 45
Baiting the Bull

For several deks, the central assignment of Filéna
Kironu had been to spy on Admiral Kurakex and his
flagship officers. During that time, she'd occasionally
visited the mind of Esteemed Valvoxa, aboard the *Fire
Lake*. Mainly she questioned him about Garthid culture.
This built understanding, and filled holes in their
knowledge.

Among other things, she validated what Lotta had
learned on the night of her abduction.

Although her questions were never military, the shafa
knew their discussions might well influence the expected
conflict. But he believed his visitor: the basic goal of
her people was to avoid war, or at least reduce its effects.

Linvo Garlaby was no longer assigned to Lord Kristal.
Lotta had long since taken back her old job. Now Linvo
was with the fleet's Home Flotilla, six billion miles off
Iryala, just beyond the orbit of Fridolf's next-to-farthest
planet, Jousk. Specifically, he was aboard the Home
Flotilla's giant Slingshot to Anywhere, sitting in the control
room with its operator. The spacecraft's small, after-end
superstructure was set off like a stubby arm on one side.
The gate field, magnetically confined, was somewhat
above the hull, invisible to the naked eye. But the six

guide-on lights, marking its 120-yard diameter, shown bright red on Linvo's faceplate display.

His immediate job was to oversee the slingshot's operator. Filéna had visited them just long enough to make sure they knew the insignia of the *Thunder Lizard*, and that of the *Fire Lake*. She hadn't needed to remind them how important it was that neither ship be hit. Especially not the *Lizard*.

This was, Linvo thought, the most important hour of his life. He found himself calm, alert, and steady. As for the slinger, Cher Bentol had a fine touch. It was she who'd gated the bulk carriers through, and taken out the munitions ship.

Alarms interrupted Admiral Kurakex sekTofarko's attention to the roast he was eating. An intruder pulsed on the screen, an icon for a small ship of unknown type. It lay a mile from the *Thunder Lizard*. As it began to broadcast on the fleet command channel, the admiral poked a control switch on his throne arm, showing the vessel in real space. An ugly craft. Its designers were barbarians with no aesthetic sense. The voice was obviously electronic, the Garthid grammar and pronunciations adequate for communication.

"You are a war fleet," it said, "trespassing within the Iryala Sector of the Human Confederation. Please identify yourself and state your intentions."

An automated sentry ship, the admiral thought, *emerged from warpspace.* "Gunnery," he growled, "*show* him our intentions. Fry him."

The battlecomp had already locked onto the foreign vessel. Warbeams lanced from the *Thunder Lizard*'s heavy guns. Almost instantly the sentry ship glowed incandescent, brightening, distorting as oxygen escaped. The beams cut off then, leaving a clinkered hulk, its glow already fading.

"There," said Kurakex. "We are committed. Put all fleet battlecomps on full-ready status."

Abruptly there was a bright flame in the distance, and simultaneous shouts of alarm from two of the bridge crew whose work station monitors had remained on the reassembly field. Again the admiral poked a switch, calling the battle display field to the main screen. The icon for the battleship *Sky Path* was gone, replaced by a flashing red light.

He stared, stunned. Fleet Gunnery ordered shields generated. Inner shield matrices formed at once, visible on the battle display field.

At that moment a file of four intruder warcraft appeared. They locked onto targets and fired torpedoes, then generated hyperspace on the move and disappeared. All in a space of 3.7 seconds. Only the inner matrices had built effective shields. The screen showed three cruisers destroyed and one a derelict. Two battleships had been disabled and another damaged. The intruders had escaped into hyperspace before fleet torpedoes could reach them.

Kurakex sekTofarko felt rage building. A cold rage, within limits rational, but permeated with hatred, powering his compulsion for vengeance. An emotion containing nothing at all of political ambition.

"Lord Admiral," said his aide, "there were no emergence waves with the last intruders, either."

The admiral nodded curtly. "So they arrived on warpdrive. They were stationed very near."

"Not on warpdrive," the aide replied. "They arrived with momentum. About four thousand miles a minute."

The thick skin on Kurakex's forehead corrugated. A moment later another ship exploded—a munitions ship, with full shielding.

«Now,» thought Filéna, to Fleet Admiral Torens Ostrak Harnel. Mentally he nodded assent, and she adjusted focus. «Now,» she thought to Rear Admiral Kori Clansig. Clansig also assented, and ordered Task Force One to generate warpspace. He gave no attention to survival. By role, by training, and by his level 6 Ostrak processing, he was strong in the T'sel. One did not throw away one's life. One played it.

Within twenty minutes, three more munitions ships had blown apart despite their shields. Then the battleship *Noble Sskachek* was disabled by another powerful explosion, its shield generator and power system burned out. Minutes after its surviving crew had been transferred to a hospital ship, the now unshielded hull blew apart.

Minutes later, a small alien vessel materialized, barely missing the battleship *Raxkess Victory*, a moment after she'd begun her move to her reassembly position. The intruder did not generate strange space—either kind. It was destroyed moments later by a torpedo, and the explosion was *far* greater than one would expect. Kurakex's eyes widened with realization: The alien craft had been a slow and primitive, but extremely large, torpedo. Delivered by some unknown means, for like the squadron of attack ships, it had arrived with momentum.

Meanwhile the *Raxkess Victory* had escaped destruction while moving. During reassembly, the position and movements of all ships were controlled by the flagship's artificial intelligence. On impulse, Kurakex ordered all ships to make frequent random shifts in position, within the limits of formation safety, momentum tolerances, and the reassembly time frame. He'd see what protection this might give. He also ordered the flagship's artificial intelligence to determine the delivery system used by the alien.

On the bridge of the *Fire Lake*, Garthid Vice Admiral Tissokt sekArrompak watched the events with Esteemed Valvoxa beside him. "These aliens," the fat shafa commented, "are more than resourceful. The grand admiral initiated hostilities by rejecting their effort at discussion, and destroying the ship they'd sent for communication. Yet the aliens waited for the *Sskachek* to transfer survivors before they blew her up."

This was not, Tissokt thought, the time or place to point out the aliens' virtues, even though the holy man's observations were correct. But the shafan had always been peacemakers. According to the philosophers, it was the shafan role. Conflicts would occur as long as Garthids were Garthids. But from earliest times, the shafan had acted to reduce the number of conflicts, their intensity, and duration. Every Garthid learned that in school, and witnessed it in their dreams.

But now the fleet was at war, and he was vice admiral. His role, as he saw it, was to obey and support the fleet admiral. If, on their return to Shuuf'r Thaak, a board of inquiry questioned him, he would speak frankly. Which, he decided drily, was why the shafa had made sure he'd noticed the facts.

Chapter 46
Battle

Clansig's task force consisted of two frigate squadrons
without escorts. Twelve ships. Like all the frigates of the
Confederation fleet, they were critically obsolete, their
design unable to accommodate shield generators. Their
normal functions had been taken on by a new and more
powerful class of ships, cruisers. The most promising
function remaining to them was surprise—striking, then
generating strange space before they could be destroyed.
Or not generating strange space, whichever the situation
required.

The Home Flotilla, starting with information from
Filéna Kironu, had given Clansig a good locational fix
on the Garthid fleet. But the Garthids had sentry scouts
parked in warpspace. Filéna had said so, and Clansig
would have assumed it anyway. So he would close in
F-space.

An hour after he'd generated warpspace, Clansig and
his force emerged. In F-space, his instruments showed
him the Garthid fleet hardly more than 1.2 million miles
away.

Frowning, Admiral Kurakex watched the alien humans
approaching in gravdrive more than a million miles
distant. Ugly craft, twelve of them in three files. His signal

ships pronounced them unshielded, but with aliens, one couldn't trust appearances. They seemed too few and small to be threats, but why then did they approach openly and from a distance? They'd already established their ability to appear without warning in the midst of his fleet.

Inevitably he wondered whether he might be attacked here by the two separate empires, perhaps coordinated, perhaps independently. But he didn't consider caution. He would do what he had to. If there *were* two, he'd defeat them both. His fame would be the greater for it, and the khanate the stronger.

Meanwhile he'd hold his fire. He might, he told himself, learn something. He'd posted a number of destroyers on the fringe of the assembly zone—standard procedure. Now he ordered several of them to lock torpedoes on the approaching aliens.

At 400,000 miles, nothing had changed except that the intruders had stopped accelerating. They were less than 40 seconds away, approaching at 10237.410 miles per second. Kurakex gave the order to fire torpedoes, and on the main screen watched torpedo icons, four for each target, head for intersects with the aliens. Beam guns also tracked them, waiting for their targets to reach locking range.

At 34 seconds, the enemy's lead ship seemed to disassemble, an apparent superstructure separating from the rest. The act was smooth, the lead segment diverging slightly, a fraction of a degree. The remaining intruders followed its example almost at once. For several seconds he simply stared. Torpedoes! The enemy ships were launching huge torpedoes!

His own ships fired another salvo, and the enemy ships released more of their huge torpedoes. At 14 seconds, a series of explosion icons began to appear. Alien ships and alien torpedoes disappeared from the main screen, marked by the icon for "destroyed," while some of his own torpedo icons proceeded *past* the alien ships, as if somehow they had lost their targets.

At 5 seconds he ordered warbeams fired. Almost at once, three more aliens were shown as hit, all three disintegrating. Two were not hit. At zero seconds, each struck a battleship, destroying its shield and leaving the ship derelict in space.

It was then Kurakex sekTofarko realized the alien ships themselves were the torpedoes! The segments had been released to somehow attract—distract!—his own torpedoes.

On the flight deck of his scout, Rear Admiral Kori Clansig leaned back in his command chair. He'd been sweating copiously. When the last of the three target ships had parted from the hull of his frigate, his scout had detached as well. He'd blacked out from the G-stress of the small divergence in course and speed. The scout had generated hyperspace automatically.

Presumably separation had made no difference to the frigate. It flew itself. His primary function had been to give two key commands: "Now!" And "Now!" He had no idea whether any other bail-out scouts had made it into hyperspace. But at least there were himself and his frigate's eight-man skeleton crew.

Perhaps a psi-spy would let him know how things had turned out back there. Meanwhile it was time to go home.

Since the firefight with the twelve alien raiders, Kurakex had sat on his command throne almost without speaking. It had been forty minutes, but to the bridge watch it seemed longer. Their admiral was in a grim and dangerous mood. A heavy pall of anger hung about him like a thunder cloud, and no one wanted to trigger its lightning. Occasionally he tapped quick notes to himself on his confidential pad.

Kurakex sekTofarko had never been a military or naval scholar. He was better read in political theory. But he had a quick mind as well as an overbearing manner. He'd read and grasped the Academy texts and other required reading, and did not hesitate to act boldly. Since the shocking surprises earlier that ship's day, he'd reviewed what he'd seen, in the light of what he knew of naval and military science—and had arrived at a set of working policies: (1) The aliens were unpredictable. Therefore he would take nothing for granted. (2) He would not take strange behavior as indicating superior military or naval understanding, doctrine, or leadership. (3) In the absence of knowledge and time adequate to strategic and tactical innovation, he would follow basic naval doctrine, applying and modifying it as indicated by experience and opportunity. (4) He would at all times act forcefully and decisively. Forceful action based on faulty understanding won far more battles than hesitancy and quibbling.

He wrote them out, and felt much better for it.

In his flagship, the *Carnothis*, Fleet Admiral Torens Ostrak Harnel had generated warpspace when Clansig began his warpdrive approach to the Garthid fleet. As Harnel traveled, Filéna Kironu traveled with him in his mind, showing him the formation the Garthid fleet was beginning to form, visualizing it for him. She was seeing through the eyes of Admiral Kurakex, viewing the main screen of his bridge. The assembly positions were outlined in soft gold. The still-dispersed ships showed black. When a ship assumed its reassembly position, its icon became scarlet.

Harnel was awed by Filéna. Lotta Romlar had told him the girl was unique in how well she dealt with two minds at once. Stylus in hand, he sketched on his notepad what she showed him. Working quickly, he blocked in battle groups and support groups without taking time to mark in the icons, simply jotting summaries.

Filéna didn't need to edit the result.

En route, Harnel took advantage of the viewing and communication characteristics of warpspace to shift his own units to his strategic and tactical advantage. From time to time he dropped forces off—had them emerge into F-space, or park in warpspace.

His fleet had maximum remote spying support. Filéna was with Kurakex and himself, Lotta with Kristal, and Garlaby with the Home Flotilla. Except for Kari Frensler, who kept track of Siilakamasu, all other RSS agents had been assigned to various fleet command personnel, providing an instant communication network. There was bound to be confusion, but the wing commanders were all good men, well trained in the new fleet tactics, and Ostrak six or better.

Garthid fleet reassembly was far advanced, and there'd been no further surprises. All its battle groups and most wings were properly formed. Two divisions were completely formed and ready. Kurakex had begun to think the aliens were leaving the next move to him. But he was not surprised—certainly not dismayed—when one of his warpspace sentries popped into F-space. It informed him that an intruder force was approaching in warpdrive, but at a fraction of warp speed. At almost the same time, his remote, in-system F-space scouts radioed him that a sizable force was approaching in gravdrive at near maximum speed, minutes away.

It was sooner than he liked, but most units were ready. Battle groups belonging to wings not yet fully assembled, he ordered to close ranks. *Now,* he thought, *we'll learn how well these aliens fight in proper battle.* Three wings he ordered into warpspace. The rest would wait.

It occurred to Kurakex that he didn't know how to recognize the alien flagship. There'd be something about it, though. Something different—some insignia, some emblem.

Harnel's command wing was alone when it emerged into F-space. The rest of his fleet had their own assignments. At a million miles, his main screen showed the Garthid fleet clearly, an open mass of warship icons forming a ragged spheroid. Enlarged and in real-space on the *Carnothis*'s screen, the Garthid ships looked unlike anything in Harnel's fleet. Confederation ships had outrigs of various functional sorts, but Garthid ships outdid them greatly. As he'd been told. They looked like junk art by some eccentric welder.

A light pulsed briefly, then another, drawing attention to two Garthid battleships. The *Carnothis*'s artificial intelligence spoke, dispassionate as always. "The two lights mark ships not to be attacked," it said. "The red light marks their flagship. Our weapons will engage neither, without overrides from the admiral's command station."

On the base of the main screen, numbers rolled, each counting down the separation by ten thousand Standard miles. Harnel spoke to the battlecomp. "Step out torpedoes and lock on targets. Launch when ready."

At intersect minus twenty seconds, the battlecomp launched them at two targets of its own selection.

At almost the same instant, Garthid torpedoes were launched. Harnel ignored them, concentrating on the icons of his own. On the screen they moved slowly, inexorably, and struck, dozens of them, all within a second. Neither Garthid ship blew, but on the battle screen, the haloes indicating shields had disappeared from both. Their shield generators would also have blown, and probably their drives.

The *Carnothis* itself shuddered from hits on her shield, briefly thrumming with a fine vibration. In real-space views, with their vast foreshortening, the battle wing seemed now to rush toward the Garthid fleet. An alarm bell began jangling. Abruptly they were among them, through them, then looking back at them shrinking with distance. Icons showed the Garthid's two shieldless battleships struck by followup torpedoes. And in the wake of their own passage were the icons of three

Confederation ships with drives down, hulls red. *Shields collapsed by torpedoes,* Harnel thought. *Warbeams finished them.*

Meanwhile more Garthid torpedoes pursued, and in the far greater distance came the next wing of Confederation warships, their icons preceded by those of their own newly fired torpedoes. The *Carnothis*'s hyperspace warning signal buzzed loudly, and the shield generator cut off. The shield took time to decay, though less than it seemed, while the torpedoes closed. Then the ships entered hyperspace, the *Carnothis* last of all.

Harnel had left the battle behind, left it to junior admirals. Then, if Lotta Alsnor's strategy didn't work, it would be his job to gather up the scattered units and do what he could with the backup plan. *Yomal spare us that,* he prayed.

Aboard the *Thunder Lizard,* Admiral Kurakex sekTofarko had simply watched through two attack waves. His battlecomp was in charge, and he'd had no occasion to override it.

It seemed miraculous to him that his flagship had drawn no fire, or at least not been hit. Perhaps the aliens didn't recognize it. Not surprisingly, the aliens had concentrated their fire on his battleships. Three had been destroyed, and two others lay dead in space. On the other hand, six alien battleships were clinkers. He'd had the best of it.

Historically speaking, those losses were light. But if they continued long enough, light would become heavy. And how could the aliens continue losing battleships like that, the survivors generating hyperspace as they fled? And in separate groups, not in formation! They'd have battle wings scattered all over this part of the sector, lost to the battle, lost to the defense of their home system. Inexplicable!

Unless their resources were far greater than his own,

or their hyperspace navigation far more precise. He'd begun to worry. Perhaps they were. Otherwise their tactics were suicide. If a third wave followed . . . But the second had already fled into hyperspace, and his instruments hadn't picked up a third.

All of that ran through his mind without words, in scant seconds. Then a scout, one of his own, emerged from warpspace and pulsed a message packet to him, a report on the fight on the other side. *Perhaps*, Kurakex thought, *warpspace is where the aliens will give their major attention. What we've seen here may simply have been an expensive diversion.*

The *Lizard*'s battle horn blared, jerking his attention from the scout's message. The alien's third F-space wave was incoming. It appeared on his main screen, and Kurakex at once relegated the scout's message to Intelligence and the battlecomp. The alien's earlier waves had consisted of a single wing each—six battle groups, each built around a battleship. They were much like his own wings, though the groups were somewhat differently composed. But this third wave consisted of two wings, and unlike the earlier, it formed a shallow wedge. What could that mean?

The battlecomp circled the apex in red. "The point ship," it announced, "has a radio insignia unlike any other in this or previous encounters." It magnified the circled ship, a battleship resembling the others, differing visually in a single respect. For just a moment, Kurakex stared. From its bow jutted something suggesting a large sword.

Abruptly the admiral jabbed keys. "All flag division commanders!" he roared. "All flag division commanders! The red-circled ship, the point ship, is their flagship! Prepare to pursue it!" He calmed then. "Maintain pressure with torpedoes, and with beams when feasible. Destroy their flagship's escorts, but use only harassing fire on the flagship. I want it captured intact, with its commander alive! Do not allow it to drop its shield and enter strange space. Battlecomps use maximum acceptable acceleration in pursuit. Maintain pressure with beams and torpedoes. Acknowledge!"

The battlecomp's voice replied unchanged. "Fleet admiral's orders received and acknowledged. All hands in flag division prepare for maximum acceleration on signal. Flag division wing commanders acknowledge!"

Kurakex paid no attention to their acknowledgements. They would obey. His attention was on the alien flagship. *Perhaps*, he thought, *they'll be reinforced from warpspace, and not run this time*.

He hoped they'd run. It would be much easier to isolate and capture their flagship if they ran.

The Confederation battleship *Makor* centered the third wave, which was Task Force Two. In his real view, Kelmer Faronya could distinguish the Garthid flagship without being able to see the distinctive icon. Its battle group had almost twice the escorts of other Garthid groups.

Pendel Gorslen's voice spoke in Kelmer's button earpiece, the words registering both on Kelmer's mind and his recording cube. "Enlarge the flagship on your real-space view. See the thing like a short spear angling out from the base of the forward superstructure? It's the Garthid admiral's insignia. Phallic I suppose. He has a radio wave signature, too. We won't be firing at him."

Won't be firing at him. Kelmer remembered that from his briefing. *I'll bet they don't have any restrictions about firing on us*. Then wondered if perhaps they did. He was aware of numbers on the base of his mainscreen, counting down the remaining distance. Switching his station screen to the real-space view, he reduced magnification, to better show the lessening distance visually.

"We've stepped out torpedoes," Pendel told him. "They're running beside us, locked on three Garthid battleships. All of them, from the whole two wings, locked on just three ships. They'll be on their way before we reach beam range.

"We won't fire beam guns. Beam apertures lessen shield integrity, and to generate beams reduces shield strength. Coming in head-on, we've loaded our shields forward, where they're most needed. When we pass through their formations, the beam load is equalized. Incidentally, at crossing velocity, a beam can lose its lock. We'll pass through in a microsecond, then load our shield strength aft."

At twenty seconds, the screen announced torpedoes launched. Kelmer switched back to the battlecomp's view, the torpedoes showing as icons. At almost the same instant, Garthid torpedoes were launched. Death, intent and indifferent, going somewhere to happen. Kelmer's body tensed as he watched. The fleet's torpedoes struck almost simultaneously. No Garthid ship blew up, but their shields were gone.

The *Makor* took no hits. Kelmer returned the magnified view of real-space to his screen. The term "real-space" was conventional and relative. The view was vastly foreshortened. The distance closed in a rush, then they slashed through the assemblage of Garthid ships and left them shrinking behind.

In the wake of their passage, five of their own hurtled on as derelicts, hulls incandescent. All were battleships; the Garthids had favored them as targets. And not only Garthid torpedoes were giving chase. A number of Garthid battle groups—a *large* number—were accelerating in pursuit, while farther back, the Confederation fourth wave came.

On the screen's lower edge a rule formed, and beneath it numbers, showing the growing distance between Task Force Two and the lead elements of the Garthid pursuit, which weren't yet up to speed. But the numbers that registered their growing lead weren't changing so rapidly. So far, so good, Kelmer thought, but things would get trickier and more dangerous. The most troublesome possibility was that the Garthid admiral would smell a rat. Almost everything so far had been pitched to discourage him from thinking analytically, but nonetheless . . .

Now the *Makor* did take hits, torpedo hits aft. Checking the real-space view showed adjacent ships taking hits as well, waves of energy playing over their shields. He didn't know whether they were in serious danger or not. He felt more hits, some in pairs or threes but nothing more concentrated. One of the *Makor*'s escorts, a destroyer, lost its shield. Before it could generate warpspace, another torpedo struck it. The ship angled sharply off course, and inertia tore it apart. Kelmer's hair stood on end.

"The Garthid's aren't concentrating their fire on battleships now," said Pendel's voice in his ear. "Lighter craft are a lot more vulnerable, and in a chase, there's more time. And destroyers and cruisers are a deadly source of return fire. I expect we won't get it too hot and heavy for a while."

Kurakex's attention was fully on his screens. The eighteen battle groups of his flagship division kept up a steady rate of torpedo launchings. A slow rate per ship, but given the number of fighting ships, it was a heavy rate of fire. Meanwhile he'd matched the alien's speed and continued to accelerate, gradually reducing the gap. The aliens had responded briefly with further acceleration, but only briefly. Perhaps their gravdrives lacked the durability of his own. In any case, speed could be a key to their successful capture.

Four of the smaller alien fighting craft had been destroyed, along with one cruiser. Abruptly the small class cut their shield generators, and before their shields decayed enough for hyperspace generation, two more were hit. Kurakex felt a surge of gratification, and reminded himself that capture, not killing, was the purpose of this chase.

It occurred to him briefly to wonder if he might be flying into a trap of some sort. He pushed the thought aside. He was here. Committed. He'd already discovered these aliens could not be predicted, and had taken the dragon by the jaws. Strength was his forte and his advantage. He would use it.

He wasn't concerned over the fighting in the reassembly area and its adjacent warpspace. Tissokt sekArrompak was an able commander; he would deal with it. His own task now was to carry out this pursuit and capture. Then everything else would be inconsequential.

Kurakex pushed the pursuit onward, out-system. Both sides became more frugal with torpedoes. Task Force Two's battleships stopped using theirs altogether, leaving it to their cruisers to return fire. The humans concentrated theirs against a single adversary at a time. Two of Kurakex's ships were disabled, but the humans chose not to spend torpedoes to finish them off. Meanwhile a second, then a third, fourth, and fifth human cruiser were destroyed.

Bit by bit, the distance shrank between Kurakex's flag division and Task Force Two. Twice the humans increased their speed slightly, but his own ships matched them and raised the ante. His battleships rotated in firing at the human flagship, not to destroy it, but to prevent its escape into hyperspace. Torpedoes struck its shield at unpredictable intervals. Several might strike it in quick order, or it might go a minute or longer without being hit. But only occasionally was its shield stressed. Kurakex wanted to be within beam range before it lost its shield.

The *Thunder Lizard*'s battlecomp tried to get a target lock for its warbeams, but the distance was still too great. A sixth human cruiser lost its shields, but before it was hit again, disappeared into hyperspace. Moments later, all the human cruisers cut their shields. Two were destroyed; the rest generated hyperspace and escaped. All that remained of the human fourth wave were seven battleships. Kurakex ordered concentrated fire on one of them. Within a few minutes, the outer layer of its shield was fluctuating erratically, threatening to go.

Another of Task Force Two's battleships had been lost while stepping out torpedoes. Ferringum's original two wings were down to six ships now, battleships without support. They'd stopped returning fire. Stepping out torpedoes required shutting down shield layers one at a time. They'd done them in batches, running them like pilot fish, in companion mode outside the shield, off the bow. From there, one by one, the battlecomp gave them target locks, and released them like magnetic mines. But those already stepped out had been released, and Garthid fire had intensified. Stepping out more was too dangerous to justify.

And the purpose of this race was not to destroy pursuers. Nor was there any indication that their torpedo fire had bought them more time.

Kelmer Faronya knew all those things. He'd been thoroughly briefed, and from that could pretty much figure things out for himself. Also, he had Pendel Gorslen's occasional comments in his ear. What he didn't have was any real sense of the prospects for success: success, survival and victory. It seemed to him the tension on the bridge had increased, but there was nothing of desperation in it.

His own situation had one drawback. He had no way of asking questions. That was no oversight, he told himself. Pendel was a communications officer, and although not on watch, was surely on standby, monitoring, staying informed. Interruptions would not be welcomed.

The *Makor* shuddered. Four torpedoes had hit its shield at almost the same time. On the bridge an alarm sounded—not the jangle of extreme emergency, but an announcement of trouble. In the shield generator compartment. With injuries. At almost the same time, one of Ferringum's battleships lost its shield, and took another hit a bare instant before disappearing into hyperspace. Leaving Kelmer, at least, not knowing what its situation was. Now they were reduced to five.

Admiral Ferringum's voice overrode the muted human and electronic murmurs. "All ships except the *Makor*, generate hyperspace. All ships except the *Makor*, generate hyperspace." Said it as calmly as if ordering a drill. Seconds later, all four had disappeared without further loss. The *Makor* was alone. Kelmer wondered what the bridge would feel like if this ship wasn't manned entirely by Ostrak 5s or higher. It was surely the only completely Ostrak crew in the fleet.

The navy's version of the White T'swa, he realized. These people would have the same reality, the same attitude toward danger, that Colonel Romlar's troopers had. He remembered his first action—the night raid on the Komarsi brigade headquarters at Hearts Content. How deathly scared he'd been, and how calm the troopers. White T'swa. He'd been baffled by them. That had been then.

It occurred to him that fleetwide, thousands of crewmen and officers had died in the last few hours. And he'd seen no blood, no bodies, and not much wreckage! Only a few tiny flashes and sparks in real-space—larger on the battlecomp screen—and the disappearance of icons. Icons! Death and destruction sanitized. He wondered how real any of this would be to viewers. He wondered whether there'd *be* any viewers.

Aboard the *Thunder Lizard*, Kurakex sat hunched forward, hands clawed unawarely with tension. His panting reflex had kicked in, and he hadn't noticed that either. This was the time of testing, he thought, both of himself and the alien admiral. Twice, multiple strikes had threatened to destroy the alien's shield. Had it been lost, its commander would undoubtedly have tried a hyperspace jump. Whether successful or not, it would have rendered this chase useless, perhaps endangering the fleet, and the whole campaign. He'd ordered the battlecomp that the fleet was not to launch further torpedoes at less than three-second intervals.

He wondered what it was like on the alien bridge. *Were I in command of it,* he told himself, *I'd have fought, and no doubt quickly died.* Yet he pictured the alien commander as not cowardly but cool-headed. The alien would *make* him catch him.

Well, he told himself, *I too am stubborn. And when my forward beam gun gets a target lock on him, I will play him like a resonator. And I will have him.*

Seconds later the battlecomp tried again to obtain a lock for the *Lizard*'s beam gun.

On the *Makor*'s bridge, another alarm buzzed, and its battlecomp announced the lock. "Shit!" Ferringum muttered. Then the battlecomp reported a beam striking the shield aft, the shield distributing the energy and dispersing most or all of it into space.

One lock, one gun, thought the admiral. *There'll be more. It's a matter now of whether he wants me alive, or whether dead is an acceptable substitute.* Filéna had said alive was much preferred. If dead, they'd want him intact, for display.

The battlecomp announced another lock, and another, and more, but only the one gun scorched his shield. Ferringum ordered maximum acceleration. It wouldn't break the locks, and the Garthid would match it, but the faster he went, the less time the Garthid had to work on him.

The battlecomp announced a second and then a third beam. A window on the screen displayed a graph of the energy received, the shield strength, shield generator status, and overall power status. He could, Ferringum knew, beef up the shield by decelerating, but he didn't consider it. No amount of shield strength could save them. Speed just might.

A fourth beam added its power to the earlier three. It occurred to Ferringum that there'd been no torpedo strikes since the first beam had engaged. *Alive*, he told himself. *They definitely want me alive. Except I'm not what they think I am.*

I have him now, Kurakex thought. *Dead or alive, I have him.* But who knew whether dead would serve? These were aliens, after all. For the first time, the thought surfaced that the aliens might not care if their commander was captured. He tried to suppress the thought, but his attention was snagged. All he could do was snarl at it. He would persist, he told himself. Either it would matter to them or it wouldn't. Even if it didn't, it would be a victory, adding to his reputation. And he was not someone who gave up, certainly not on the basis of some groundless fear.

He hadn't expected the alien to accelerate. The *Lizard* was holding its own, but didn't have much in reserve. One could travel indefinitely in gravdrive at cruising speed. But running so near full emergency speed strained the drive system and reduced shield strength.

But the alien knew, of course, that his shield could be overwhelmed regardless of what he did. *Perhaps he needs reminding*, Kurakex thought. *Or perhaps he is testing me.* "Fire two more beams," he ordered the battlecomp, and the battlecomp passed the order to two more battleships. After a minute he added, "And another torpedo." *Just to add a little pressure.*

The shield had held well, the energy overload partly in the visible range, multicolored luminescence playing over it in flickering waves. Then the torpedo struck, the outer shield layer collapsed, and generator stress prevented regeneration. Kelmer swore silently, and looked around at the bridge crew. The worst he saw was annoyance; Ferringum was frowning.

The ship spoke. "Admiral, the Garthid commander is trying to communicate with you. Shall I give him an open channel and filter the shield effects? If I do, he may well gain a visual of your bridge. Also, judging from the Klestronu experience, there is a risk of his gaining access to my data banks, with a theft program or a sabotage program."

Ferringum didn't answer at once. After a moment he said, "Reject him."

"Yes, sir."

Pendel's voice spoke in Kelmer's ear again. "The Old Man was tempted. It might have accomplished some delay. But it wouldn't be worth the risk."

Kelmer nodded, as if the lieutenant was in front of him. "Right," he said.

He watched the battlecomp display. Shield strength, shield generator status, overall power status, all were edging slowly downward. Another beam added its power, and the drop steepened. The mid-layer, the outermost now, fluoresced more strongly, the waves quicker. Abruptly it pulsed once, twice, flared brightly for a glaring instant, a blinding picosecond, before the ship damped the image. Then the mid-layer collapsed, leaving only the inner. The afterimage on Kelmer's retina faded slowly.

The emergency alarm began to jangle now, and reaching, Ferringum shut it off. There was nothing anyone could do about it. All but one of the Garthid beams had cut off. The one remaining played on the inner layer, where the waves of fluorescence were not yet alarming.

Pendel's voice spoke to Kelmer again. "The Garthid definitely wants us alive," he murmured. "He's not pumping it to us like he could. Otherwise shield collapse might parboil us."

The battlecomp showed shield strength low and dropping. The overall power status was in trouble, and the shield generator was in the red zone. Kelmer wondered what would happen if they lost power. The weakening inner layer replayed the event sequence of the mid-layer, but less intensely.

Two minutes later, Pendel spoke in Kelmer's ear again. "The Garthid's a master; he really knows his stuff. He's reducing beam strength as our shield layer weakens."

When it finally collapsed, it was not cataclysmic, but it put the power system in the red zone, fluctuating up and down. Ferringum responded at once. "Cut the matric tap!" he snapped. "Activate emergency backup—life support and basic ship functions only."

The command startled Kelmer. Cut the matric tap? He wondered whether the command was subterfuge, or a quick response to save life support. The Garthid kept a beam on the *Makor*, at greatly reduced intensity now. Particles of hull metal boiled off, scintillating in the blackness of space. *Somewhere back there*, Kelmer thought, *it is getting hot*.

Even bridge illumination had dropped; that took Kelmer by surprise. Station screens and main screen remained on, showing the progress of system shutdowns. Some systems had cut off at once, weapons for one. Some were dropping gradually or by steps. Instrument systems remained on full. Most artificial intelligence functions had reduced to standby. Reengaging them would require a stepwise restart. Even some life support subsystems were off entirely; others were at reduced levels. The cooling system was on full.

And the gravdrive had shut down. They were continuing on inertia. *I wonder*, Kelmer thought, *how much of this the Garthid admiral knows. And what he'll do with what he thinks he knows.*

Kurakex sekTofarko stared at his screen. His battlecomp reported the alien's main power had shut down. It must be on a backup system. Exactly what ship systems were up and what were down was not knowable. But at that level of total output, the gravdrive would definitely be down, and there'd be insufficient capacity to generate strange space. *Now they can't get away.* "Find out how much reserve their backup system has. Surely they have an emergency braking system, and power enough for it."

If they didn't, they couldn't decelerate. And he very much wanted them to.

His main AI undertook the checks he'd asked for. It could not determine how much reserve the alien's backup system had, but it was definitely not enough for gravdrive.

Kurakex's face was a grim mask. "Ship!" he ordered, "Give me acceleration that will catch him within an hour."

The AI read his tone, and perhaps his body language. "Lord Admiral," it replied, "given our present extended velocity and the alien's inertia, that is beyond my capacity. By stressing our gravdrive to the limit, it is possible to catch him in one-point-seven-one-eight hours. Assuming that neither our matric tap or gravdrive break down. I cannot compute a probability, but the risk is substantial. On the other hand, it would be strongly reduced at an acceleration that would allow us to engage his docking locks with our docking tractor in approximately three hours."

Kurakex's parietal hood flared. *Ships are always conservative,* he thought. "Split the difference," he said. "And apply more heat to the alien's tail. If he has power enough to brake, perhaps we can inspire him."

Carrying his shoulder cam, Kelmer had found his way to the engine section through passageways already hot. When he got to the engine department, he didn't want to know the temperature there. About right for a T'swi, he thought. The chief engineer and the chief machinist's mate were in the power section, working on the matric tap. Their faces looked oiled with sweat. It dripped from their noses, and their coveralls were stuck to their backs. Despite the heat, they wore heavy gloves. Presumably the matric tap had been heated by conduction from the hull. The two men ignored Kelmer, and he kept well clear of their working zone. In editing the cube, he'd leave in their occasional oaths. They'd help make the situation real to viewers.

Nearby, a PO1 with a long wrench was removing the nuts on an access panel. He too wore heavy gloves. "How's it going?" Kelmer asked.

The man answered without turning. "Be bloody impossible, if the Old Man hadn't shut her down." Grunting, he loosened a nut, then screwed it off rapidly by hand and laid it on the deck beside the bulkhead. He wiped sweat from his eyes with a sleeve, then started on a third nut. "It was one hundred thirty-two degrees in this compartment, last I looked," he said, "and we've got lots to do to get this bruiser running again. The Garthids might like it this hot, but no human being this side of Tyss could work in it for long." That nut too came off. He laid it by the first, then gestured farther aft before starting on the next. "That's where the shield generator is. And it's hotter back there—we've already dragged two guys out for the medics—and there's work needs done on it." That nut didn't come off as easily. He swore, removed it with the wrench, then loosened the next. "If we don't fix it, we'll finish burning out the system when we try to use the matric tap again." That nut joined the others. "The chief's got guys getting into hot suits. Clumsy to work in, especially in small spaces, but . . ."

He got the next to last nut off. The one remaining was on the bottom. The PO1 unseated the panel and lowered it, letting it pivot down and hang from the bottom bolt. Without finishing what he'd started to say, he switched on his helmet light and climbed into the opening. Kelmer recorded him crawling back into the work space. Looking after him through the access opening, Kelmer

found it substantially hotter in there. If the guy passed
out, no one would know. He'd die.

Two men in cumbersome firefighter's suits waddled
through the power section. Each wore a pack frame
with what presumably were air tanks. Refrigerated?
Kelmer didn't know. The chief stopped them, gave them
instructions, then followed them to the shield generator
room, Kelmer a few feet behind. One of the two
crewmen turned the handle of the heavy door and
pushed it open. A billow of hot air came through it,
and the chief staggered back, arm raised in defense.
After a moment the two men in hot suits went in and
closed the door behind them.

The chief slumped for a moment then, straightening,
took a deep breath of hot air. For the first time he seemed
to notice Kelmer. "We're going to lose it back here," he
muttered. "Backup system and all. If they don't take that
bloody beam off us." Then he started back to the matric
tap, stumbling once on nothing. Kelmer wondered how
far the man was from heat collapse.

Pendel spoke again through the button in Kelmer's
ear. "Kelmer," he said, "better get back to the bridge.
The microwave marker has shown up against the
background radiation. The navcomp's identified it."

The passageways were much hotter than before, but
not remotely like the bake-oven heat of the engine section.
A crewman he passed gleamed with sweat, and Kelmer
realized how wet he was himself. His skivvies were stuck
to him. Even the bridge, when he arrived there, was a
hundred degrees or more, he was sure, remote though
it was from the site being heated by the warbeam.

The calm on the bridge both surprised him and it didn't.
The intentness didn't surprise him at all. From his backup
station, Pendel Gorslen spoke again in Kelmer's ear. "The
icon on your battlecomp view is the gate. Two-point-
eight million miles ahead—about four-point-one minutes.

The Garthids have accelerated further; their flagship is at one hundred eighty-nine miles and closing. But they're stressing their gravdrives severely."

Kelmer sat down at his station, glad that his cube was recording Pendel's words. His eyes went to the battlecomp view. The Garthid flagship had turned off its warbeam. Another beam, showing green instead of red, ended at the icon of the *Makor*. There were similar beams from the ships ranked beside the Garthid flagship.

"Tug beams," Pendel said. "Barely perceptible now, but locked on. With so many, we'll begin to slow measurably, at about ten miles separation. In about three minutes. And the effect is exponential, of course."

Kelmer stared at the real view, not the battlecomp view. *Microwave marker.* He wondered if the Garthid flagship's instruments had picked it up.

"It's a race," Pendel said.

"Lord Admiral." The officer speaking was the *Thunder Lizard's* captain. "Let me have the drive slowed. Slightly. The diagnostic shows incipient failure in the grav converter."

Kurakex sekTofarko didn't reply at first, but his parietal hood flared in irritation. His eyes were on the separation numbers at the bottom of the main screen. There were only two digits now, the second digit changing flick-flick-flick, the first less quickly.

"And we are locked on," the captain added.

The reply was growled, the admiral not turning as he spoke. "Leave it as it is, and do not bring it up again. You anger me!"

"Yes, sir."

The signals officer stepped over to the captain and spoke quietly. "Captain, we have differentiated what appears to be a weak microwave signal at fifteen-fifty megacycles. Dead ahead."

"At what distance?" the captain asked. Also quietly.

"Point-seven-one million miles."

The captain sucked in his leathery cheeks. "Watch it closely," he said.

The screen showed the fine lines of tug beams, from all vessels to the prey. On the screen they arrived at quite different angles, because of the foreshortened view. In reality the angles were decimal parts of a second of arc, their separate forces aligned, arithmetically combined. Very soon now the quarry would slow perceptibly.

The captain tapped a key, getting the signals officer's attention, and beckoned. Best to keep this off the system. The officer came over to him.

"Put the suspected microwave signal on the battlecomp screen," the captain said. "But make it inconspicuous."

"Yes, sir."

The captain watched him return to his station. A moment later the reported signal appeared on the captain's battlecomp view. *If the admiral asks what it is,* he thought, *I cannot be faulted for answering.*

On his own screen, he created a window around the source of the apparent signal. Definitely a signal, and virtually on line with the alien. *It resembles an astrogation beacon or pod station,* he thought, *but out here? More than 300 billion miles from their primary?* And dead ahead! As if the alien was homing on it. A signal needed a source, but he could not see one. Of course, it need not be large. He frowned. A mine perhaps?

The signal icon disappeared. The alien, hardly a dozen miles ahead now, was in the line of sight, he realized. If it was a mine, the alien would either hit or avoid it. Locked as they were, they'd share any avoidance maneuver, but with their inertia, avoidance would have to start very soon.

The icon of the human ship began to flash. A footer caption reported that they had functional tractor force, which meant the beginning of deceleration. They felt it aboard the alien ship, he had no doubt.

❖   ❖   ❖

The *Thunder Lizard*'s signals officer had thought his way through much the same steps, to much the same conclusion. The beacon would be visible by ships on the division's flanks. He keyed a closed comm line to a ship on the extreme left flank. "Calling *Ice Mountain*, signals officer on watch. This is the flagship. Do you see the beacon on the alien's course?"

"We do."

"What does it mark?"

"Something that registers only as mass, in the range of 10 to 20 kilotons. We get no reflections, no outline, and almost no thermal emissions. The alien will impact it in approximately . . ." He paused. "Fifteen seconds."

The signals officer felt himself panting. There was still time, barely. If he had an override at his station . . . He looked at the captain, who was looking toward the admiral. Who was facing the screen, seeing God knew what.

Rear Admiral Arnoth Ferringum's eyes were fixed on the screen. On the *Makor*'s bridge, all eyes were. It showed the navscreen view, and the icons of six marker lights. In a window at one side of the screen, the seconds wound down, each equivalent to some 11,000 miles: five, four, three, two, one . . .

They felt a brief twinge of disorientation, then they were speeding through another part of space, hyperspace weeks from Iryala. Four miles behind them, the *Thunder Lizard* followed exactly, decelerating. The Garthid flag division, which had swept past the gate, was in another sector of space, parsecs distant. No doubt bewildered, dismayed. Where had their flagship gone? The two flagships? They wouldn't find the beacon, either. The gate ship was to generate hyperspace after the Garthid flagship had gated through.

Meanwhile the *Lizard*'s solitary tug beam had disengaged at crossover. Ferringum called the engine department, and waited a few seconds for an answer.

"Second Engineer Wallbaron. The chief is in sickbay."

"Wallbaron, do we have enough backup power to decelerate?"

"Yessir. If you're not too ambitious."

"Give me half a grav and I'll make do."

"Yessir. We can manage a half gee."

The screen showed tugs and an ambulance ship chasing the Garthid flagship, which showed no sign of armed response. Ferringum visualized the Garthid bridge watch convulsing, or sprawled unconscious on the deck. Lormagen had assured him the only question was how severe their gate shock would be, but up till now he'd feared privately that they just might prove immune.

The next uncertainties were whether existing gate-shock therapy could keep them alive. Especially since Garthid biochemistry and nutrition was highly speculative, based on the chemistry of two not-very-freshly-dead Garthid fliers. And how—this one he hadn't thought of before— how the T'swa would get inside the ship. Surely someone would have worked that out.

But those were someone else's problems. His—actually Torens Harnel's, but he was Harnel's right hand man— theirs would be to get the fleet ready, in case they still had to fight the Karghanik Armada. The Armada had substantially outnumbered and outgunned them before, and now the Confederation fleet had had serious losses fighting the Garthids.

...

Chapter 47
The Surrogate Concurs

Esteemed Lomaru walked into the kitchen. He'd just
come from the House of Sitting, where he'd supervised
novices.

"Ah, Master!" said the cook. "You've come to feed your
children! Or so you claim." It was cook's little joke,
repeated daily with minor variations. Like many other
Garthids who'd lived and worked long enough among
shafan, he'd developed a rudimentary sense of humor.

Lomaru grinned as the cook handed him a stainless
steel pail containing twelve pounds of meat in modest
chunks, fresh and bloody. "My children thank you,"
Lomaru said. "I will not eat a bite of it, I promise."

He left by the back entrance, passing the neatly fenced
herb garden and crossing the landscaped rear lawn to a
strongly fenced area of several acres. He yodeled as he
went, not very loudly, but loudly enough. Three yearling
killer lizards, males of a quarter-ton each, came out of a
grove at a leisurely half gallop, a gait surprisingly graceful.
They met the old Garthid at the gate, greeting him with
snorting hisses, like strange, steam-driven automatons.
He fed them by hand, a piece at a time, the alpha male
first, respecting their self-imposed ranking.

At one point he paused and spoke aloud, as if to
someone unseen. "Ah, Tso-Ban!" He laughed. "Shortly,

shortly. I am with God's other children now. He loves us all, you know."

The big saurians offered no threats as he fed them, nor was there any scuffling among them. When the meat was gone, he presented first the pail, then his bloody hands to the alpha male, who licked them clean with a rough and muscular tongue. Then by turn, they exposed to him the relatively soft undersurface of their jaws, which he scratched with stubby claws. They purred like great cats. They were pushier for his petting than they'd been for meat.

After a few minutes, Lomaru turned and left with his pail. They did not try to get out when he opened the gate. They simply stood, their intent saurian eyes watching him leave. Their longish tails waved slowly, free of the ground. Later that day a prey animal would be released in the enclosure, to be cornered, killed, and devoured.

After returning the pail, Lomaru washed his hands and retired to an arbor in the lawn garden. There he settled into the ukshaf meditation squat. He'd been peripherally aware of the quiet visitor waiting patiently in his mind. Their communication was of images, concepts and feelings. Translated into words, it ran as follows:

«So, Tso-Ban. You have not visited me for a while. You have concrete matters to discuss today.»

«Indeed. Warriors of our two species have been in conflict. The fighting has been resolved, and an armistice concluded. Esteemed Valvoxa guided Admiral Tissokt sekArrompak through the negotiations. Now they wish the Surrogate's approval. With you as intermediary.»

«Tissokt, eh? An interesting development. You have activated my liveliest curiosity. As for my intermediary services—we are within an hour's drive of the palace. And of the Surrogate, if he is at home. Tell me all, dear Tso-Ban, tell me all.»

«I will undertake to show you the live images given to me through another seer.»

«Hmm! My friend, you are a source of revelations and wonders. Proceed! Proceed!»

Lomaru met with the Surrogate on the Surrogate's south balcony, from which they could see the roseate sunset in the west. In the east, the red giant "Eye of the Dragon" had risen. It was not as baleful as it had seemed to their remote and superstitious ancestors.

"What you told me on the comm is truly astonishing," the Surrogate said. "It is hard to conceive of a commander being captured alive in a space battle. With his flagship! How did it happen?"

"It was a result of great daring, of advanced souls and advanced science. And of the desire of the alien humans to minimize deaths. Like yourself, their rulers are not fond of killing and destruction. Happily, neither were their fleet commanders. Many were sacrificed to the greater good—a concept often used in our history to justify great wrongs. But this time both honest and effective."

"How did they come to fight?"

"First let me describe how I learned it. I have told you about the human shafa known as Master Tso-Ban. He had visited the minds of those involved: Tissokt, Valvoxa, and the human vice admiral responsible for the capture. He saw the images of what they had seen, and showed them to me."

They talked for hours—till the Eye of the Dragon had crossed the meridian. When Lomaru had finished his report, the Surrogate asked questions, and they'd discussed the probable long-term effects. But there'd been no disagreement on terms. In the morning, the Surrogate would dictate and sign his approval. When Tso-Ban next made contact—he'd planned to within one of his own planet's days—Lomaru would forward that approval mentally. Tissokt sekArrompak and Valvoxa could sign a copy in the Surrogate's name. It was a strange way to carry on the business of state, but there was no acceptable alternative.

Meanwhile, a Confederation ambassador would be sent, a human named Dho-Kat, one of Tso-Ban's race. He could tolerate the Shuuf'r Thaak climate. He'd be equipped with appropriate breathing apparatus, and was familiar with Confederation monetary and legal systems. With him would come Esteemed Valvoxa, as an eye witness to the events, and a principal participant in the negotiations. Indemnities to the families of Confederation dead and reparations to the Confederation government would be worked out. Then a trade agreement would be explored, though at such distances . . .

"One term I'm surprised they didn't ask," the Surrogate said. "Our help in ousting their invader from the world he has claimed. If the invader's Armada is as powerful as described . . ."

It was a question the old shafa could not answer.

Alone in his bed that night, the Surrogate found sleep elusive. *Kurakex taken alive!* he thought. *For that by itself I owe them gratitude. His gross violation of orders was high treason, and by law requires execution. But not before a public tour of the Khanate, thoroughly publicizing his actions and defeat. Display him in chains on every world. Hold him up to public contempt.* Briefly he rehearsed the scenario, and found no pleasure in it. *The arrogant fool refused even to talk to the humans,* he told himself. *He attacked a peaceful but dangerous nation against which the Khanate had neither grievance nor quarrel. The indemnities alone will break the power of the Tofarko Clan forever.*

Chapter 48
War Council

Lord Kristal's gray eyes looked at the people at his conference table: Lord Carns, the Emeritus Kalif, Kusu Lormagen, Artus Romlar, Lotta Alsnor-Romlar, and Kari Frensler were there. Along with Master Deng-Vaht of the Lodge of Kootosh-Lan, who'd gated in the previous night from Tyss. And Torens Harnel, who'd just gated in from his flagship.

"Good morning," Kristal said. "I thank you all for being here. As you know, the purpose of this meeting is to explore the problems of liberating Aslarsan. We won't be making decisions this morning, but I will need consensus on an outline plan by Threeday. Lord Carns and Colonel Romlar have been asked for brief preliminary proposals, which we will get to in due time.

"Most of you have been heavily involved with the Garthid threat, and are not well informed on events in the Aslarsan System. So to begin with, we'll review what's known."

Kristal's eyes settled on Kari Frensler. "Miss Frensler, update us on what you know from remote spying."

Kari stood to answer. "Your lordship, the Armada arrived at the Aslarsan System four days ago, and sent a strong flag command group in-system. By that time I had help from some agents Lotta assigned me.

John Dalmas

"The queen and her government, of course, pretended surprise. Actually only Eldra and her Privy Council knew in advance. They're all fives and sixes. So the surprise and shock of everyone else was genuine.

"Siilakamasu isn't worried about us at all. The only thing he feels concern over is the Garthids. He assumes they suffered losses here, more or less heavy. And he pretty much expects them not to stay around longer than it takes to give Iryala a good scorching. But he also worries that they just might make the rounds of the other worlds, including Aslarsan. And that he'll have to fight them. He's afraid of them, of their alienness, though he'd never admit it."

She turned her eyes to Torens Harnel. "Meanwhile his fleet has largely completed reassembly, ready to engage any intruding forces. Destroyer squadrons are posted at strategic locations for prompt reaction. He's not allowing any non-Armada craft to leave the planet, and he controls the pod station. And of course he's intercepting and interning any incoming merchant ships. So he feels reasonably secure there, certainly from us. He's convinced himself that whatever forces we have left are fugitives, and pose no real threat. But he's got the system well monitored, and his warships are in position to move quickly and decisively."

She turned to the Defense Minister, General Ircon Thromlek, Lord Carns. "Initially, Siilakamasu talked about destroying two or three small Aslari cities with warbeams, but he wasn't more than half serious. He enjoys annoying General Vrislakavaro." She glanced at the Kalif. "I assume your Eminence finds that believable. But the admiral is quite capable of doing it, and without provocation.

"The general told him to go ahead. That if he wanted to destroy otherwise useful property, create a vast pool of hatred and future difficulties, and ensure a bill of complaint in the first pod to Varatos, that would be a good way to do it. He surprised the admiral, but didn't really worry him. The admiral believes that if it comes down to it, he can have the general done away with. Meanwhile the elite 1st Heavy Infantry Division, and the two marine divisions, are under the general's command. Along with engineer battalions, of course. They're the only ones on the ground yet.

"That's the marine *divisions*, not the fleet marines. Since then the admiral's played nice, but he believes that when the time comes, he can subvert the marine divisions.

"Meanwhile, the general is following the basic takeover plan he'd developed for Iryala, modified as appropriate. Just now he's got engineer battalions building base camps at strategic locations around the perimeter of the capital. The climate is tropical, and for now he's got his troops bivouacked. He refused to billet them with the population. Believes it would hurt discipline, and cause trouble with the Aslari."

She looked around the table. "For those who don't know, Aslarton, the capital, is on a plateau at about three thousand feet. So the bases will be of squad-tent camps initially. They'll have raised floors, open-weave walls for whatever buildings are necessary, outdoor shower facilities without roofs . . . You get the picture. Quick, cheap, and reasonably comfortable. They'll move in more divisions as they complete sections.

"The general has thoroughly impressed his staff and upper-level command officers with the importance of starting off on the right foot. And he hasn't messed too much with Aslari government and business. He's officed his Control and Expropriation people in the executive palace, where they're observing and asking all kinds of questions. Learning the system.

"The rest of the planet is untouched. But formations of assault fighters have made low-level flyovers of all prefecture capitals and other major cities, in a show of force. And of course, every broadcasting station has shown imperial cubeage of beam-gun ships parked off the planet, able quickly to scorch any area on the surface."

Kari looked around. "Those are the basics. Lotta can describe the situation from the Aslari point of view."

She sat down, and Kristal nodded. "Go ahead, Lotta."

Lotta stood. "The first thing the Armada commanders did," she said, "was televise a bombardment flotilla parked above the capital. Then they buzzed the government district with assault fighters. At the same time radioing the queen an ultimatum, demanding the immediate surrender of the government. Eldra complied. She had no real alternative, and of course she knows we're working on it. Now the entire government district is under imperial martial law.

"And while the troops are bivouacked, Vrislakavaro's upper echelon staff is billeted in the homes of high-level government people. With orders to behave themselves, or experience the wrong side of a court-martial. He's given his deputy, Major General Meksorli, the provost marshal's hat. Meksorli's main responsibility is troop behavior toward civilians. Vrislakavaro considers him both realistic and hard-nosed, and they both see the job as vital to getting off on the right foot.

"And of course, the high-level government people are Alumni, fives and sixes.

"Things have started out pretty smoothly. The general's staff is intelligent and well-trained, and the people they're working with are being cooperative." Lotta turned to the Kalif. "The general addressed an auditorium full of bureaucrats, and did it without arrogance or bullying. He spoke to them through a translation program by SUMBAA, good enough to handle the subtleties. He didn't even lie. His key facts were wrong, but he didn't know it. And ninety-nine-point-nine-nine-nine percent of the Aslari don't know the true facts. Most of them believe there is no more Confederation, and that these new people might turn out not too bad. The choices seemed to be to collaborate and live under a new and basically parasitic overlayer, or resist and live under harsh repression."

Lotta looked around, her expression mild. "I've visited the minds of a few ordinary people, and had some apprentices sample others. Not much of a sample, but instructive. Almost all of them were resigned to the situation as they saw it.

"This is good in two respects. There's not apt to be a blowup with consequent bloody reprisals, and the imperial troops and their commanders are likely to get a bit slack about security." She sat back. "That's how it looks now."

"Thank you, Kari and Lotta," Kristal said, and turned to the Kalif. "Does Your Eminence have any comments at this point?"

Chodrisei Biilathkamoro's expression was wry. "Only that their observations fit what I know about the admiral, the commanding general, and the general's deputy."

After Artus and Lord Carns had presented their suggestions on strategy, Torens Harnel added his. This was followed by three hours of discussion. The liberation of Aslarsan required that the White T'swa mission be successful, and it promised to be the trickiest, most difficult part of the whole operation.

Only Artus and Master Deng-Vaht felt happy with it, but no one offered an alternative. They'd have to see how it worked.

Chapter 49
People, Viewpoints, and Threats

"Well, Deng, what did you think of our meeting today? I'm sure things are done differently on Tyss."

The large, grizzling black man put down his cup and wiped his lips with a napkin. "Our business is much different, Emry. Over the decades since my retirement as a fighting man, my duties have been the gathering of relevant information, the evaluation of potential employers, the drawing up of contracts, and providing the assigned regiment or regiments with appropriate equipment, information, and transportation."

Deng-Vaht glanced around the table at the other guests. "This requires considering both the war level, the nature of the contending parties, and of course the environment, whatever it might be: climate, urban, rural, forest ... Within broad limits we seldom consider the merits of the war itself. Or of the employer, beyond his credit status. We are simply a provider of highly skilled warriors."

He returned his gaze to Kristal. "Nor, with one exception, have we ever involved ourselves with intrigues. You know, of course, the exception I refer to. I was the commander of the Ice Tiger Regiment on Kettle, and I was briefed on the unusual circumstances before I left Tyss. And it was you, of course, who signed our contract for your king."

The old nobleman's eyebrows rose slightly. Thirty years earlier, as His Majesty's personal aide, he'd coordinated the Orlanthan insurrection. With its layers of apparent purposes. He'd still been young: forty-seven years old. "Ah, that!" Kristal hadn't met the young T'swa commander, had merely signed the contract. "And now you are your lodge's ambassador to the Confederation." He paused. "You know, as much as we've learned from the T'swa, and borrowed from you, at times bought from you, we still don't understand you well." He laughed. "Certainly not as well as you understand us."

White teeth flashed in a gun-metal face. "True. Though the Colonel's wife knows us quite well." Again his teeth flashed, this time toward Lotta. "I doubt that anything we do would greatly puzzle her." He gestured farther down the table. "And Filéna would be puzzled even less. Her life and training with us began at age three, I believe." Filéna nodded. "And continued till this past year. Both are deeply immersed in the T'sel. And the colonel, after all, is a graduate of the same Lodge as I. Six years of training under T'swa veterans . . . But still you are different. Inevitably."

He turned to Artus. "I recall the lodge's review of your regiment's graduation maneuvers. Your 'White T'swa' regiment, so named by your original cadre, T'swa veterans all. A name given in affection, with admiration. Grand Master Kliss-Bahn was deeply impressed by your troopers." Grinning at the young colonel, he added, "And their commander." He looked at Lord Kristal again. "Kliss-Bahn invited Artus to comment on his newly completed training, an unusual honor. And I recall the colonel's words—not all of them, but those which most impressed me. In fact, I believe I can recite them rather closely."

His large eyes fixed on Artus. "You said, 'We are not truly T'swa. Our scripting and imprinting have been different. But the Ostrak Procedures, and our training by your lodge and the Order of Ka-Shok, have made us close cousins. In most ways we have become closer to you than to our families. But we remain Confederat'swa, and more specifically Iryalans.'

"Your insight, Artus, made us feel closer to you than ever. Truly you are *not* T'swa. But at that moment we felt very much your brothers. As I do now."

No one spoke. Coso Biilathkamoro squeezed his wife's hand, and felt hers squeeze back. On the other side of the table, the Romlars had done much the same. It was Kristal who broke the brief silence. "What do you see as the principal difference between yourselves and us? Ignoring the superficial."

Deng-Vaht grinned. "You are, in your own words, a Movement. With a major goal. And its survival is threatened. Thus you are notably more *serious* than we are. Which makes your association with the T'sel less intimate. And in general, the more highly ranked you are, the more serious.

"So far it has not weakened you. To salvage your Confederation—and the word *salvage* is not too strong— is very worthwhile. It impacts the spiritual evolution of many billions of humans. And to a large degree the lives and conditions of living and learning for many generations to come."

He grinned again. "But enough of that, or I'll become serious myself. T'sel Master Alsnor-Romlar found it difficult not to laugh when I said that as a people you are serious. She recognized it as both accurate and amusing. Colonel, I cannot congratulate you too strongly on your excellent judgment and great good fortune in becoming her husband."

He paused, his calm eyes scanning his lordship's dinner company. "And while I am being talkative, let me comment further on your goal. As I indicated, this is only the second time my people—in the person of my Lodge—have ever, ever, actively involved ourselves in anyone's intrigues. Each time it was because of the respect in which we held your goal, and wished to advance it. That is why Kliss-Bahn sent me here. It is why I agreed to come."

He looked at the fruit compote on the table in front of him. "And now I will find another use for my mouth, and take a second serving of this delightful preparation."

Lotta pulled off the unaccustomed party dress she'd worn, hung it in her closet, then laughed. She'd been laughing at intervals since they'd left Emry's penthouse. "Serious!" she said, and laughed again. "How much that word explained! Did you see Filéna's aura when Deng-Vaht said it? Afterward, in the ladies' room, she almost collapsed laughing. And calm is her trademark! She laughed herself into hiccups before we came out, and that made her laugh even more."

Lotta paused, appraising her husband. "You're not laughing though. Not close."

He shook his head ruefully. "Deng-Vaht hit it square, and I knew it. But I still feel dead serious about this."

Lotta stepped to him, reached up and put her arms around his neck, drew his face down to hers and kissed his lips, just a peck. "I worried about that when you were on Maragor," she said. "Especially after you started having bad dreams. But it was nothing I could do much about. There's something really heavy, back in your past. Way back. I've known it since you were a recruit. And it's not anything our procedures can deal with. Wellem agreed.

"I told Emry about it when you were on Maragor. It's why we wanted you to assign someone else to lead the field operations here. And you agreed. So he was concerned when you changed your mind and decided to lead the hit yourself.

"I talked him out of a veto. I pointed out your success on Terfreya, where the odds were heavily against you, and you were already worried about 'wasting your regiment.' And how, on Maragor, you outfoxed a larger T'swa regiment, not once but twice."

Artus chuckled. "You'd have loved its CO, Colonel Ko-Dan. We got together and exchanged stories after the peace was signed. To him, everything was amusing. He had some marvelous bits about Engwar II, for whom he actually developed a kind of affection, incidentally.

"But the one he thought funniest was finding Coyn Carrmak pulling guard duty outside Undsvin's office. To him that was hilarious. An OSP major, presumably on a spy mission, in an enemy uniform, guarding the office of an enemy general! He said it told him right away the kind of warriors he was up against."

He gazed thoughtfully at his wife. "You know, it just struck me. The reason that whatever it is didn't screw up my decision making. It produced depression instead of anxiety. And it didn't hit me at decision-making time. Only afterward, after the action. I never had trouble making the hard choices. One would feel right, so it was the only choice. And it always did the job. It will this time, too."

The two got ready for bed, and to Lotta, it was obvious from his aura that her husband was feeling serious again. "What's going on, lover mine?" she asked.

"It's about Carrmak. Looking back at the things he did on Maragor, maybe he *should* be leading the hit."

She looked long at Artus. "No, my dear, *you* should. It's true that Coyn Carrmak has a great combination of both intelligence and wisdom. From stories you and Jerym tell, he's been proving it since your first week of training. But so do you. You showed it first in your squad's first orienteering problem, that same autumn. My big brother's told me about it more than once.

"Ask Dao or Voker or Dak-So. They had seventeen hundred trainees, and it came down finally to you and Carrmak. And they chose you."

She laughed again. "Ask Brigadier Shiller, poor man.

Or poor, frustrated Saadhrambacoora! You didn't send them to their graves, but you certainly embarrassed them. Ended their careers."

She was standing almost toe to toe with him. Reaching, she touched his nose with a small finger, and when she spoke again it was more softly. "And now I'm going to tell you something else, something that may sound strange to you. It's opinion, but it's a damned good one, because it's mine. You've been waiting for this mission, this encounter actually, for a long long time: twenty-one thousand years and change. Since the Great War. And if you pull it off, it will have a bigger impact on the species than if Coyn Carrmak or anyone else did the same thing."

He looked down at her soberly without speaking. "You know what?" he asked. "The way I've felt lately— I haven't been depressed. I've been grim. And you're right. I'm the only one to lead this hit. I've known it all along, and been afraid of it. It'll be a culmination and completion."

She looked long at him, then grinned. "Huh! All that seriousness got me sweaty. Now I'll have to take a shower." She paused. "Not alone, I hope."

It was Artus's turn to laugh. Softly. With his hands beneath her arms, he picked her up and kissed her.

"Gone for a whole dek? Oh Kelmer, no!"

"As much as a dek. Could be less."

"You were gone for weeks, training, and then in that awful battle. Can't you . . ." She stopped in mid-sentence. She knew the answer, or one answer. Perhaps he *could* take her, but she'd have to drop out of school. And it was going too well. So instead she finished: "Can't you talk your way out of it?"

"No, I can't. It has to do with the war. And I'm the only one trained to carry this out."

She didn't argue, didn't plead. Instead she said, "Do you worry about . . . me? That I might do something foolish again?"

He smiled slightly. "You were honest with me. And earlier, we'd been through a lot together. No, I don't worry about that."

It troubled her slightly that he wasn't angry. Didn't seem angry. And she wouldn't have told him, if she hadn't been in trouble with Interior, for her association with Jarnell Walthen. During interrogation, Jarnell had said he'd learned about Lotta from her, but Interior had decided it had been an act of simple ignorance on her part.

"I'll tell you what I will do, though," Kelmer added. "When the war is over, which shouldn't be too long, and if we win, I'll tell them at the office that I want a year off. A year to write a holo novel. I've gotten enough public attention from the Komars-Smolen War, and the war with the Garthids, I can sell it as a project. Get an advance, and write the script at home." He grinned at her. "Maybe you'll find a role in it."

In his office on Aslarsan, Chesty Vrislakavaro stared at the comm on his desk. The voice issuing from it was Loksa Siilakamasu's, reconstituted after security scrambling. The communication lags were minute. The admiral was only 67,000 miles out, about to generate warpspace after his first surface visit.

"Chesty," he was saying, "I've been reviewing what you showed me, and I don't like the way you're doing things. You're too damned soft! Put the fear of Kargh into them, man. Let them see what we can do to them. That'll help the missionaries, too, when we put them down."

The general's answer was testy. "I don't send reports for anyone's approval. They don't require anyone's approval but my own. I send them up for your information, and SUMBAA's. As for the proper approach in dealing with the Aslari, that's mine to decide. As I've made clear before.

"As for establishing our ability to punish possible crimes

against the Army of Occupation, some ninety-nine percent of the people on Aslarsan have seen your bombardment flotilla on television. Probably half have seen an actual overflight of assault craft. Meanwhile things are functioning smoothly. The original absenteeism from work . . ."

"Absenteeism? Bullshit, Chesty! All that is bullshit! Timid bureaucratic bullshit! You're a military man, and don't forget it! If you don't show people what you're made of, we'll be in serious trouble."

The general's fist slammed his desktop. "Look, admiral." His big voice boomed. "*I* am in charge of surface operations, and don't you forget *that*! I'm open to advice, but we've been over this before. And I am not going to create centuries of turmoil and sabotage by carrying out stupid suggestions just to please you!"

"Ah." Loksa Siilakamasu's voice had turned soft. "So my suggestions are stupid."

Chesty stared at the blank screen. *You overstepped that time, Arbind,* he told himself. *You and your damned temper.* He wished he could see the admiral's face, read his eyes, but the ultrasecure scramble program didn't accommodate visuals. "Hell yes!" he answered. "Maybe tomorrow you'll say something that makes some damn sense."

"Very well, *General*." The words were little more than breathed, yet clearly audible. "But keep in mind that your authority is restricted to the *surface*. The *surface*, general. Everything above the *surface* is in my jurisdiction."

He paused, letting the words sink in. The general's swarthy complexion had darkened with blood; Tagurt Meksorli was afraid his commander was about to have a coronary. "And General," the voice continued, almost conversationally now, "that includes mail pods. Pods and the pod station are also my responsibility."

The words *communication terminated* flashed on the general's computer screen. "Shit," he breathed, and turned to Meksorli. "I guess you know what this means."

"I know what it looks like. Whether he'll follow through though . . ."

"What do you think, Tagurt? Could he be right?"

"Shall I be blunt?"

Chesty scowled. "My name's not Loksa Siilakamasu. If I didn't want an honest answer, I wouldn't have asked."

"Got that. All right. The admiral is psychotic. It's that simple. He wants to kill people. Terrorize them. Blow things up. He'll do what he wants to, with or without justification."

Chesty Vrislakavaro sighed gustily through pursed lips. "I've got one solution open to me. I'll call him back and challenge him to a duel."

"Can you take him?"

"I don't know. If the challenge is mine, the choice of weapons becomes his. He'd probably turn me down anyway. In the forty years since duels became illegal in the services, there hasn't been a single one between senior officers. Not more than two or three a year among junior officers." He gnawed a lip. "Do you have any suggestions?"

"I'm not urging it, but I see one possibility. You can bypass him, take it to the fleet on the work channels. Remind them what really happened to the Kalif and the survey base. Charge the admiral with treason, and with the attempted murder of the Emeritus Kalif, the Grand Admiral, personal representative of the Emperor Kalif. And name one of his vice admirals as the new fleet admiral.

"They already know, of course. Most crewmen were awake and heard it direct. Those who were in stasis have heard about it since. I have. My troops have. There were crewmen on the troopships who made sure of it, after we woke up. Told the story or played cubes of it surreptitiously. And the word spread.

"Deadly dangerous business. Which tells you about the level of loyalty he has up there. If he gives an order to fight, or to scorch some Aslari city, they'll do it. They're service. They're trained to obey orders, especially orders to fight. But they do not like their admiral. Give them a choice; see what happens."

Inciting to mutiny? Chesty Vrislakavaro looked acutely uncomfortable. "See what happens? What do you think would happen?"

"I can see maybe a dozen scenarios. One is favorable, the others various degrees of bad. Especially if the aliens show up in force."

Chesty nodded thoughtfully. "I know Loksa well enough to know he's about fifty percent bullshit. Unfortunately the other fifty percent is snake venom. For now, at least, I'm going to bet on bullshit and do nothing. Tomorrow he could call and ask me how I liked his little joke."

"And if he has his gunboats shoot up—say Golden Bay?"

"Then you and I will have a very large salvage job to handle down here with two-point-two-seven billion Aslari. We'll do what we can. Hopefully without incinerating a bunch of them."

Kari Frensler emerged from the mind of Chesty Vrislakavaro and for a moment sat blinking on her trance cushion. *Someone needs to know about this right now!* she thought, and getting to her feet, stepped quickly to her comm.

Chapter 50
Shoot-Out in Space

Beneath the personnel carrier, the countryside was new to Sublieutenant Yesik Abreekas, but he wasn't paying much attention. It didn't seem greatly different from his home state on Varatos, and anyway he'd never been interested in nature. His universe consisted of the real stuff and staff of life: contracts, tables of organization, tax records, spreadsheets . . . That and the army, especially the Expropriations Section, Imperial Army of Occupation.

The world of opportunity for a young and ambitious gentry officer with a business education. And since yesterday, things were looking up. His group was getting away from the Old Man.

Regular Army people insisted that Chesty Vrislakavaro was a good CO, that when things were going decently, he could be almost affable. But recently he'd been grouchier than a master sergeant with an abscessed tooth. The rumor was, he'd crossed swords with the admiral—this supposedly from a warrant officer on the general staff's staff, who'd overheard a bit of it through a door. Sublieutenant Abreekas was always skeptical of rumors, but certainly something was bugging hell out of the Old Man.

Another rumor had it, the Old Man was worried about

an Aslari uprising. It was one of those rumors that made sense if you didn't look too closely. The Aslari police formed layers: planetary, state, prefectural and local, all of them armed of course. And if it came down to it, you couldn't know which side they'd go with. But they were no real threat. They weren't organized, trained or armed to fight military forces.

More worrisome, but not much—every one of the planet's 312 states had a planetary defense armory. The 5th and 9th Light Infantry Divisions had been shuttled down, and scattered by companies all over the planet, occupying the principal armories. There they inventoried and disabled the weapons, then moved on to others. The word was, they weren't finding many discrepancies with the government's preexisting inventories.

Which wasn't surprising. The Aslari would have to be crazy to start anything, with all the ordnance parked overhead. Especially as good as they had it, even now. People got up in the morning, went to work, got paid, and lived pretty damned well. And no one was hassling them. It was your ass if you did, or your head, depending on the crime. And the provost marshal had a reputation.

Anyway, all that was Civil Control's hat, not Exprop's.

But whatever the reason, with the Old Man breathing fire and wearing his spurs to work, it was hard on everyone. Then the goddess of luck smiled, and Yesik's office had reassignment orders for Banner Lake, a prefecture capital 287 miles from Aslarton. The word was, there were recreational opportunities there, if you could find time for them with all the rush-rush.

Yesik looked forward to the day when the overstructure was in place, and he could have a fief of his own—a retail chain of some sort—and a nice home, with a sexy, long-legged Aslari wife . . .

He was roused from his reverie by someone saying, "There it is. Banner Lake." Yesik Abreekas looked out the window again. A considerable city sprawled by a very large blue lake, with forested hills on the far shore. It looked pleasant enough, and they probably wouldn't see the general once a month.

The Banner Lake Exprop team was officed on the upper floor of the prefectural executive building—had been there for three days. As with the planetary records, it was difficult to sort out the ownership of wealth. In Banner Lake Prefecture, income properties—agricultural land, rental properties, mercantile, industrial and service businesses—were in the hands of innumerable private and corporate individuals, very largely in the form of shares. In the Empire, most would be sole ownerships held by noble families. Expropriations promised to impact directly a very large part of the population—people. This wasn't looking as good as it had.

Yesik Abreekas sat at his terminal—not really his, but his for now—with his liaison beside him. His knowledge of Standard was rather good, learned with a tutorial helmet before he'd left Varatos. But the vocabulary had been compiled by the Klestronu military expedition on a backwater Confederation trade world. A liaison was necessary to help him over the humps and gaps of language, custom, and business law.

Sharol Venling was a strikingly handsome woman, albeit nearing middle age. And with auburn hair! She was taller than he; on Aslarsan, many women were, perhaps most. And long legged; very sexy. He wondered if she was married, and if she was, whether she took lovers on the side. Perhaps here, 287 miles from the provost marshal, he might explore the question with her. Or perhaps not. Certainly not at their work station. They had far too much to do.

In the distance a sound began, but he was concentrating, and at first didn't notice. It got louder, a peculiar and somehow disturbing sound, a crackling sort of rumble. People began getting to their feet. A few steps away was

one of the ever-open balconies, and Abreekas stepped
out onto it, seven stories above the street.

Stretching across the residential suburbs above the river
was a long line of flame and black smoke, one end cut
off from sight by nearby tall buildings. The sound
continued, growing louder, as if approaching; an endless,
popping, snapping roar. Then its devouring head swept
into view, slashing diagonally past, deafening now, scything
swiftly a few blocks in front of him through the central
business district, buildings bursting into flame and debris.
It sped toward the suburbs again, leaving a wake of flames
and oily black smoke. And a hundred-yard-wide gash of
destruction. If the wind were different, the reek would
be choking.

He knew what he was looking at. Far overhead, a
"gunboat," a bombardment ship, was attacking the
undefended, unoffending city with its great beam gun.

"The bastards!" Abreekas said it aloud, then became
aware of the woman beside him. Sharol, his liaison. Where
did she live? Somewhere in that broad strip of burning
wreckage? What did she think? What could she think?

Then the roar, and the all-devouring head turned and
started back toward them.

Chesty Vrislakavaro seethed with anger as his signals
aide set up the program for him. "There it is, sir," the
man said. "Ready to play on every work channel in the
Armada."

Chesty picked up the microphone, thumbed the switch
and began, his big voice heavy and hard, the words like
hammer blows. "Spacemen, soldiers and marines of the
Imperial Armada!" he began. "As commanding general,
appointed by the Emperor Kalif, I order you to arrest
and imprison the traitor and murderer, the ex-admiral
Loksa Siilakamasu. Vice Admiral Garpind Tellesaveera
is now command admiral.

"Admiral Siilakamasu is charged with the following

crimes." He began to enumerate, beginning with the day's attacks on two Aslari cities, with scores of thousands killed, including imperial soldiers detailed in one of them. From there he reiterated the crimes the Emeritus Kalif had exposed in the Hope System, a year earlier.

The general's signal beam took six hours to reach the Armada, near the orbit of the system's farthest planet. When the general's voice sounded over the bridge's command speaker, the admiral listened for just a moment. Then "Turn it off!" he shouted. "Off! Off!"

The comm officer on watch began tapping keys, but the voice continued, so he tried turning it down. The admiral could hear it from every work station on the bridge. Lurching from his throne, he rushed around the room, uselessly jabbing MUTE keys. For a long moment he stood in the middle of the bridge, his broad Maolaari face swollen. His body shook. All eyes avoided him. Abruptly he left, his personal aide a stride behind. In the passageway outside the door, he snatched a blast rifle from the marine on guard. The man watched big-eyed and silent as the admiral stalked off with it.

His target wasn't far away. He was certain the problem lay with SUMBAA. No matter that he'd had the powerful AI cut from the ship's data and servomech systems weeks before. It was SUMBAA who was humiliating him. SUMBAA was the villain in this. Another marine stood guard outside the door to SUMBAA's compartment. Blaster in hand, the admiral brushed past the man and pushed the door open. His eyes went directly to the AI's integration module, the muzzle of his blaster following, and he played a lance of energy against its face till he'd melted a hole through it. The systems no longer showed life, and the general's voice could no longer be heard from the passageway speakers outside.

The wild glare left Siilakamasu's eyes, and for a moment he stood silent, frowning, jaw clenched. Then he strode from the compartment with its scorched and smoking integrator module, the smell of hot metal, burnt plastics, and boiling quasiorganics thick in the air.

Back on the bridge, he could still hear the general's voice from work stations, condemning and indicting, now partly obscured by orders, reports and queries from various stations and ships, a kind of audible accompaniment. He ignored it. Sitting down again, he barked orders into his microphone.

"Now hear this!" he said. "Now hear this! This is command Admiral Siilakamasu! This is Command Admiral Siilakamasu! All work boats in! All work boats in! Fleet security will prohibit any craft from locking out without flag clearance. No further craft will be allowed to lock out of any ship without flag clearance."

He turned to Captain Nakarasama, on the commander's seat beside his own, and spoke with a chuckle. "Now," he said, "we will learn who the serious traitors are. And deal with them appropriately. The great traitor we already know. I will deal with him first."

Then he went to his office, called up his confidential signals file, activated a prepared message with precoded recipient, and pressed SEND. A scrambled radio pulse left the *Sambak*'s signal gun for the six-hour trip to Aslarsan. When it arrived, Marine General Snake Butarindala could adjust his timing to fit the circumstances.

The Confederation Home Flotilla was nothing at all like, say, a battle wing. Its ships were a motley assemblage subject to change as needed. Its flagship was a packet, a small, leased merchant ship, with a suitable combination of cargo holds and adequate passenger accommodations. Linvo Garlaby had a modest stateroom that served as his home there.

Various small craft were parked alongside. A few hundred meters distant lay a Slingshot to Anywhere, a converted space barge, its gate visible only by its marker lights.

Occasionally the packet-flagship housed guests—personnel in training, or waiting to be gated on some mission. At present it held the six squads of a White T'swa task force. For them it was "night"—their sleep time. The alarm in their bunking bay ignored that as irrelevant, its strident racket jerking them from their bunks. They pulled on uniforms and boots, donned gear, grabbed weapons, all of it waiting on hooks.

Within a minute, the troopers had cleared the compartment, boots thudding down the passageway toward the assembly hold. There the squad leaders took silent muster, with eyes alone, reporting quietly to their commander when all were there. The troopers stood at ease, relaxed but intent.

"That's all of you, right?" Linvo Garlaby asked. The psi-spy stood in loose pajamas, rumpled, unkempt, and out of shape. No one faulted him for it. In a general way they knew what he did—the hours and importance of it—and that he was one of the best.

"Affirmative," Artus Romlar answered.

"Okay, here's why the rush. Siilakamasu's gunboats scorched a couple of Aslari cities. Killed an army detachment, along with tens of thousands of Aslari. So Vrislakavaro tried ousting him from fleet command; basically he called on fleet personnel to mutiny. The admiral is taking various steps, but the one that concerns you is he just called in all work boats. All of them at once. And no further craft are to lock out. That means you have only minutes to hit him. It also means he's watching for attack by possible mutineers. You may be detected as bogies, and they're preparing to repel possible boarders."

He didn't suggest canceling. If that was an option, and the situation called for it, the colonel would order it. To Linvo, the mission had seemed extreme before Siilakamasu's psychotic break. Now it seemed doubly so.

But all Romlar said was "All right, guys, let's load up." Then they double-timed through passageways to their boats—two work boats in the packet's docking hold, and a much larger pinnace. The pinnace was clamped to the packet's outer hull, a sphincter giving access through a gangway. The troopers boarded, their helmeted combat suits simulating those of imperial marines. In the deliberate gloom of ship's night, they looked ominous, not quite human to the packet's crewmen standing soberly at their posts. The boats bore imperial symbols and markings, to look as much like imperial craft as possible. After securing for separation, they pulled away on gravdrive, piloted by troopers.

Five minutes earlier the troopers had been in bed. In three more they'd be light years distant, surrounded by imperial warships.

When they were gone, it took the gate master several minutes to locate and close on her next target. It was harder to find, and required more precision. The barge-like lighter she gated through on it amounted to an unmanned, ultra-short range, point-blank missile intended for stationary targets. In this case the heavy gunboat parked 200 miles above Aslarton, her beam gun several times as powerful as those used on Banner Lake and Parmall. A destroyer squadron would follow as soon as the gate master shifted coordinates again.

The pinnace moved at a leisurely speed toward the imperial flagship, following the two work boats that had gated through ahead of it. Kelmer Faronya sat on the flight deck beside Corporal Bertol Bromens, who was piloting. The pinnace had a 360 degree external viewer on both top and bottomside, and Kelmer had plugged in. He had the same spectrum of view choices the pilot did.

Kelmer had participated in the mission preparations

at the shipyard at Varodin, where a realistic 1:50 scale
model had been built for them. Thus he recognized the
flagship's relevant external features. There'd also been
diagrams of the ship's interior, and a full-scale mockup
of its pertinent passageways and spaces, jerry-built into
the stripped-down hull of an obsolete battleship.

The exterior model had been based on drawings by
the Kalif, and pictures taken by the robot signals ship
that had broadcast his message to the Armada. Before
the signal ship was destroyed, it had beamed thousands
of photographs of the Armada to another signals ship,
parked a few hundred million miles in-system. It, in turn,
had gated them to G-2 on Iryala.

The flagship's interior had been rough-sketched by the
Kalif, and proofed and refined by Kari Frensler through
the eyes of unsuspecting crewmen and officers. The
mockups were reasonable approximations, with particular
care given to the flagship's Engineering Department and
the near vicinity of the bridge.

But none of it, Kelmer knew, meant a thing if the
pinnace and work boats didn't pass the ship's security
surveillance. Therein lay the advantage of arriving with
other craft returning under urgent orders, with a
deadline.

The initial difficulty would be getting inside the docking
lock. That would be mainly a matter of luck; it was pretty
much out of their hands. Once in, they'd have to pass
for an imperial craft, and the pinnace was not an exact
replica of any of them. On the other hand, imperial models
were more diverse than Confederation craft. As for
disembarking: almost every trooper was taller than the
Kalif, who'd warned them he was taller than most
imperials. When they disembarked, their height would
be visible. Colonel Romlar had selected entire squads—
men who'd lived and fought as a team—rather than
assembling a force of the regiment's shorter troopers.
This made his own size less conspicuous. And unless there

were imperials in the lock just then, their height might go unnoticed.

That was the theory. If it didn't prove out, they'd blast their way in. They'd have to fight soon enough anyway.

They pulled close to the *Papa Sambak*, approaching the Command Section A lock, the only one suited to the mission. There was no lineup, and as Kelmer watched, the entry irised open. Before the curve of *Papa's* hull had intervened, they'd seen the two work boats in a short line waiting to enter the Engineering Section A lock. It accommodated only work boats, two at a time, and hopefully was unpoliced. The idea was for all to enter at about the same time. Bromens might have held back, to better match the estimated timing of the work boats. But it wouldn't do to draw attention by stalling conspicuously, so he retracted the bottomside viewer, drew through the round, well-lit opening, and slid smoothly into the landing dock. It was large enough for a craft half again the pinnace's length.

The lock looked much like the mockup. The large window of its control room was at the head end, near the portside corner. Kelmer could see two men inside. Beneath the window, a light shone red. Interesting that in the Empire too, red meant unsafe, or wait.

Kelmer felt the magnetic hull locks engage with a mild bump, and the lock iris closed. On a dial beside the red light, the atmospheric pressure reading began to climb. He realized his body had grown tense. *You're supposed to breathe*, he told himself wryly, and exhaled, then inhaled.

The pressure stopped climbing and the red light flashed off. Beside it, a blue light flashed on. Had theirs been an actual fleet pinnace, Kelmer knew, a buzzer would have sounded inside it, activated automatically via the hull locks. Apparently their pinnace didn't make the appropriate connection. What he didn't know was whether the instruments in the control room registered the lack.

"Face shields down and secure!" Romlar's voice ordered. In Imperial, as in the drills. "On your feet!" Pause. "Shoulder sling arms! Stand in the door!" Pause. Kelmer stepped into the cabin and stood at the end of the line of troopers, recording with his helmet cam. "Open the gangway!" Behind him, Bromens pressed the gangway release. Through his helmet's ears, Kelmer heard the soft sound of the gangway door striking the magnetically padded stops. He was aware of Bromens behind him.

"Disembark!" The line moved, turned right at the gangway, and stepped out of whatever illusory security the pinnace offered. This, it seemed to Kelmer, was the moment of truth. The first. His guts insisted on it. He followed out the gangway and down the short extruded ramp. At the head of the file, Colonel Romlar had already strode briskly through the door, out of the lock and into a passageway familiar from the mockup. As Kelmer neared the door himself, he glanced up toward the control room window. A face stared out, mouth open.

"We've been noticed!" Kelmer said into his throat mike, and crowded the man ahead of him. Through their helmet comms, every man in the file heard him. Bromens had hardly made it through the door when it slid sharply shut. An alarm began jangling in the passageway, and a speaker called out: "All those just disembarked in Command Section A docking, stop and remain where you are for security check."

The command was redundant. Ahead of them, a security door had slid shut. The troopers waited till it slid open again, disclosing a number of marines, blasters held waist high. Kelmer's guts twisted. The marines saw the troopers' blasters shoulder slung. "Raise your hands!" one of them ordered.

As one, the troopers dropped to the deck or threw themselves sideways against the walls, blast rifles somehow in their hands, firing. There were shrieks. Marines fell almost en masse, some, in their moment of death, returning fire. Of the forty-two troopers, thirty-six followed their commander down the passageway, boots thudding on composition matting. Unlike the troopers, Kelmer Faronya's glance took in the carnage as he ran, dodging or jumping corpses, his silent helmet cam recording.

The speaker system warned crew and marines of armed intruders, and ordered crew to stay out of the corridors. The Kalif had said that crew had no weapons. Kelmer hoped he was right.

Almost at once the passageway ended at a cross passage. The troopers turned right, running hard. Ahead another passage crossed theirs. Marines appeared around a corner, and instantly the troopers dropped, firing. Marines fell; others jumped back into the safety of the cross passage. Between them and the troopers, another security door slid shut. The troopers got up, and several trotted to it.

One, instead of a beam gun, carried a heavy-duty beam torch. He began to cut the steel door like a welder cutting plate. Some of the others moved back the way they'd come. A crewman peered out a door and fell shot. Boots could be heard thudding down the passageway they'd left, and several troopers hustled to the crossing, heavy concussion grenades in hand.

The admiral's eyes were fixed on his screen. It showed a passageway diagram for the Command Section. The section of passageway occupied by intruders showed red. The sections with marines showed blue.

"Who are they?" the admiral demanded. "From what ship?"

"We don't know, sir," said the voice on the comm. "The pinnace identification number belongs to, ah, one of ours, but it does not belong to a pinnace."

"What *does* it belong to? And what ship did it come from?"

"Sir, the number belongs to the scout the Kalif was sent off in, sir."

"The *what*? I want at least one of the intruders alive! *Alive*! I'll cut the information out of him piece by living piece!"

"Yes, your lordship!"

The admiral's eyes swept the bridge as if looking for someone to kill. They settled on the watch's comm officer. "What do they report from Engineering?"

"Nothing further, sir. There was just one call, reporting intruders. I heard shooting, quite a bit of it. Projectile weapons. That was all. Marines are on their way there."

"I'll have someone's balls on my saber if any harm comes to the drives! Tell them that! Tell them!"

"Yessir! Right away, sir!" The man poked keys, misdialed, cleared, fumbled again and started over. The marine duty sergeant answered. His CO was off with 2nd Platoon, he said, directing the isolation and destruction of the intruders from Command Section A docking. The XO was with the troops gone to Engineering. He'd inform him of the admiral's orders.

Behind Kelmer, the firefight around the passageway corner had quieted. Farther away, boots thudded. Someone not using a helmet mike shouted orders. Several troopers stood with grenades ready as the cutting beam approached completion of the oblong it was making. Anyone on the other side would be ready. When only a narrow piece at the bottom held it in place, the colonel slammed it with a powerful jokanru side-kick, bending it partway back. Troopers threw grenades through the gap. They roared, even as blaster beams struck the sagging steel oblong from the other side. There were screams, muffled by helmets. Two more grenades were thrown through. The trooper with the beam torch stepped up and cut the last uncut metal. The door crashed down and troopers rushed through. But not far. Ahead another door had closed. From the rear came more shouted orders, nearer now. Blasters hissed. There were more explosions.

"Lord Admiral, sir!" called the con officer. "The hyperspace generator has been disabled."

"Kargh *damn* them all! Someone will pay for this with their lives! Their family's lives! What are those fucking marines doing about this?"

The marine CO's voice spoke from the comm officer's speaker, and the comm officer turned the volume well up. "Repeat," he ordered. The voice repeated, then continued, calm, and assured. "The intruders in the Command Section are isolated between passageway doors. We have a launcher coming up with armor-piercing rounds. It'll kill them all."

"I want one alive!" the admiral roared. He was stiff, shaking with anger. "I must have at least one alive!"

The comm officer repeated the order. "We already have prisoners," the marine's voice answered. "Wounded but alive."

The admiral relaxed progressively, as if willing it. "Tell him good work," he said huskily. "I'll see him promoted."

Lotta Romlar whispered in her husband's mind. "They're going to fire armor-piercing rockets through the door."

His reaction was instantaneous. "Out of the corridor!" he said into his helmet mike. "Into the side rooms!"

In seconds only bodies remained—marines and troopers, their uniforms indistinguishable. Seconds later a rocket burst through the door, a swarm of white hot fragments streaking down the passageway. Instantly side doors opened, inward, the only way they could. The passageway security doors opened almost as quickly, and from both ends marines rushed in, blasters leveled. Trooper grenades roared.

❖   ❖   ❖

Engineering reeked with burnt plastics, insulation, and flesh, overlying the smell of scorched metal and the pungency of explosives. Like the troopers there, the marines who'd arrived had carried projectile weapons, in an effort to reduce random, incidental damage to equipment.

Captain Jerym Alsnor stood beside the body of a ship's engineer. One of three tech personnel whose sidearms and grim determination had dangerously delayed his access to the control panel he was frowning at. Jerym had been crammed on it, preparing for this mission, and knew the relevant panel and keypad notations. His eyes found one with the abbreviation for ingress. He pressed it. A diagram of the entire ship appeared on the monitor, showing passageways and docking locks. With a stylus hanging by a cord, he touched a work boat lock he recognized, then two more. Their symbols changed from blue to red, with the iris symbol indicating "open." He keyed in the lock instruction.

«That's it, Trini,» he thought to the psi-spy assigned to him, and received an acknowledgement. He didn't need to specify which locks. Carrmak and the others knew. Then, blaster ready, he knelt out of sight between the heavy housings of two large machines. He had to keep control of the panel as long as needed, and without help. So far as he knew, he was the only one of his squad alive and functional.

He didn't worry about his life, or wonder about his commander, his brother-in-law. His focus was entirely on his mission.

His brother-in-law didn't have any attention on Jerym, either. With six troopers and a uniformed journalist, he was inside a cabin. One of a series belonging to bridge officers, and they'd killed those they'd found. The trooper with the cutting beam was working on a side wall. It would be the fourth room they'd cut their way out of. Compartment walls were much easier than security doors to cut through. If they'd figured it right, and if the heavy-duty power slug held out, cutting their way out of the next room would get them into a narrow utilities passage with access to the bridge.

Of course, marines might open the security doors into the passageway they'd left a few minutes earlier. Then they'd check the side rooms, and follow them through the series of holed compartment walls. It was surprising they hadn't already. Perhaps they were running short of men, though they shouldn't be.

He certainly was. What he needed now was for Carrmak and his force to arrive. But for that to happen, Jerym's people needed to hold the security control panel in Engineering.

Loksa Siilakamasu felt more incredulous than alarmed. The bridge was the most secure place on board, its heavy door substantially stronger than almost any other on the *Sambak*. It wasn't subject to control from anywhere other than the bridge itself.

Just now he was staring at the screen. Three docking locks had opened. That could have only one purpose. And not only was the hyperspace drive disabled. The gravdrive was down. Otherwise he could foil boarders by moving around.

The marine CO was in touch again. Of the intruders who'd fought their way through the passageways, 34 were dead, or wounded and in custody. Only between five and ten remained uncaptured, and some of those were no doubt wounded. He didn't know how many others were in Engineering. He'd sent a squad to root them out, and close the opened locks.

The admiral had always supposed the controls in

Engineering could be overridden from the bridge. Now he'd learned that security commands could not. When this present outrage was handled and things back to normal, he'd have that changed. Even if Engineering had to dismantle the whole system to do it.

Right now though, they had to mop up the intruders and repel any further boarders. The battlecomp insisted that none had shown up on the screens. And none of his own were outside now to confuse identification. The master at arms insisted the intruders were Confederation troops in imperial uniforms, but that was preposterous. Now what was left of them, or of their main force, was isolated just one security door from the passageway section outside his bridge.

According to the marine captain, the mutineers had used up not only their men but their tricks. And their luck. Meanwhile his company armorer had contrived a powerful petard, which was being brought, along with a welder, to blow the door. It would kill anyone between the enclosing doors. Intruders who'd taken refuge in side rooms would have nothing stronger than a cabin door to protect them. Those could be blown with a simple door charge, and grenades thrown inside.

He'd rather, the admiral thought, take them all alive. But to insist on it would cost him more marines. And they'd likely be needed to repel boarders, if the opened docking locks weren't soon secured.

The marine captain hadn't volunteered his casualty count, and the admiral hadn't asked. Heavier than the Old Man thought, he supposed. Still, the captain felt confident. No bogies were reported in the vicinity of the ship, and his men would soon take back Engineering's control panel. Then they'd close the opened docking locks, and no one short of the Old Man himself could get him to open them again.

The captain didn't suspect how many of his men had died in the difficult maze of Engineering.

Not ten feet from the control panel, Marine Sergeant Vindoka could see the end of a strap lying on the deck between two housings of some sort. It appeared to be a strap on a musette bag. The intruders carried musette bags. He felt quite sure an intruder crouched concealed between the two housings—had taken it off and laid it on the deck.

He could lay fire into the gap, but the angle was such the bullets would probably smash when they hit the steel of the housing. If, on the other hand, he shifted to a housing to his left, he could move around behind it and fire straight into the intruder's cover from the far side. He wished he was left-handed. As it was, he'd have to sight and fire from his off side, and he'd never done that before. Too bad they'd been ordered to take rifles instead of blasters. He would, he decided, empty a whole magazine into the space. That would take care of whoever was in there.

Quickly and softly, he moved across an aisle and into cover. Then, rifle ready, he slipped along the back of the housing, paying no attention to a small housing behind it. He hadn't heard anything when a forearm clamped across his faceplate, and a long-bladed boot knife slammed upward beneath his ribs, through pleura and right lung, into the heart. The sergeant collapsed instantly without crying out, his life's blood gushing into his abdominal cavity.

The men in support of the sergeant crouched waiting. He'd ordered them to hold their positions, cover the aisle leading to the panel, and shoot anyone not wearing a white rag around their sleeves. They felt uneasy, waiting, but in a combat situation, they were not about to disobey their sergeant's order.

✧   ✧   ✧

On the bridge, the admiral could hear and feel the petard explode. Now he'd see the end of this ridiculous situation.

What he didn't see was the utility panel open. Blasters hissed, cutting down most of the bridge crew, and both the marine guards inside the door. At almost the same moment, the battlecomp's crisp voice reported intruders in the opened docking locks, though no bogies had been reported approaching.

For just a moment the jangling distracted the admiral, then he reached for his sidearm. Someone else's sidearm boomed, and the slug tore through the reaching hand. He staggered backward. Half a dozen intruders were on his bridge. He stared at one of them, tall as himself. Roaring with rage, he drew his belt dagger and charged the man. Who gripped his knife arm and slammed the admiral to the deck. The impact drove the breath from the admiral's lungs, leaving him gasping, flopping with pain. Kneeling, Artus rendered him unconscious.

A moment later, Artus's voice was heard throughout the ship, in Imperial that was accented but easily understood.

"Attention all crew and all marines. All crew and all marines. We control your bridge in the name of the Kalif, and have your admiral prisoner. In the name of the Kalif, put down your weapons and remain where you are! Put down your weapons and remain where you are."

With the *Papa Sambak* in trooper hands, it was safe to gate the Kalif through. Like Carrmak's troopers, he arrived on a space scooter a few yards outside an open docking lock. Minutes later he was on the bridge. Twenty minutes after that, he had Vice Admiral Garpind Tellesaveera's agreement to accept command of the

Armada in the name of the Kalif, if enough captains agreed to support him.

The Kalif then described a virgin world, newly named Glory, ceded to him by the Confederation.[1]

Several commanders of "pastor" ships and troopships radioed their agreement almost at once. The commanders of fighting ships agreed more slowly. After twenty minutes, however, the trickle became a flow. When more than half the ships' commanders had agreed, the request for support became an order. Several crews mutinied against holdout captains, whom they shackled and locked in the brig.

Not one ship took the opportunity to generate hyperspace. Where could it have gone except home? And messages would precede it there by pod.

The Kalif set up his command center on the *Sambak*. After the Armada's surrender, he sat down with Artus Romlar in the dining room of the admiral's suite, for a private meal and conversation. Whatever else might be in disorder, the command galley was functioning. The two men didn't say much. Forty-one troopers had died, and more than three times that many marines and spacers. Four billion miles away—six hours for a radio message— perhaps 100,000 Aslari had died. And powerful imperial ground forces remained to be pacified.

---

[1]Though the Kalif didn't say so, the Confederation had itself just formally claimed the planet, for the sole purpose of giving it away. It was the best of three suitable but remote worlds found and surveyed during an official exploration program 14,000 years earlier, when the Confederation worlds were officially "the Iryalan Hegemony."

The decision had then been made to forbid settlement of planets farther than three hyperspace-deks from Iryala, as too distant for proper central supervision of the Sacrament, and proper enforcement of Iryalan law.

By tying the ruling to the Sacrament, there'd been little argument with the decision.

Yet the colonel seemed to be in a strange, exalted state, a sort of calm serenity. When he spoke at all, it was quietly, briefly, smiling. When they'd finished their dessert and brandy, they returned to the bridge again, the nerve center of the Armada.

Chapter 51
Liberation

Tagurt Meksorli had been quartered with the family of Dorva Arvalin, Lord Felthos. It was appropriate: Tagurt was provost marshal, and Arvalin headed the Interior Ministry—basically planetary law enforcement. Nor did it hurt that Sendra, Arvalin's daughter, was small for an Aslari, pretty, and conspicuously intelligent. The Meksorli clan had always favored intelligence, and Tagurt had begun cultivating her, with courtship a definite possibility.

Just now though . . .

Given the destruction of Banner Lake and Parmall, General Vrislakavaro was concerned over a possible public backlash, and the safety of public officials who'd been working with the occupation army. There'd already been a shooting. Lord Felthos, however, had refused a detail of military guards. His own men were capable, he said, and the presence of imperial guards would be provocative. Which was true. But next to Queen Endra, Dorva Arvalin was the most important person in government these days. So the general had told Tagurt not to work late that night. "Go home. Stay with him. Get him to spend the night on his yacht."

Tagurt had to settle for an evening on the lake.

The Arvalin city residence was in an aristocratic exurb on the south shore of thirty-mile-long Sapphire Lake.

He kept a forty-foot yacht there, for quiet evening cruises, and holidays along the irregular and forested north shore, seeking wildlife and birds with binoculars and spotting scopes.

They'd eaten dinner as if two cities had not been razed that day. As if an estimated 60,000 hadn't been brutally murdered. Meksorli had phoned Dorva as soon as he'd heard, expressing his outrage. And Chesty had spoken to the planet by television and radio, expressing his. There were elements within the fleet, he'd said, who favored violent subjugation. They would be suppressed.

He hadn't added that the "elements" were led by the command admiral, with the entire warfleet at his disposal. Or that his own available forces were limited to the army's 1st Infantry Division and the marine's 2nd and 4th, with the allegiance of the marines uncertain. Even adding the 5th and 9th Infantry, scattered all over the planet, didn't change the picture, because he had no defense against attacks from space.

Over joma that afternoon, the grim army commander had made clear to his deputy that what he now feared most was an Aslari uprising. Quelling it would mean a bloodbath that would weigh heavily on the perpetrator's soul. He swore he'd do no more than necessary to safeguard his forces. Kargh judged all men, he said, and General Arbind Vrislakavaro would not arrive in Kargh's Hall of Judgment arm in arm with Loksa Siilakamasu.

Tagurt Meksorli's theology was much less orthodox than his commander's, but neither would he play butcher. He didn't articulate this to himself. It was simply there, a fact.

Dorva Arvalin did not take his house guards with him on the *Lady Milri*. When it drew away from the family pier, it carried only himself, his wife and daughter, two quiet servant-crewmen, a single unobtrusive bodyguard, and Tagurt Meksorli. Meksorli wondered what the crew thought of his inclusion.

Remarkably, the family showed no hostility or even coldness toward him. Their attitude was quietly, casually correct, as before. His lordship himself had the helm; apparently this was customary. Lady Felthos sat beside him, tall, regal, and still beautiful at what Tagurt guessed might be fifty years of age. Tagurt himself sat beside their daughter on the foredeck, leaning back in his deck chair, gazing up at a star display somewhat thinned by the sky glow of Aslarton. Both of them saw the brief flash, far brighter than any star. Tagurt knew instantly what it was—a warship exploding, hundreds of miles overhead. Presumably one of the bombardment flotilla the admiral had stationed there. For just a moment his hair stood on end. *We might,* he thought, *have effective allies in the fleet after all.*

"What was that?" Sendra asked.

"There seems to be a fight up there," Tagurt said. "Someone was blown up. Let's hope it wasn't a friend."

Almost at once there were smaller flashes, quick bright sparks like stillborn first-magnitude stars. They were farther northward, in the darker sky across the lake, away from the city. *Torpedoes,* Tagurt thought.

He wondered if Lord Felthos had seen them. Seemingly none of the crew had. Meanwhile the yacht continued out onto the lake, and after a few minutes there were no more flashes in the sky. Tagurt was tempted to call headquarters and ask what they knew, then decided not to. Chesty would call him if there were things he needed to know.

"The show," Sendra commented mildly, "seems to be over. It would be interesting to know what went on. And who won."

Tagurt wondered if her nerves were really that good, or if she was naive enough not to realize that fighting up there could lead to fighting down here. He did not, he realized, know her very well.

He shared Chesty's doubts about which side the marine

CO would favor. A week previous, the admiral had appointed Major General Sopal "Snake" Butarindala as overall commander of marines on the ground—the 2nd and 4th Divisions. Butarindala was CO of the 2nd. This appointment made him senior to Major General Barni Vorkalasama, CO of the 4th. It also preempted an appointment authority that properly belonged to Chesty, as commander of the Occupation Army. But Chesty had swallowed hard and said nothing. Loksa had all the leverage.

As provost marshal, Tagurt had access to personnel records, and had looked up the two marine generals. Butarindala was younger in age, years of service, and years in grade, and his file had considerably fewer commendations. He had, however, been CO of the marine contingent aboard Loksa's first command. They'd have known one another well, might even have been close. Vorkalasama, on the other hand, had been deputy commandant at the Marine Academy when the Kalif-to-be had been its honor student. Had signed, and probably written, a laudatory commendation of the fourth-year cadet.

Loksa Siilakamasu undoubtedly expected the support of his old shipmate, and they'd probably plotted something. Or rather, Loksa had planned something and Snake was his agent on the ground.

The brief, twinkling light display was grounds for hope, but hardly for festivity. When a crewman asked what he'd like to drink, Meksorli answered simply, "Joma." He expected his belt comm to twitter before long, and order him to headquarters.

Meanwhile here I am, he told himself, *sitting beside a pretty girl on a yacht, on a scenic lake. And what am I thinking about? A psychotic admiral!*

As they left the city farther behind, the skyscape became more beautiful. The only sounds were the soft rush of water around the streamlined hull, a barely discernible engine hum, and the occasional soft murmur of voices. Mainly from the con, whose roof was retracted to expose the stars. Ahead was the high forested ridge on the lake's north edge, seen as the starscape's bottom edge.

"What," Sendra murmured, "do you suppose tomorrow will bring?"

Before he could reply, his comm twittered. "Wait a minute," he said, "I might have an answer for you."

He held the comm to his ear. "General Meksorli," he answered quietly in Imperial.

A soft double beep sounded, telling him the message had arrived in scramble pulse. The voice was Chesty's. "Tagurt, I'm in my backup office in the Ag Ministry's Executive Building. Are you aware of the fight overhead?"

The backup office? "Affirmative."

"Unidentified warships attacked the bombardment flotilla. The rumor is, they were mutineers from the fleet. No one knows how many gunboats are still up there, or in whose hands. Or how Loksa's puppets down here will react. With all those trees, groves and hedges around the palace, headquarters is hard to defend, so I came over here, where we're surrounded by empty parking lots: excellent fields of fire. Two companies of the 1st Infantry just arrived for security.

"What I want you to do is put on your provost marshal hat, go to 1st Division headquarters, and question Denni Faradalarsa. G-2 told me Denni'd had a visit from the Snake, earlier today, but they don't know what was talked about. Find out. If you need to, relieve him, and take command of his division."

Tagurt frowned. Relieving Denni Faradalarsa wouldn't be easy. He could feel the blouse gun in his left armpit. Shoving it against Denni's breastbone would probably work, but he'd have to keep it there. Pulling the trigger would definitely work, but he'd probably be shot himself—locked in the stockade at least—instead of in command. *Well,* he told himself, *Grampa said interesting lives aren't easy.* "I'm about five or six miles out on the lake," he answered. "It'll take a little while, unless you send a floater."

There was a pause. "No," Chesty said at last, "have Lord Felthos take you ashore. Lean on him if necessary. And call when you've done it."

"Affirmative." Tagurt returned the comm to its belt case. "Excuse me," he said to Sendra, and getting to his feet, went to the helm.

"Your lordship," he said, "please return to shore at once. I've had an urgent call. I'm needed by the commanding general."

The Interior Minister looked down at him in the darkness. Tagurt Meksorli was of ordinary height for a Vartosit, while Dorva Arvalin was tall for an Aslari. Arvalin turned the wheel and increased their speed, the yacht swinging around in a tight curve, hull slapping as it crossed its own wake. Distant city lights now formed the backdrop.

Arvalin gestured skyward. "Does your order have anything to do with the light display we had up there?"

"It might." Tagurt considered for a moment, then added: "What you saw up there—it's grounds for optimism."

Dorva Arvalin didn't reply, simply increased their speed further. Before long, Tagurt could make out what he assumed was the minister's lakeside home, its grounds larger than most, bordered by spirelike trees with dense crowns. At three hundred yards, Arvalin cut his engine well back, letting the craft slow. A moment later they saw bright, wire-thin lances of blaster fire near the Arvalin residence, and heard the sharp staccato of automatic rifles. His lordship veered off eastward, paralleling the shore, increasing his speed. Headlights crossed the broad lawn. Stepping back from the raised helm, Tagurt moved quickly to the stack of small life rafts on the afterdeck. There were four of them, awkward to handle. He grabbed the top one.

"I'll help." The voice was Sendra's. Together they threw

the raft over the side. Then, startling both of them, Tagurt picked Sendra up and threw her in before jumping himself. Hampered by his clothing, he began to swim toward the raft, then heard an explosion. Stopping, he turned and looked back. The yacht had been hit by a rocket, and the stern blown off; it continued eastward on momentum, settling in the water as it went. Another rocket hit at about the helm, and a third the bow. In seconds, what remained of the craft had sunk, leaving floating debris.

Tagurt began swimming again toward the raft, aware of Sendra swimming near him. She was, he knew, a strong swimmer. "Don't stop," he said, "but don't climb in."

When he reached the raft, he paused, clinging to the hand line, and looked back. Most of the wreckage was more than a hundred yards away. A spotlight played over it, paying special attention to the other life rafts. At one point a blaster fired, its beam boiling water where it struck. What its target had been, Tagurt didn't know.

Finally the spotlight switched off, but still the swimmers waited. A minute later it switched back on, poking again among the floating debris for half a minute before slowly sweeping the area around it. At one point it reached dangerously near the swimmers. Finally three more rockets were fired. The rocketman was good! He hit each of the other rafts, blowing them apart. Then the spotlight switched off again.

Those were not local rebels, Tagurt thought. They knew their weapons far too well.

After another minute, he climbed onto the raft and helped Sendra aboard, then unshipped the short oars from their brackets and began to row. For a moment Sendra simply knelt, staring back toward where the yacht had been. *Assholes!* he thought. Pulling strongly, he paralleled the shore. He would, he decided, put about half a mile behind him before landing. The girl seemed to be crying. Silently. *Thank Kargh for that,* he thought.

He'd highjack a car, but it wasn't 1st Infantry head-quarters he'd drive to. Siilakamasu, or at least his people, had gone out of control, beyond all tolerance. There was, Tagurt told himself, something more important to do than relieve Dengkato Faradalarsa of his 1st Infantry command. Something nearer the core of the problem.

The psi shop on the ridge above the OSP building had been outgrown, and supplemented by another built at the foot of the ridge. In one of its trance rooms, a recently graduated apprentice knelt on a small platform, frowning at a map of Aslarton. After checking the index covering the bottom third of the sheet, her eyes found the Agriculture Ministry Executive Building. *Now,* she thought, *comes the hard part.* "Thanks," she said to the page who'd brought it. "Wait in the hall. I may need you in a hurry."

Almost as soon as the youth had closed the door behind him, she was back in trance. And in the mind of General Arbind "Chesty" Vrislakavaro.

There really wasn't much he could do, Chesty told himself. He had little information, and not much in the way of reliable resources. There were two rifle companies from the 1st Infantry on the bottom three floors, protecting the building, with two squads on the roof watching the surrounds. Facing them was a battalion of marines, occupying tactical locations outside the parking lot, positioned to attack. So far they hadn't. He'd tried again to contact Tagurt Meksorli, and failed. Tagurt, the best man he had. Probably dead, Chesty decided.

If he were commanding the marine battalion, he'd wait all night and save his troops. Because General of the Army Arbind Vrislakavaro was a cipher, a non-player. The game had been changed, and his cards taken. He'd radioed Faradalarsa for a squadron of armor and a flight of ground assault fighters, to demonstrate, and disperse the marines.

"Right away," Denni had said. That had been forty minutes ago, and not even the fighters had arrived. And his personal floater, circling overhead, had seen no tanks en route.

Personal floater! thought the psi-spy. With no more information than that, she transferred to the mind of the pilot, a kind of transfer not generally thought possible. *It's remarkable,* she told herself fleetingly, *what necessity can do.*

With the pilot, she watched the government district below, recognizing the Ag Ministry Exec Building by its location and her host's recognition. With his night vision visor, the young man could see considerable detail, and didn't like the situation at all. *The fucking marines have thrown in with the fleet,* he thought. *You might know.* He'd never liked marines. Now it seemed to him he'd end up fighting them.

The psi-spy hadn't stayed long enough to hear the pilot's brief soliloquy. When she'd gotten the layout of the roof, she withdrew, returning to her body in Psi Shop II. A notebook and stylus sat beside her cushion. She activated them and began to sketch.

An APCL arrived, a large armored personnel carrier with a platoon of T'swa. It appeared seemingly out of nowhere, a few hundred feet above the Ag Ministry Exec Building. The gate operator had guided on a map and sketch, hand-delivered via gate from Iryala to the recently set-up gate facility at the Kootosh-Lan Lodge on Tyss.

That had been twenty minutes earlier, and thirty-three hyperspace days distant. Captain Gokan gave the building and surroundings a brief lookover. That was the place. Had there been a question, the firefight would have settled it. Because one thing had changed in the forty minutes since the RSS agent had prepared her sketch and short written message: The marines had begun laying down desultory fire on the building.

There was no sign of an armored force, and neither side had sent fighter craft. Perhaps they didn't want to escalate the conflict or increase their commitment. Captain Gokan decided not to either, at least not yet. He radioed his observations and intentions to the APCs and ground support fighters that had followed him through, some 15,000 feet higher.

Then he ordered the sergeant-pilot to land on the roof. "Between the stairhead and outer wall," he said. "The roof should be strongest there."

Chesty Vrislakavaro sat glumly in his dimly lit office—dimly lit so the light wouldn't show through the drapes. He was glad shadow glass hadn't been used. Drapes provided a degree of protection against flying glass, if the marines decided to fire at the upper-story windows. If they did, he'd take shelter in the hall. He wasn't doing any good here anyway, he told himself. All he was was a target. Not even a target; a prisoner waiting to be captured. That sonofabitch on the bridge of the *Papa Sambak* wanted him alive. Probably so he could execute him.

Again he tried to contact Meksorli on the comm, and this time got an answer. "This is General Meksorli. Over."

"Tagurt! Good god, where have you been?"

"Someone—some of ours, marines probably—hit the minister's yacht with rockets. Apparently killed everyone but his daughter and me. Right now I'm driving a stolen car. Sendra's with me."

And she doesn't speak Imperial, the general thought. "Good! Good man! I'm still here in the Ag Ministry Building. The marines are shooting at it. And they shot down my floater. My men are shooting back, but neither side is trying very hard. Look, get to Division at once, and arrest Denni. He's refused to send the armor and fighters I ordered. He won't even acknowledge my calls now. Over."

The Old Man sounds dispersed, Tagurt thought, *as if he's losing it.* "Affirmative. Any other instructions or information? Over."

There was sudden excitement in Chesty's voice. "Something's happening on the roof here. Something landed, ours or theirs. Hold on a minute."

He paused. "It's theirs. There's shooting . . . They're in the corridor now."

Tagurt could hear the shooting but not the boots. The comm didn't pick them up, nor show him the general crouched behind the desk with his pistol in his fist. The pistol hammered, but the only answering fire was the pop of the gas grenade, which Tagurt barely heard and didn't recognize.

Then someone else spoke—just a few words, none clearly audible. After a minute, Tagurt put his belt comm back in its case. There was nothing more from Chesty.

"Sendra," Tagurt said, "it's time for you to leave. Go to an apartment house and get someone to let you in. I have orders to carry out. Dangerous orders."

Her gaze was neither frightened nor confused, and the initial shock at the death of her parents was no longer evident. "I understand," she said, and got out. He watched her go to an apartment building entrance, pause beside the call panel, and half a minute later go inside. It seemed doubtful he'd ever see her again. The odds of his being alive at daylight were not good.

Activating the motor, he pulled out into the empty street. *Too damn late to follow orders,* he told himself. *They'd arrest me instead of Denni.* Besides, his first decision was the right one. Get to the nub of the problem. If it worked, Chesty would thank him. And if it didn't, there'd be no one to complain.

General Sopal "Snake" Butarindala drummed his fingers on his desk. Half an hour earlier he'd gotten word that an APC had landed on the roof of the Ag Exec

Building, and minutes later had taken off again. Had Chesty been arrested? Rescued? If so, by whom? Denni's people? Reportedly the APC had left troops on the roof, and perhaps inside the building. And someone was still shooting at his marines. Maybe Chesty was still there.

Butarindala realized what his own problem was. He'd been ordered to arrest Chesty and hold him for transport to the flagship. But he hadn't tried very hard. It hadn't seemed necessary. Denni Faradalarsa had agreed not to send troops to defend the building.

So much for agreements. Denni's excuse was, he'd been out of his office when Chesty's order arrived, and his XO had sent them. And it wouldn't do to withdraw them while marines were there to arrest the commanding general.

The marine general knew bullshit when he smelled it. But at least Denni *hadn't* sent the armor or air relief Chesty had ordered. He'd cooperated that far.

Snake slammed a fist into his palm. It was time to take the bull by the horns. He'd been afraid to order Barni Vorkalasama to commit 4th Division. Afraid he'd refuse. If Barni refused, he'd either have to back down himself, or fight, and neither was acceptable.

He called his aide. "Vendil, get Barni on the comm. Even if he's sleeping. Tell him I need to see him. Here. Tell him we've got a big problem." He looked at the clock dial above his monitor. *Rush him,* he thought. *Don't give him time to think about it.*

"Tell him midnight," he added. "Not a minute later. And when you've done it, you're done for the night. Go to bed."

It wouldn't do to have witnesses.

"This is Captain Sork Kovensi, 1st Shuttle Squadron, calling General Dengkato Faradalarsa. Over."

Denni Faradalarsa scowled at his radio. He'd ordered someone sent up to see what had happened to the bombardment flotilla. "This is General Faradalarsa. What did you learn? Over."

"Sir, I've found three Kesriki-class gunboats, all wrecked. The other two are missing. One of the three has since lost residual gravitic resonance and fallen into the atmosphere. That may be what happened to the two I didn't find. I've spent a lot of time hunting, and I don't believe they're out here.

"I also found a section of hull that I believe belonged to the *Emperor*. It has a large radius and very thick hardshell. It reentered the atmosphere just a couple minutes ago. You may have seen the light streak. Over."

Shit! "Any sign of other than gunboats? Over."

"Not a thing, sir. Over."

The general exhaled gustily, wondering if he'd backed the wrong horse. And if he had, if he could fake his way out. The admiral still seemed to hold the best hand, but now he wasn't sure. "Anything else to report? Over."

"Nothing sir. Over."

"All right. Get your ass back down here. And Captain, good work. Faradalarsa out."

He pressed thin lips together, picked up his comm, and spoke a code into it. A human voice answered. "General Butarindala's office. Sergeant Major Jeslati."

"This is General Faradalarsa. I need to speak with your general."

A moment later he had Snake Butarindala on the comm, and told him what he'd just learned.

"Blessed Flenyaagor!" The marine general looked almost sick. *The* Emperor *too!* he thought. *Kargh! What could have done that?* "Thanks, Denni." He paused. "About the Ag Exec Building—"

"Do what you have to," said Faradalarsa. "Just don't tell me about it. I'll be informed, of course, and I may have to mount a response. If I do, I'll give you a chance to pull back first."

❖   ❖   ❖

The marine general disconnected, looking suddenly older. One heavy infantry division had more firepower than his two marine divisions combined, and until he handled Barni Vorkalasama, he only had one of them. He couldn't imagine Barni obeying an order to attack another imperial unit. Not without severe provocation.

He should be on his way here by now. Snake glanced at his clock, opened the desk drawer where his pistol lay, checked the weapon and put it back, then closed the drawer again.

Meanwhile it was time to make another move. He'd thought these things out earlier, part of contingency planning, but they hadn't seemed as dangerous then. Buzzing G-3 Special Ops, he ordered a preplanned mission carried out. Kill Denni and there'd be confusion in 1st Division, the degree of it depending on who died with their general.

Next he placed a call to his division's light armored squadron, already in ready status. He ordered a troop sent to clear the Ag Building of defenders. And to use artillery if necessary.

Finally, at his keyboard, he called up his Fleet Secure File. A minute later, a scrambled radio pulse left for a relay buoy parked off Aslarsan's major moon. A secure message from the admiral. Doing it scared hell out of Snake Butarindala. He knew in a general way what it ordered. He hoped devoutly that the *Retributor*'s captain would use care and judgment.

By the time Snake Butarindala had poured a brandy and sat down again at his desk, a prebriefed assassination team was driving away from marine Special Ops, in a command car with 1st Infantry markings.

Captain Gokan's helmet comm beeped softly in his ear. "Gokan," it said, "this is Koju. A light armored troop is moving out of the 2nd Marine encampment, through the gate leading to the city. I am going to put down ambush parties along the avenue between their camp and your position. Not to prevent their progress, though it may have that effect, but to inflict casualties on personnel and equipment, and produce confusion. I am also putting down skirmish parties to engage your playmates from the rear. How is your ammunition supply?"

"We've been using rifles. Sniping. Our blaster men haven't fired at all. The imperial troops on the lower floors are using blasters however."

"It's remarkable they haven't come up to see who their allies are."

"Someone, probably the general, had the stairwell doors locked and the elevators shut down. It would be possible to break through, but they seem content to have our support without requesting our credentials. The general's comm buzzed several times, but I haven't answered." He paused. "Do you plan to engage the armor with your ground support fighters?"

"Not at this point. I will if necessary to evacuate you. Meanwhile intensify your fire. The apparency is, the imperials are not personally committed to this fight, and their morale is flabby. But they are well trained, well equipped, and probably adequate technically."

When they'd finished talking, Gokan gave orders to fire at will, blastermen as well as riflemen. This was, he thought, an interesting exercise. Their training had included Level One warfare, of course, but his was the first T'swa unit to actually fight at Level One since the Technite War.

Tagurt Meksorli drove up to the checkpoint barrier, where a marine guard stopped him. Apparently the marines weren't letting anyone, certainly no one in a civilian vehicle, drive up to the entrance of the fenced 2nd Marine encampment.

Several guards waited, blasters poised. One of them stepped over to the driver's window, his blaster in Meksorli's face, fingers on the firing lever. Peering in, he recognized the twin sunbursts on Meksorli's shoulders, but the face was unfamiliar. And in a civilian vehicle? "Sir," he said firmly, "you'll need to get out of your vehicle for identification."

"Certainly."

The marine stepped well back, blaster still pointed at him. Tagurt opened the door and got out grinning, raising his arms to his sides, displaying his wet, disheveled uniform. "My girl friend and I got dumped in the lake when my boat got shot out from under us," he said, then gestured at the car. "I requisitioned this from a civilian. Now I need to report to General Butarindala. He seems to be the senior commanding officer."

The statement didn't explain much, but the marine relaxed a bit. Boat, girl friend, take a car from a civilian, and grin about it? Maybe freer times were on their way. "Yessir. Come with me, sir."

The sentry led him to a guard shelter. A corporal watched them come. Tagurt drew out his sodden wallet, showed his wet ID card with photo, and seconds later the corporal was on the comm.

Within minutes a car arrived with the officer of the day. He'd already checked with General Butarindala, who'd seemed delighted. The OD didn't know it, but his general had gotten the notion that the provost marshal wanted to make a deal.

No one had told their general, or the OD, that Tagurt Meksorli had arrived in a wet uniform in a civilian car. His wet, unkempt appearance flummoxed the OD a bit, enough that he repeated the corporal's request for ID. But the name was familiar, the faces matched, and the man's Imperial was typically Vartosu. The OD's initial caution faded.

No one thought to pat down a major general. The OD

drove him to division headquarters and conducted him into the sergeant major's office, which served as reception and filter for the general's visitors. By that time, Tagurt had taken his provost marshal's axe insignia from his pocket and pinned it back on his collar. The sergeant major rose promptly and saluted—a courtesy to the provost marshal's twin sunbursts. Go right in, sir," he said. "General Butarindala is expecting you."

The OD led him in. The CO had told him to, on the comm. Entering the office of Sopal Butarindala, they found the Snake already on his feet. He ignored Tagurt's appearance, stepping around his desk to shake the provost marshal's hand. "Nice to see you," he said. "Have a seat." He gestured to a straight-backed chair, then returned to his own seat behind his desk. "I've tried to get in touch with you. Didn't realize you were off duty. I suppose you know our commanding general has disappeared. I got wind of an Aslari plot to kidnap him, and sent a company to guard the building. They were too late. He was whisked away by a civilian floater on the roof. As I see it, that leaves you acting commander here."

He looked quizzically at Meksorli. If this gentry general was willing to cooperate, it would solve his problems. Tagurt, in turn, found Snake's approach transparent and interesting. He'd wait a bit, question him. Let the man incriminate himself. Maneuver him into a threat if he could, before killing him.

Second Division headquarters was its only proper building, a molded, modularized prefab that the Snake regarded as necessary to his dignity. And his privacy. Tent buildings, with their breezy, open-weave walls, required speaking in undertones, if confidentiality was wanted.

Nonetheless, both generals heard the strong voice in the reception office, overriding the sergeant major's objections. It was Major General Barni Vorkalasama who pushed open the door and strode in, chin jutted. "Good evening, Generals," he said. His eyes took in Meksorli, and he grinned. "Tagurt, it's customary to disrobe before swimming. My apologies if I'm interrupting, but Sopal demanded to see me by twelve. It is less than a minute to twelve now."

Snake waffled for just a moment. He'd planned to shoot Barni Vorkalasama, and the provost marshal if he didn't seem pliant enough. But now . . . If he killed these two, and his people did their job on Denni Faradalarsa, he'd be the only general officer left on Aslarsan. And he wouldn't have to worry about the commoner double-crossing him.

"Of course," he said genially, and gestured. "Have a chair. I'm glad you've arrived." He looked at the officer of the day. "Captain, your services here are no longer needed. Return to your duties."

The OD saluted and left. When he'd had time to drive away, Snake opened a desk drawer, closed his hand on his pistol, and got to his feet. "General Vorkalasama," he began, pointing the weapon, "I know about your conspiracy to assassinate and replace . . ."

He should have kept one eye on the provost marshal. When Tagurt saw Snake's hand reach into the drawer, his own slipped inside his rumpled shirt. Now it emerged with his light, short-barreled blouse gun. "Drop it!" he snapped. "I'm arresting you . . ."

He'd practiced avoidance moves while provost on the prison planet, Shatimvoktos, where assassination attempts were a way of life. And he'd had no doubt what Snake's reaction would be. When the Marine general swung his heavy pistol toward him and squeezed the trigger, Tagurt was already throwing himself sideways, his chair falling with him, while his finger squeezed and held down the trigger. The marine general's big slug plowed through the wall behind Meksorli, while four light slugs of his own tore into Butarindala's chest. The stricken man's mouth opened in apparent astonishment, the pistol dropped from his hand, and he fell forward across his desk. The provost marshal ignored the other general, turning his attention to the door.

"Sergeant major!" Tagurt bellowed, "Come in here! I have just shot your general for treason, resisting arrest, and deadly assault. You are ordered to examine him and determine whether or not he is dead."

Sergeant Major Jeslati entered slowly, his expression wary. "General Vorkalasama witnessed his criminal act," Tagurt continued. "As acting commander of forces on the ground, I hereby appoint General Vorkalasama commander of all marine forces on Aslarsan. He is herewith ordered to withdraw the marine forces besieging the Agricultural Ministry Executive Building."

At almost precisely that moment, and six miles away, one of the assassination team fired his silenced pistol into the forehead of General Dengkato Faradalarsa, while another was doing the same to the general's sergeant major, who would otherwise have investigated the muffled sound.

It was a tough night for generals.

Like most of Aslarton's residents, the Felderlis and their unexpected guest had been listening to the distant sound of automatic weapons. The firing had grown more intense. It was almost midnight, but not many people had gone to bed.

Now another sound reached them through the open windows. To Sendra Arvalin it sounded like the heavy glass security doors being broken. Less than a minute later they heard booted feet thudding down the hall. Sendra turned worriedly to the elderly couple who'd taken her in. *Why*, she wondered, *would soldiers have broken into this building?* The only reason she could think of was, they were looking for her. Unlikely as it seemed.

Something slammed against the door. The latch broke, and the door flew violently open. Mrs. Felderli screamed

and fainted. Shocked, wide-eyed, Mr. Felderli caught
her. She was too heavy for him, and both fell to the floor.
The intruders wore black uniforms, and the open visors
on their helmets showed black faces with large eyes.
T'swa! Sendra realized. *But how . . . ?*

With their weapons, the T'swa broke the large, single-
paned windows and cleared the shards from the frames.
The balcony doors were already open; they simply
fastened them against the inside walls by the magnetic
pads. The sergeant looked quizzically at Sendra. She was
dressed in a far too large blouse of Mrs. Felderli's, and
a pair of slacks with the waistband folded over and secured
by a belt. The legs were folded up at the bottom.

"An imperial marines armored troop is expected to
pass this building in a few minutes," the sergeant said.
"We are part of an ambush. I recommend you move to
the rear of the building, where the danger is less."

Mr. Felderli had gotten warily to his feet. "Zho!" the
sergeant said, "help this gentleman to the rear of the
house. Carry his wife for him."

The trooper knelt, hoisted the limp bulky form over a
shoulder and stood, then trotted from the room, Felderli
following, more wide-eyed than before. Sendra watched
them leave. "I advise you to go with them," the sergeant
told her, then turned the lights out, and crouching, went
onto the balcony carrying a rocket launcher.

Sendra couldn't have said why she didn't leave. Nor
did she wonder. Possible factors included that she was
a fourth-year nursing student and might be useful there.
That she'd lost her family that evening, almost certainly
to imperial troops. Also she'd never experienced war in
her life—not in that life; perhaps she simply wanted to
watch. Stepping to an open window, she knelt, looking
out. The T'swi with whom she shared it glanced, then
ignored her.

Abruptly, gunfire and larger explosions broke out, in
the other direction than she'd been hearing, much closer

and more intense. Her eyes widened. "Another ambush," the T'swi said. It occurred to her that he looked as young as she did.

"Will they still come past here?" she asked.

"Unless they are easily discouraged. The ambush is partly to test their reactions. Now I will not speak further with you. I must give my attention elsewhere."

His helmet, she realized, would contain a radio. He probably wore an earphone.

He listened, utterly calm. Most of what he heard, he'd already known. The armored troop formed a short column—ten light tanks with five-inch guns, and six armored ground personnel carriers, apparently carrying a squad of infantry each, plus light turret-mounted blasters. The ambush was in a wooded park, where the ambushers could more easily withdraw, and the supporting infantry was more likely to be committed.

After a minute or two the firing slackened, then stopped. Again the T'swi spoke to Sendra. "You are on the dangerous side of the window, the side toward which fire will be concentrated."

She looked around the room and decided to stay where she was. As a daughter of Ostrak Alumni, and an Ostrak level four herself, she regarded death as interruption rather than extinction. And she really did want to watch.

Meanwhile, from the government district, the firing had intensified further. She wondered if T'swa were involved there, too.

"They are nearing," the T'swi said. He spoke without looking at her, his assault rifle ready, his head at windowsill height, peering around the edge. Apparently he intended to fire left-handed.

The armored vehicles were gravitic hovercraft, their engines making little noise. Sendra saw them before she heard them, coming down the avenue with hooded headlights. Rapidly, as if to speed through any further ambush. She heard the swoosh of a rocket launched, heard the explosion, multiple explosions, accompanied by flashes. The two lead vehicles, APCs, hadn't been fired on, but the lead tank was hit. It lost its gravitic cushion and skidded on the turf of the street, slewing sideways. The tank behind rammed it hard, rolling it onto its side. The second tank's turret swiveled. Its gun banged, belching flame, and a shell roared, dominating but not discouraging a storm of lesser gunfire. The T'swi was firing into the street below, almost beneath their window, and she turned her eyes to his targets. The APCs had stopped, were unloading their troops in the middle of the avenue, under fire. Even she realized they should have pulled close to one of the buildings before unloading. Soldiers fell, some immediately, some after running a few yards. One she saw reach the shrubbery in front of the opposite building, disappearing under it as if for protection.

Marine Gunnery Sergeant Gadib Sidhmaga was not an excitable man. Just now he was exasperated. They'd been sent expecting no trouble till they reached the government district. Then they'd been ambushed, and that changed the whole situation. They'd lost two tanks and an APC with its squad, along with other riflemen before the ambushers had pulled out. The captain had radioed for backup. Then, in spite of the demonstrated presence of hostiles, he'd started again for the government district. A single armored troop, especially without strong infantry support, had no business on a hostile city street.

The column had closed up at the first ambush, and had stayed that way, without proper intervals. And now this. The tank lay on its side, Gadib hanging down in his harness. He was lucky, he realized, that the rocket had hit the engine instead of the crew space. Meanwhile, the captain was no longer with them. The damn fool had been sitting in the open turret hatch and been thrown out. Gadib had difficulty reaching his microphone switch, and realized his right arm was broken. He was surprised it didn't hurt.

A voice from headquarters spoke into his headset. "All 2nd Division units in contact with hostile forces," it said, "disengage if possible and surrender if necessary. I repeat: disengage if possible and surrender if necessary."

The sergeant began to swear. Some minutes later, large men with black uniforms and black faces eased him from the tank. When Gadib saw the bodies and the wreckage, curses gave way to tears of anger. How had such fuckups ever been given command? He didn't see the captain's body. It was, he hoped, under the tank, smeared into the ground.

Some 160,000 miles out, the *Retributor* had made one of its periodic, covert emergences from its parking location in warpspace, traveling from one universe to another without moving. Whenever Captain Zarbosh Kozkoraloku thought about it, he was amazed. This time, however, he hadn't thought about it, because the relay buoy had a message waiting for him. Unscrambled, it took less than a minute to play. He could hardly believe his luck. The Kalif was down there, in the Aslari palace! The man his father had so hated, who had driven him to suicide.

Admiral Siilakamasu knew the captain's great button, and had pushed it hard.

Kari Frensler had left the mind of Chesty Vrislakavaro when he was rescued by the T'swa. After a brief break, she'd transferred to the mind of Snake Butarindala. Then Tagurt Meksorli had shown up. When Butarindala laid his hand on the pistol in his desk drawer, she'd withdrawn reflexively. For half a minute she'd sat wide-eyed on her trance pillow, her skin a field of gooseflesh. Finally she reached hesitantly back, ran into the general's shocked, disembodied soul, ricocheted, and found herself in the mind of Tagurt Meksorli. She stayed there while Barni

Vorkalasama ordered the marine armored troop back to base, then withdrew again and reported it all to Lotta.

The next report to Lotta was from the T'swa, via a Ka-Shok adept who monitored Captain Gokan. The marines who'd besieged the Ag Exec Building had surrendered and been disarmed. They were being returned to their base, which was guarded now by T'swa and OSP regiments gated in. All marine and army officers above company levels were being rounded up and interned in their divisional stockades.

Meanwhile signals, with video, had arrived from the fleet. They showed Loksa Siilakamasu in chains, and the Kalif on the bridge of the flagship. The new command admiral was Garpind Tellesaveera, whom the Kalif had promoted to full admiral. The videos would be shown to all interned imperial officers and men.

Lotta Alsnor-Romlar liked to meditate on the Logos before retiring, but lately she hadn't had time. Now it seemed she did. She folded herself into the customary lotus, closed her eyes, regulated her breathing, and recited her mantra of Logos meditation. Her body seemed to lighten. Then something like a magnet tugged on her. She relaxed to it, and found herself in an unfamiliar mind, on an unfamiliar ship's bridge.

It took awhile for Zarbosh Koskoraloku to move from the vicinity of Aslarsan's principal moon, and position the *Retributor* 200 miles above the capital. His instruments exposed the city and its environs in detail. His DAAS identified for him what he looked at. He had his battlecomp fix the great beam gun on the palace. And on the Kalif. Zarbosh scanned his bridge crew at their stations. The command admiral had allowed him access to fleet personnel records, back on Varatos, and he'd made the final choice of his officers based on instrumented interviews. These were men who would not hesitate to follow orders, however extreme, and they need not know the Kalif was down there.

The original plan had been to raze the capital of Iryala, destroying the sites and instruments of its government. To destroy the bureaucracy and put all power in the hands of imperial nobility.

This was far better. He'd never imagined he'd have the Kalif himself in his gun sight. Kargh had truly blessed him, chosen *him* to destroy the renegade murderer and profligate who'd dishonored the Prophet's throne.

He ordered the great beam gun charged, the most powerful in existence. It would, Zarbosh told himself, blast the Kalif's soul as well as his body. And punish the Aslari for their insolence.

Directly over the palace! Lotta transferred to the mind of Linvo Garlaby. Linvo was dozing at his desk, and awoke with a start at her urgent meld. In less than twenty seconds he was on the horn to the gate master, the lighter pilot, and all ships' bridges. He'd kept them on standby because of the number of imperial warships.

The lighter would go first. The battleship *Pertunis* would follow. A battleship had far greater fighting ability than the gunboat, which was designed to attack stationary ground targets, but it lacked the capacity for the quick kill of something as durable as the *Retributor*. While the destroyers already gated into the Aslarsan System lay parked outside the radiation belts. They'd take far too long to arrive.

It took about two minutes for the gate master to find the *Retributor* with her scanner. It was stationary. Before she could move in closely enough, a great shaft of energy appeared beneath the bombardment ship, stabbing downward at light speed. Then the *Retributor* began to move, accelerating quickly to perhaps a mile a minute. The gate master flicked on her comm and told the lighter pilot, who was piloting from an ejection module atop his craft.

"Position me abaft him!" the pilot barked. "Quickly! Don't worry about aim or distance!"

The gate master didn't argue, didn't point out the unlikelihood of hitting a moving target. From its distance a mile away, the lighter started toward the gate, accelerating. The gate master watched for its ejection module to separate at about the four-fifths point. It didn't. She stared, realizing what the pilot intended.

The lighter emerged more than a mile behind the *Retributor,* at three times the speed, and closed quickly. At about a half mile separation, the bombardment ship began a turn, in a maneuver to torch another swath across the city. Seen from the side, it was less than a fourth the length of a battleship, though perhaps two-thirds the diameter. And *ugly,* thought the lighter pilot. *Ugly!*

He didn't hesitate, but accelerated, cutting the angle. Till then the gunboat's bridge had either overlooked or ignored the lighter. Now it reacted, generating a shield. Only the inner layer had formed when the lighter struck. The explosion was awesome, driving the gunboat sideways, her shield blown out of existence. The galaxy's greatest matric tap flared in an incredible burst of electrical energy that instantaneously heated the bulkheads incandescent. The monstrous beam gun's condenser blew then, bursting the heavily armored hull.

Of the lighter and her pilot, nothing would be recovered.

Chapter 52
Wind-Down

On the third day after the *Retributor's* destruction, Lord Kristal called a conference of his War Council, its staff, and upper level commanders. The overall situation seemed secure, stable, and safe. The people summoned were highly informed on their areas of responsibility, but beyond that there were holes in their knowledge. The conference would answer questions, help them clear their registers. Free their attention from the war, as they settled into post-war functions.

Because the king would attend, it was held in the lesser auditorium at the palace. Forty-three persons seated themselves facing the speakers' table. Cameras would record the proceedings.

Lord Kristal waited to preside. At eight sharp he tapped his bell. "This meeting will come to order," he said. "I anticipate a full day. We will take a half hour at eleven and three, for lunch. I will try to wind this up in time for supper at seven."

He paused. "Before we begin today's agenda, I want to announce a news item some of you may have missed this morning. Last night, ten retro terrorists were arrested by Interior Ministry strike forces. Three were taken while they waited in ambush outside the residence of a member of His Majesty's cabinet. My niece Clianna, actually. Three others were taken in the process of abducting whom they supposed was Mayor Emmith Kurssbann, in the parking lot outside Symphony Hall. In fact, however, the person they laid hands on was a ministry agent, chosen, made up, and dressed to resemble the mayor.

"Two other terrorists were arrested by a police ambush, leaving the residence of a third. They were armed with a blaster, an automatic rifle, and sidearms. The terrorist carrying the blaster was shot by a ministry undercover agent who had accompanied them. Their targets were two people prominent in His Majesty's government. The man whose residence they were leaving was also arrested. His home contained an arsenal of illegal weapons.

"The tenth arrested was someone some of you may know, for his support of the musical arts: Bariss Fildkarm, publisher of the *Weekly Review of Music*. He was the organizer of all three terrorist teams, and we had no notion of his retro involvement until a few days ago. He has been charged with criminal conspiracy, conspiracy to abduct, conspiracy to murder, the purchase and possession of illegal weapons, and hiring to commit murder."

Kristal's eyes scanned the audience. A hand rose. "Yes, Colonel Romlar?"

"If it wanted to, how many people could Interior arrest for sedition and other retro crimes?"

Kristal smiled ruefully. "I haven't a count. Thousands, on existing evidence. With a little effort, tens of thousands planetwide."

"Then why arrest just ten?"

"The retro movement overall is not an actual threat to government, nor a major threat to public safety. Most of its people are not violent. Its attraction will decline, and in fact has already begun to. And the less attention we appear to pay it, the briefer and weaker that attraction will be. Best let it die on the vine, if it will.

"And consider. Our own Movement, in its necessary work, caused the changes that have upset so many. That's right: we are the primary and adequate cause of their disaffection. Therefore, Crown policy is to overlook what we can. We are content simply to arrest any who undertake crimes against persons. As we did last night."

He smiled. "Incidentally, Artus, the undercover agent who exposed all three would-be abductions, and took part in the exchange of hostile fire, is a friend of yours. He saved your life on Maragor, and credits you with his rehabilitation."

Artus stared. *Gulthar Krol!* In the press of war-time duties, he'd lost track of the Maragoran.

"And now let's get on with the business of the day. Judging from questions I've already heard, many of yours can best be answered by the Remote Spying Section. So I'll call first on Lotta Alsnor-Romlar."

Lotta adjusted her microphone. When she looked up, hands had been raised. "Your Majesty," Kristal said, "we'll begin with you."

Marcus's delivery was casual. "Lotta, some of Admiral Siilakamasu's decisions and actions are difficult to understand. Given your—um—inside view, what light can you shed on him?"

"Loksa Siilakamasu had a compulsion for dominance and authority. It underlay almost everything he did. His ambition was to be an absolute monarch over a sort of layered autocracy. With everyone accountable to him, and himself accountable to no one.

"Overlying that, and permeating it, was a sort of low-intensity paranoia that colored all his thinking and actions. All this in spite of being very self-confident and chronically optimistic. He considered himself at risk of plots, but more than a match for them. At the same time, he was always on guard, ready to act ruthlessly.

"He tended to treat people with contempt. Some he treated with open, even scathing contempt, so no one wanted to get on his bad side. Also, while he didn't lose his temper very often, his rages were extreme, and led to severe punishments. All in all, the people around him lived with a chronic sense of threat.

"He knew that, of course, and fed it. At the same time he realized it led to hatred, which reinforced both his paranoia, his abusiveness, and his secrecy. Paranoia typically leads to secrecy.

"And that," she finished, "pretty much describes the admiral."

Hands raised, and Kristal recognized another questioner. "How could the *Retributor* be as big a surprise as it was?"

Lotta frowned thoughtfully. "That," she said, "takes us back to the admiral. He preferred to act on impulse. He didn't like formal planning; considered it restrictive and burdensome. On the other hand, he kept himself very well informed, and his impulses were rooted in his knowledge as well as in his paranoia and greed for power. His responsibilities, of course, required formal planning, but he assigned it to others, then approved or rejected what they produced.

"But some planning he couldn't assign. In matters he didn't want his 'enemies' to know about. Including the matter of the *Retributor*.

"The officer corps in general subscribed to the concept of ruling the conquered worlds with as little upset and destruction as necessary. It would be less dangerous and more productive. The admiral, on the other hand, wanted to destroy the system and replace it with his own.

"Before he ever left Varatos, he'd set up expedients to bring it about, though we didn't know about them. The *Retributor* was one. But it had to be covert.

"The *Retributor* and *Emperor* were built thirty years ago by Kalif Gorsu Areknosaamos, to discourage revolts by the Empire's subordinate planets. When the admiral wanted them included in the Armada, the new Kalif"— she gestured at Coso—"vetoed them. In the end he settled for half a loaf. The *Emperor* would go, and the *Retributor* would be left behind.

"In either case, his Eminence hoped and intended to dispose of the admiral en route, and command the fleet himself.

"But the admiral managed to, ah, smuggle the *Retributor* in. It didn't travel as part of the bombardment flotilla, but at the trailing fringe of the Armada, where it was not conspicuous. It was virtually identical with the *Emperor*— had even been given the same ID markings. So if the bridge crew of another ship saw it, they'd assume it was the *Emperor*, and that it was where it was for some good reason. And of course, the Armada was in hyperspace for almost the whole time, visible only as unidentifiable blips.

"I doubt very much that even the bombardment flotilla's commodore knew the *Retributor* was with the Armada." She paused. "The admiral was not a highly satisfactory source of remote spying information. His internal monologues, such as they were, tended very much to be on current or personal things. Once he'd set something up, he pretty much dismissed it from conscious attention till he needed it. In fact, some of what I know from him, I learned only the day before yesterday. I gated out to the flagship to question SUMBAA. And while I was there I questioned the admiral. Now the *ex*-admiral. Covertly, of course, through Colonel Carrmak. Carrmak fed him questions while I eavesdropped in his mind.

"It was easy to get him to talk, incidentally. Carrmak simply dished him a little admiration. The admiral has a large appetite for it. He told the colonel verbally a lot of what I wanted to know. He still gloats over what he considers his successes."

She stopped again, and Kristal recognized Lord Carns. "My impression," Carns said, "has been that SUMBAA had a great deal of power. Why didn't it intervene more than it did? It obviously preferred the Kalif."

"Keep in mind that we have a very incomplete understanding of how SUMBAA interacts with DAAS. There seems to be a kind of psychological relationship. Kusu's shop is trying to work out its physico-chemical basis. Also, the flagship's SUMBAA is a limited version of the planetary SUMBAAs. It has as much computational power, but it lacks most of their accessories.

"It is *not* the brain of a giant, fighting servomechanism called the *Papa Sambak*. The flagship's DAAS comes closer to that. But unlike a SUMBAA, a DAAS lacks volition, in the strict sense of the word.

"Basically, though SUMBAA communicated with DAAS, it has no actual authority over it, except as assigned from the bridge. I suspect, though, that SUMBAA played logic games with DAAS on that. Ordinarily, any instructions SUMBAA gave it had to be compatible with senior orders. And though DAAS used data from SUMBAA, if the data were inconsistent with sensory or command data, it was ordinarily rejected.

"Also, almost any instruction SUMBAA gives can be overridden from the bridge. So SUMBAA tried to keep its activities unnoticed, except when special opportunities arose."

Lotta paused, then continued. "Beyond SUMBAA's technical limitations was its personality, so to speak. Its designers programmed it to be skeptical, even of its own conclusions. This involved broadly cross-checking the data received and the conclusions drawn. So it was also programmed to scan for data providing a probability basis for acceptance, rejection, or modification. Which resulted in an intelligence that was alert and observant, as well as skeptical.

"To that built-in skepticism was added SUMBAA's awareness that it lacked something—some mental component that humans have. It has an awareness-of-awareness unit, but it's a designed artifact, and at first was fairly crude. An artifact it refined for itself, with time and experience.

"Furthermore, SUMBAA is unemotional and highly rational. In fact, it says, lack of emotion was an early problem in understanding the social and economic phenomena it had to factor into its computations. But bit by bit it developed a calculus to handle that. It learned to more or less 'understand' emotions and their effects, which is something quite valuable.

"Meanwhile it learned to tap electronic sensors indirectly, in a manner analogous to the way RSS agents meld with humans."

Lotta looked her audience over. No one seemed to have picked up the implication of what she'd said. Kusu, of course, had drawn the same conclusion independently. She went on.

"All of this was driven by the Basic Canon—'to serve the welfare of humankind.' And SUMBAA reacted the way government bureaus do to carry out a legislative decree: It created rules and policies to restrict and guide its own actions in complying. And while my main source of information has been the flagship SUMBAA, it tells me that all SUMBAAs share the same policies.

"In the process of obeying the Basic Canon, SUMBAA evolved a philosophy on the nature of Homo sapiens, and what human welfare really involved. And decided it was the nature of humankind to self-evolve toward a higher state. 'Self' being the key term.

"So one of SUMBAA's policies is not to take external actions that might interfere with humankind evolving in whatever direction it chooses. In fact, for more than a thousand years it restricted itself almost totally to protecting the Empire from collapsing under economic, social, and governmental aberrations and complexities. It was giving society time to evolve. All while recognizing that the species might scuttle itself instead."

She turned to Kristal. "Am I spending too much time on this?"

Kristal smiled. "It's intriguing. I'll cut you off if I need to."

She nodded, took a sip of water and continued. "When

the Klestronu expedition discovered our existence, it drastically changed SUMBAA's picture of humankind. Because we became part of it. And even before it knew about us, the Vartosu SUMBAA had decided that Kalif Chodrisei Biilathkamoro was an important step in a new evolutionary direction. Sufficiently important that during the coup attempt—I suppose you've read the background sheets on the Empire—during the coup attempt, SUMBAA electrocuted several insurgency soldiers to save the Kalif's life. It was the first such intervention in SUMBAA's history.

"It intervened again when it instructed the DAAS in the Kalif's scout not to detonate the bomb intended to kill him. And again in refusing to allow the Kalif's message to be cut off. And later, General Vrislakavaro's message. When I asked how it succeeded in those interventions, it said that when we understand its physiology better, we'll know.

"At any rate, these were extreme interventions. They openly thwarted the admiral's orders. They also exposed his corruption, and damaged his image of invulnerability. Both of which helped make him susceptible to rejection, when the time came.

"And disconnecting SUMBAA from the ship's systems took more than just pulling a plug. SUMBAA had programmed multiple, and sometimes hard to find, connections through various of the ship's systems and subsystems. When the recording of the Kalif finally stopped playing, the admiral thought he had SUMBAA entirely cut out of the system. Actually, SUMBAA stopped on its own, to protect itself, leaving the admiral and his technical people thinking they'd succeeded.

"You get the picture."

The King's hand raised. "Yes, Your Majesty?" she said.

"I take it you couldn't meld with SUMBAA. Despite its being quasi-biological, and having an awareness-of-awareness. Apparently, then, it doesn't produce a mental field, so to speak."

"Actually it does, Your Majesty, and in a sense I did

meld with the Varatos SUMBAA, years ago. Got away with it, too, very briefly, though not long enough to learn much. Then it discovered me, and that was the end of that."

She turned to Kristal, who pointed at another raised hand. "Torens," he said, "what is your question?"

"I still don't really understand why Siilakamasu went to so much trouble for *Retributor*."

"You're not used to insanity," Lotta answered. "A lot of people act, and react, more or less insanely from time to time, so Ostrak operators develop a feel for it. Taking *Retributor* along was partly a result of the admiral's political ambition, partly his paranoia, and partly because *Retributor* was a symbol and source of great power."

And partly, she thought, *for reasons I won't go into.*

"To Loksa Siilakamasu, people were properties on the stage of what he considered his universe. And as the self-appointed producer, director, and main act, he felt free to do whatever he wanted with them. So he brought the *Retributor* along to provide control, and the destruction of any place he saw fit to destroy."

Kristal got to his feet, smiling at her. "Thank you, Lotta. We'll get back to you later, if need be. But just now I want Linvo Garlaby to answer questions."

That evening the Romlars drove a roundabout route home, that took them along the bluffs above the river. None of the moons were up, the night was clear, and the city center several miles behind them. At Lotta's suggestion, Artus stopped at one of the tiny parks overlooking the river.

After a few minutes of gazing at river and sky, Artus spoke. "It'll take some getting used to."

"Peace you mean."

"Right. Not that the war lasted so long."

"Longer for me than you."

He nodded.

"What are you thinking about?" she asked.

"About Siilakamasu. And capturing him. Do you know what ship was first named *Retributor*?"

"The mad emperor's planet killer. You told me that after one of those bad dreams you had on Maragor. But I already knew it from the T'swa. What about capturing Siilakamasu?"

"When I had him, I felt enormously—fulfilled, you could say. Light. Ecstatic. Although I couldn't have told you why. I knew we'd just settled the war, but it went beyond that.

"Then, that night I dreamed; I can't remember just what. But when I woke up, I knew. I couldn't remember the details, or who'd been what. But Coso, the admiral, me—we'd all played roles on the old *Retributor*, and this time we'd straightened them out.

"It's not important to know more," he added earnestly. "In this life, the importance was an illusion. That was the key. That's what I had to get. The life we're living is the one that counts."

"Of course," Lotta said. "And the illusion is just as important as you think it is."

She didn't tell him what *she* knew. Because he was right: it wasn't important. Not any longer. But she was Wellem Bosler's consultant for particularly sensitive Ostrak cases he ran into. Including Coso Biilathkamoro's. The being who was Coso had spent numerous lifetimes, over 21,000 years, working off the enormous burden of karma he'd created. And transforming himself in the process. This one had probably finished the job. And the being who in this life was Artus had owed him. Now that debt was paid.

As for Loksa Siilakamasu—he'd been the mad emperor's dwarf, as insane as his master. He'd died envying him, wanting to be him. *Some choice of role model*, she thought, and leaned against her husband's shoulder.

Epilogue

The Armada

Within days of the Armada's surrender, all its beam gun generators had been disabled beyond repair, and its torpedoes launched into the inferno of Aslarsan's sun. Armored vehicles, assault aircraft, and assault spacecraft had followed via slingshot.

The Armada's crews and troops were given a choice: they could colonize or go home. The decision process had included viewing new holography of Glory. More than eighty percent of ex-serfs chose Glory, with the agreement that wives and prospective wives would be sent. Nearly forty percent of gentry personnel also opted for Glory, and surprisingly, nearly twenty percent of the nobles, mostly junior officers of non-affluent families. A sizable contingent of technical personnel were required to go with them—physicians, engineers, etc.—and serve till replacements could be recruited and sent from the Empire.

The Emeritus Kalif opted to go with them, not as monarch, but as colony director, serving a renewable six-year term. The kalifa would join him after completing her training as an Ostrak operator. Rami would continue to reside and attend school on Iryala, at the Lake Loreen Institute. His parents would gate in to spend holidays and vacations with him, till he was old enough to be gated himself.

More than twenty percent of the Armada's pastors also opted for Glory. These were the chaplain-missionaries sent to minister to the armed forces, improve their literacy, and convert Confederation heathens. Some went as teachers or pastors, others as pioneer farmers and civil servants.

The colonists rode troopships, almost all of which would then return to the Empire. Most of the supply ships accompanied the colonists, to provide supplies till colony farms and Confederation trade lines were functional. Some, with volunteer crews, would remain as merchant ships.

The Garthids

The peace treaty with the Garthids was simple. The Confederation and the Khanate would each send an embassy to the other. Because of the Garthid inability to adapt to cold, the Garthid embassy would be located on Tyss. The Confederation ambassador to Shuuf'r Thaak would be T'swa, as would his staff.

Reparations were assessed; the Garthids had to pay the Confederation for ships lost, and to compensate families for crewmen lost. The Khanate, in turn, charged the Tofarko Clan for the reparations, so far as its resources allowed. Its ranking member, Kurakex sekTofarko, had been fully and criminally responsible for refusing negotiation with a Confederation representative, and for deliberately and wrongfully initiating hostilities. The Tofarko honor, wealth and influence were destroyed. The clan would dwindle toward extinction.

To satisfy the diplomatic technicalities, a quick political promotion of Tyss was necessary, from trade world to associate world. This in turn required that it have at least a nominal planetary government. As the principal organization on Tyss, the Order of Ka-Shok was accepted as its "government," and Grand Master Ka its "president."

At T'swa insistence and with careful wording, nothing changed except on paper.

The Karghanik Empire

Because of complex and always contentious imperial politics, development of a formal and friendly relationship with the Karghanik Empire was less straightforward.

It began with Coyn Carrmak being gated to the Kalif's garden, in the kalifal compound on Varatos. The garden was just outside the Emperor Kalif's office. So when Carrmak arrived, he simply sat in an arbor, to wait till the Emperor Kalif came out for his midmorning stroll. He would then introduce himself.

Carrmak's large powerful figure was dressed in a reasonable facsimile of a wealthy Vartosit's business suit. His formal position was Confederation legate to the Emperor Kalif, whom he was to inform of the war and its outcomes. Including the colony world of Glory. He was to carry out preliminary negotiations for a Confederation embassy, with headquarters and residence grounds of its own.

In his briefcase he carried message cubes and numerous other documents to the Emperor Kalif, Jilsomo Savbatso. One of the cubes was from Jilsomo's ex-mentor, the Emeritus Kalif. The other was from Marcus XXVIII. Carrmak was in daily meld-communication with what had been retitled the Remote Communication Section.

Other cubes included detailed coverage of the bombardment and other war damage on Aslarsan, and interviews with a boastful, unrepentant Loksa Siilakamasu, interviews covertly recorded on holo. And of course, extensive holography of Glory, particularly its virgin prairie "grasslands."

Meanwhile, Lotta and Artus were being trained as ambassadors to the Empire. Lotta would be the actual ambassador. However, because the Empire was not ready for a woman with such authority, Artus would wear the title, and perform its public functions. His actual, principal functions, however, would be deputy ambassador and military attaché.

One of their first tasks would be to initiate reparation negotiations with the Empire, for damages, casualties, and survivor benefits. These were owed mainly to the government of Aslarsan and its citizens. Next in priority was the exploration of trade possibilities.

The ambassadorial couple and their staff would be gated to Ananporu well before Lotta gave birth to their child.

They would be accompanied to Varatos by General Tagurt Meksorli and his wife, Sendra Arvalin-Meksorli. Meanwhile, on Iryala, Tagurt was training intensively as a candidate for imperial ambassador to the Confederation. His acceptability to the Emperor Kalif and the College of Exarchs seemed a foregone conclusion, given the support of the Emeritus Kalif. Given his gentry origin, his acceptability to the Diet was less certain but probable. Remote spying had found Jilsomo's relations with the House of Nobles to be reasonably good.

If acceptable to the imperial government, Meksorli would be further trained and briefed at Ananporu, under the Emperor Kalif and the College of Exarchs. By that time a teleportation gate, and gate staff, would be gated to the Confederation embassy there. Two Ostrak operators would go with them to prepare any imperial citizens, officials, and businessmen who might need to gate to the Confederation.

Other

On his deactivation as legate to the Emperor Kalif, Colonel Coyn Carrmak would begin an apprenticeship as Deputy Governor of the Office of Special Projects. He would assume the governorship on the retirement of Lord Kristal.

Kelmer Faronya's first holo drama was quite successful, and his wife Weldi received favorable reviews in a key supporting role. Both would go on to major careers, Kelmer as a producer-director of historical dramas, Weldi as an actress.

Gulthar Kro, an Ostrak 6, gated to Tyss, where he was accepted as a Ka-Shok novice. After a period of meditation and training, he would leave Tyss as part of a long-range expedition to explore as-yet-uncharted space.

Author's Notes

One of the people who read an early draft of this novel asked how the characters in the story could be drinking coffee and eating chicken, for example.

First of all, the terms provide a sense of the meal. But their justification goes deeper than that. Historically, human colonists have taken livestock and seeds with them, for propagation in their new home. This will be easier in a future where frozen embryos or discarnate DNA can be transported, then nurtured to maturity on the new planet.

Also historically, colonists needing names for native animals and plants have frequently named them for things "back home" that they more or less resemble. Sometimes less rather than more. The "beech" of Australia doesn't much resemble the beech of Europe, and is no kin to it. The "elk" of America is a very different looking animal from the elk of Europe. And what we call "cedars" often do not much resemble cedar. This tendency in naming may be even stronger where there are no intelligent natives from whom to borrow names such as moose, tamarack, kangaroo and kookaburra.

This is the fifth and final novel of the *Regiment* series. The earlier novels are: *The Regiment*, *The White Regiment*, *The Kalif's War*, and *The Regiment's War*.

" SPACE OPERA IS ALIVE AND WELL! "

And DAVID WEBER is the
New Reigning King of the Spaceways!

The Honor Harrington series:

On Basilisk Station
"...an outstanding blend of military/technical writing balanced by superb character development and an excellent degree of human drama.... very highly recommended...." —*Wilson Library Bulletin*

"Old fashioned space opera is alive and well."
—*Starlog*

Honor of the Queen
"Honor fights her way with fists, brains, and tactical genius through a tangle of politics, battles and cultural differences. Although battered she ends this book with her honor, and the Queen's honor, intact."
—*Kliatt*

The Short Victorious War
The families who rule the People's Republic of Haven are in trouble and they think a short victorious war will solve all their problems—only this time they're up against Captain Honor Harrington and a Royal Manticoran Navy that's prepared to give them a war that's far from short...and anything but victorious.

continued ☞

DAVID WEBER

continued ☞

DAVID WEBER

On Basilisk Station
0-671-72163-1 ◆ $6.99   (available May, 1999)

Honor of the Queen
0-671-72172-0 ◆ $6.99   ☐

The Short Victorious War
0-671-87596-5 ◆ $5.99   ☐

Field of Dishonor
0-671-87624-4 ◆ $5.99   ☐

Flag in Exile
0-671-87681-3 ◆ $5.99   ☐

Honor Among Enemies(HC)
0-671-87723-2 ◆ $21.00   ☐

Honor Among Enemies(PB)
0-671-87783-6 ◆ $6.99   ☐

In Enemy Hands(HC)
0-671-87793-3 ◆ $22.00   ☐

In Enemy Hands (PB)
0-671-57770-0 ◆ $6.99   ☐

For more books by David Weber,
ask for a copy of our free catalog   ☐

BAEN

If not available through your local bookstore fill out this coupon
and send a check or money order for the cover price(s) +$1.50
s/h to Baen Books, Dept. BA, P.O. Box 1403, Riverdale, NY
10471. Delivery can take up to ten weeks.

NAME: _____

ADDRESS: _____

_____

_____

I have enclosed a check or money order in the amount of $ _____